It begins with a

NAMED A MOST ANTICIPATED BOOK BY

New York Times; Time; People; Washington Post; O, The Oprah Magazine; Elle; Marie Claire; Real Simple; Harper's Bazaar; BuzzFeed; Huffington Post; and many more!

"This is a true beach read! You can't put it down!"
—JENNA BUSH HAGER, *TODAY SHOW* BOOK CLUB PICK

"A moving tale that, while billed as a mystery, transcends the genre. . . . This is a beautifully written story in which the author evokes the hard reality of being an immigrant and a woman in today's world." —*WASHINGTON POST*

"This novel is part mystery, part saga of an immigrant family. It is both gripping and emotionally resonant on every page—a remarkable achievement."
—SCOTT TUROW, *NEW YORK TIMES* BESTSELLING AUTHOR OF *TESTIMONY*

"It's a thriller, and it's an immigrant story, and it's also a romance. . . . This is a story like no other." —*MARIE CLAIRE*

"Dazzling. A heartbreaking, tumultuous ride of a novel that upends our expectations—about family loyalty, cultural identity, and the very nature of love itself."
—JULIE OTSUKA, *NEW YORK TIMES* BESTSELLING AUTHOR OF *THE BUDDHA IN THE ATTIC*

"A mystery about a daughter's disappearance that will have you on the edge of your beach chair." —THESKIMM

"*Searching for Sylvie Lee* is so much more than a globe-trotting suspense novel."
—*HARPER'S BAZAAR*

"POWERFUL. A TWISTING TALE OF LOVE, LOSS, AND DARK FAMILY SECRETS." —PAULA HAWKINS

Praise for

Searching for Sylvie Lee

"Kwok's story spans generations, continents and language barriers, combining old-fashioned Nancy Drew sleuthing with the warmth and heart we've come to expect from this gifted writer. . . . I lost myself in the music of Kwok's story and heard a family trying to find their own harmony. If there's a more familiar and beautiful sound, I don't know what it is." —*The New York Times Book Review*

"I was only about two-thirds of the way through Jean Kwok's '*Searching for Sylvie Lee* when I began telling everyone I know: 'I've found this book, you need to read it.' . . . It's a thriller, and it's an immigrant story, and it's also a romance. I love a lot of books, but none quite like this one. The moment I finished it, I tried to restart it, but trust me, the first read is the most magical. This is a story like no other."

—*Marie Claire*

"Like all most compelling mysteries, Jean Kwok's *Searching for Sylvie Lee* has a powerful emotional drama at its heart. A twisting tale of love, loss, and dark family secrets."

—Paula Hawkins, #1 *New York Times* bestselling author of *The Girl on the Train* and *Into the Water*

"*Searching for Sylvie Lee* is so much more than a globe-trotting suspense novel—it's a moving portrait of the unintended consequences that stem from an immigrant family's efforts to adapt, survive, and provide their children with a better future."

—*Harper's Bazaar*

"A satisfying hybrid of mystery and family drama." —*People*

"A moving tale that, while billed as a mystery, transcends the genre. . . . When family secrets are revealed, we feel Sylvie's unbearable pain. Kwok cracks open Sylvie's heart, spilling its sorrowful contents for all the world to see. This is a beautifully written story in which the author evokes the hard reality of being an immigrant and a woman in today's world." —*Washington Post*

"*Searching for Sylvie Lee* is riveting. A dazzling, talented woman disappears, leading her younger sister to search the Netherlands—and the past—for the truth. This novel is part mystery, part saga of an immigrant family. It is both gripping and emotionally resonant on every page—a remarkable achievement."
—Scott Turow, *New York Times* bestselling author of *Testimony*

"Piercing, inventive novel." —*O, The Oprah Magazine*

"Masterfully written, this suspenseful story of two sisters, and the power of long-buried secrets, is also a profound exploration of one immigrant family's search for identity and belonging in an increasingly global world. *Searching for Sylvie Lee* will haunt me for a long time." —Sari Wilson, acclaimed author of *Girl Through Glass*

"*Searching for Sylvie Lee* is part mystery, part emotional drama, and the book you need in your beach bag this summer." —PopSugar

"*Searching for Sylvie Lee* made my pulse race and my heart ache. This novel takes readers twist by twist down an unpredictable path. Guided by Jean Kwok's masterful writing, we move toward a conclusion that we never see coming—and that we realize afterward could have been no other way. But this is not simply a thrilling mystery. It is a wrenching, rich, and emotionally resonant work of art. Kwok writes about identity, longing, language, and loss. She writes about how our cultures form us—how family members who grow up in different countries are divided by their experiences and bound together by their love. *Searching for Sylvie Lee* combines extraordinary events with the beauty of people's ordinary lives. It is unforgettable."

—Julia Phillips, acclaimed author of *Disappearing Earth*

"More than a simple suspense tale of a missing young woman, this novel explores the complicated dynamics of immigrant families and the universal quest for belonging and identity." —*Town & Country*

"This compelling mystery will scoop you up from page one and won't let go until the very end. . . . Come for the mystery surrounding Sylvie's disappearance, and stay for Kwok's empathetic and masterful exploration of the painful choices one family makes to survive and the unintended consequences of intergenerational secrets and misunderstandings."

—The Daily Beast

"*Searching for Sylvie Lee* had me in its grip from the very first page and didn't set me loose till the last. Apart from a moving portrait of two sisters, so very different in character, it also showed me my own country—The Netherlands—and its people from a perspective in which we Dutch seldom see it. Jean Kwok has the sharp and intelligent eye of the newcomer who has lived here long enough to know perfectly well what she does and doesn't like about her second country. A wonderful portrait of an immigrant family life and one of the best 'unputdownable' suspense novels I've read in a long time."

—Herman Koch, *New York Times* bestselling author of *The Dinner*

"Like many contemporary mysteries, *Searching for Sylvie Lee* begins with a missing woman. But Kwok isn't interested in playing out the conventions of the genre, instead opting for a narrative structure that focuses on the missing woman and the sister who searches for her, both of whom must face questions of identity and justice in a complicated, hybridized world that offers no easy answers."

—Thrillist

"Dazzling. A heartbreaking, tumultuous ride of a novel that upends our expectations—about family loyalty, cultural identity, and the very nature of love itself—at every twist and turn. Kwok is a wise and knowing story-teller who keeps us under her spell until the very last page."
—Julie Otsuka, *New York Times* bestselling author of *The Buddha in the Attic*

"Kwok tells this story of an immigrant family with lucidity and compassion. . . . A profoundly moving portrayal of the complicated identities that exist even within a single family. . . . A graceful portrait of the sacrifices we make for love."
—*Nylon* magazine

"This isn't a novel—it's a puzzle box of familial secrets, some dark, others luminous, all of it haunting, mysterious, and completely satisfying. I was utterly spellbound."
—Jamie Ford, *New York Times* bestselling author of *Hotel on the Corner of Bitter and Sweet*

"*Searching for Sylvie Lee* by Jean Kwok is a mystery about a daughter's disappearance that will have you on the edge of your beach chair."
—theSkimm

"Jean Kwok's *Searching for Sylvie Lee* is the smart literary thriller you want to read this summer."
—The Amazon Book Review

"When brilliant, beautiful Sylvie Lee suddenly vanishes, brave Amy Lee embarks on a heart-stopping mission to find her lost sister. Crossing continents and generations, this magnificent and enthralling story unfolds with the intricate suspense of a classic mystery novel and blooms into a radiant tale of intergenerational family love. The haunting path of Amy's search for the exquisite, lost Sylvie is both mesmerizing and illuminating, spanning oceans and cultures, revealing secret promises and unforeseen passions."
—Lan Samantha Chang, award-winning author of *Inheritance*

"The beauty and tragedy of *Searching for Sylvie Lee* is in how much these sisters love each other because of—or in spite of—their upbringing. . . . Readers interested in the family drama are sure to be drawn in by Kwok's undeniable gift for creating memorable, intimate portraits of characters struggling to find their place in the world."

—*Los Angeles Review of Books*

"Written in prose as mesmerizing and full of depth as a perfect pearl, Kwok's new literary masterwork explores the Chinese immigrant experience both in New York and in Holland, but what it's really getting at is what it means for anyone to belong—to both your community, your family, and to yourself—even as it explores one of my all-time favorite questions, 'How well do we know the ones we love? And how well do we know our own selves?' So smart about the price of being a sibling, the way families shift and change, and how secrets can damage as much as they can free, this is a novel that I loved and admired so much, and I want everyone else on the planet to feel the same."

—Caroline Leavitt, *New York Times* bestselling author of *Cruel Beautiful World*

"A compelling story of how the unsaid can powerfully shape families and lives. . . . Sharply observed, with a plot as unpredictable as its moody Dutch landscape, Kwok's novel is a powerful meditation on loss, identity and belonging."

—Shelf Awareness (starred review)

"Reading Kwok's third novel is like watching an artist create a pencil drawing; she lays down the initial outline, then builds on it with shading and nuance until everything comes together at the stunning end. Her sharp and surprising language transports readers across the globe on a breathless and emotionally complex journey. Excellent from every angle, this is a can't-miss novel for lovers of poignant and propulsive fiction."

—*Booklist* (starred review)

"Part domestic suspense, part generational saga and all heart, *Searching for Sylvie Lee* unfolds in an enthralling way that will upend all readers' expectations. . . . An unforgettable and powerful story of love, loss and truth."

—Bookreporter.com

"Deftly moving between generations and from New York to the Netherlands, *Searching for Sylvie Lee* is a page-turner, and a suspenseful journey of secrets, family, loyalty, and loss."

—Lisa Ko, award-winning author of *The Leavers*

"Though the novel is rife with romantic entanglements and revelations that wouldn't be amiss in a soap opera, its emotional core is the bond between the Lee sisters, one of mutual devotion and a tinge of envy. Their intertwined relationship is mirrored in the novel's structure—their alternating chapters, separated in time and space, echo each other. . . . But the book is a meditation not just on racism, but on (not) belonging. . . . A frank look at the complexities of family, race and culture."

—*Kirkus Reviews*

"A favorite of Paula Hawkins, this literary novel will take you on a rollercoaster of emotions this summer. A must-read for fans of Celeste Ng."

—She Reads

"When the eldest daughter of an immigrant family goes missing, what ensues propels us through the depths of a family's secrets, complicated discoveries and what makes us individuals." —*Newsweek*

"[A] thoughtful thriller. . . . Kwok builds suspense by alternating between the points of view of Sylvie and Amy. The story is at its best when it delineates the struggles of second-generation Chinese immigrants in the two countries." —*Publishers Weekly*

"A dazzling display of the unique bonds among women, mothers and daughters. It's a suspenseful read detailing what happens when the oldest daughter in a Chinese immigrant family disappears."

—CNN.com

"This powerful novel is a must-read." —Women.com

"Told with gorgeous prose, the strongest aspect of Kwok's storytelling is the revelation of how differently these characters see themselves versus how they are seen by the world. . . . These characters prove the resiliency of the human spirit in the face of social and personal challenges and our ability to become the people we're meant to be."

—New York Journal of Books

Searching for Sylvie Lee

ALSO BY JEAN KWOK

Girl in Translation

Mambo in Chinatown

Searching for Sylvie Lee

A Novel

Jean Kwok

wm

WILLIAM MORROW

An Imprint of HarperCollins*Publishers*

This is a work of fiction. Names, characters, places, and incidents are products of the author's imagination or are used fictitiously and are not to be construed as real. Any resemblance to actual events, locales, organizations, or persons, living or dead, is entirely coincidental.

HarperCollins books may be purchased for educational, business, or sales promotional use. For information, please email the Special Markets Department at SPsales@harpercollins.com.

A hardcover edition of this book was published in 2019 by William Morrow, an imprint of HarperCollins Publishers.

FIRST WILLIAM MORROW PAPERBACK EDITION PUBLISHED 2020.

Designed by Leah Carlson-Stanisic

Handlettering by Joel Holland

Library of Congress Cataloging-in-Publication Data has been applied for.

ISBN 978-0-06-283432-4

20 21 22 23 24 LSC 10 9 8 7 6 5 4 3 2 1

To Erwin, Stefan, and Milan

In memory of
my beloved brother, Kwan

Searching for Sylvie Lee

Part 1

CHAPTER 1

Amy

Monday, May 2

I am standing by the window of our small apartment in Queens, watching as Ma and Pa leave for their jobs. Half-hidden by the worn curtains Ma sewed herself, I see them walk side by side to the subway station down the street. At the entrance, they pause and look at each other for a moment. Here, I always hold my breath, waiting for Pa to touch Ma's cheek, or for Ma to burst into tears, or for either of them to give some small sign of the truth of their relationship. Instead, Ma raises her hand in an awkward wave, the drape of her black shawl exposing her slender forearm, and Pa shuffles into the open mouth of the station as the morning traffic roars down our busy street. Then Ma ducks her head and continues her walk to the local dry cleaners where she works.

I sigh and step away from the window. I should be doing something more productive. Why am I still spying on my parents? Because I'm an adult living at home and have nothing better to do. If I don't watch out, I'm going to turn into Ma. Timid, dutiful, toiling at a job that pays nothing. And yet, I've caught glimpses of another Ma and Pa over the years. The passion that flickers over her face as she reads Chinese romance novels in the night, the ones Pa scorns. The way Pa reaches for her elbow when he walks behind her, catches himself, and pulls back his hand. I pass by my closet of a bedroom, and the poster that hangs on the wall catches my eye—barely visible behind the teetering piles of papers and laundry. It's a quote I've always loved from Willa Cather: "The heart of another is a dark forest, always, no matter how close it has been to one's own." I'm not sure I believe the sentiment but her words never fail to unsettle me.

Our cramped apartment still smells faintly of the incense Ma burned this morning in front of her mother's altar. Grandma died in Amsterdam a week ago. She lived there with the Tan family: Ma's cousin Helena; Helena's husband, Willem; and their son, Lukas, who is thirty-three years old, the same age as my older sister, Sylvie. I never met Grandma but Ma's grief has poured over me like a waterfall until my own heart overflows as well. The skin around Ma's eyes is rubbed red and raw. The past few evenings, while Pa hid in their bedroom, I held Ma's hand as she huddled on the sofa, stifling her sobs, attempting to stem the endless stream of tears with an old, crumpled tissue. I wear black today too, for Ma's sake, while Pa dresses in his normal clothing. It's not that he doesn't care. It's that he can't show us that he does.

Sylvie lived with Grandma and Helena's family in the Netherlands for the first nine years of her life, and flew back there a month ago, as soon as she heard Grandma was ill. She's handling a consultancy project for her firm there as well. Dazzling Sylvie, seven years older than me, yanked from her glamorous life in Europe back to our cabbage-scented apartment in Queens when I was only two years old. Often there's a dichotomy between the beautiful sister and the smart one, but in our family, both of those qualities belong to my sister. And me, I am only a shadow, an afterthought, a faltering echo. If I didn't love Sylvie so much, I'd hate her.

How did a brilliant creature like Sylvie arise from such mundane stock as our ma and pa? Any time I had a teacher in elementary or high school who'd taught Sylvie, they'd say, "Ah, you're Sylvie Lee's little sister," rife with anticipation. I would then watch as their high hopes turned to bewilderment at my stuttering slowness. This was followed by their disappointment and, finally, their indifference. Sylvie went to Princeton undergrad, earned a master's in chemical engineering from MIT, worked a few years, then went back to school for her MBA from Harvard. Now she's a management consultant, which is a profession I'll never understand no matter how many times she tries to explain it. Like me, Sylvie adores all sweets, but unlike me, she never gains an ounce. I have watched her eat one egg tart after another without any effect on her elegant hips, as if the sheer intensity of her will burns the calories, consuming everything she touches. She used to have a lazy eye when she was little and wore an eye patch for years. Now the only imperfection in her lovely face is that her right eye still shifts slightly outward when she's tired. Most people don't even notice, but I sometimes console myself with this tiny fault of Sylvie's—*See, she's not so perfect after all.*

I go to the pockmarked cabinet where I have carefully wrapped and hidden a cluster of small orange loquat fruits. If I'd left them on the vinyl kitchen tabletop and Pa had caught sight of the vulnerable snail hidden among the pear-shaped fruit, he would have killed it. Pa works in a fish market in Chinatown. He's been forced to become insensitive to death—all those fish gasping on the wooden chopping block until he ends them with his cleaver.

The tiny snail with its translucent shell is still perched on one of the loquats and seems fine. Anything strong enough to survive such an arduous journey from China deserves a chance to make a life for itself. I take a used plastic bag, gently lower the loquat and snail into it, and head for the door. I shrug into a light jacket and grab my wallet and cell phone. Before I step outside, I remove my thick purple glasses and shove them into my pocket. I don't bother to put in my contacts. Vanity plus laziness add up to my living in a blurry world much of the time.

I trudge the few blocks to the small park near our home. It's early enough that some of the shops are still gated and I shiver as a chilly breeze sweeps down the concrete sidewalk. A bitter stink arises from the wide impersonal asphalt of the road, lined by blank buildings that have always intimidated me. A mother dragging a small, grubby child behind her averts her eyes as she passes. No one makes eye contact in this densely populated, lonely, and dispiriting place—no one except for guys trying to hit on you. A group of them are hanging out now in front of a broken store window with a large sign that says something about fifty percent off. They are mere bruises in my peripheral vision as they yell after me, "*Ni hao!* Can I put my egg roll in your rice patty?" and then break into raucous laughter. Do they have to say the same dumb thing every day? As long as they maintain their distance, the vagueness of my vision is as comforting as a cocoon. When I'm practically blind, I can pretend I'm deaf too.

One day, I'm going to return to my program at CUNY and finish my teaching credential so I can get out of this place. I'll move Ma and Pa too. It doesn't matter that I dropped out last year. I can do it. I already have my master's in English; I'm almost there. I can see myself standing in front of a class of kids: they are riveted, laughing at my jokes, eyes wide at the brilliance of the literature they are reading, and I don't trip over a single word.

Wake up, Amy. All you are now is a savior of snails, which is not necessarily a bad development.

Sylvie and I were both raised Buddhist, and some ideas, like all life being precious, have stayed with us. When we were little, we'd race around the apartment with butterfly nets, catching flies and releasing them outdoors. However, as evidenced by Pa and the killing-fish-and-many-other-sea-creatures thing, religion only goes so far when confronted by the harsh grind of daily life.

The park is still recovering from the severe winter we had and I struggle to find a nice, leafy area. I am bending down with the snail held gingerly between forefinger and thumb when my cell phone rings. I jump and almost drop the snail. I set it down, manage to pull my phone out of my jacket, and squint to read the number. I am just about to answer when the caller hangs up. The number's long, beginning with +31. I've seen this before on Sylvie's phone. It's someone from the Netherlands—probably my distant cousin Lukas, except he's never called me before. He only speaks to Sylvie.

I consider the cost of calling Lukas in Amsterdam and wince. Hopefully he'll try me again soon. Instead, I head for the local music shop. I love to linger in one of their listening stations but almost never buy anything. My stomach clenches at the thought of my staggering mountain of student loans, built up degree by degree. Years of flailing around, trying to figure out what I wanted to do with my life before deciding on teaching—and then, that old stutter of mine resurfacing as I stood in front of the group practicing my teaching assignments. I have outgrown it, most of the time anyway, but the fear of my stutter proved to be as powerful as the thing itself: all those blank faces, my panic suffocating me like a thick blanket. Sometimes I think I should have stayed an uneducated immigrant like Ma and Pa. Some fledglings leave the nest and soar, like Sylvie; others flutter, and flutter, then tumble to the ground. In the end, I couldn't face my classmates and teachers anymore. And Sylvie, of course, was the one who bailed me out when my loans passed their grace period. She took over the payments without a word.

Sylvie's rich, at least compared to me, but she's not so wealthy that she can shoulder that burden without feeling it. She and her husband, Jim, are even more weighed down with student debt than I am, and Jim doesn't make much money as a guidance counselor at a public school in Brooklyn. Even though he's from old money, Jim's parents believe that kids should make it on their own, so he won't see a cent of his wealth until they pass on. That is, except for the ridiculous present they gave him when he married Sylvie. As for me, instead of helping Ma and Pa, who have already spent so many years working their fingers to the bone, I'm living in their apartment and eating their food. I temp here and there but despite my ability to type really fast, the only true skill I have, work has been scarce. It's the economy, I tell everyone, but of course I know better. It's me. Sylvie tells me I'm not fulfilling my potential and I tell her to shut up and leave me alone.

Inside the shop, I head for the classical section and begin to relax as soon as I hear the lustrous and velvety voice of Anna Netrebko floating from the loudspeakers. She's singing Verdi. Neat racks of CDs sit beside rows of musical scores and bin after bin of vinyl records. Old guitars and violins line the walls. I love the way it smells of paper, lacquer, and lemon detergent. Zach, the cute guy, is working again. At least, I believe he's attractive. It's hard to be sure without my glasses, which I wouldn't be caught dead in around him. To me, the lines of his face and body are appealing, and I love his voice—warm, rich, and clear. He always sounds like he's smiling at me.

"Hey, Amy. What would you like to listen to this week?"

I try to express friendliness with my face but think I've wound up contorting my features into something extremely awkward. "D-do you have any suggestions?"

He's only supposed to allow paying customers to sample the music but never seems to mind my lingering visits. "Well, how about some Joseph Szigeti?"

In my enthusiasm, I forget to be shy. "I just read an article about his version of the Prokofiev Concerto no. 1 in D."

"It's phenomenal," he says, pulling out a CD. "He's proof that technical perfection isn't everything."

But as we walk over to the listening station together, my phone rings. "I'm so sorry," I mumble. "I have to take this call." I duck my head and leave the store. I manage to answer my cell in time and the moment I hear Lukas's voice, I know something is wrong.

The line is full of static, probably due to the transatlantic call. I cover my other ear with my hand to try to hear him more clearly.

"Amy, I must speak to Sylvie right away," Lukas says. His voice is strained with urgency and his Dutch accent is heavier than I'd expected.

I wrinkle my brow. "But she's in the Netherlands right now, with you."

He breathes in so sharply I can hear it over the phone. "What? No, she is not. She flew back on Saturday. She should have arrived by now. Have you not heard from her?"

"W-we didn't even know she was coming home. I just spoke with her after Grandma's funeral. When was that? Thursday, right? I thought she'd stay awhile longer. She also mentioned her project there wasn't finished yet."

"Sylvie is not answering her phone. I want very to speak with her."

Precise, responsible Sylvie would have let us know right away if she were back. She would have come to see Ma and tell her about Grandma. My heart starts to throb like a wound underneath my skin.

There must be some simple explanation. I try to sound reassuring. "Don't worry, I'll find out what's going on."

"Yes, please see what the situation is. When you find her, ask her to call me, okay? Immediately." There is a painful pause. "I hope she is all right."

I quickly put on my glasses and hurry to the dry cleaners where Ma works. The faint smell of steam and chemicals engulfs me as I push open the door. I find Ma standing behind the long counter, talking in her broken English to a well-dressed woman with sleek, honey-blond hair.

"We were quite horrified to find one of the buttons loose after we picked this up," the customer says, pushing a man's pin-striped shirt toward Ma.

"So sorry." Ma's small face looks wan and pale against her black clothing, her eyes puffy from crying. "I fix."

The woman taps a manicured nail against the countertop. Her tone is both irritated and condescending, as if she's speaking to a child who has misbehaved. "It's not really the quality we expect, especially after your prices went up."

"So sorry," Ma repeats.

I glare at the woman's bony back. I want to tell her that the owner hiked up the prices. Ma had nothing to do with it. She's never even gotten a raise in the long years she's worked here—standing on her feet all day, lifting heavy bundles of clothing, steaming, ironing, and mending. But I keep my mouth shut. I wait until the customer finishes berating Ma and leaves.

A smile lights up Ma's face, despite her grief, when she sees me. Even though I can understand some Chinese, I never learned to speak it well, so Ma always talks to me in English. "Amy, why you here?"

I had resolved not to worry her but find myself grabbing her wrist, crumpling her thin polyester blouse. "Cousin Lukas just called. He says Sylvie flew home this past weekend, but she's not picking up her phone."

"Ay yah." Ma covers her mouth with her other hand. Her large dark eyes show too much white. "She not tell us she coming home. She must be okay. Just a mistake. You call ah-Jim?"

"I tried all the way here but he's not answering. There haven't been any plane crashes or anything, right?"

"Of course not! What you saying!" Ma brushes her forehead three times with her delicate left hand to ward off the evil of the words I just uttered. She stares at me until I lean in so she can do the same to me. We're almost exactly the same height and when I catch sight of our reflections in the store mirror, I'm reminded of how much we look alike—except that I wear thick glasses and can't compare to the photos of Ma in her youth. She had been the loveliest girl in our village in Guangdong. Now in her fifties, her skin is still fine with only a light etching of lines, a silky cream that sets off her warm eyes, and there's something gentle yet wild in her gaze, like a deer in the woods. "You go to their place. See what happening. Use the key, in dry ginger jar at home."

"I have my own key. Sylvie gave it to me before she left. But are you sure, Ma?" I cringe at the thought of entering Sylvie's house without permission. My mind races: What if Jim's there? What's happening to us? What could have happened to Sylvie?

"Sure, sure," she says. "You go now. Quick."

CHAPTER 2

Ma

Monday, May 2

I was as ignorant as the frog at the bottom of the well when I let Sylvie return to Holland. How many times must I surrender my daughter to that land of wind and fog and loss? She already spent the first nine years of her life there—and then, one moon ago, when she heard my ma, her grandma, was facing death, she rushed to book her ticket for Amsterdam. Sylvie was but a leaf, withering from homesickness, fluttering downward to return to the roots of its own tree.

I was so busy with Mrs. Hawkins, whose fair skin hid ugly features, that I did not notice when Amy entered the dry cleaners. My poor younger girl, her face stunned with fear, chewing on her chapped lips without realizing. I did not want to reveal my soul-burdens to her, especially since she was wearing her eye lenses for once. Her heart knows enough as it is.

I sat down to sew tighter the button Mrs. Hawkins complained about. I had shown it to Mr. Hawkins when he picked up the shirt and he had said it was not a problem. But he must be more than sixty years old and Mrs. Hawkins closer to forty. He is an old cow eating young grass, and so he must pay the price for his pleasure. As I worked, my mind wandered back to the blackest time in my life. It was more than thirty years ago, when I gave my six-moon-old Sylvie to Grandma to be raised in Holland. The worst thing about it was that I knew what I was doing. I had no excuse.

Pa and I had just moved to the Beautiful Country, and on all sides were the songs of Chu—we were isolated and without help. I already had the big stomach with Sylvie. There was no way to mend the pen after the goats were lost. Neither of us could speak a word of the Brave Language, English. Pa hunched over his bowl of bare rice with no meat or vegetables, only soy sauce, hiding his eyes with his roughened hand as he ate. He still loved me then with the innocence of his green years, and the hollows of his young face filled with guilt rather than accusation when he gazed at me.

We ate bitterness and tried a thousand ways, a hundred plans, but when the tiger ventures from the mountains to the plains, it is bullied by dogs. No one would help us or give us work until, finally, Pa found a job at the fish market in Chinatown. That was but one strand of cow hair among nine cows. How could it be enough? And things would only get worse after I delivered my baby. Many other couples like us sent their little ones back to China to be raised by family. That was their plan before they ever came to the Beautiful Country. But I swore I would never let go of my lovely swallow-girl.

Then Ma's letter arrived. She had moved to Holland with my possessing-money cousin Helena and Helena's husband, Willem, and they had just birthed a baby boy named Lukas. Grandma spoke of the cool air conditions, the ample broadness of their house, how Helena burdened her heart that Lukas would grow large as the only child of the Central Kingdom in their neighborhood. There were too few Chinese in Holland, as Helena herself knew well. That was the reason she'd returned to our village in the Central Kingdom to snatch up the good-to-look-at Willem as her own.

I scanned the letter, jealous that Helena had stolen my ma to care for her son. I would have given anything to have Grandma with me here in this strange and hostile Beautiful Country. But when I looked around the tiny space Pa and I were crammed into, I brought my heart in accord with both emotions and reason. Helena's family possessed money and they could provide for both Grandma and their baby. I made myself eat my discontent. Helena's own parents were too busy with their multipatterned lives to help Helena and Willem with their child. I should be grateful they had offered Grandma a better health situation than she had had in China.

I read on and realized Helena was putting forward more than that. *My heart stem,* Grandma wrote, *if you were to entrust your most precious fruit to me, perhaps it might alleviate some of your burden. It is at the asking of your cousin Helena that I write this. She and Willem would care for your child like their own cub until you are able to care for her yourself. Or come to Holland simply to see your old ma and accept the gifts only a mother can pass on to her child.*

I puffed air. Helena's flowery words and cunning language did not deceive me. She did not like me very much. From one fact, I could infer three. Her offer was to her own advantage, of course. She did not need to worry about my taking Grandma away, her babysitter and serving woman, and she would gain a play companion for her son. To be fair, Helena was asking for another mouth to feed, a body to clothe, and for that I was grateful. She would even pay for my flying machine ticket. But I would only bring my child to her as a last resort.

Then Sylvie was born. Sally, I named her in English. That is still what is written on her birth certificate. But in the language of the Central Kingdom, she has always been my Snow Jasmine, Sul-Li. It was the Holland people who did not recognize the name Sally, the Holland people who renamed her. She left me as Sally and returned as Sylvie.

She was so dainty, a small people-loving bird, clutching my finger as if it were a branch, Pa's great hands caressing her cheek, which was as flushed and tender as a peach. We had exhausted our meager savings by then. Earlier, no one wanted to hire a big-stomached woman who did not speak the Brave Language, and now, no one would allow me to come to work with a baby. What path would the fates have chosen for us, my Snow Jasmine, if only I had kept you here with me?

In that blistering New York summer, Sylvie wept sobs, and the little wind stirrer in that narrow room, stuffed with me, Pa, and her, offered no relief. I did odd jobs—bits of sewing, stringing fake pearls into bracelets—to earn more money. I washed her pee cloths in the bathing vat. Pa started a second job, standing tables at a meal hall until deep into the night. It ground us down until, in the eighth moon, the white ghost took my purse bundle.

I had gone into Chinatown with the hope of finding a job in a bread-baking shop. They had taken one look at Sylvie strapped to my back with a piece of cloth and sent me out the door again. With low breath and no strength, I was the last off the underground train at our stop in Queens. I was half running, trying to catch up to the other passengers, when the white ghost cut them from my view. He had eyes as blue and flinty as the blind old beggar of our village in the Central Kingdom. With one hand he grabbed my purse strap and with the other he shoved my shoulder so hard I stumbled and fell to the ground.

Desperate, I twisted to avoid landing on Sylvie. A flash of agony burned its way up my arm, footsteps running away. The white ghost wailed over his shoulder, "Fokkin' Chinee!" That much of the Brave Language I already knew. I lay there, stunned, with my cheek bleeding against the concrete, glad to hear Sylvie weeping on my back, glad she had survived to cry. What if he had grabbed the straps of the baby carrier cloth along with my purse? What if I had landed on top of her? What if we had fallen onto the train tracks?

I wrote to Helena to say I would bring my baby girl in the tenth moon. I still should not have done it. But I was twenty-three years old, newly married, newly emigrated, and struggling not to drown in this vast ocean called the Beautiful Country. I told myself it was only for a year, and then we would bring her back. I did not know it would be nine years until I saw her again.

I held my girl close to me that endless time in the flying machine until we landed in Holland on a black day of excessive water. Then I understood: I had brought my daughter to a landscape of tears.

CHAPTER 3

Amy

Monday, May 2

Sylvie's fine, of course she is. I hang on to my seat as the subway car rattles its way to Brooklyn Heights and try to think. Aside from all of her other qualities, Sylvie's like a female James Bond. *Overachiever* doesn't even begin to describe her. If our faucet leaks, Sylvie fixes it. She's enhanced my old laptop with so many extra drives and so much memory that I nicknamed it Frankenstein. Even if her plane crashed, Sylvie would be the one to parachute to safety, after saving all of her fellow passengers. I've never been on an airplane, but she's told me a million times to always count the number of rows to the nearest exit door, so that in case of an emergency, I could crawl there in the dark. She even learned how to shoot a gun at a shooting range. You never know, she said.

One of the few things Sylvie can't do is swim. When we were born, Ma and Pa had our prophecies written by the monks at the temple and Sylvie's forbade her to go near water. When I'd heard this, I'd said, "Isn't that kind of self-fulfilling? If she doesn't learn to swim, she'll definitely drown if she falls into the water, right?" But Sylvie didn't want to take swimming lessons anyway and everyone ignored me as usual. Our parents didn't share anything more about our prophecies. When I pressed Ma years ago, she said, "Must not open book too far. But your bone weight is heavy. Good fortune will come to you."

"And Sylvie?" I asked, proud to have a substantial bone weight, whatever that meant.

Ma's lids lowered, shuttering her thoughts. "Mountains of gold everywhere, but thirst too."

I get off the subway at Brooklyn Heights and try to call Jim again. It goes straight to voicemail. How can a guidance counselor be so hard to reach? If I were a suicidal student, wouldn't I be dead by now? I leave another message and try Sylvie's number too. Again, it goes straight to voicemail.

"Hey, it's me," I say. "People are getting worried about you so please get back to me, okay? I'm going to use that key you gave us for emergencies and break into your house. I hope you're okay with that and that Jim isn't there, showering or something. All right, bye."

Not that I'd mind seeing Jim nude. He's pretty hot, if you're into the blond scruffy type. But ever since Sylvie brought him home from Princeton, I've always been slightly irritated by the way he leans in too close to everyone, his hand casually resting on their arm or shoulder. We Chinese are pretty much the opposite of touchy-feely, although Sylvie drinks up his warmth like a thirsty plant—and I'm happy for her. Sylvie needs to be in control and hides her affection most of the time, but I've caught her watching him, the look in her eyes so tender and open. I'd give anything to experience that kind of love. At first, Ma and Pa didn't like that Jim wasn't Chinese, but since he was Sylvie's boyfriend, they accepted him. Sylvie always could get away with anything.

I exit the subway station and step out into the kinder, gentler world that money can buy. I brush past a nanny pushing a pram along the shady, tree-lined cobblestone sidewalk and hurry to reach the waterfront, where Jim and Sylvie live. Along one side of their street, sloping walkways lead to the Promenade. As I hurry past, I glance down at the long esplanade and see a model surrounded by reflective screens posing against the spectacular view of the Manhattan skyline. In the distance, I hear little kids whooping as they chase each other around the large playground at the end of their block. What Sylvie and I would have given for a place like that when we were small, filled with tire swings and a huge jungle gym.

"So Jim and I will be moving again," Sylvie had told me a few years ago, right before they married. I was meeting her for lunch at Rockefeller Center, where she had just started a new job as a management consultant. She was rubbing her short, roughly bitten fingernails against the gleaming tabletop. They had moved back to NYC a couple of months earlier, after Sylvie finished her MBA at Harvard. They were renting a studio apartment in the East Village.

They wouldn't leave New York so soon, would they? I'd just gotten my sister back. "Where are you going?" I'd asked, taking a big bite of my burger to cover my alarm.

"His parents have given us an apartment in Brooklyn Heights as a wedding present." Her voice was determinedly casual, as if gifting someone a place worth more than a million dollars happened every day. She didn't meet my eyes and toyed with her salad with her fork.

I stopped chewing. I'd heard Jim's family was rich but it had always been theoretical, with his battered car and wrinkled T-shirts. I'd even wondered if Sylvie had invented that part of his background to appease Ma and Pa for her marrying a white guy.

Sylvie looked up and saw my face, her eyes bright. Her dimple appeared in her left cheek. "Close your mouth, Amy. You're going to choke."

I finally managed to swallow. "Now I feel bad. I'm getting you guys a blender."

We both giggled.

I exhaled. Sylvie was staying. That was the important thing. "How do you feel about it?" I asked.

"Fine, of course. It's a lovely present," she said, but I heard the undercurrent of shame in her voice. Sylvie loves to show off her nice things, but she's also proud. In high school, she once had a math teacher who was infamous for saying girls didn't belong in his classroom. I still remember her intense, rigid back as she bent over her math books night after night until she'd beaten everyone in that class.

When I arrive at the tall, sleek brownstone where their garden apartment is located, I open the gate next to the outside staircase and pass by the large glazed dragon pot Ma and Pa gave Sylvie. It's filled with some indestructible shrub she never remembers to water. I go down three steps and reach their blue front door.

I ring the doorbell a few times. *Come on, Sylvie, open up. You're inside sleeping off the jet lag. Your phone broke, that's all.* My breath quickens as I wait. Finally, I pull their key from my pocket. But when I unlock the heavy door and try to push it open, it jams.

A large pile of newspapers and mail blocks the entryway. What the hell? Sylvie's been away for about a month, but where on earth is Jim? The air in the hallway is still and musty. I step inside and look around.

The apartment has been beautifully renovated, with tasteful recessed lighting, large bay windows, and a sleek modern kitchen, but Sylvie and Jim still live in it like two college students. There are piles of books everywhere and stacks of magazines on their upright piano. Sylvie has never cared about anything remotely domestic. She's a terrible cook, blackening every slice of toast and attempted pot roast. A couple of months ago, I accompanied her and her colleagues to a Broadway show when their company had free tickets. The conversation was stiff and none of her coworkers asked me anything about myself. After a while, I felt like I was interviewing them. How did Sylvie survive among such uptight people? At one point, I mentioned what a disastrous cook Sylvie was in an attempt to lighten the atmosphere and she glared at me, later chewing me out for my unprofessionalism. I wanted to say, *Sylvie, if people know you're human, they'll like you more,* but I remained silent, as usual.

I peek in a few kitchen cupboards and find the pots and pans pristine, of course. Neither of them ever cooks. They live on takeout sweet-and-sour pork and tikka masala. Despite Sylvie's chronic messiness, I'm unprepared for the chaos I find when I open their bedroom door.

A pair of slacks has been tossed across the turquoise footboard of their large bed. Wrinkled shirts are strewn all over the floor and small piles of scarves and earrings lie scattered on the mattress, as if Sylvie packed in a hurry. Then I notice that every item I see is Sylvie's. Where are Jim's belongings? I open their closet door. It's a violation of their privacy, but I need to know—and, indeed, only Sylvie's pressed suits are hanging there. The other half of the closet is bare.

My chest constricts. It's clear no one has been here for a long time.

CHAPTER 4

Sylvie

Saturday, March 5
Two Months Earlier

People call French the language of love, but the only language lodged deep in my heart was that of my childhood, Dutch.

He had told me his name was Jim. It was only later that I learned his true name. My first semester at Princeton, I focused solely on my grades and my future. After all, when poverty enters, love flies out the window. I understood better than anyone that smoke does not come out of the chimney from love alone—and never forgot that Amy, Ma, and Pa were counting on me back home.

In a writing seminar, my second semester at Princeton, I noticed Jim. We were working on a practice exam in a lecture hall with soaring, pointed arched windows and slender columns that made the room feel like a Gothic church. I finished long before the others and rechecked my paper for style, spelling, and grammatical issues but was still surrounded by bent heads and pens scratching lined notebooks. I gazed out the window, watching as the angels shook out their cushions atop the backdrop of trees. At first, I was so hypnotized by the snow I did not notice how the cool sunlight cast a halo of gold upon the guy sitting in front of the glass. His hair curled in loose gleaming waves, unrestrained and free. He was sprawled in his chair—legs spread wide, jeans so torn I could see bits of hairy leg through the holes. I could never take up space like that, as if I had been born unfettered, as if this world were my birthright. Then I met his eyes. So warm and wicked, I could drown in them. He had been studying me the whole time. I quickly looked away, but found him waiting for me by the doorway as we left.

"I'm struggling in this class," he said, his mischievous eyes now entreating. Even his feathery eyelashes were golden. He bent closer and almost breathed into my ear, "Please help me."

It was a lie and also our beginning. For many years, I found the excuse he had used to meet me charming.

Jim was the perfect combination of high- and lowbrow. He bought a wreck of an automobile for six hundred dollars and named it after Grendel from *Beowulf.* I was delighted to have a boyfriend with knowledge unfathomable to Ma and Pa. We rode around in his car, feeling young and carefree. Jim wanted to do things that would never have occurred to me, like scoring beer even though we were underage. Neither of us liked the taste but we drank it because it was the sort of thing normal college kids did in the movies—and that was what we wanted to be. I sputtered, unused to alcohol, and Jim, driven by his desire to seem ordinary and manly, disguised his distaste. He was more accustomed to the fine wine of his parents' collection.

I wanted to escape my poor background and forget about ugly Sylvie with the crooked tooth and eye patch, and he was pretending to be someone other than James Quaker Bates II, a name I never even heard until he took me home for Christmas during our second year. I should have known that was why the prep school kids always trailed after him and laughed too hard at his jokes. I had naively thought it was his charisma that overcame all boundaries. It was not until Grendel drove through the gate at his family's coastal estate on Lake Michigan and continued past a half kilometer of landscaped garden before reaching their Georgian mansion that I began to understand that he had a life like a god in France.

Now, many years later, I was not sure if we had truly loved each other or merely the versions of ourselves we had seen reflected in the other's eyes—as if we had acted out a play together, both of us player and audience alike. I was what he had dreamed of as well: someone who had gotten into Princeton based on drive and brains alone. My lack of connections and money had reassured him that he too had made it there on his own.

My heart ached at this realization. The revelations and drama of the past week had gone straight through my marrow and bone. Who was the man I had married: Jim, James, or someone else I never knew at all?

CHAPTER 5

Amy

Monday, May 2

My palms are wet and clammy and my heart is running a marathon inside my chest. The robust security guard behind the desk stares at me as if she's wondering whether I should be at a mental hospital and not at the high school where Jim works. I give her my name. She calls him, listens to something on the other end of the line, and says he's unavailable.

"Please," I say. "H-his sister, I mean, my sister—"

"I can't help you, ma'am," she says. Her tone is polite but firm. "Please exit the school premises."

I stand outside and wait among the pushing, writhing crowd of raucous teenagers for what feels like hours. A group of them lean against the gate, smoking pot; the musky odor clings to my hair. Jim will come out for his lunch break. He's one of those overly energetic people who's always taking long walks or jogging places when he should be resting like a normal person. I hate myself for waiting. Why didn't I have the guts to elbow my way into the school? I'm nauseous with worry about

Sylvie yet still a coward. How could Jim be unavailable? He's family and Sylvie is missing.

Finally, I catch a glimpse of his light hair. It's immediately visible, like an albino rabbit. He's surrounded by adoring teenage girls, mostly Latino and African American, all laughing up at their cute young guidance counselor.

"Jim!" I call out. When he finally sees me, he immediately averts his eyes and shoves his way in the opposite direction.

I am so shocked that it takes me a second to move. Jim is rather broad, and the girls tag along, still chatting, so it takes him longer to worm through the crowd than me.

I maneuver myself in front of him so he can't avoid me. "Hey, Jim!" The teenagers take one look at my strained face and disperse.

"Oh, hi, Amy," he says with a weak smile. I have never seen him look so terrible, not even when he was in grad school and pulling all-nighters. His eyes are bloodshot, his hair greasy, and he's sporting a few days' worth of stubble.

"I-I tried to see you at school but you weren't available."

He rubs his hand over his forehead as if he's tired. "What? I was in a meeting all morning. I wasn't even told you were here."

I press my lips together but decide not to confront him about this. What would be the point anyway? "Where's Sylvie? Have you seen her?"

A fire engine screams past us, distracting me, sirens blaring. When I turn back to Jim, his gaze is calm. Was he surprised at my question? "She's still abroad, isn't she?"

"Our cousin Lukas says she flew back this past weekend, but no one can reach her. I was just at your apartment and it looks like nobody's been there for ages. What's going on?"

He pinches the bridge of his nose like he's in pain. "She didn't tell you? Of course not."

"Tell me what?"

"We're separated."

"What?!" That was too loud. The kids standing nearby are staring at us now. Images of a happy Sylvie and Jim flash through my mind. We spent this past Christmas at their house.

Jim bends closer to me and lowers his voice. "Since March. She kicked me out, Amy."

"Why?" My eyes narrow. "What did you do?"

He holds up his hands in protest. "Look, you know Sylvie's not the easiest person in the world."

The blood rushes to my head. "D-don't you insult my sister. If she threw you out, she had a damn good reason."

He clenches his square jaw. "Oh, right, can't taint the altar of the holy Sylvie. Well, hero-worshipping little sister, don't let your illusions blind you."

"What do you mean by that?"

He huffs out a deep breath and then easygoing, charming Jim returns. "Forget I said anything. I'm just upset by the whole thing and she's refusing to be reasonable. Is she okay?"

"I wouldn't know. No one's heard from her." Despite my frustration, I am desperate enough to ask, "Do you have any idea where she could be?"

His face is still. I catch a flash of genuine fear in his eyes. "I'm the last person Sylvie would contact or want to see. Believe me, I've tried. But come on, Amy, this is Sylvie. She's fine. She probably just wants some time to herself."

Sylvie is the most dutiful person I know. She would never make us worry like this. I turn on my heel and walk away. Jim calls after me, "Look, I'm sorry, Amy. If there's anything I can do . . ."

I'd like to go back and punch him in his face. Sylvie's marriage has been on the rocks for months and she didn't tell anyone. She didn't tell me. When we were little, I'd lie with my head on her lap as she stroked my hair and I'd tell her every tiny thing that happened to me at school: the girls who'd giggled over my cheap pants, the impossibly densely freckled boy I'd liked, the mean teacher with the face like a prune. She would laugh or commiserate and I'd always say, "Sylvie, we tell each other everything, right? Right?" And she'd answer, "Right." But now I'm beginning to realize that maybe I've always been the only one doing the telling.

The shadows grow long as Ma and I wait for Pa to come home. Ma seems to have crumpled and shrunk over the past few hours, this blow coming on top of her mother's death. As she prepares dinner, her hands shake so much I'm afraid she will cut herself. Several times, she stops and prays to our gods, her lips moving silently. We have carefully avoided any further conversation or decisions. There's still no word from Sylvie. My head is spinning with the news that she and Jim broke up. I'd tried to find out if Sylvie had boarded any flights but the airlines wouldn't disclose that information and we don't have access to her credit cards.

I think back to Christmas at Sylvie's apartment. It had been a bit stressful, but the holidays are always somewhat strained. Ma and Pa's English is so poor and Jim doesn't know any Chinese. Furthermore, Sylvie feels like that's the one time a year she should cook—big mistake right there. Jim tries to help, but that's pretty much the blind leading the blind. It's as if Sylvie is trying to fulfill some fantasy of a real American Christmas, when none of us even know what that means. We're still foreigners despite the years we've lived here. I may have grown up in Queens but my entire home life has been Chinese—chopsticks, bitter melon with carp on Sundays, Buddhist holidays, respect your elders—and Jim's as close to royalty as you can get in this country. We always sit at the table while Ma and Pa struggle with the cutlery ("ay yah—knives on the table," Ma whispered in Chinese the first time, staring), burned stuffing, cranberry sauce, and the language barrier.

I don't remember this past Christmas being any different. The best part was always after dinner, when Jim played their piano and Sylvie and I sang Christmas carols and top forties hits together by candlelight. Even Pa would sit back, his eyes shining; listening to words he didn't understand but carried along by the river of feelings conveyed through the music. Sometimes I'd even play a little guitar. I'd begged for lessons growing up, but we could never afford it. Still, Sylvie had bought me a guitar a few years ago and I've taught myself a few songs. Christmas at Sylvie's had been the only time I was the center of attention and felt competent, joyful, and free. Despite the awkward dinners, those holidays together were some of my happiest memories: all of the people I loved at peace with each other and the world.

Of course, Lunar New Year is the most important holiday to the Chinese, but it's hard to celebrate with all your heart when your festivity isn't reflected by the society around you—no films on television, no displays in department stores, no friends with gifts, and no propaganda about peace and love whatsoever. Sylvie and I always had to go to school on Chinese New Year.

Sylvie, where are you? How could you not have told me what was going on with Jim? I've seen her often since they broke up in March. We talk or text several times a week. She must have been in so much pain and didn't let me help her. That hurts me more than anything. Ma told me not to tell Pa about their marriage problems, that it would only upset him.

When Pa finally comes through the door, he doesn't realize anything is wrong. He is carrying a wrapped bundle of seafood from the store, as usual. After we greet him as is proper, he puts the package in the refrigerator and hangs his jacket on one of the bent wire hangers in the closet. He sits at the fold-out table in the kitchen and waits for his dinner, like he always does. He's a large man with reddened hands that smell like fish. He scrubs them daily but can never entirely rid himself of the scent. Ma always says how much Sylvie takes after Pa, though I'm not sure I see it, with Pa's hulking bulk and Sylvie's greyhound leanness. She does have a dimple in her left cheek, and Pa, ridiculously, has one in his right—another similarity Ma likes to bring up. I'm always surprised when it appears on his hard face. Sylvie isn't much like Ma either. They are both beautiful, but where Ma's delicate and yielding, like a coconut rice ball, Sylvie is all long limbs and sharp edges, more a broadsword saber.

Pa unfurls the Chinese newspaper he's brought home and grunts. He's always been like this, as far back as I can remember: a taciturn, old-fashioned man. It must have disconcerted him to have two daughters. He would have preferred sons. They tend to chatter less. The old faded posters of chubby boys riding on carp and carrying gold and peaches that cover our apartment are remnants of his failed hopes, his thwarted attempts to bring male energy into the womb of his pregnant wife. But there's something gentle about Pa too, a tenderness to the way he brushes Ma's cheek with the back of his hand every once in a while. After they shop for groceries in Chinatown, he carries as many of the heavy plastic bags as he can, leaving as few as possible for Ma. He stands the entire day at work but if a seat opens up on the crowded subway, he guards it until Ma can drop her tired body into it. He makes sure our winter coats are warm and thick but has refused to replace his own shabby jacket for years, despite the way I catch him shivering through the bitter winters.

I'm his favorite daughter. Why, I don't know, but he and Sylvie have never gotten along. Like ginger dipped in sugar, Ma says, simultaneously delicious and explosive. Sylvie's even allergic to fish and seafood, which has been a source of irritation to Pa through the years. When we were younger, he used to growl about how it was a waste for Ma to cook separate dishes for Sylvie, as if it were Sylvie's fault that she broke out in hives after eating shrimp. He seemed to believe that Sylvie was allergic because she thought she was too good for his food, and thus too good for him too. Now he looks up, sees me watching him, and smiles, unveiling his straight white teeth. That easing of the daily strain on his face makes him suddenly as handsome as a movie star. Pa used to pat me on the head when I was little and call me "my girl, my very own Amy."

I exchange a glance with Ma, and then gently say, "Pa, we have bad news."

He startles, sits upright. His English is a bit better than Ma's. "What is this?"

"Sylvie's missing." The color in Pa's skin drains away, turning it slowly to ash. I swallow hard and press on. After I tell him the whole story, carefully omitting the part about Sylvie's problems with Jim, he hides his eyes with his hand until he finally pronounces, "Jim is her husband. He must act now. It is his duty."

"I spoke with him today." I decide to lie. "He's too busy at work.

He can't get away to do anything and he thinks she's just taking some time." I'm a terrible liar. "For her career." Anything to do with work is sacred as far as Ma and Pa are concerned.

Pa nods. "Jim knows best. We can do nothing anyway."

I don't have Pa's faith in Jim. I say hesitantly, "Should one of us go to Holland?" Who? Me? I am terrified at the idea of traveling to another country. I don't even like the thought of going to New Jersey. Ma? She can't speak English. And Pa could never leave—he's needed at his job, anyway. The image of Ma and Pa on an airplane is incongruous. They can hardly navigate this country. How would they ever manage abroad?

"No," he says, anger filling each word. "Too dangerous and what you can do there anyway? You just little girl. Cousin Helena and her family know what to do."

I have to bite back a retort at that. Ma doesn't speak up. She never does. Whenever Pa is drunk and angry, she only becomes quieter. I suppose I've learned my silence from her. Their marriage, like many others of their generation, was arranged because their families knew each other. Pa often feels to me like he's holding his breath, filled with frustration and rage at some wrong that's been done to him in the past. Sometimes I spot a look that might be longing on his face but then I blink and it's gone, as if it had never existed.

There were nights when I was little when they'd fight and Sylvie and I would clutch at each other in our room, hiding behind the walls that were too thin to muffle any sound. My memories begin a few years after Sylvie was brought home to Queens to live. I was about four years old. I couldn't understand the Chinese words Pa called Ma then, but Sylvie's cheeks would glow bright red. It often happened after he'd been drinking rice wine, and the next day, it'd be life as usual.

Sylvie confronted him once. I tried to stop her, clutching at her sleeve, but she marched down the hall and pounded on their door.

When Ma opened it, Sylvie said, "You waking Amy."

Ma was horrified, more so than Pa, and quickly bundled Sylvie out and back to our room.

"You must never do that again." Ma was a pale ghost standing in our doorway. "Never, never. Promise!" And we did, though we didn't know if she was afraid for us or for herself.

"We have to do something," I say to them now. But as I look around the room, I realize that none of us have any idea what our next move should be. Sylvie was the one we always called for help. There's no one else, no one except me.

Telephone Call

Tuesday, May 3

Bethany: Hello, Bethany Jones speaking. How may I help you?

Amy: Bethany, this is Amy.

Bethany: What a surprise. What can I do for you?

Amy: I'm calling about Sylvie. [Voice breaks] She's disappeared. No one knows where she is.

Bethany: What? I'm so sorry. Is there anything we can do?

Amy: Well, I would really like the contact information for that consultancy project she's doing in the Netherlands.

Bethany: I'm a bit confused.

Amy: Your company sent her there, right? Maybe she's left a message or something. I don't know how to get in touch with them.

Bethany: . . . I'm afraid Sylvie doesn't work here anymore. She left more than a month ago, at the end of March.

Amy: What? B-but she never said anything . . . Are you sure? Why did she leave?

Bethany: I truly apologize but I'm not permitted to disclose that information. She's probably been sent there via a new employer and this is just some sort of mix-up.

Amy: I'm scared something's happened to her. [Chokes back a sob] I can't believe she didn't tell me she left your company.

Bethany: I wish I could do more for you. But don't worry, Sylvie is extremely competent. She doesn't need anyone's pity.

Amy: Why would I pity her? Was she fired?

Bethany: Well, we don't let anyone go here. People sometimes are encouraged to explore new horizons—that's all. Of course, it's not up to me to say what's fair or unfair. When you reach your sister, I'm sure she'll tell you all about it.

Tuesday, May 3

Amy Lee

Everyone, sorry to bother you but has anyone heard from my sister Sylvie in the past week or so? Do you know anything about a possible new job of hers by any chance? It's really important. Thanks.

Like Comment Share

Don McConnell

Nope, but isn't she abroad? She's probably just caught up with her work.

Like Reply

Katie Che

Sorry, haven't heard from her. But she doesn't tend to write much. Probably just a time difference thing. Don't know anything about a new job. Hey, when are we getting together for a drink? Been too long. Noah says hi, by the way.

Like Reply

Etienne Sarski

She went to Denmark or Finland or something, right? Always get confused with those foreign places. I'm up for a drink, can I come?

Like Reply

Amy Lee

She went to the Netherlands. Has anyone heard anything? **Min Ho Chung**? **Fred Gap**? **Judith van Es**? **Michelle Silva**? Please tag anyone else you think might have heard from her. We're getting pretty worried.

Like Reply

Amy Lee

Hello? Has anyone heard anything from her?

Like Reply

Amy Lee

Hello?

Like Reply

Telephone Call

Wednesday, May 4

Sylvie (recording): Hi, this is the voicemail of Sylvie Lee. Please leave a message after the beep and I will get back to you as soon as possible.

Amy: Please pick up. We're scared. It's been so long. It's totally not like you to disappear like this. I've checked with Lukas again via email and there's still no sign of you. If you can hear me but for some reason can't answer, it's going to be okay. We love you and I'm flying to the Netherlands tonight. I know, I'll probably die of fear before I even arrive. Ma and Pa don't want me to come but I used my bank account money, you know, all those red envelopes we saved our whole lives. And at least I have a passport. It's a good thing you always make us keep our passports valid, in case we need to flee a sudden war or something. Of course I didn't dare to actually tell Ma and Pa I'd bought the ticket, I just left the confirmation page on the table for them to find. Pa turned quite red but he didn't say anything. I'm so nervous about leaving the country. I practically threw up after booking my seat, but you're more important.

You hang in there, Sylvie. I don't know what kind of trouble you're in but we'll get through it together. I'm coming for you.

CHAPTER 6

Sylvie

Friday, April 1
One Month Earlier

It was late in the evening and I sat on the airplane at JFK, waiting for it to depart and bring me home to the Netherlands. When I was little and still living there, I had chafed at the bit. I was a troublesome child, had already started the dolls dancing even then. *She has pepper in her butt*, the Dutch kids had said. In a society that graded you down if you wrote extra pages for an exercise because you had not followed the rules of the assignment, I had always wanted too much, tried too hard. *Just do normal*, the Dutch said, and I was many things but never that.

But as I fastened my seat belt, I felt as if I was returning to a safe haven—east, west, home was best. I was going back to the place where no one had ever needed me to be extraordinary. How many times had I dreamed of going home over the years? Why had I never returned before now? It had been a long trip of the spotted cow, filled with trials and tribulations.

When I was nine years old and newly arrived in the United States, I had to wear that hated eye patch and the American kids had laughed at me; for that and for my accent and my crooked front tooth. I could speak only a few words of English then. Even after I learned the language, I kept the accent that, for many years, they thought was Chinese—*chink, go home to China, you can't even talk right, stupid Buddhahead*—but was actually Dutch. And I had watched as those syrup lickers fawned over the girl with French parents because her accent was so European. Only Amy would dance with joy when she saw me each day. Amy, who slipped her tender hand in mine, wrapping it around my icy heart.

Where I was cold and false—a beast of artifice like the bejeweled mechanical nightingale the Chinese emperor bought to replace the one of flesh and blood—Amy was genuine, a sweet little piece of licorice, always true to herself. She had a habit of pushing up her glasses with her middle finger, as if she were giving everyone the bird, and I found it incredibly endearing that she had no idea she was doing it. She was a giver while I was a consumer, burning up everything and everyone I touched. Naturally, I had been jealous of Amy ever since she was born. Amy, the wanted child, and the only reason my parents brought me back to the United States, so I could babysit her. Ma cared nothing for what I did. I could go to bed past midnight and she would not even mark it. I often left the apartment without eating breakfast because I wanted, just once, to hear Ma's soft voice say, "Sylvie, come back," but she never did. Meanwhile, Amy had to button her coat. Amy could not leave without a warm little bite in her stomach. Amy had help in everything.

When I had nightmares, Amy would bounce me awake in that little bedroom we shared and say, "You're speaking monster language in your sleep again." No matter how many years I lived in America, I always dreamed in Dutch. Dutch was something that belonged to me, or so it seemed when I left the only country I had ever known. It was a complex language, filled with challenging sounds and a wrapped-up word order. Despite its intricacy, it was the language of my soul. Nowadays, we all lived in a time boundary when emotion defeated logic, an era when gut feeling reigned over rationality. There was no patience for the difficult, the indecipherable, yet what else was the human heart but that?

While at Princeton, I joined the Dutch language table for our weekly meal to converse among others who spoke it. Their surprise, when they first saw me, turned to shock when I started to speak Dutch, at first with some hesitation, then ever more fluently. They delighted in teaching me everything I had missed, from sexual organs to curses that often embarrassed them but not me: *cancer, typhoid sufferer, raisin snob, poop catcher, lamb balls*. I had to hold myself in so I did not laugh out loud. From this, I learned that curses were impotent unless powered by shame and the appeal of the forbidden.

And naturally, Lukas wrote to me in Dutch, but our correspondence tapered off as we grew older and were drawn further into our separate lives. When we were little, we would go to the library in our village and Lukas would pore over the art and photography books, inhaling the scent of each page as if he wanted to absorb every image into himself. Off and on through the years, I would receive a letter from him in his beautiful slanted handwriting about yet another new girlfriend ("you would like her, Sylvie, she is as brilliant as you"), his study by the famous Rietveld Academie ("the world has cracked open its lens for me")—and then, as he was struggling to establish himself as a photojournalist, a view-card only once in a while from places like Bolivia ("freezing my butt off in the Andes Mountains"), Turkey ("stray kitten here has been waiting for me every day outside my door, bringing her home"), China ("leaving Guangdong behind me now"). He was less good with electronics: erratic and confused, sometimes writing me emails that ran on for pages, then not responding to my reply for months, only to later send an apology that he had found his unsent email in his drafts folder.

I told Amy she should not lose herself in her fantasies, but I was the one who had spent my life on dreaming. When I was living with Helena and Willem in their cold house, I longed for my own ma and pa, whom I had never met, parents who would love and accept me as I was. Then, when I was finally allowed to return to my real parents—*They only need a child minder for their new daughter,* Helena had told me—I clung to memories of Grandma back in the Netherlands. Her warm arms, her smell of Nivea cream and Chinese hair gel, of the rice and meat porridge she made for me and Lukas after school, of warm caramel waffles from the street markets and licorice in long, pointy plastic sacks. Lukas, who always had a new joke to tell me as we walked to school each day, and who made me toss stick after stick into the swirling water so he could capture just the right photo. Fool that I was, I always yearned for that which I did not have.

It was a risk, returning to what I cherished as my homeland. I dreamed of plaice and yet I ate flatfish; I always expected too much. Yes, that was the reason I had never gone back to the Netherlands on vacation, not even on our marriage-trip. I had changed and I was terrified that my dream of the one place I truly belonged would be overwritten and I would have nothing left, no solace at all.

But then Grandma called, her voice so weak on the phone. *Sylvie, you must travel back to see me. Quickly. Quickly.*

There were only a handful of people whom I genuinely loved in this life and Grandma was one of them. She reached out because she was on the edge of her grave, close to being with the ants. My sweet grandma, who had held me as I cried over some cruel words Helena had said to me. I clutched at the raw pain that convulsed my chest. How many years had it been? Now, suddenly, there was almost no time left—and, even if only temporarily, the trip would allow me to leave behind the wreck that was Jim, my career, and the rest of my life.

When I had repeated Grandma's words to Ma, Pa, and Amy, Ma had stiffened, and I knew that she too grasped what Grandma truly wanted. We had never spoken of the jewelry, but Grandma must have revealed her secret to her only daughter.

"I want to say goodbye to my mother—I mean, Grandma," I had said. Ma had flinched. I had kicked her in her tender leg on purpose and I was glad. She had not been there for me when I was a child, and Grandma had. Then I had lied as hard as glass, telling them that work was sending me there. I knew that would pull Pa over the rope like nothing else, and Ma always did whatever Pa said, as if she were paying penance for some crime she had committed. If only they knew that the successful, competent Sylvie had nothing anymore. Would they be disappointed in me?

Then Ma had surprised us all by saying, "Maybe I go with her."

We all stared. Ma never went anywhere. She was afraid to burn herself with cold water. Even when I tried to take them out to dinner, she protested about the expense, the trouble, the unsafe world outside of our apartment. What the farmer did not know, she would not eat. Go nowhere, do nothing, then you'll be safe.

Pa turned to her, angered, rearing on his back paws. "What?"

Ma looked down, blinked away tears: I spotted a ship with sour apples on the way. She said in a choked voice, "She is my mother." Guilt engulfed me like a cloud of hot steam and I could hardly breathe for a moment. How could I have overlooked this? Always only concerned with myself. Grandma would be filled with joy to see Ma again.

"No," Pa said, his face hard and stern. Sometimes I hated him. "Amy need you here."

At this, Amy's jaw slackened. "Are you crazy? She doesn't need to change my diaper."

"I can pay for the tickets," I said, even though in my head, I watched the figures dwindle in my savings account.

But Ma was already shaking her head, always the peacemaker, her own needs buried under a mountain of obligation. "No, I must work. You go, Sylvie."

"She has the right to see her mother," I said, facing Pa. I was not afraid of him, not like Ma and Amy. My own guilt at neglecting Ma's feelings built up in me like hot air, egging me on. Pa was so unfair, so old-fashioned and sexist. My voice rose. "Why are you stopping her?"

A dark streak of red raced up his rigid neck, the strained tendons prominent. "You have no respect," he ground out.

"No, stop," Ma said, stepping between us with fluttering hands. She spoke so quickly, I could barely make out the words. "No matter, no matter. I not go. I not want to. Sylvie, please stop. Please." She was almost in tears, a pale pink flush drowning her eyes.

I watched her with sharp and painful pity and sighed, my anger deflating like a pricked balloon. How could I ever convince Pa if Ma insisted on fighting against herself? I turned to Amy. "Do you want to come?"

Amy, so much like Ma, had eaten from frightened hare meat. Her eyes enormous behind her thick lenses, she said, "A foreign country? Thanks, but I haven't even been anywhere else in the U.S.—unless you count Hoboken. Strange language, weird food, terrorists . . . I'll stay right here."

"You need to expand your horizons."

"I like my boundaries just where they are, thank you very much," Amy said, and that was the end of our discussion. Secretly, I was relieved. I would be able to return alone.

The flight attendant's voice came on through the intercom, telling us to get ready for departure, first in English, then in Dutch. I felt her words sink into my bones. The engines roared and we took off.

Part 2

CHAPTER 7

Amy

Wednesday, May 4

I spend the entire flight counting the number of rows to the emergency exit in case we crash, not only due to fear but out of loyalty to Sylvie. The plane is too hot. The huge, heavy man next to me keeps claiming the armrest with his plump elbow and I decide to cede him this battle, scrunching myself as small as possible in my seat. I'm thankful I have the window. I'm so worried about Sylvie that I don't have much anxiety left to wonder if we'll crash. Any terrorists can wait until after I find out what happened to my sister. I'm too nervous to sleep, even when they turn off the lights. There's a wide selection of movies available in the screen built into the back of the seat in front of me, but they all seem to revolve around murder or sex. Finally, I plug my headphones in and tune in to the music station, trying to relax. The constant hum and vibration of the engines makes me feel nauseous, and that giant man looms beside me. It's like there's no way out. I don't have enough air. But I can't panic. Sylvie needs me. I breathe shallowly for hours in the dark.

After what feels like an eternity, the lights come back on and the flight attendants hand out cardboard boxes filled with our prepackaged breakfasts: a flat container of blueberry yogurt, a little closed cup of orange juice, plastic utensils so we can't attack anyone, and a cold turkey and cheese sandwich on hard bread, plus coffee or tea. I ask for tea. I'm already vibrating with tension, lack of sleep, and fear; I don't need much caffeine. The man next to me has slept soundly with his special neck pillow and now stretches. Since he's awake, I slide open the window shade and a shaft of the bright morning sunlight slices into the dark cabin like a knife.

Below me, I spot flat, inscrutable postage-stamped parcels in various shades of green, pieced together like a puzzle, lit up here and there by geometric slashes of brilliant orange, white, and yellow: the famous tulip fields. No hills, no skyscrapers, no forests. This alien landscape seems bizarrely orderly and unreal. I, an urban introvert, am disconcerted by all of this verdant openness.

The flight attendant announces that we're about to land, in both English and Dutch. I wish she'd stop doing that. I know we're going to a foreign country, but the constant Dutch on the flight hammers the point home. What am I doing? Of all people, I'm completely unprepared for this. What can I do for Sylvie anyway? Sylvie is extraordinary.

Sylvie was named a Baker Scholar at Harvard Business School, and graduated in the top five percent of her class. When I was flailing around after college, I asked her how she'd done it. She had just started her management consulting job and, like old times, we were following Ma around the temple in Chinatown after Chinese New Year.

"A lot of it is keeping your head clear, Amy," she said, holding the tip of her bundle of three incense sticks into the flame of the oil lamp until they caught fire. "Princeton, MIT, Harvard, it's the same pressure. Everyone's just razor sharp. At Harvard, this one woman was so fast with numbers, it was like she'd swallowed a calculator. People would open their mouths and words like 'IMF austerity measures' and 'trilemma of free-capital flows' would pop out. I was very intimidated at first. Sometimes people think it's about competing with each other because they divide you into sections and everyone inside a section is graded on a bell curve. That kind of thinking makes you insane. I never considered anyone else. I only made sure I competed against myself."

I fanned my incense sticks and hers to put out the flames. Thick plumes of smoke spiraled upward. "Umm, so positive thinking saved you?"

She flushed a bit, the dimple in her cheek appearing. She carefully wedged her incense into the sand-filled urn in front of the enormous golden statue of Kuan Yin, goddess of compassion, and bowed low a few times, her posture perfect. Then she turned to face me. "That and I figured out how every syllabus was structured and only spent time on the important issues. I had no choice—I had the receptionist job at the construction company in the afternoon and waitressed until late at night. I only had the morning to get my work done. I had to be really efficient. I'd let the others take the easy questions in class and wait to answer the hardest ones. I'm Asian and a woman, which shouldn't matter but did anyway. It was clear sometimes that no matter how hard I worked, I didn't qualify to be a member of the in club. But the worst was the money." She sighed and rubbed her eyebrow. "Everything cost hundreds of dollars. I didn't know that an unspoken part of the Harvard MBA was the social aspect—all those invitations to events and galas where you could rub elbows with powerful people. There was no way I could keep up, so I didn't try. I'm no good at making people like me, anyway."

I had finished my bows and knocked her with my shoulder. We'd had this conversation before. "That's ridiculous, Sylvie."

She hugged me then, enveloping me in her scent of smoke and oranges. "That's your superpower, Amy, not mine."

My throat chokes up. Why haven't I heard from her? Like I said, Sylvie is extraordinary. Remove the *extra* and that's me: ordinary. I've just wasted so much money buying this expensive plane ticket to the Netherlands, where I won't be any use at all. I am sick to my stomach. What will happen to me and my loans now that Sylvie's—I stop myself before even thinking the word. How could I be so selfish?

I'm overwhelmed the moment I step inside Schiphol Airport, a name

I can't even begin to pronounce. It's futuristic and spotlessly clean, a spaceship complete with a disembodied female voice reminding me to "Mind your step" at the end of every automatic walkway. The people seem to be uniformly tall, their heads hovering far above mine. I am lost in a forest of trunks. The babble of incomprehensible words around me forms a stream of sound that I wade through, ignorant and alone. I long for home, and Ma and Pa. How can the signs be in so many different languages?

I walk to one of the huge bathrooms. The stall doors run all the way to the floor. I have a hard time figuring out how to flush the toilet. I try to check myself in the mirror but the mirrors are hung so high that I can only see the top of my head and a bit of my glasses. Beside me, a tall woman washes her hands efficiently, then strides toward the exit without a glance at the mirrors, which are exactly the right height for her. In fact, no one puts on lipstick or powder. I smell no perfume either.

Did Sylvie really live here for much of her childhood? The one she had before I existed. She doesn't often speak about her life in the Netherlands, but when she does, her skin flushes, her eyes soften. I know she loved it and longed to return. How could Ma and Pa have sent my own sister here? Had they planned to give me away too? Ma, who holds and pets me, but whose eyes follow Sylvie with so much yearning—Sylvie wriggling away whenever Ma had tried to wrap her arms around her until Ma stopped trying; Sylvie leaning against me every time we watched TV together; Sylvie holding my hand in the street. Even now, we always walk arm in arm. When Sylvie went away to college, I sobbed myself to sleep, counted the days until the too-short breaks when she came home again. That had always been Sylvie's role, to go forth and have adventures. My job was to wait for her to return home safely. Now the country mouse has been forced into the great devouring world.

In a daze, I stand on one of the automatic walkways and let the scenery pass me by. I am herded in the only possible direction by the planeload of passengers. We stand neatly in line at passport control, where the young military guy behind the counter glances through my passport before saying in crisp English, "Welcome to the Netherlands."

I can't believe I'm in Europe when I've never really left New York. The enormous baggage hall is brightly lit with more than twenty different belts and I wait at the wrong one until I realize that I'm supposed to be in another section altogether. I half panic, rush to the right place. When I finally manage to collect my bags, which have all miraculously arrived, I wheel my things out the door below the green NOTHING TO DECLARE sign. I look so nervous that one of the customs officers asks, "Are you feeling all right?" before letting me through.

I exit to find a wall of faces—a lot of white people in the Netherlands. I feel short and puny as the lanky Dutch hurry past me to embrace one another. I move forward, and suddenly spot three dark heads: two men and one woman. Must be my cousins Helena and Willem and their son, Lukas, none of whom I've ever met. They're clad in black, which sends fear stabbing into my heart until I realize that they're in mourning for Grandma, not Sylvie. The woman's clothing seems fluttery and filled with lace.

I step tentatively toward them. They are the only Chinese here but I am still unsure. The presence of the large, shaggy dude especially worries me—probably Lukas? He's in his early thirties, unshaven, with long black hair that looks like he hacked it off himself. His eyes—brown, with a touch of cinnamon—are slightly swollen, like he's been crying or beaten up by someone, and his clothes seem worn and sanded down, as if he's been crawling through a desert. A permanent scowl appears etched into his spidery eyebrows and forehead. This is Sylvie's childhood playmate? I heard he's a photojournalist, and indeed he looks like he's just ventured out of a war zone.

The other man is older, probably in his fifties, long-limbed and sophisticated in his suit and tie, which even I can see is well-made—likely Lukas's father, Willem. He's clean-shaven, smooth, with aristocratic features, still a very handsome man. I wonder if Lukas would look like this if you cleaned him up. There's something about the way Willem stares at me, as if he's not quite right in the head. Meanwhile, the woman, most likely his wife, Helena, has a face that's too smooth, lipstick a smidgen too bright. Black hair tamed into one slick wave falls neatly against the pressed collar of her lacy shirt.

Then her face splits into a smile. She lifts a hand, says something to me in rapid Chinese. I am too overwhelmed by all the strangeness around me to understand her.

I blink, unmoving, and Lukas steps toward me. He says something in rapid Dutch to his mother, then turns to me and says in English, "Are you Amy?"

Relieved to hear the words in my own language, I say, "Y-yes."

Helena peers around him to say, "I am your cousin."

She reaches out her arms to me but when I try to hug her, she holds me firmly by the shoulders and kisses me on the cheeks, alternating three times. After each kiss, I try to pull away only to realize she hasn't finished yet. I hang on and try not to screw up the side-to-side cheek rhythm. I am afraid I'll wind up kissing her on her sticky lips.

"We are all very worried about Sylvie." Her English is quite good, though accented. I realize that English is a third language for her, after Chinese and Dutch. She's left traces of some spicy perfume on me. The scent makes me queasy.

"Your English is v-very good." With all my stress and nervousness, my stutter has returned.

"We have many tourists as customers. You should learn Chinese, though. Lukas will teach you." Helena nods at Lukas, confident in his compliance, then checks out my crumpled black shirt and baggy jeans. "You do not look much like your sister." Strangely, there's approval in her voice.

Helena waves a hand at Lukas and he reluctantly kisses me three times too, his skin scratchy with stubble. He smells like something wild and smoky. I've learned to stay still and let them do the weaving around. Then I do the three kisses thing again with Willem, who handles me gently, like someone precious to him.

Someone calls out, "Hoi, Lukas!" I look up to see a flight attendant emerge from the gate behind us. She's wearing an unusual uniform and strides toward us. She grabs Lukas and kisses him full on the lips—wow—and I notice the four stripes on the sleeves of her arms, which are wound around his neck. She's a pilot, not a flight attendant. She's still kissing him. No three kisses this time. Finally, they say something in Dutch to each other; he smiles and tosses his arm around her in a loose hug.

Helena and Willem look on, not quite frowning but not beaming either. They probably don't approve of his non-Chinese girlfriend. Lukas gestures to me and the female pilot turns toward me and grins, extending her hand. "So you are the sister of Sylvie. I am Estelle."

Her handshake is as confident as her gaze. She and Lukas make a striking couple. Her hair is so light it's almost white and, with her beside him, Lukas is transformed from shaggy wild man into sexy artist, as if she were a light cast upon him, throwing his features into sharp relief. "I just flew back from Nairobi."

Something falls out of Estelle's large sloppy handbag onto the floor and Lukas releases her. He retrieves the silky thing and hands it to her. "Careful. What is this?"

"My headscarf. Carry one with me everywhere I go, have to hide my hair in Muslim countries. I never know when I will need it." She winks at me as she tucks it back into her purse. I can't imagine a life that would require such a thing in the handbag. Does she mind needing to hide her hair? Or does she accept that it's her choice to go there? She speaks English almost as well as a native speaker—only it seems to cost her a bit more effort to shape her mouth around the words.

Lukas says to her in a voice that isn't completely stable, "Sylvie is missing."

"What?" She goes completely still. "Did you get in a fight?" A fight? My eyes fly to her face. Her brows are furrowed and her jaw clenched. She's glaring at Lukas, as if blaming him. Why would Lukas and Sylvie fight?

"I will fill you in later." Lukas shoots her a quelling look.

Estelle clearly wants to question him further but glances at Helena's frozen face.

I ask, "Do you know her?"

Her voice is now clipped, the earlier effervescence dissipated. "We were kids together, good friends until she went back to the U.S. I was so happy to see her again this past month." She shoots another pointed look at Lukas.

"We are all from the same village," Lukas explains to me, avoiding her eyes.

Helena interrupts, "We'd better go now. Willem and I still have to work today and Amy must be tired after her long flight."

"You have to work? But it is Liberation Day," says Estelle. I hadn't realized today was anything special in the Netherlands.

"Holidays are the busiest time for our business," says Helena, and I realize that's why she and Willem are dressed so formally, not for me but because they need to run their large Chinese restaurant in Amsterdam.

"I want to talk to you," says Estelle to Lukas, her voice steely. "Call me as soon as you can." Then she turns to me with a smile. "Amy, after you recover a bit from your jet lag, why do you not come out for lunch with us? Maybe tomorrow?"

"I-I'd like that," I say, even though Lukas looks like he's swallowed something unpleasant. Not only does Estelle seem kind but I want to find out what she knows about Sylvie.

I am crammed into the back seat of the car with Lukas, who seems to take up all the available oxygen with his general air of surliness. It's not just his physical size, although he is big; it's the feeling of wildness around him, like he's capable of anything. I eye his huge hands, which he flexes often. But then I study his averted profile more carefully, his raw eyes, and I wonder if I've mistaken misery for bad temper.

I turn my attention out the window. We pass fields shrouded so thickly in the early-morning mist that I can't make out the ground underneath. The fog gathers and drifts, collecting in folds around mysterious objects below its unfathomable surface. The disgruntled sky lies low across the land, its gray clouds restless. I gasp in surprise as a ghost boat sails right across the billowing fields, but then Helena turns in the front passenger seat to say, "It is just on a canal that cuts through the middle. There is water everywhere here."

I say, "It's strange f-for me to think that this was Sylvie's home. It's a bit spooky."

"Spooky is no problem for Sylvie." Lukas's voice holds real affection, which makes me warm to him for the first time. "She is fearless. She can take anything."

Helena says in a singsong voice, "Oh, Sylvie can take anything and everything, all right."

My head swivels back and forth between them. What is she implying? What kind of crazy family is this? I remove my glasses to clean them and, when I put them back on, notice Willem watching me in the rearview mirror. His gaze is both intense and tender. Then he focuses on the road again. It could be that he's a bit dimwitted. Perhaps Helena chose him because of his good looks and decided to overlook any mental deficiencies. I am beginning to feel sorry for Sylvie that she had to live with this group of people for the first part of her life.

The clouds darken and a slow, steady drizzle drums against the outside of the car. After a long silence, I venture to say, "I thought you lived in Amsterdam?"

Lukas scoffs. "All Americans think everyone here lives in Amsterdam. We're about half an hour away."

We approach a small village, with old, well-maintained narrow houses no more than three stories high. It looks like the sort of place Hansel and Gretel would have lived, where children could venture forth and be lured into cottages by witches or eaten by wolves. Many of the houses have flagpoles attached to their facade and fly Dutch flags, which flap heavily in the rain and wind. Although the heater in the car is on, I shiver. A tall church looms in the distance, and then we pass into a slightly more modern part of town, with redbrick houses and slanted roofs.

The wheels of the car bounce against the cobblestones and I try not to throw up. A group of men too old to be seen in the skintight black Lycra that they're wearing zoom past us on racing bicycles, heads ducked against the driving rain, disappearing into the distance like a flock of misshapen crows.

We drive up to a detached house with a separate cottage that looks like it might have been a garage once. The large two-story house stares blindly into the road, its dark windows bleak underneath the slanted roof. Willem parks under a long carport.

Helena says, "It is probably small by your American standards, right?"

I had not been thinking anything of the sort. I'd been wondering what it must have been like for Sylvie to go from this Grimm fairy-tale existence to being cooped up in our tiny apartment in hectic New York City. "W-why, no—"

She proceeds as if I hadn't spoken. "We pay a lot of taxes. If you sneeze, you pay a tax. I will open up the house. Lukas, help her with her bags." She opens the car door and strides off to the main house, head high in defiance of the rain. Gusts of wind assail the car windows as the deluge intensifies, and by unspoken agreement, the three of us huddle a moment in the car, waiting for the downpour to lessen.

"It is not so bad here," Lukas says. "I was just in Honduras last year, and kids were running barefoot in rags through the buses, trying to sell snacks to the rich tourists instead of going to school. Taxes are good for something. There is even an animal ambulance to free the swans that get frozen in the canals during the winter."

To my surprise, Willem turns around and speaks for the first time. "Do you remember when you and Sylvie found that blackbird when you were little, Lukas?" His voice is rich and sonorous. Although his English is heavily accented, he speaks slowly and clearly to make up for it. Thus, he is not an imbecile, which leaves creepy and possibly malevolent. "A cat had attacked it. Those two called the animal ambulance late in the evening without telling anyone, and before we knew it, a large white van was stopped in front of our house with all the neighbors staring out their windows." He shakes his finger playfully at Lukas.

Lukas grins. "Pa, you are just as tenderhearted about animals as Sylvie. Once you found out, you filled its shoebox with so much cooked white rice, we were afraid it wouldn't be able to breathe anymore. Sylvie had chased the cat away. She was so worried about that bird. 'It needs its mama, it needs its mama,' she kept saying. We searched for the nest for hours with no success. I still remember that man in the white suit. He took the blackbird away in a cage and the next day, they called to tell us it was doing fine. It was being raised with a foster bird mother and a group of other baby blackbirds and would be released once it was fully healed. You told Sylvie, 'Do not worry, it has a new mama now.'"

How many moments like this have I missed? The enormity of the existence my Sylvie had before me yawns at my feet like an abyss. She had another family, these strangers I'm now meeting. For a second, I wish Pa were like Willem, sophisticated and well-spoken, someone who could joke with his children.

"Does she have any pets in the U.S.?" Lukas asks me, not quite meeting my eyes, almost shy.

"She still loves animals," I say, with more heat than I'd intended. Sylvie's mine. No matter how many stories they have about animal ambulances, I know her better than anyone. "But she and Jim can't have any pets because Jim's allergic to everything."

At this, Lukas's face closes up. "That is a pity. It looks a bit lighter outside. I will take your suitcases."

As I step out I wrap my jacket more closely around me. The storm has turned day into evening. It is freezing for May. The wind feels different here, more penetrating, piercing the thin cocoon of warmth I'd found in the car. We race into the main house. Helena has turned on only a few lights, and it somehow manages to feel even chillier than the bleak weather outside. I stare at the darkened stairwell, which has steep, tiny steps that look like they would only fit half a normal foot. The living room is depressing and tasteless, as if someone flipped through a pile of decorating magazines from different decades and copied the pages at random. The walls are modern in dark gray, clashing with the orange-and-gold marble floor. A brown leather couch dominates the room, forbidding and stern, bracketed by two puritanical armchairs that face off against a traditional Chinese wooden opium table. None of the stiff furniture seems to go together, despite the apparent expense of each individual piece. Willem flips on more of the lights and I catch sight of my reflection against the main window, pale and wrung out, like an old dishcloth.

There are framed photos of Lukas everywhere—very handsome, now that I can see his face without the overgrown stubble. Impish, long-lashed dark eyes, his father's fine features. Gangly adolescent. Estelle and Lukas, laughing together into the camera, like two teenage models posing for a perfume ad. Lukas, small and skinny, missing a few teeth, wearing swimming trunks and holding up a piece of paper that reads *A*. A family photo of Helena, Willem, and Lukas in front of the Eiffel Tower. They all squint into the sunlight as if they've been blinded. A studio shot of Helena and Willem's wedding: A young Helena sitting in a cake of a dress and Willem awkwardly poised with his arm around her. A small basket filled with what looks like identical triangular bits of folded paper sits beside a half-assembled paper sculpture of a creature—a coiled cobra, perhaps.

I search for a picture of Sylvie and can't find anything: only there, a small stubby finger on Lukas's shoulder; in the background, strands of black hair over a purple jacket; part of a knee, resting next to Lukas's leg. Sylvie has been deliberately excised, made into nothing more than a fall of hair, a disembodied hand. With painful pity, I think, *Sylvie, was this the home you longed for?*

At the far end of the living room, a long hard dining set looks like it's been bolted to the floor. Helena is bustling around in the open kitchen, where I also find an altar for Grandma. I clasp my hands together and bow low. The incense holder overflows with ash. Finally, something I recognize here.

As I straighten, Helena watches me approvingly. "Let me show you to your room."

Even with my small feet, I am careful climbing the shallow stairs. My bags have disappeared, which means someone has probably already brought them upstairs, thank goodness. Helena and Willem's bedroom is on the second floor as well, along with the main bathroom and a little room filled with cabinets and boxes. There's another room that smells faintly of medicine, an old person's room. I know instinctively that this must have been Grandma's. An empty key chain and a few pieces of china are all that remain—a Kuan Yin, serene on her lotus blossom, sits on a small raised altar in the corner. A bracelet of polished wooden temple beads, like the ones Ma wears, lies abandoned next to the bed.

Helena pauses by the doorway and I see grief shadow her face. She wraps one arm around herself as if she is cold.

Impulsively, I touch her shoulder. "I'm so sorry you lost Grandma. You must have loved her very much."

Surprised, she blinks rapidly before pulling away, but the smile she gives me is genuine. "Yes, you are quite different from your sister. Thank you, Amy."

I'm placed in the attic, in what was probably once Lukas's room. I can hear the deluge pounding against the roof tiles outside. The air smells wet and a bit musty. The space is large since it stretches across the length of the house, and it has been stripped bare. The bed is made up with a green coverlet. I see my bags sitting beside a simple desk and office chair underneath the dormer windows, which intermittently flash with the lightning outside.

I shiver. "Is this where Sylvie was staying?" At Helena's nod, I turn around slowly. There's no trace of my sister anywhere. I had been hoping to hold something of hers in my hands. "Where are her things?"

Helena shrugs dismissively. She waves her hand in the air. "She packed everything and took it with her. That is why we thought she flew back to America. And she was in Lukas's cottage most of the time anyway. I think she liked it better over there."

Despite the moment of intimacy we shared earlier, I am irritated by Helena. What is she trying to imply? I turn to face her directly. "S-strange, Sylvie's not one to complain."

Helena's smile reminds me of a mannequin's, plastic and fake, and her eyes remain cold. "Well, she was also practicing that cello day and night. It was disturbing Grandma. We decided it would be better if she was not here all the time."

I blink. Are we talking about the same person? "Sylvie doesn't play any instrument. She's never been interested in music."

Thunder booms and Helena crosses over to pull the shades shut. She yanks the curtains closed with an aggressive flick of her wrist. "She started taking lessons while she was here—with that handsome music teacher, of course. Good looks never hurt, right? Old friend of

Lukas's. And no, she does not play. She was terrible." Helena emits a short laugh, devoid of humor.

I stammer, "B-but Sylvie's married . . ." Then I remember her separation from Jim. "Anyway, she never looks at men like that." Sylvie, who would breeze by as male heads turned, only ever focused on whatever her next big project was. I had once arrived late to a party given by one of her colleagues and peered shyly into the packed room to find her sitting on a couch surrounded by admirers. Sylvie had beamed, rushed over, linked her arm through mine, and whisked us away without a single backward glance.

Helena walks to the door and leans against the frame. She taps her finger against her cheek. "Your heart is too big and"—I can tell she's about to say *stupid,* but instead she chooses—"innocent. You should be careful. People will take advantage of you." Then with another false smile, she leaves.

After she's gone, I collapse into the chair and think about what she said. My body is clammy with cold sweat. I brush my forehead three times with my left hand, like Ma would tell me to do, to ward off her words, and I realize my hands are shaking. Who might take advantage of me—she herself or some other member of her family? Or does she mean Sylvie somehow? And what in the world was Sylvie doing with a cello?

CHAPTER 8

Sylvie

Saturday, April 2
One Month Earlier

As the plane descended, I remembered the game Lukas and I had played as children—rock, paper, scissors—and so I felt: plummeting downward onto the flat sheet of the Dutch landscape, the Netherlands wrapping around me like a sheet of paper, cradling my worn stone heart. I was finally coming home from a cold carnival, disappointed after a long trip.

In the confusion of my departure all those years ago, the doll Grandma had made for me, Tasha, had been lost. Tasha had always been by my side and then, suddenly, she was gone. Lukas and I had looked everywhere. We had avoided each other's eyes, throwing ourselves into the hunt, knowing with the instinct of children that after this day, we would be searching for each other instead. And my ma was nothing like I had imagined. She was thin to the point of frailness, tiptoeing around the house like an unwanted guest. In my fantasies, she had been warm, plump, and strong, filled to overflowing with love for me. This woman spent hours in Grandma's room, whispering secrets, and when I crept into Grandma's lap instead of hers, she stared at me with trembling lips, as if it had been my fault that she had abandoned me. Helena's sharp eyes never let Ma out of her sight, like she was afraid Ma would steal something precious to her.

Until the last moment, I had believed we would find Tasha somewhere, but we never did. I had burst into tears, grief for my doll overlaying my sorrow for leaving Grandma, Lukas, Willem, even Helena. Lukas, always my loyal companion, bawled right beside me. Willem had taken me into his arms then, sheltering me from Helena's cold gaze.

"Shhhh." He kissed my forehead and tucked a lock of my hair behind my ear. "Tasha will always sit in your heart, just like I will. Now, if you hold up with crying, I have a surprise for you."

I sniffed, blinked away my tears, and peeked at Helena. She never liked it when Willem and I were too close. I had called him "Pa" once when I was little and she had dragged me by the arm to my room, and made me swear never to do it again. "You have your own pa, you little fool, do you understand?" she had hissed, red with fury. Now Helena glared at us, but with Ma looking on, and this being the last day of mine in the Netherlands, she did not dare say anything.

Willem pressed a small red silk envelope into my hand, just like the ones Grandma had. His eyes clouded with tears. "One day, you will grow up to become a beautiful woman. I will not be there to see it but I want you to wear these for me."

I unzipped the envelope and tipped the contents into the palm of my hand. A pair of sparkly stud earrings fell out and twinkled against my skin. I gasped and threw my arms around his neck. He smelled like grapefruit and cedar, as he always did. "They are so shiny! But my ears are not pierced."

"They will be," he said, his voice low with promise.

I felt someone pry my fist open. It was Helena. She took the earrings from me and held them up against the light, her hands shaking with anger. "These are real."

Willem laughed his deep melodious laugh. He released me and went to his wife. He put his arm around her and hugged her to him, like in a scene from a film, while we all watched. "Silly one. Of course they are crystal. But set in silver and still very pretty, right, Sylvie?" And he had winked at me.

I always suspected, especially because those earrings had never tarnished. So I had them appraised a few years ago—nearly flawless diamonds, more than half a carat each, in a platinum setting. It was a wildly inappropriate gift for a little girl but I still wore them today. Willem had always been the generous one. He would take flat squares of origami paper and, like magic, dinosaurs and butterflies, dragons and airplanes would bloom from his fingertips, delighting Lukas and me. I never saw Willem follow a design from a book. He must have known hundreds of patterns in his head.

"I am a bad Chinese," he would say, shaking his head. "Resorting to Japanese arts. But it soothes me."

"It is because you have no family, no roots," Helena answered. "Wasteful habit. Uses up so much paper." But despite her scolding, she had sought out beautifully patterned origami paper and left the packages around the house for him to find, as if by accident. Helena was kind to everyone except me.

The last time I had been at Schiphol Airport, I had taken the hand of a woman I did not know and walked away with her to start a new life. She was the mother I had yearned for, but my heart had no more room for her. It had been too late. Turning back to look at them: little Lukas with his woebegone face, Helena's thinly hidden relief, Willem filled with regret, Grandma staring at both me and Ma as if she wanted to run and join us.

And what had I accomplished in all these years away? I wanted so much and had been able to hold on to so little of it. When had it begun to fall apart with Jim? Was it after our conversation on the way home from his friend Caitlin's baby shower?

Of course, Jim had tons of female friends. Caitlin and Jim had gone to the same exclusive private school before Princeton. She was tall, freckled, adored horses and sailboats. In college, we had spent a weekend with her and her then-boyfriend, now-husband, Xavier, on her father's ranch in Wyoming. "Would you mind terribly if the rest of us went out for a ride?" she had asked me apologetically, assuming that poor immigrant me would be at a loss. "Oh, I think I'll join you," I had answered, "I love horses." It had been satisfying to see her mouth slacken as I swung into the saddle and nudged the mare into a trot. I did not tell her that my old friend Estelle had been horse crazy, like so many Dutch girls, and had dragged me along to groom and ride her horse Umbra every week. I had shoveled lots of horse shit with Estelle.

About a year and a half ago, Jim and I were in the car on the way home after congratulating a heavily pregnant Caitlin when he said, "What about us?"

I stared out the window as the highway sped by, pretending I had not heard him. I jumped when he reached over and touched my hand.

"I know you don't want to talk about it, but time's running out. We've been married a year now. I'd hoped—" I heard what he was not saying. *You're going to be too old soon.* When I finally met his gaze, his blue eyes told me what he longed for: a tiny soft being dependent on him, coming home to a wife baking banana bread, a faded landscape where he would be loved and admired as a king.

I tried to gentle my tone. "You know I work eighty hours a week, Jim. And my mentor says I'm doing so well."

Jim gave a half shrug, like he did not care.

I rolled my eyes. So typical. "This current project, I'm involved from the conceptual stage to the completion and operation of the facility. Do you know what that means? I'm not saying never—just another year or two, that's all." I was not going to throw away everything I had done, everything I was. Why did it not matter to anyone else?

"Sweetheart, you know how proud I am of you. But aren't *we* important too? We already waited so long to get married because of your career," he said softly. The autumn sun was setting and as it soaked through the windshield, it turned his face into a pale golden mask. Brilliantly colored leaves were torn from the trees as we sped by, swirling in the air while they searched for a final resting place.

"Of course. But it's my body that's going to be taken over, Jim. My life that will be put on hold. It's up or out at the company. If I don't get promoted to engagement manager in the next year or so, I'm out. The coming period is critical." My heart rate quickened at the thought of it—a crying baby, like when Amy had been a toddler with one of her tantrums and I was alone with her and all I wanted was to do my homework in peace and be free to play at other girls' houses. This was my fault. If I had not wasted those years working as a chemical engineer, searching for who I was, I would not be older than the other associates. I would have had time to build my career and then have a child.

The car next to us beeped, suddenly veering into our lane.

Jim hit the brakes in time to slow down. "Jerk," he muttered. His fingers clenched the steering wheel. "I can take time off too."

I bit back the words: *You don't really have a career. You always have your parents' money and family name, a nice cushy safety net to land on.* But some of my guilt and bitterness escaped me anyway. "You have no idea what a baby would mean. I always have to be the practical one."

The tendons on Jim's forehead protruded and a flush darkened his cheekbones. He raised his voice. "You always have to be in control and you can't bear to loosen up. Well, I'd like to come first in this relationship for a change."

"You're jealous." I spat out the words. "You feel emasculated to have a wife who earns six times what you do." There was a dreadful silence. I had gone too far. Jim had turned into a statue beside me. He squeezed his eyes shut for a moment. I was such a horrible person. "Jim, I'm sorry."

He took a deep breath and gave me a cold smile. His voice was polite. "Let's not talk about this anymore." And we had not.

God, I was glad to get away from everything. We exited the plane and I quickly strode through the airport. My soul leaped as if it had been freed of its bindings. I had left the jungle of New York City and was back in the warm and welcoming plains. What a gorgeous and efficient airport. How many cities had I been in by now? So many flights for work. A week in a hotel in Atlanta, another in Chicago, then a couple of days in San Francisco. It had not been easy for Jim either. *No more of that, Sylvie. Leave it all behind.* I took a deep breath. My shoulders started to relax against the musical background of Dutch voices all around me. I almost shivered with pleasure. I could still understand everyone perfectly. *Little treasure, have you seen my boarding pass? Hallo, taxi, we have landed, where should we meet you? Now you have to stop that up immediately or you may not have any licorice.*

I quickly found my bags and exited through the arrivals gate. My eyes scanned the crowd, looking for Helena, Willem, and Lukas, especially Lukas. Had he not come? Where was he? But then, there was a great Asian man standing before me instead of the little boy I had subconsciously been looking for. I did not recognize Lukas in him at all. The adorable chubby cheeks had turned into a sharp, angular face; where did this square jaw come from, the high forehead? Where were the scrawny, vulnerable shoulders? This was a stranger. My heart deflated like an old bicycle tire. The man was clean-shaven, his long hair neatly combed back, still wet from the shower. I spoke Dutch for the first time in years, my tongue slowly growing used to the twists and turns once again. "Are you Lukas? I recognize you not."

He smiled and then gave me three kisses on the cheeks, with none of the forced intimacy of American hugging, where you have to keep your breasts away from the closeness of the other person. But still, my body remained stiff. He held me at arm's length, an intense burning in his eyes I now remembered. "You are unchanged."

His voice was so deep, not squeaking like it used to when Lukas laughed himself sick. I searched for something to say to this person I no longer knew. I wanted my old Lukas back. "So you came back from Nepal?"

"I had enough of the continuous traveling anyway."

I did not mention Grandma. A cloud of grief hid behind his eyes. I already knew why he had returned. There was another awkward silence. I looked around for Helena and Willem. They had not come. She had outsmarted me once again. What a fool I had been, choosing my expensive, seemingly casual slacks and blouse with such care. Fixing my hair and makeup in the mirror on the airplane, to ensure Helena would know that a new Sylvie had returned.

Lukas's quick eyes understood without my saying anything. He stumbled over the words, his cheeks stained with shame. "It was not possible for my parents—"

I cut him off. "I understand." We both knew what an insult this was.

He slung his large black camera bag across his back, then took my suitcase with one hand and started shouldering his way through the crowd. As we dodged past people on our way out of the terminal, he said, "I thought about picking you up with my scooter but we could not fit your luggage. Is the train good or do you want to take a taxi?"

Helena and Willem had not let him use the car. "I love the train."

"Did you ever ride on one before you left?" Lukas punched the buttons and bought two tickets from the yellow machine.

"Class trip to that museum in Amsterdam, do you remember?" I smiled at the memory. He had been my partner, as always. We used to hold hands as we skipped across the schoolyard, even though some kids tittered at us for being a boy and a girl and still so close—my best friend and my cousin. On Sinterklaas, we both had pathetic surprises made by Grandma, who knew nothing of Saint Nicholas. As the other kids unveiled huge papier-mâché creations of robots and hockey fields filled with candy and presents, we had thinly curled cardboard surprises that barely resembled anything but the toilet paper rolls they were. For the first time, I wondered what Lukas had endured after I had left.

He grinned. "I remember we fought about who would sit next to the window until the teacher threatened to separate us." Anything but that—we had quieted down immediately.

"How is everyone?" I asked as we strode down the motorized walkway to the lowered train platform. The wheels of my suitcase emitted a high-pitched whine as they scraped against the ribbed metal floor.

We waited for the train in the underground station as he filled me in. Estelle was flying for KLM; his photojournalism was going well, he had spreads in a few good Dutch and international magazines, but it took time to break into such a competitive field; he was renting that garage apartment from his parents and hating it, even though it was practical for now.

Then our sleek train arrived and we got on. I sat across from him and studied him as we traveled back to our little village along the coast.

Underneath the lean sculptured lines of his face, I could just make out the boy he had once been: shy, loyal, mischievous. His eyes were still warm, lit with humor and intelligence, and slowly, he came into focus for me again, my Lukas. When you truly love someone and you see them again, even if it is many years later, their new face blends back into their old face and it is like no time has passed at all. We sped onward through the tunnel and, finally, burst through the other side. I now saw the orderly green countryside that was so familiar to me, like a half-remembered memory of a lullaby that had comforted me as a child. Even from inside, I could feel the difference in the wet and caressing air. The clock at home ticked in a way it ticked nowhere else. The rain beat steadily above our heads. "How does it come that you have grown into such a giant?"

He laughed—a booming sound that surprised me. "How is it you are not different at all?"

"What?" I said with mock outrage. "How can you say that? Look at this." I point to my right eye. "And this." I bare my perfect teeth. "Years of wearing that eye patch. And it cost me a fortune to get that tooth pulled and a fake one put in its place. I had it done the moment I went away to college. Now you say I am no different!"

"Actually, I still have regret about that accident with your tooth."

I sniffed. An accident is hidden in a little corner, where no one expects it. When I was seven years old, I had been riding on the back of Lukas's bike when we crashed and almost knocked out my front tooth. "Well, it was a tiny bit my fault too."

"You were swinging back and forth, singing with a full chest. You did your best to make us fall. That you succeeded in too."

Outside, it began to rain cow tails and I traced my fingers along the streaks the water left on the exterior of the windowpanes. We were warm, safe, and dry. The patter of the rain beat against the steady roar of the train and, between the beading raindrops, I caught a glimpse of our reflections in the glass. Lightning flashed and for a moment, it was as if our images flickered between the children we had been and the man and woman we were now.

"I cannot believe how long it has been," I said.

"You never came back." There was sadness in his voice.

"You did not come to visit me." Then we were both silent, thinking of the intervening years. How I could not bear to have one foot in both countries. How I had become aware of Helena's underlying hatred of me once I grew older. How my love for him and Grandma had not been enough to overcome my fear of Helena. And my complicated, twisted relationship with Willem had not helped matters.

Finally, I dared to ask, "How is Grandma?"

"She does not have much time left. She has been waiting for you." When we were seven years old, a stray kitten, a puff of gray fur and bright blue eyes, had followed us home from school. Lukas had not let it out of his sight, crawling around on the floor with it, creating toys for it out of newspaper and cardboard. Despite all of our begging, Helena had made us give the kitten to the animal asylum after only a few days. Lukas's eyes had looked like this then, as if they could not contain the depths of his hopelessness.

I pressed my lips together and nodded. We were silent again.

Then abruptly, Lukas said, "My parents would have come but there was an emergency at the restaurant." A flush mottled his neck.

Why did this still hurt after all these years? "You do not need to lie to me. Did I ever tell you? I phoned the restaurant of your parents last year to congratulate you on your birthday since I could not reach you on your mobile."

"I think I was in Africa covering a story then. No reception."

"A woman speaking perfect Dutch answered the phone. She told me you were not there and then asked who I was. She had me spell my name. At first I had not recognized her voice and thought it was an employee, but, slowly, I realized it was your mother, pretending she did not know me." I swallowed down echoes of the anger and humiliation I had felt. "I did not confront her."

Lukas winced. "I am sorry, Sylvie."

I reached over and laid my hand on his arm. "It is no use."

His head was resting back against the seat, but he studied me as if he could not believe I was truly there. He pulled a huge camera from his bag and asked, "May I?"

I nodded. When we were little, Lukas had used up the film in his Polaroid camera at an amazing rate. He spent the rest of the train ride taking photos of me, the landscape, a tear in the seat next to him. The jet lag was beginning to catch up to me. I half closed my eyes, leaning my forehead against the window, and continued to dream.

Luckily, in one of those abrupt changes of schizophrenic Dutch weather, the rain had stopped by the time we got off the train. I breathed in the gentle air. It smelled like cut grass. Clouds danced in the bright blue sky. As soon as I saw the uneven brick streets, I paused for a moment, shook my hair loose, and sat at a bench to change out of the heels I had worn to impress Helena into flat shoes. Their house was not far from the station and it was an easy walk along the Vecht River. Lukas pulled my bag, the wheels bumping against the smaller bricks that made up the sidewalk.

People nodded to us as we passed. I had forgotten. No more of that strict avoidance of eye contact learned in New York City. They considered me with curiosity, but as long as I smiled and said *good day* back to them, they were satisfied. There were a few changes to this former medieval fishing village. A large modern supermarket in the center, a bank, ATMs, an office building with only four stories. There was a little red mailbox beside a large blue trash receptacle that looked so much like the mailboxes in the United States. When I had first arrived in New York, Ma barely stopped me in time from throwing my sticky crumpled tissues into the mailbox, which I had assumed was the garbage can.

There was the house again. My stomach clenched. It was just as I recalled—dark and cold with impenetrable windows. They had built an apartment above the separate garage for Lukas. No, I had never missed this house, only some of the people in it. As Lukas let us inside, I was surprised by how much I remembered.

The way the front door stuck and would not click shut behind you unless you gave it an extra push with your hip. The key rack was still there, with extra sets to the house and garage, now Lukas's apartment. I had grown tall enough to reach it easily. They had changed the interior to modern: the old dark wood replaced by gray and orange garishness.

The room simmered with flickering shadows. The lights were off to conserve electricity, as was the case in most Dutch homes. The heat was set low as well—*Thick sweater day: why not wear one, it is better for the environment and your energy bill.* My feet knew where to slip off and leave my shoes. My arms recalled the coat hangers that jangled against each other. My hand reached for the light switch half-hidden behind the old Vermeer print on the wall without a thought, even though I no longer had to go on tiptoe.

How I had dreaded the mornings, the time Helena and Willem were home before leaving for the restaurant and returning late in the night. The afternoons and evenings had been lovely, only me and Lukas and Grandma, eating our simple meals of fresh rice in the lamplight instead of the rich restaurant fare Willem and Helena brought back. Most days, I was in bed before they came home. I made sure of it.

But there had been good times with Helena too. Days when she took me shopping for dresses, bought me colored elastics for my hair. One winter, the Vecht River had frozen over. I was amazed to find it packed with people I recognized as neighbors. I hugged the shore, expecting the ice to crack and swallow everyone whole. It was one of my nightmares, to be trapped underneath the surface of the water. But earlier that morning, Helena had rooted around in the garage until she found pairs of skates for Willem, Lukas, me, and herself.

"I picked these up at the open market during the last Queen's Day," she explained. People sold their used toys and clothing for almost nothing then. "The children's skates are adjustable, so they should still fit the two of you."

Then, while Willem taught Lukas, Helena pulled me into the center of the river, the ice smooth underneath my feet, the treacherous water tamed into submission. I hung on to her and she laughed. Then she unfolded the plastic chair she had brought for me. I held on to its back like many of the other children around me.

"Push with your legs," she said. "Keep your weight forward. You are doing fine."

I used the folding chair as a skating aid and learned to glide across the ice with Helena by my side. I remembered my initial surprise that she could skate perfectly, but of course, she had grown up in the Netherlands. It had been a glorious day.

Now Lukas was watching me. "Welcome home," he said, his face falling into serious lines. He knew better than anyone how bittersweet my childhood had been.

Although everything in the house had been replaced by something more expensive, the furniture was equally ugly and grim. I could see from the uncomely marble tiles that they had floor heating now. The old flowery couch wrapped in vinyl was gone. The fireplace still sat cold and empty because the smoke would damage the furniture. There was no cozy rug to dispel the chill because rugs collected dust. The curtains were as gloomy as ever.

No books, no music. But all around the room, photos of Lukas: on the beach, at preschool, wearing an enormous paper hat with a number 4 stapled to the peacock-like tufts—his fourth birthday, ready to leave and start elementary school the next day. That was my hand on his shoulder. I was not in the photo but I had been there, watching him, trying not to cry that my Lukas would be departing our preschool while I had to stay until I too turned four. Lukas holding up his A diploma for swimming, beaming, missing his two front teeth. Helena had used the silly prophecy that I would die by water as an excuse to stop me from taking swimming lessons, which every single other child in the neighborhood did. In the Netherlands, water was everywhere. Kids could fall into canals next to their house, by school, in the fields. The danger of flooding was always imminent, and the Dutch were forever aware that it was the nature of water to flow back to reclaim its own.

Swimming lessons were expensive but I suspected it was more about the humiliation of Grandma bringing me along to Lukas's lessons. I was the only child who sat on the bleachers next to the adults instead of being in the water. But Grandma could not leave me alone at home and she was so superstitious that she thought this was a fine idea. At school, all of the kids chattered: *Did you get your B diploma yet? I'm already starting my C.* The birthday parties held at the swimming pool, which I was not allowed to attend; the outings to the beach. Trips out on that flat-bottomed family boat they moored on the Vecht. I felt myself a foreign leg, a misfit. There were so many occasions to exclude me. So I pretended I did not want to learn how to swim anyway, until my imagined disinclination became reality, like so many things we desired as children.

Now I saw the years I had missed—Lukas on the cusp of puberty, half child, half adolescent, sitting on an adult bike that was far too big for him. At his high school graduation, awkward and gangly, with my old friend Estelle—she was so tall!—her teeth a flash of metal braces, her white-blond hair in a ponytail, hugging him as they laughed together. I felt a flash of loneliness, a retroactive longing to be by their side in all those intervening moments. There was not a single photo of me. I had been erased as if I had never existed.

I stared at a small basket to keep from crying. It was filled with tiny folded bits of origami paper. So Willem still had his hobby—and what about his furtive affection, his clumsy attempts to offset his wife's hostility toward me? I was a grown woman now. Why had Helena treated a child like that? Why did she take me in at all if she hated me? I wanted to ask her but despite all I had accomplished since I had left, I doubted I had the nerve. I could hardly breathe through the emotions that were running across my face like a sheet of shallow water.

Lukas came and slipped his arm through mine. "Is it going all right?"

I could not trust myself to speak. My heart was beating quickly, my eyes burning. I had not expected this room, remodeled for the outside world yet at its heart unchanged, to do this to me. I had chosen to forget as much as I could.

But as always, Lukas understood.

"I left here as nothing and I have returned as nothing." My voice cracked.

His intelligent eyes dropped to my left hand, where I still wore my wedding ring. I could not bear for Helena to know of my failure. His voice was low and warm. "You were always something, Sylvie. You shone like a light in our class. Do not let my mother . . ." He broke off. "I am so sorry she . . . and I never . . ."

"But you did. You used to sneak me food when I was being punished, remember? And you were just a child yourself." That word, *punished*, stuck in my throat. Lukas had never let me down.

"She was not always like that. It was as you grew older that she—" Again, he could not finish.

I did have vague memories of a warm and comforting Helena, one who hummed as she braided my hair, but somehow, she had stopped loving me, as everyone else did, except for Lukas and Amy. Helena made sure I knew she was not my mother. Those disembodied voices on the telephone that I heard once in a blue moon were my real parents. How helpless I had been. No more. Bitterness in the mouth makes the heart strong. I realized then that perhaps I had not been working so hard all these years just to earn the love of Ma and Pa, but to become an equal adversary to Helena.

CHAPTER 9

Ma

Tuesday, May 5

One year turned into two, then three, and more. There was never enough money for the flight, for another mouth to feed, never enough time to leave the workplace. It would be nine years before my girl returned to us. It was after Amy, Mei-Li, my Beautiful Jasmine, was born and had grown to two years old. When I gave Snow Jasmine away, I did not realize I would never fully get her back. Sylvie left a piece of her spirit behind in Holland.

She was a quiet, listening-to-orders child, always trying to blend into the woodwork, so unlike Amy, who laughed and sang more than she spoke. Sylvie did not speak any words of the Brave Language when she arrived, only Holland talk and Central Kingdom talk. Her speech of the Central Kingdom was good, far better than Amy's would ever be. And despite the mouth-suffering of Amy's stutter, I could only think of that as yet another failure on my part. Grandma had succeeded in transferring our language and culture to Sylvie, whereas I had failed with Amy. Of course, my ma was free to spend all her days with my girl, while I worked for almost all the days of their childhood.

Sylvie had lost the baby loveliness. Her lazy eye, her bent tooth, and that haunted look made her too intense and foreign for the tastes of the Beautiful Country. When I tried to make up for the years I had not been able to hold her, her body stiffened and pulled away, scrambling to get as far away from me as she could. She missed Helena, Willem, and Grandma, no doubt.

Slowly, she spoke the language of the Central Kingdom less, or perhaps she was only not speaking much to me in general. I felt her moving further away. Sometimes when she would look up from her homework, with a quick wary flicker of her eyes, I would see it: she did not trust us. I did not blame her. Who believed in parents who sent you away so that someone else could raise you? The distance between us never disappeared. It only became obscured by the daily pattern of life. Pa and I scrimped to raise our children. I searched the secondhand shops or did my best to replicate on my sewing machine the Western costumes I saw. I tried to feed them enough white vegetables, buy them snake gourd peel and wood ear mushrooms when they were ill, praying that nothing in the apartment broke that we could not fix ourselves because the landlord never did anything.

I made my girls sweet egg drop soup on wintry days but Sylvie scorned it, sweeping out the door most mornings without a mouthful. I accepted this, knowing she was accustomed to better food from Helena. Then Pa and I were gone until late in the evening and it was Sylvie's task to care for her younger sister. I marveled that she did it so well, and with the burden of her own schoolwork. It did not occur to me until it was too late to wonder where Sylvie's friends were, if she had ever wanted to do anything other than her duty. I admit it; I had not wanted to know. My ignorance had been self-serving.

I became jealous of my own mother, Sylvie's grandma, who in some ways was more her ma than I could ever be. I wondered what Sylvie's relationship was like with Helena and Willem but she never spoke of them. They never contacted us either. The only person Sylvie loved with all her heart was Amy. She clutched Amy to her, lavishing kisses upon Amy's rounded pink cheeks like she was devouring a delicious apple. It was as if Sylvie poured all of her warmth and laughter into Amy, and she had so much to give. Pa and I only received a few droplets once in a while, more out of duty than anything else, I suspected.

Then Sylvie left elementary school, tested into one of those special New York City schools for smart kids, and it was as if she had been launched into orbit. She was spectacular—one perfect report card after another, despite the fact that she sold newspapers and ran errands in her free time now that Amy was bigger. She was so independent, so important. The truth was: I was afraid of her. I could not understand her or her life. I was, after all, only a simple woman from a little village in China.

There descended such a barrier between me and my daughters, like a curtain through which you could only vaguely make out the figures on the other side. The Brave Language belonged to the devil with all of its strange consonants, a puzzle I could not solve, and they were constantly chattering in it: stories, joys, and pains. I desperately tried to understand. I never could. I could not reach them and they barely noticed me. I asked them to speak Central Kingdom talk but they ignored me as if I had been playing the lute for a cow.

I knew I could not do the things for them that other mothers did. If there was a problem at Amy's school, Sylvie had to take care of it. If there was an issue with Sylvie, she solved it herself. When the stuttering mouth-suffering of Amy became a headache, Sylvie skipped her own classes to speak with Amy's teachers. Even with her brilliant mind, so like her father's, Sylvie often stayed up until late into the night to finish her schoolwork. When I tiptoed to her bed to lay a blanket across her thin back or offer a cup of oolong tea, her answer was always, "Do not fuss over me, ah-Ma. Go sleep. You cannot help me anyway." And Pa and I were always working. The children came home to an empty apartment and all they had was each other. Who could blame them?

There was so much wisdom I could never manage to pass on to them. I never even taught them how to pray, though I believe we all find our own path to the gods. I closed my eyes, sitting in front of rows of mummified clothing in the dry cleaners. *The great gods have great compassion. Let the good draw near, let evil desist. Please protect my Sylvie, let her be safe, let her be healed.*

And then Grandma fell ill. I would never see her again, my heart stem, and Sylvie had gone to hold her as she passed. Now Sylvie was missing as well. I had lost them both. I put my head down on the table and wept.

CHAPTER 10

Sylvie

Saturday, April 2

"Are you ready?" Lukas asked.

I nodded and we went up the stairs. They seemed shallower than I remembered. Before we entered the room, I could smell the sickly scent of medicine and death. There was Grandma. Had she always been so tiny? Her body was barely a lump underneath the covers. Her little feet ended somewhere in the middle of the bed and she was sitting upright, propped against a mountain of pillows, staring at me.

With a gasp, I rushed to her side and took both of her hands in mine. I rested my cheek against hers. I did not kiss her, as Grandma had never taken to that Dutch custom—*Why do they all lick me on the cheeks, and three times too? Is once not enough?*

Even with the oxygen glasses, the small flexible plastic tubes directing air to her nose, she was breathing quickly. I had not known she was on oxygen therapy. She said in Chinese, "Snow Jasmine. You have returned."

I switched to Taishanese, the dialect of her old village in China. "Grandma. It has been too long."

I could see the bones of her skull clearly through her thin, fine skin. Her skeleton was beginning to triumph over flesh, her bright eyes sunken and dimmed; her thick black hair had gone fine, wispy and completely white. Bits of pink scalp showed through. Had it truly been so long?

Grandma wore a long-sleeved flowery shirt she had doubtless made herself. She was so small that nothing store-bought in this country of giants ever fit her. The blouse hung on her gaunt frame, her emaciated hands and wrists protruding from lace sleeves, limp against the coverlet. Where were the strong hands I remembered, the ones that guided me home after school each day and stirred the flour for wontons and dumplings?

She smiled at me, happiness brightening her eyes, and I caught a glimpse of the elegant woman she had once been, always immaculately dressed and made-up, waiting for me and Lukas each day after school. We would often find some other kid's grandpa towering over her, laughing and trying to communicate with her despite how few words of Dutch she'd learned. She was so unlike Ma and Amy, who never cared how they appeared. Now her lips were white and bare, vulnerable flesh. All these years, when I had thought about Holland, Grandma was the one I held to my heart. I had blocked out Helena. That was how the mind worked, deceiving us so we could bear the many sorrows of life.

My voice was thick with unshed tears. "I should have come sooner." My regret was as plentiful as the hairs on my head.

"You are back now. And you are as lovely as ever." Her voice was thin, the words slurred. Underneath the hooks of the oxygen tubes, I could see she had hearing aids in both of her large ears. Next to her, on the table beside the oxygen tank, sat a photo in a silver frame: me and Lukas, the day after my birthday, both four years old, hand in hand, my first day at elementary school. For Grandma, I had always existed. The image was from the time before the crooked tooth, and before my right eye started to move away. Yes, Grandma would remember me as beautiful.

"As are you," I said.

She barked a laugh and shook her head. I heard her fight for each breath. "My heart has borne too much through the years and now it is failing. No one should see me like this."

"Only because you do not have the right help." I reached out and touched her cool fingers. "I could get gloss for your hair, if you want, and put some makeup on you."

Her lips swept upward, and she said, "Would you? I hate looking like an old woman."

Lukas, who stood by the door, laughed, and Grandma and I joined in. "Who is minding her?" I asked him.

"The home care. She is coming later today."

I turned back to Grandma. "I will speak to the nurse and if it is allowed, I will make you up, okay?"

Her eyes were tremulous. "It is good to have my girl back. I have something for you. It is in the drawer next to the bed."

I slid the rickety wooden drawer of the bedside table open and gasped when I saw what was inside. "Tasha!" My old rag doll, the one Grandma had made for me—and so much smaller than I remembered. I smoothed her black yarn hair back with a finger. The first time I had seen her, I had been amazed at a doll that was dark like me, instead of blond like the Barbies in the stores. The rip in Tasha's red satin dress had been repaired, her dark brown eyes restitched with care. I could still see the stain where I had once spilled grape juice across her leg. I pressed Tasha to my chest. "I have missed her."

"I know. She has been waiting here for you," Grandma said, and my heart smote me again, because I knew Grandma was speaking of herself.

I set Tasha on the bedside table and arranged her in a sitting position. "For now, she shall watch over you and keep you company."

"She is yours."

"I know but there is time enough for that." We all knew what I meant. I felt bereft at the thought of taking Tasha away from Grandma, after Grandma had kept her safe for me all these years.

Grandma quirked her lips into a smile. "Well, I must say I have gotten used to having your doll around. And now that you are back, I can depart in peace."

"None of that kind of talk, Grandma."

"No worries, Snow Jasmine. I will not pass on before I give you my treasure."

Once we were outside and the bedroom door was closed, I turned to Lukas. "Is she truly getting home care?"

He hesitated, and said, "It is palliative care."

I became very still. My blood felt like it had pooled in the bottom of my stomach. I had looked this up before I came. In the Netherlands, you only received palliative care if the doctor had issued a statement that you had less than three months to live.

Lukas went on, "We thought about moving her to a hospice. There is a beautiful one close by, almost completely volunteer-run, where they would cook her anything she wanted, wait on her day and night. But she prefers to stay here."

"Of course. Did she make any other arrangements?" I knew from my many discussions with the Dutch students in college how different the options were here for the dying.

"She has been approved for euthanasia if she should request it."

Euthanasia. Three months or less. My dear grandma, she had been invincible when I left her. I leaned my head against the wall for a moment and closed my eyes. I felt a tear trickle down my cheek. "Has all hope already sailed?"

He nodded. The deep lines around his mouth betrayed his grief. "She is too weak. Old age comes with defects. You know Grandma has swallowed high blood pressure pills for years and now her heart and lungs cannot keep up with the demands of her body."

Then we heard the front door open and we exchanged a look. I rubbed my aching forehead and composed myself before going downstairs to greet Helena and Willem.

Helena's eyes, cold and calculating, watched as we descended the stairs. I felt dizzy; a sudden wave of jet lag, depression, and grief swept over me and I swayed for a moment, holding on to the railing to stay upright. I recovered and straightened, making sure I descended with the dignity of the former queen Beatrix. This woman before me was the Helena I had known, and she was not. She was older than I had expected. It was like I was seeing her for the first time. What was an adult to a child—a head in the distance, a voice, a force for kindness or cruelty. She had cut her hair, which used to lie halfway down her back. I had loved to hold it between my palms in the small moments of peace we had shared.

The years had begun to reveal the truth of her face, as they did to all of us. The superficial prettiness I remembered had yielded to something stiff and unrelenting in the set of her lips, the frown between her eyes. I had grown into a woman in the years I had been gone, and she—what had Helena become? Her fair skin had turned mask-like, and harsh grooves lined the sides of her nose. She wore an outdated Dolce & Gabbana tuxedo jacket that did her hips no favors over an ankle-length leopard-print fringe pencil skirt. Trying to look younger than she was and failing miserably with chunky Van Cleef & Arpels jewelry that only emphasized her short neck and arms. Even if an ape wore a golden ring, it was and remained an ugly thing.

I felt a surge of triumph that as she had grown less, I had come into my own. Her eyes drifted up my Loro Piana outfit, from the pressed cream slacks to the white cap-sleeve blouse to the silk floral-print stole knotted around my neck. Then she checked out the Hermès Kelly bag I had tossed onto the chair in the hallway, and eyed my reversible cashmere coat in pearl blue and silver myrtle, which hung from her coat rack. Ah, she spoke my language; I loved it. I had suspected she would. Finally, we were legible to each other. My designer clothing had always been invisible to Amy and Ma. Amy and I had often fought when we were younger because she did things like tromp around the room playing cowgirl in the three-hundred-dollar Yves Saint Laurent suede ankle boots I had found at a sample sale. Even paying discount prices, I had worked and scrimped for months for each purchase. Now I saw the silent assessment in Helena's eyes, the hatred kindling once again.

As always, Helena eclipsed Willem, who was staring up at me with the secret affection he had always shown me that had turned into something hungrier over the years. As a child I'd needed it, but now I despised him for it, for his ravenous eyes, for his fear of Helena. His love for me had always bowed to her will, like a plant grown within the confines of a box. If he truly cared for me, he would have dared to stand up to her. He would not have hidden every caress of my hair, every tiny gift.

I felt the solid warmth of Lukas at my back.

Helena smiled and spoke to me in Dutch, probably hoping for me to stumble. As always, her accent was flawless. She had been born here. "Sylvie, you are exactly what I had expected."

I replied fluently in the same language. "As are you, Cousin Helena."

She blinked a moment, taken aback, and then we exchanged three empty air kisses, neither of us touching the other's skin. I turned to Willem and we did the same, but I felt the urgency of his lips against my cheek, the way his hands clutched my arms. He whispered, his voice trembling with emotion, "I have missed you so, Sylvie."

He had always loved me too much, albeit surreptitiously. I pulled away before Helena could notice but also knew it was too late. She had always seen us. I smiled at him and said nothing, only tossed my hair so the diamond studs he had given me glittered. By his quick intake of breath, I understood he recognized them.

"How is your ma?" he asked, with a furtive glance at Helena, as if trying to distract her.

"Fine." I exhaled, relieved. I was glad to distance myself from this excess of emotion. "Ma and Pa are both in good health."

Helena chattered as we all went into the kitchen. She was playing the gracious hostess. I had not noticed earlier that they were carrying bags of food from their restaurant, which smelled delicious. But as they were unpacking, Helena said, "This is a bit of a celebration lunch to have our Lukas return to us."

I glanced at him. "When did you get back?"

"Last night. My project was coming to an end and this seemed like a good time not to take on anything else yet." I heard the words he had not said: *since Grandma is dying.*

"Anyway," Helena said, stepping between us as she set the table with the traditional red glazed Chinese plates I still remembered, "we have brought back his favorite dishes—Szechuan prawns and sea bass braised in black bean sauce. I completely forgot that you are allergic to seafood. I hope you do not find it a difficulty, Sylvie?"

I stood there a moment, as if she had slapped me. This was the Helena I knew. So quickly did we shed the wisdom and kindness of accumulated years, how easily we reverted to our former selves in the company of those who had known us before. I had just arrived, jet-lagged and exhausted, to the house where I had been a member of this family for the first nine years of my life, and Helena wanted to remind me how much of an outsider I was, how much they did not need me. The ground sank away beneath my feet. The worst was seeing how Lukas's head snapped up, his eyes widened in shock and cheeks reddened with shame. Willem too stared at Helena, aghast. He clearly had not known what they were bringing home and the message it would send.

"Mother, I am sure we have food for Sylvie in the refrigerator," Lukas said, pulling open the fridge door with unnecessary force.

"Naturally," said Willem, making an effort to smile at me. We all did such a good job of pretending we believed in Helena's "accident." "I can also cook something fresh for you, Sylvie."

"Not a problem." I knew how this game was played. When I was little, I would have slunk to my room and hidden in the blankets, willing myself not to cry. No more. "I am as full as an egg. The way they feed you in first class, it is like they think you are starving," I lied. Fortunately, I had learned all about humble-bragging from my so-called friends. They often came up with statements like *Oh, we're flying private to our vacation house on the island, not that we do that all the time—just when it's more convenient.*

Lukas said, "Are you certain, Sylvie? We have—"

"Oh no," I said, even though I was willing my stomach not to growl.

Hunger makes raw beans sweet, but I smiled and sank with deliberate grace into the central chair at the table. "I could not eat another bite."

Helena stared at me a moment. Then she continued setting out the food as Willem helped her. Lukas gave me a half smile. He understood exactly what I was doing, and poured me a glass of Spa red, bubbly mineral water with lemon. No ice, of course, unheard of in Dutch homes.

Helena said, "You go ahead upstairs to unpack and relax, Sylvie."

"I have no haste." I leaned back in my chair while they filled their plates, playing with my scarf between my fingers. Lukas kept glancing at me and hardly ate any of his own food. I could see he felt terrible, which I regretted, but I enjoyed making Helena aware of every bit of her rudeness to me. She had ensured that even the fried rice had shrimp in it. Despite my hunger, I smiled throughout the meal, so every time they passed the food or took a bite of fish, they could sense how un-Chinese this behavior was, to treat a guest in this way. Willem's forehead held a ruddy glow and even Helena knocked her chopsticks onto the floor in an uncharacteristically clumsy move.

The home care nurse arrived midway through the meal, a sturdy young woman named Isa with red hair, a nose ring, and two large disc earrings that created one-centimeter holes in her lobes. She had a wide friendly smile and made up a plate for Grandma, which she then took upstairs.

"Make sure you take some for yourself too, Isa," Helena said. This too I remembered, how everyone else thought she was so kind, lovely, and polite. In some ways, that warmth was real. I was the only one she disliked. What was it about me that brought out the worst in people? When Isa hesitated, Helena pressed a full plate into her hands and gave her a heaping scoop of fried prawn rolls to top it off.

After the awkward meal, Lukas carried my suitcase to the attic, which had been his room when we were little. Grandma's door was shut and we heard Isa chatting away inside. We passed my old room too, so tiny that it had been turned into a closet, filled with odds and ends. We had always spent our time in Lukas's room anyway. All of his things were gone but the lines of the rafters, the red checkered curtains by the small circular window were the same, as were the dormer windows that extended the length of the room. I could have navigated the space blindfolded.

"Do you remember how often we bumped our heads against the ceiling?" I asked.

"That was because you never looked when you launched yourself off the bed," he said, grinning.

Suddenly, it was too much for me—the air in this house, so still and contained, smelling of Helena's perfume and Grandma's medicines. I felt like an animal caught in a trap. I tossed my suitcase on the desk and said, "I can unpack later. Show me where you are living now."

Lukas took me to the large separate garage. He had converted it into a living space with a second story built above the original area. The old garage door had been removed and now a neat red door sat in its place, beside wide curtained windows. As Lukas fumbled with the key, a little orange cat bolted into the garden and then skidded on her hind legs. She scampered back to his feet and batted at the shoelaces of his dusty hiking boots.

"Who is this?" I cried, scooping the cat into my arms.

Lukas shook his head. "She is incorrigible. Her name is Couscous. I found her half-starved in Turkey a while ago. I could not leave her there so I brought her home. She will get dirt all over your shirt."

"Who cares about a stupid shirt when there is an incorrigible Couscous? You little heart-thief," I crooned. The cat blinked at me with her amber eyes. The tip of her creamy snout was light apricot brown, as if she had been caught drinking chocolate milk. She was alternately white and orange like a candy cane and when I cradled her, she began to purr, her fur so dense and soft. "You have good taste to come here instead of the main house, Couscous. I wish I could take you home with me."

"I know so little about your daily life," Lukas said. "Do you have a house? A flat?"

"You should come. Jim and I live in an apartment." I felt a pang. Jim was not there anymore. I had managed not to think about him for a few hours now. We stepped inside the dark converted garage and, for a moment, I was blinded by the change in lighting. Unlike most Dutch, Lukas had all his drapes closed, probably because of his photography equipment.

He closed the door behind him and the shadows wrapped around us. Couscous was a warm silky weight in my arms, her steady purr a comfort. I exhaled. Here I was with Lukas, who had known and loved me before I became somebody and before I lost it all too. Being with him was as natural as breathing. My cousin, my friend.

Lukas leaned against the wall. He still had not switched on the lights, and he carefully asked, "How goes it with Jim?"

"Fine, he is just diving in bed with someone else." My mouth dropped open. How had that popped out?

In the half-light from the curtained window, Lukas's eyes widened but he showed no other reaction. Yes, he had always been like this. He was the calm itself. "Is he enjoying himself?"

"Seemed like it to me." Then we both chuckled, even though my throat burned.

He came over and touched me gently on the arm. "Serious, goes it all right?"

Couscous started to wriggle and I set her down. I shrugged. My heart was throbbing as if it had been punched. "You are the first person I have told."

"Sometimes it is easier to confide in a stranger."

Now my voice broke. "You are no stranger." And, despite myself, a few tears escaped my eyes.

Lukas took me in his arms then and I rested my head against his chest. He smelled of basil and ginseng and I felt the words his body said to mine: *You are safe here. Everything will be all right.* He whispered, "Why did you not come back to visit?"

I sniffed and pulled away. I cocked my head toward the main house. "I was not welcome."

He didn't meet my eyes, stared at the floor. "I—I wish I had some-place else you could have come back to."

For a moment, I was confused. Then I understood. "No. You did not choose an easy path and it made sense for you to stay with your parents. Jim's parents gave us our apartment too, so it is not so different."

"I used to daydream about going to see you. I think that is what first made me want to travel," he said in a low voice. "But by the time I was old enough, you were with Jim. I felt like I would be intruding on your life."

"That is ridiculous." I shook my head, shedding the intimate, serious mood. "Come on, turn on the lights and show me around."

When he flicked on the track lighting, I was delighted to find the room arranged like a theater or movie set. There were no boring couches or oppressive sideboards. Long rolled-up backdrops leaned against the walls behind stacks of photography equipment. Lines of lights hung above us, angled in all directions like birds perched on a wire, covered with filters in yellow, blue, green. I picked up a small umbrella, opened it, and twirled like a girl in a black-and-white movie. "I love this."

I stepped over to a rack by the wall that was stuffed with silk scarves, Balinese sarongs, Indian saris, flapper dresses, and tuxedo jackets. I arched an eyebrow at him. "Cross-dress much?"

He laughed. "All for photo shoots. I have to work, you know. He who sits on his butt must also sit on his blisters." He led me to the back, where a wall had been erected next to the staircase, separating the last part of the garage space.

"I built this myself." As he stood by the doorway, I noticed that the two doors attached to either side of the wall had two separate sets of hinges. I swung one outward and the other inward. We entered and Lukas drew back a thick black curtain that ran across the length of the room, separating us from the inside.

I made an appreciative noise in my throat. "A darkroom. I assume the second set of doors and curtains are so no one can walk inside and accidentally expose your film to the light. But who would come in here anyway?"

"My parents, the cleaning lady. You." He tossed a key chain at me. I caught it on reflex—the keys to the main house and to his place. "My spare set."

"I would not want to disturb your privacy."

He rolled his eyes. "Right. Who was it who never knocked when she came to my room? Who would not even let me go to the toilet without chatting away about something?" He mimicked in a high falsetto, "'Pee later! This is important!'"

I punched him in the arm. "I never did that. I am a very respectful person."

Lukas flicked on the red lightbulb attached to the ceiling. It turned him into a long ruby sculpture. The glow reminded me of the red light district in Amsterdam, where the lingerie-clad prostitutes stood lit up in windows. Suddenly, I was aware that the boy I had known had turned into a man and we were alone. I coughed, mortified by my thoughts. For goodness' sake, he was my cousin. I could barely get out the words. "Could—could you please turn on the regular light?"

He turned on the main lighting and then fanned his face. "Sorry, it stinks an hour in the wind here, heh?" Even though the windowless room was spotless, it still smelled of the strange and exotic chemicals stored inside the canisters and jugs that lined the shelves.

I recovered quickly and moved away from him. "No, I sense invention and possibility." How to change the subject? I gestured toward his long workbench and the three deep sinks. "I did not think anyone did darkroom work anymore. Is it not all digital these days?"

Now a glow lit up his eyes. He ran his hand through his rumpled hair. "I am in love with imperfection. Some of my mistakes wind up being the most interesting work I have ever done. Come upstairs, I will show you."

We entered his living room and kitchen, which only consisted of a combination oven/microwave, a mini fridge, and a stovetop. A low coffee table that had lost one leg was propped up by thick art and photography books—Basquiat, Dorothea Lange, Mondrian, Jerry Uelsmann, Vermeer. There was a door at the other end of the room. I assumed it led to his bedroom and bathroom. Everything was as neat as Lukas's room used to be. I was the one who had always rebelled against Helena by living as messily as possible.

I snickered. "It is so bare here, a blind horse could do no damage."

Lukas barked out a laugh. "I do not have time to collect thingies."

I scanned his apartment again. "It feels more like a train station than a home. Like a stopping point before you arrive at your destination."

He sat cross-legged on the floor, pulled out a thick black portfolio, and started flipping through the photos. They were mostly in black and white. I plopped down beside him, looked over his shoulder, and stopped him at a page: the hands of a workingman, crusted with dirt, callused, cradling a tulip bulb. "I love this one."

He grimaced, rueful. "The client rejected it." He tapped on the sheet beside it, which held a color photo of the farmer, cleaned and shaven, complete with a fake smile. "This is what they bought in the end. I keep this here to remind myself not to get too carried away when I am being paid by the client. I am a photojournalist. I should document, not dominate."

We paged through the warm-toned photos. They were almost three-dimensional with the depth of the developing he had done on them. I felt I could reach in and touch the images: a bat the size of a small dog hanging upside down with gleaming red eyes, a flamingo poised at sunrise, a child in rags peddling rice wrapped in leaves—and then his more commercial work: pouting models, tropical flowers and landscapes, all lush, colorful, filled with brilliance.

"I do not know, Lukas," I said. "You, the camera, the subject. They all become one in the photo. Maybe you need more of yourself in your work, not less."

Now his voice roughened, became more intimate. "I am fascinated by the way the process influences the result, the ways I can manipulate the images. A grain of dirt, a flash of light—I am crazy about the physicality of film. We are tangible beings. I revel in that."

On some, he had colored in the negatives or clipped out a little girl and transferred her so that her ghostly image floated above her father who had just tossed her in the air. From the girl's angle, I could not tell if the man was poised to catch her in his arms again or if he had launched her into the great world. There were even a few shots of Lukas from his trip to South America last year. He stood knee-deep in water, wearing tall rubber boots, his teeth white in the midst of his unshaven face, holding a line with a fish with large teeth dangling from the end.

I leaned closer to the image. "Is that a piranha?"

"Our dinner that night. The river was filled with them."

"Bet you were glad for your boots. Who took the pictures of you?" I said, turning to another photo of him. Lukas smiling into the camera, a black spider monkey with one arm wound around his neck while licking its own fingers.

"My guide wanted to try out my camera. I believe the monkey had found a flea in my hair and was very happy about eating it."

There was an old woman sitting in a ramshackle hut, her leathery skin illuminated by the weak flames in the tin can before her. A sheet filled with holes hung next to her and kept out the night, both serenity and struggle plain on her face. Then a faded Polaroid of me fell out. I took one look at my homely eight-year-old self and flipped it over. Some things I did not wish to remember.

"What is this doing here?"

"It was the first good portrait I ever took."

"You were always sneaking around with that Polaroid camera. Did you not get it for your birthday?" I had not been allowed to touch it. Even though Lukas did not mind, I had understood the difference between Lukas and me then, between blood and child companion. Film was expensive. I had never taken a single photo with it.

He nodded. "Do you remember how the teacher made us sing that song for my birthday?"

"It was horrible." I still remembered the lyrics, sung to the tune of "Happy Birthday to You."

Hanky panky Shanghai
Hanky panky Shanghai
Hanky panky
Hanky panky
Hanky panky Shanghai

How the Dutch people loved this song. They would stretch their eyes into long slits and move them back and forth as they sang. To make things worse: that teacher had been our favorite, a friendly woman with long red hair who fed us tea and caramel waffles when we behaved. In that moment, the gulf separating Lukas and me, the only nonwhite children in the group, from the rest of the class grew into an abyss. That space had always existed, I realized then, I had just not been aware of it. Lukas had scrunched his face into a scowl and looked at me. I had pressed my lips together, unsure what we could do to stop them.

"Do not be shy," the teacher said with her customary cheer. "Come up, sing along!"

At our silence, she took us both by the arm and led us, humiliated, to the front of the room. "Okay, everyone together. Again."

The children obeyed. Lukas and I looked out over the classroom, surrounded by an ocean of singing pale heads.

"You too," she said, nodding at us. She clapped her hands in encouragement.

Lukas wrapped his arms around his skinny frame and glowered. I burst into tears.

"Oh, sweetie," the teacher said. She felt my forehead. "Sit down, then. You must not be feeling well." As Lukas and I slumped in our chairs, I heard her say to the student teacher with a shrug, "I thought they would enjoy it, something fun from their culture."

Now, Lukas said, "They still sing that song at children's birthday parties, you know, to this very day. But a few years after you left, I went to the director and told her how racist it was and they never sang it at school again."

"You have changed, Lukas." He had once been a quiet child, like me, and now he was this.

"Yes and no. But I learned that if you do not speak, no one will ever hear you."

At that moment, my stomach rumbled so loudly we both jumped. Hiding a smile, Lukas said, "Okay, enough of this. Shall we go get you something to eat? You lied about the airplane food." He stood and held out his hand to me.

I let him drag me to my feet. "How did you know?" I stretched and groaned. It had been a long day.

He was already headed for the doorway and said over his shoulder, "You paid for the ticket, right? You would never purchase first class for yourself. When we were little, I always ate all of my candy in five minutes, but you would still be munching away many days later. Despite your expensive clothing, you are frugal."

I used my haughty voice. "Oh? You are a fashion expert now?"

He scratched his head. "Umm, no. But I saw your bag in a magazine I worked for. And your clothes seem very—" He was bounding down the stairs in front of me; his broad back barely fit in the narrow stairwell. He fluttered his arms in the air. "Fancy. But you buy them as a soldier collects weapons. In the end, you are practical. You would see flying first class as wasting money on yourself."

I flushed as red as a beet, happy his back was to me and he could not see it. He had it right. Indeed, I used those designer labels as armor, to communicate my status to my clients and colleagues, nothing more. I never indulged in extravagances just for myself.

He continued, "Come on. We can go to the snack bar and stop by Estelle's. She would love to see you. Maybe she has an old bicycle she can lend you."

We went outside and he wheeled a black bike out from underneath the carport. A gentle breeze tousled his hair.

I whistled. "Now you are riding a lady's bike?"

"You are out of touch, Sylvie. It is hip for guys to be on grandma bikes nowadays. I am just being a modern man, although Estelle tells me I need to work on becoming more metrosexual."

I burst into a laugh as he climbed onto his bicycle and waited for me to hop onto the baggage rack behind him. It was just like old times. The metal was bumpier than I remembered but I held on, and as we swung off, Lukas pedaling hard, I leaned my shoulder against his strong back and breathed in the clear Dutch air.

CHAPTER 11

Amy

Friday, May 6

When my alarm clock rings the next morning, I am completely disoriented. Last night, sleep fell upon me like a concrete blanket. My body knows it is actually the middle of the night back home and fights my attempts to wake up; the weight of my limbs binds me to the coma-like darkness. I struggle and crack open my eyes. It takes a moment to realize I'm not in my own bed, or even my own country. This isn't a nightmare. Sylvie's missing. I grab my phone. Still no word. I close my eyes and clutch my cell to my chest. How can this be real?

I haven't seen Helena and Willem since they left for work yesterday. I understand they are generally home in the mornings and gone until late in the night, returning after their restaurant has closed. They work through the weekends and their free days are Monday and Tuesday. For dinners, I was told to help myself to the restaurant food they bring home every day. Their enormous fridge is packed with spicy beef in black bean sauce, grilled shrimp, and pork skewers in hot peanut sauce. Normally, I would have been beside myself. I love to cook and to eat.

Yesterday, we all sat around the table for lunch. They served an Indonesian *rijsttafel,* composed of fried rice and Indonesian yellow rice and forty smaller dishes: hard-boiled eggs in chili sauce, chicken coconut curry, duck roasted in banana leaves, aromatic caramelized beef in spicy coconut milk, and more. Although I didn't have much of an appetite, it was one of the best meals I'd ever tasted. Maybe later, after Sylvie was safely home, I would ask them for the recipes. When I told Helena I'd never had Indonesian food before, she said, "We need to serve every type of Asian cuisine here. The Dutch cannot tell us apart, so when they come to a Chinese restaurant, they expect Indonesian and Japanese food too." I spent the afternoon unpacking and then attempted to make up for my restless night on the airplane by going to bed early.

I check the time. It's almost nine in the morning and the police family liaison officers are supposed to arrive at ten. There's a bathroom attached to my room, so small I can barely squeeze between the toilet and the sink to brush my teeth. A radiator in the shape of a towel rack hangs beside the tiny shower, draped neatly with two white towels. Before I step into the shower, I realize I've forgotten to pack shower gel. There's a huge green bottle labeled DOUCHE GEL but I'm afraid of it for obvious reasons. I grab the antibiotic hand soap from the sink instead. I close my eyes and wash off the stink of the airplane, which has somehow clung to me all these hours. The disorienting feeling of jet lag remains, as if my brain has been packed in wool.

I dry off with a warm towel and pull on jeans, a plain long-sleeved black shirt, and my glasses and head downstairs. I hang on to the railing to ensure my feet don't slip off the shallow steps.

Couscous, the stripy cat I met last night, is rubbing herself against Helena's legs. Helena is dressed for work in a fluffy black outfit but she isn't wearing any shoes. As she fries some fresh fish in the wok (for breakfast?), she scolds Couscous in Chinese for being too greedy. Lukas is sitting at the dining room table, drinking what smells like coffee from a traditional Mun Shou Chinese mug, the type where the ceramic looks like it's been embroidered with blue lotus flowers. Behind him, the morning light, clear and merciless, streams in through the windows of the large double doors, illuminating his unshaven face and shadowed eyes. I can see the back garden, the lawn pierced by sharp white stones.

Helena blows on the fish fillet to cool it, then cuts it into little pieces. She arranges them on a plate, first feeling them to make sure there aren't any bones, and sets the dish on the floor. So the fish is for Couscous.

"She is getting fat, Ma," Lukas says. "You should stop spoiling her."

"How can you say that about a lady?" says Helena, indignant. She bends to stroke the cat, now gobbling the fish. "She just has big fur."

I jump as Willem comes up behind me, passing me on his way to the kitchen counter. Does he need to come so close?

"Good morning, Amy. Would you like some tea or coffee?" he asks.

"T-tea, please." I sit at the table across from Lukas. There's a loaf of bread, boxes of what appear to be cupcake sprinkles, butter not in sticks but shaped into a block, a large wedge of uncut cheese, and various jams and other condiments. No cereal. No toast. No oatmeal.

Willem sets my mug of tea before me. "Sugar?"

"Yes, with milk, please." I notice Willem raises his eyebrows when I say this, though he gets the carton out of the refrigerator for me. "Don't p-people drink tea with milk here?"

"Umm, no. Only very small children." Willem gestures at the sprinkles. "As you can see from the things on the table, we practice being Dutch in the mornings. Would you like to try some *hagelslag*? Sylvie used to love it. You butter your bread and shake it on. We have fresh *tijgerbrood* from the bakery—that is the bread over there."

I relax a bit. Finally, a comment about Sylvie that isn't laced with aggression.

Willem passes the loaf to me. It's light brown, with a crisp puffy top, and smells delicious. He asks, "How is your mother doing?"

"She's fine, working hard as always." I try the *hagelslag* and butter like he suggested on a corner of my untoasted slice. The sprinkles are bright orange and yellow and taste exactly as they look—like sugar on bread. I recognize a jar of peanut butter with relief. After I've spread it over the rest, I spoon some strawberry jelly on top, then realize they're all staring at me.

"You eat peanut butter and jelly together?" Lukas asks.

With my mouth full, I nod.

He scrunches up his face and taps the middle of his forehead a few times with his index finger. "Crazy."

I try not to be freaked out by the Dutch hand gestures. "How do you eat peanut butter?"

"Plain. Sometimes with butter and cheese."

Right. I turn to my meal. Willem places the basket filled with bits of folded paper I saw earlier on the dining room table beside the half-finished paper-formed beast. He sips his coffee as he inserts new pieces into the creature with careful and precise hands.

"What are you doing?" I ask.

"Modular origami," he answers with a smile. "I began with regular origami and moved on to the 3-D version."

"Is that a snake?"

He shakes his head. "A Chinese dragon."

Willem's hobby, the flavorful bread, the cheerful domesticity of Helena cooing over the cat in the kitchen: it makes me miss my own family. If only Ma and Pa were here. If only Sylvie were here. It all rushes up into my throat and I worry I'll choke on my fear. "I'm so scared about Sylvie."

Helena pauses, her hand suspended over Couscous's fur. The warmth drains from her face. "You do not need to worry about that one. She always lands on her feet."

I bristle at the bitterness of her tone. "I-I know Sylvie's good at everything, but no one's heard from her in a week. There must be an explanation." I can hear the desperation grate my voice raw. "I hope she has enough money to survive."

Lukas's hand clenches so tightly around his coffee mug that his knuckles turn white. "She is fine."

I stare at him. "What do you mean?"

He stares into the back garden, avoiding my eyes. "She is just taking some time for herself." His voice cracks and he looks furious at himself for it.

"She has enough means, I am certain." Helena's tone contains more accusation than reassurance. She doesn't add anything else.

In the silence that follows, the doorbell rings. The police are here.

An enormous man enters the house, stooping to avoid the low-hanging lamp in the hallway. He must be at least six foot five, with protruding red ears and a squashed, intelligent face like a French bulldog's. His head is shaved bald but judging from the gray hairs in his scraggly eyebrows and the lines around his eyes, he's in his early fifties. He's accompanied by a younger woman, perhaps late twenties. Her dark blond hair is pulled back into a ponytail and she has a firm, determined mouth. They are both dressed in regular clothing rather than police uniforms.

They shake hands with everyone, including me. Thank goodness, no three kisses for them. Helena slips on her pumps as we move into the living room. Willem pours everyone a coffee or tea. Lukas pulls up a chair from the dining room table and sits. I find myself wedged on the couch between Willem and Helena.

The policeman's knees seem to come up to his ears when he sits in the stern-looking armchair. A torrent of Dutch pours from his mouth.

Willem responds in kind, gesturing at me.

"Oh, I am sorry," the man says with a thick accent. "You speak English only?" At my nod, he says, "My name is Pim de Jong. This is my colleague, Danique Smits. You are Amy Lee, the sister of the . . ."

As he searches for a word, Danique leans forward in her armchair. She smiles and manages to look both competent and warm, and her English is much better than his. "The missing person. You are from the United States? And Sylvie Lee, she is also American?"

I say, "Yes," at the same time Lukas says, "No, she is Dutch."

Then Helena smiles and says, "She is Chinese," as if that settles the matter.

Willem says, "Sylvie has dual Dutch American nationality."

Pim writes this down in his notepad. He jerks his head slightly at his colleague and I see they have decided that she will do the talking as he takes notes.

Danique says, "We already have the basic information you gave us over the telephone and now we can officially begin."

I say, "Wh-what? You are o-only starting now? Why?"

"She is an adult, with a good mental and physical state. There is nothing to show she may be in danger or dangerous to other people. There is no signal of a crime."

"Sylvie would never just disappear like this."

"Most missing persons return by themselves and the police have limited resources. For a child or an older person, we take immediate action. For a healthy adult, we wait. But we will do our best to find your sister, I promise you this. Do you have a recent picture of her?"

I want to smack myself. Why hadn't I thought to bring one with me? My eyes flit over the many images of Lukas in the living room. Obviously no one here ever cared enough to photograph her. But Lukas pulls a large envelope from a folder he's stashed beneath his chair. He passes it to Danique.

"Where did you get that?" I ask.

"I took it myself."

Of course, I'd forgotten he's a professional photographer. Danique opens the envelope, slides out an eight-by-ten, and holds it up so we all can see. She raises her eyebrows. "Is this a good likeness of her?"

It is a stunning portrait of Sylvie. She's slightly turned away from the camera, the angles of her high cheekbones and straight nose highlighted by the golden sunlight that glides over her skin and gathers in her glossy hair, her eyes so sad beneath the winged eyebrows. Helena's lips are pressed firmly together, simmering, and Willem stares at the photo with so much open longing I am embarrassed.

Danique takes our silence for acquiescence. "How would you describe her character?"

"Secretive," Helena says.

I want to kick her. But then I think about all the things I didn't know, and still don't, about my sister. "P-private. Loyal. Brilliant."

Danique's sharp eyes are trained on Helena. "Why do you say 'secretive'?"

Helena shrugs, an abrupt, aggressive movement. "She keeps her thoughts to herself."

"Would you say she is introverted or a loner?"

"She never fits in," Helena answers.

"We do not either," says Lukas, glaring at his mother. I'm happy I'm not the only one who doesn't like hearing these negative things about Sylvie. This warms me to him.

"What do you mean?" Danique asks.

Lukas shifts on his chair. "It is not always easy being one of the few Chinese families here."

Pim's mouth falls open, and if he still had hair, I'm sure his eyebrows would have disappeared. "But there is no racism in this village."

Lukas cocks his head, his eyes burning. "Really? Well, you are a white man and a police agent, so people are not likely to treat you in a different way, are they?"

"This is all beside the point," says Willem. "The most important thing now is to find Sylvie."

Danique turns to me. "Would you agree that she is an outsider, Amy?"

"Well," I say slowly, "Sylvie has always been special, so by definition, she is different from normal people."

"I understand she was here because her grandmother was dying. Did she seem depressed after her grandma passed on?"

Helena snorted. "She was off having a grand time celebrating her birthday in Venice when her grandma died."

"Wh-what?!" I protest. "Sylvie wouldn't do that. She loved Grandma deeply. She came all the way here to be with her." Venice! Why in the world would Sylvie go to Venice? Had she gone alone? But indeed, Sylvie hadn't called me on her birthday. She'd texted me that she had too much going on with the family and that with the time difference, it was too hard to talk. My gaze darts around the room. Lukas has averted his eyes and his neck has reddened.

Helena presses her lips together, as if she's holding the words inside by brute force alone.

"Did Sylvie ever talk about hurting herself?" Danique asks.

"Sylvie d-did not commit suicide," I say.

"When somebody disappears and does not return within three days, there are usually only four main possibilities: suicide, murder, kidnapping, or flight."

I gasp at her plain words. Pim shoots her a look, and says, "We do not know the reasons yet."

Looking mildly chagrined, Danique continues her questions. "She has many impressive diplomas, is that correct? And a very good job? Sometimes, a person who is very successful, if they lose face, can become depressed. They can do something about it or they can flee. Perhaps it can be issues in their relationship. Were there any changes in her circumstances recently?"

I don't want to reveal Sylvie's troubles in front of Helena, but I want the police to be able to help her too. Before I can decide what to say, Lukas speaks up. "She was having problems with her marriage. Her husband was stalking her. He even showed up here. They had a fight."

I drop my teacup onto the saucer with a loud clank. Hot tea splashes in my lap but I don't feel it. "Jim was in the Netherlands?" Did Sylvie go to Venice with him after all? Helena tsks and rubs at my jeans with a napkin. I take it away from her. "I'm fine, thanks."

"About a week before she disappeared. She thought he had gone back to the United States. But no one knows for sure."

"I saw Jim on Monday, before I flew here," I say. "He did act a bit strangely. What did they fight about?"

Lukas draws his eyebrows together and slams his fist into his palm as if he wished it were Jim's face. "I only overheard the last part of the conversation. He asked her not to destroy his life and she said she had no choice. He had grabbed her and was threatening her when I walked in."

I can't imagine easygoing, patrician Jim doing such a thing. Destroy his life? Threatening Sylvie? This was crazy. What could Jim have to hide? Or did he mean the divorce? Were there parts of Jim that I never suspected existed? If a woman disappears, the husband or lover is often involved. But Jim? Or is Lukas not telling the truth?

"So it is possible he left the Netherlands only after Sylvie disappeared," Danique says. They ask me for Jim's contact information. I am still so stunned by the revelations that Willem has to nudge me to answer. Then Danique says, "Amy, what was Sylvie's life like back home? Would you say she was happy?"

A week ago, I would have said yes with complete confidence. Now, I hesitate before saying, "I don't know."

"Would she have any reason to run away?"

After a moment, Helena answers for me. "I think anything is possible. After all, our own house was broken into just a few weeks ago."

Pim checks his printed notes. "Yes, there is a record. Nothing was taken."

Helena laughs shrilly. "My inheritance was stolen. A fortune in gold and jewels."

Danique steps over to Pim and they both scan the papers. Pim clears his throat. "That was the claim but there was no proof."

"It belonged to Grandma," Helena said. "She never wore any of it and we did not think to take photos. She was very secretive. Did not show it to anyone, or tell us where it was hidden."

Danique asks carefully, "Are you certain it existed?"

"Absolutely," says Helena, the color rising in her face. Her eyes are two black furnaces. "That treasure was a legend in our family. I saw it myself, many years ago."

"Back to Sylvie," Willem says gently. "That has nothing to do with her disappearance."

"Of course not," says Helena, but her tone belies her words.

"Can't you set dogs on her scent or something?" I ask, knowing I sound like a cliché from a television series. They are the professionals here. Aren't they going to take action?

"She disappeared with her rental car," says Danique. "The dogs will not be able to track anything. There is no scent trail and the car has not been found."

"Maybe she was in an accident." I get up and move behind the couch.

I can't stand being stuck on the sofa. "Somewhere no one can find her—in the woods or mountains. Maybe she's wounded right now." My breath comes quickly. Sylvie with a broken leg, dying of thirst, lying next to her car.

"There is no great wilderness in the Netherlands," Danique says. "We are a very civilized country. It is difficult to leave no trace. The healthy people who disappear usually do not wish to be found."

Willem asks, "Have you been following her bank accounts and mobile telephone?"

Danique looks uncomfortable. "We are not permitted to access that information due to privacy laws unless we have reason to suspect criminal activity."

"But it's completely out of character f-for Sylvie not to tell anyone where she is. I'm afraid something happened to her." I wring my hands. How can we all be sitting around drinking tea when Sylvie might need us?

"I am sorry, but we need special permission from the public prosecutor to get into her records."

Pim speaks up, his low voice confident. "You will not get it. For this case, I am sure. I have many years experience."

Danique asks, "Did she leave a note or something else?"

Lukas squirms in his seat but again we are silent. Finally, the police liaison officers stand to leave, after more promises to do their best for us.

After the front door closes behind them, I say, "I'm not sure they're going to be very effective."

Willem rubs the skin behind his ear. "To be fair, they do not have the legal right to do much in this situation."

Lukas is staring out the window, as if he expects Sylvie to materialize in the front garden. "She is an adult and maybe she just wanted to think things over."

I say, enunciating each word carefully, "Sylvie would let us know. She wouldn't worry us like this." Then I take a deep breath and crumple into a chair. I'd had such hopes for the police. What else is there? "I'm sorry I made them speak English. Pim is the older officer. You might have gotten more out of them if I hadn't been here."

Helena stands and starts clearing the cups. "It would not have made a difference. But enough of Sylvie at this moment. Nothing was ever enough for her. Even now, she has gone somewhere and all we can do is talk about her. Sylvie, Sylvie, Sylvie."

I draw in a sharp breath. I want to stalk over and slap her. How dare she? From the way Lukas's head whips around, I know he feels the same. "How can you say that? Don't you care?"

"Of course I do. But I am sure she is fine."

Despite my anger, hope rises inside my chest cavity like a bubble. "What do you think happened to her?"

Helena gives a short laugh, devoid of humor. "I have no idea." There is rage and an old pain in her eyes. She steps out of the living room and I hear her heels click their way upstairs. This woman, who seems to hate my sister so much, was the one who raised her? Does she know something about Sylvie that I don't?

Dutch Local Newspaper

NOORD NEDERLANDS DAGBLAD

Friday, 15 April

Yesterday on Thursday, 14 April, in between 13.15 and 14.00, a house on the Prins Bernhardstraat was broken into. It is lucky that there was no damage and nothing was stolen. The police believe the in-breaker was surprised by the return of the elderly inhabitant, who was taking a walk, and thus the thief could take nothing.

Alas, not every burglary walks off so good. Please remember to set your doors and windows to locked and to ring Burgernet if you see any sign of strange incidents. If anyone has any other information about this break-in and attempt at thievery, please contact the local police.

Part 3

CHAPTER 12

Ma

Friday, May 6

Pa and I silently revolved around the absence of our two girls, circling this core of emptiness until we collapsed inward. Neither of us wanted to give voice to our dark thoughts.

My poor Amy sounded so distraught when she spoke to me from Holland. It was even harder than usual to understand her English over the phone and I had to do my best to keep up with the conversation.

I asked her, "How are Helena and her husband?"

"They're a bit strange, Ma. Helena is kind to me, but sometimes, I'm not sure how she feels about Sylvie. And I can't figure out Willem."

"Why not?"

"He seems to be watching me a lot, when he thinks I'm not looking."

I caught my breath. Then I gave a little laugh. "Oh, all girls think he was very handsome back in the village."

"That's not exactly what I meant." Amy lowered her voice. "Ma, do you know anything about a treasure?"

I said in my careful, useless English, so long trained not to speak of it, "What you mean?"

"Cousin Helena was going on about some incredibly valuable jewelry that she thinks Grandma had. There was a burglary and then it disappeared. Helena seems to think it has something to do with Sylvie."

That Helena dared accuse my daughter of such a shameful thing. But if Sylvie had taken the jewelry—not stolen, because my ma would have meant to give it to her—then it might mean she was still all right. Rage and hope warred inside me. Perhaps Sylvie was waiting for the calm to come and then she would reappear, as the goddess Kuan Yin manifested herself on the surface of a muddy lake, the beauty of a lotus that bloomed above the muck.

"There was something," I said. "But it has been many years since anyone has seen it. I not know if it still there. Maybe Grandma sold it."

"Helena says she saw it herself. Do you think there's any chance Sylvie took it?" Amy sounded so young, a cub reaching out for her mother. If only I could tell her that when we get to the mountain, there will be a way through it. When the boat reaches the bridge-head, it naturally goes straight with the current.

Instead I said, "Try find out. If treasure still there, Grandma give to Sylvie. Will be okay. Not worry."

After we hung up the phone, I thought about the gold. Of course Helena wanted the jewelry more than anything. We were distant cousins who had never met until she returned from Holland with her wealthy parents. Some who would put the tall hat of flattery on my head had called me the beauty of our village, but Helena had something more valuable to offer: a foreign road. Any man who married her would be able to leave the Central Kingdom and all of his family could follow, one by one. She was a lifeline. She had no trouble finding a husband there.

Helena did not want the gold for the value of it. She had enough wealth of her own. She desired it to spite me, to take something of mine from my mother. She had already had Grandma to care for her boy all these years—must she steal my inheritance as well? That jewelry had been passed down in our family from mother to daughter, hidden away through wars and revolutions, accumulated through pain and death.

I had seen it long ago and remembered it: the finest jade, which grew greener and more vibrant against the skin of the deserving owner; twenty-four-carat gold, untainted, unlike silver, considered undesirable because it tarnished. That gold was too soft, helpless in its purity, too yielding to be of this world. Like my mother and me, it belonged to an age gone by. Its strength was in its ability to bend, but how much could it withstand before it broke for good?

CHAPTER 13

Sylvie

Wednesday, April 6

After excluding me from their meal last Saturday, Helena had tried to make up for it in her own way.

The next morning, she had spoken to me at breakfast. "I got you a few things. Here is an OV-chipcard. Do you know what that is?"

I shook my head.

"You can use it to check in and out on any type of public transportation. It is loaded with enough money for you to travel for a while. I also bought you some toiletries."

I opened my mouth to say I had plenty of my own, but recognized this as a peace offering and thanked her instead. "That is very kind of you."

Helena handed me the OV-chipcard and a wicker basket filled with shampoo, conditioner, shower gel, and hair gloss.

I pulled the familiar large green bottle of shower gel from the basket, flipped open the lid, and sniffed it. Mmm, green tea and cucumbers. "I used to love this. You remembered."

"Of course, I took care of you for all those years," she said briskly. She held her head high and cleared her throat. "I apologize for the confusion yesterday. There is plenty of food for you in the refrigerator when Willem and I are working. Please help yourself, Sylvie."

Since then, we had all coexisted in peace, but as was always the case with Helena and me, our tranquility was short-lived. I spent much of my time helping Isa with Grandma, her labored breathing acting as a constant backdrop. I escorted her to the toilet and bath, exposing pale skin untouched by the sun, arms and legs grown so spindly and frail, an intimacy she had never shared with me before. Grandma's chin had trembled the first time, but I said, "When you love someone, there is no shame. When I see you, I only know that you are my grandma and you are beautiful. You did this for me when I was young. Now it is my turn. You always said, the old become children once again."

The first time I tried to make rice congee, I set off the smoke alarm (Grandma: "Lukas! Can you get to the batteries? Quick! What will the neighbors think?" Lukas, balancing on a stool to reset the shrill alarm. Grandma, muttering, "How can a person burn congee? It is all water.")—and so I was no longer allowed near the stove. Instead, I cut her steamed chicken and vegetables with rice and fed her bites on the bad days, the ones when she barely moved, her thin hands picking listlessly at the coverlet.

Mostly, Lukas, Isa, and I took Grandma outside for walks. After carrying her wheelchair downstairs, Lukas would guide her down, walking backward, one slow step at a time, a sturdy buttress should she fall (Grandma, giving Lukas's biceps a good squeeze: "So strong and handsome like his father. A tiger father does not beget a dog son."), Grandma gripping the banister with her left hand as I held tight to her upper arm, Isa behind us with the oxygen tank and other equipment. We would pause often so Grandma could take a few shallow breaths, trading alarmed looks if she seemed to overexert herself. Once outside, her faded eyes would brighten as she smelled the wind, delighting in the green blades of grass that had survived the winter and the ever-changing swirl of clouds across the sky.

"The water wind is good here. Better than people mountain, people sea," Grandma had said one morning—she had always hated crowds—and suddenly her eyes were awash with unshed tears. "But it is still not the Central Kingdom."

My heart ached, understanding how she must long for the land of her youth as she neared the end of her life.

Lukas stepped closer to her and laid his arm across her frail shoulders. He dipped his dark head to rest his cheek gently on top of her dandelion hair. His Chinese had never been as good as mine, but it was far better than Amy's. He said, "But your granddaughter with her limpid eyes of autumn water is not in the Central Kingdom."

I flushed as Grandma smiled through her tears. "This is true. You both accompany me with the grace of floating clouds and flowing water, and open the heart of this old woman with joy."

This morning, I had a special treat for her. I could not wait to show her the photos and videos of Ma, Pa, and Amy that I had brought on my phone. But after a few minutes, Lukas placed his broad hand on my shoulder and gestured with his chin toward Grandma. I had been so absorbed in my presentation that I had not noticed she was weeping silently, her mouth gaping in mute anguish.

"Oh, Grandma," I said, folding her in my arms. "I did not mean to throw stones down a well at you."

"I will never see my daughter again," she wailed, gasping for air. "I shall never meet your sister, Beautiful Jasmine."

Lukas patted her back as I said, "You shall gaze upon us all after you pass the red dust of the mortal world. You will shed your body and exchange your bones."

Slowly, Grandma quieted. "I should like to rise to our ancestors." She raised her small face and blinked at us with her swollen eyes. "You will burn offerings for me after I am gone? So I have gold to spend and silk to wear in the afterlife."

"Of course," I said, my heart full to overflowing. "They now make Mercedes and flat-screen televisions in paper for people to incinerate for their loved ones."

She cocked her head to one side. "No Mercedes. I want a Jaguar."

Lukas emitted a choked sound that was somewhere between a laugh and a sob.

I said, "Why don't I sing to you now? I still remember some of the old songs you crooned to us:

Little sparrow
So young and new
Your mother sought for worms
So that you might grow strong."

And with Lukas listening intently, I sang to her until she fell asleep again.

That afternoon, I asked nurse Isa for permission to buy some makeup and tinted hair gloss from the pharmacy. I wanted light, natural shades for Grandma. When I was younger, I had practiced my makeup in front of that mottled bathroom mirror in our New York apartment for hours, trying to adjust for its yellow cast as I applied my colors for a professional look. I loved doing Amy's makeup too, but she never cared about the end result, nor could she ever remember how to replicate it. Then she would insist on reciprocating and paint me up like a clown. But Amy did not need cosmetics. Her beauty glowed from within, whereas I was all about the surface.

The shop woman watched me with suspicion, an immigrant and stranger in this small town. She thought I was a pocket-roller and subtly followed me as I brushed past another customer. Did she really think I would pick that elderly man's pocket right in front of her? She stared at me as I selected some hair clips for Amy, probably because they were small and she was afraid I would slip them into my bag. I held up a set studded in rhinestones. Amy would look pretty in these. They would add some sparkle to her thick, unruly hair when she pinned it back from her heart-shaped face.

The saleswoman was starting to annoy me now. This close to Amsterdam, and she acted like she had never seen a person of color before. I knew we Chinese only made up one-third of one percent in the Netherlands as a whole, but this was ridiculous. I turned to her and said in perfect Dutch, "Do you think you could help me choose a hair color for my grandma?"

She jumped in surprise. Her shoulders relaxed and a slow smile spread across her face. If I spoke Dutch that well, I could not possibly be a criminal. "Of course, ma'am. This way."

When I brought the supplies to Grandma's room, I could smell the disease eating at her heart and lungs underneath the sharp cool scent of the tiger balm we'd rubbed across her chest earlier. She had mostly recovered from the emotion of the morning but pain still filmed her eyes, clouding their original golden brown. It went straight through my soul to see her like this. I pulled my hair into a sloppy ponytail so it would not get in my way as I worked. As Isa and I shampooed Grandma's hair, her breathing grew so shallow I was afraid I had made a terrible mistake, overexerting her like this.

Isa exchanged a glance with me. "No worries, it is going good."

I had picked a simple odorless hair glaze with a honey-brown tint. After I applied it onto Grandma's white locks, her hair held a light coating of color. I then gently penciled in subtle eyebrows over her prominent skull bones, dabbed her dry lips with a natural peach gloss, and brushed a bit of blush over her fading cheeks. I had her close her eyes and finished her off with a pale pink powder that offset the pallor of her skin.

When I held the mirror in front of her, she smiled, as if recognizing an old friend. "Take this oxygen thing off my face and get that good-looking boy in here so he can see me. Tell him to bring his camera too."

After Lukas had admired and photographed her to her satisfaction, we tiptoed from her room so she could rest. Outside her closed door, Lukas looked at me, then raised his hand and pulled my ponytail loose. My hair tumbled down around my face. He brushed a strand back, then bent down and whispered, "Thank you."

That evening, as I often did, I went to bed before Helena and Willem returned from the restaurant for their late dinner.

There was a knock on my attic door. When I opened it, I could see

Helena had shot out of her slipper with fury. Her nostrils flared and her legs were planted wide. She raised a finger, visibly shaking, and the thick gold-and-jade dragon bracelet on her wrist trembled in the hallway light.

Where I once used to cower, I decided to confront instead. "Is there something, Cousin Helena?"

She gritted out her words through a tight jaw. "What have you done to the hair and face of Grandma?"

Was that it? I should have known. I kept my voice calm. "It made her happy."

She pointed her finger at me, two centimeters from my nose. "It exhausted her. You could have hurt her. She is in the last stage of her life. From a beautiful plate, you cannot eat. No need for her to be made up like pussycat. For whom?"

I knocked her stupid hand away from my face. "For herself."

Helena reared and for a moment, I thought she would slap me. I almost wanted her to do it. I would hit her back so hard her head would spin for a week. She finally hissed, "Do not think you are so clever. I know why you came back, even though no one invited you."

I raised an eyebrow. "Oh?"

"You want her favor again. Now that she is old and ready to pass on her inheritance, after you left for so many years. While I was the one who was always here for her. Me and my family." She emphasized every phrase with a bob of her head.

My anger rose up in me. I had to voice my words before they exploded into the humiliating tears I refused to shed. I clenched my hands into tight fists. "And why did I not return to this house for so long? Where I had been treated so well? Was it because of Grandma that I stayed away?"

Helena puffed up like an envious dog tied to a short rope. She was not used to this version of me, the one that spoke. She sputtered, strangled by rage and shame, "Grandma always loved you best, like everyone else. You and your mother."

I could not keep my voice from breaking. "Why did you stop caring about me?" I half lifted my hand toward her: this woman who should have been everything to me, who had instead taught me to beware of love.

Caught up in her hatred, Helena went on, ignoring my words. "That gold of hers belongs to us. We housed and clothed her all these years. I am more her daughter than your mother ever was."

My arm dropped back to my side. "You never paid her for all those years she worked here for you as babysitter, cook, and maid. You only gave her pocket money to spend. The least you could do was to provide her with food and a place to live. Now you want the rest of her jewelry too?"

"We are family. Who pays family? Should I get money for all the diapers of yours I changed? Anything she asked for, we gave her. I deserve her legacy." Helena's eyes glittered with naked intensity. I could not tell if they were filled with greed or a desperate need to be loved. I was not even sure if it made a difference: it came down to hunger. Perhaps those desires all stemmed from the same place in our broken, burdened hearts.

"Grandma has but one child and that is my mother." I saw I had hit a sensitive string in Helena. She paled and I was ashamed. I tried to gentle myself. "Grandma loves you and I know she has already given you some valuable pieces, like that dragon bracelet you are wearing now. She wants to pass something on to Ma too, that's all. Is that so wrong?"

Helena covered the jewelry with her other hand, as if she believed I would wrench it from her wrist. "Did Grandma call and ask you to come?"

"Yes."

The flash of hurt in her eyes was quickly swallowed by fury. Beneath the hallway light, her face was a patchwork of white and red blotches. "That treasure belongs to me and my family. I will do anything to stop you from leaving with it. Do not cross me in this, Sylvie."

Without another word, she turned and left.

When I still lived in the Netherlands, Grandma used to let me play with her jewelry if we were alone in her room. It was the one thing she never shared with Lukas, the only way she let it be marked that I was her direct blood relative. Our family had been rich before the Communist Revolution took over China and much of our wealth had been hidden in the form of jewelry. Some pieces had been in our family for generations. When I was little, I especially loved the articulated carp pendant set with imperial jade. The emerald-green stones were so translucent and vibrant that the fish seemed alive, and I would make it swim across Grandma's bed.

"You were made to wear jade, Snow Jasmine. See how it comes to life against your skin," Grandma said.

But I never dared. I was a coward, a hero with only socks on, because of the one time I had skipped down the stairs while admiring a marquise-cut gold ring set with diamonds that was much too big for my finger, and Helena had caught me.

The anger on her face had been as clear to read as parts of a book. "Where did you get that?"

I had turned and fled back upstairs to Grandma's room, where the treasure was still spread across the bed. Helena had burst into the room and we all stood there, the three of us, as silent and unmoving as blocks of ice. Grandma gestured with her fingers. I took off the ring and handed it to her. Without a word, Grandma gathered it all up and put it back in her jewelry bag. She waited until Helena had left to hide it again. None of us had ever spoken of the incident.

Grandma did not like to mention death because it was bad luck, but she had said to me many times before I left for America, "If anything ever happens to me, Snow Jasmine, you must take this. It is for you, your sister, and your mother. This was given to me by my mother and to her by her mother, and so it must remain."

It was the morning after I had colored Grandma's hair. Only Lukas and I were in the house with her, and she sat upright in her bed. This was a good day. She said, "Sylvie, show me you still know where it is hidden, get it out."

I glanced at Lukas, who looked confused.

"It is all right. He is a good boy," Grandma said.

And so I did. I went downstairs and removed the screwdriver from the toolbox, came back and went to the small closet in Grandma's room. I unloaded pile after pile of boxes filled with brocade and cotton, coils of old knitting yarn, outdated blouses that smelled of mothballs, and cheap Dutch souvenirs until I found the worn carpeting underneath. I pried open the loose piece I knew was in the back left corner. Then I brushed away the dirt, uncovering what appeared to be nails in the floorboards but were actually screws. I loosened them, lifted the floorboards, and pulled out Grandma's treasure.

The embroidered velvet bag was compact and heavy for its size. I set it upon Grandma's bed and, when she did not move, opened the drawstring to slide out the small, bulging, zipped red silk envelopes. Lukas came to stand behind me and I opened a few to show him their contents as his bushy eyebrows disappeared into his forehead. Was that hurt on his face—because Grandma had shared this with me but not him?

A jade-and-gold necklace with shimmering diamond accents, each piece dangled on a delicate shiny stream of gold. A ruby-crusted beetle brooch—when I was a child, the beetle and the carp had many adventures together. Heavy necklaces and bracelets of braided pure gold, delicate flowers and sprays of water frozen into precious stones, a small satchel filled only with wedding rings, the twenty-four-carat gold bent and scarred from years of wear, yet still glowing with gentle radiance. I tried to slip one of the rings onto my finger and it was much too small now, as if it had been sized for a child bride.

Then the two smaller silk bags, one filled with gold coins and the other with fine jade pieces. I had learned a few things since I was a child and now knew that the best jade could command a fortune on the market, especially the types I recognized here: kingfisher, moss-in-snow, and apple jade, but mainly, and the most desirable of all, imperial jade.

Grandma lifted her limp hand. Her low voice cracked. "This bag bears the weight of years, Snow Jasmine. It is as rare as phoenix feathers and unicorn horns. From the women of our line, drawn from their happiness and their sorrows, this passes on to your mother and later, to you and your sister."

I tried to swallow. "Grandma, I do not want to take this from you."

"You must resound like thunder and move like the wind. Act now. I have kept it safe all these years for your mother. Do with it as you will. Tell your mother she should sell whatever she needs. This gold is meant to serve the living, not to enslave them."

I thought about the costs piling up now that I had no job and no husband. I thought about the credit card bills lying unopened in my hallway. I thought about Amy's student loans, Ma and Pa, and their apartment. I had not cared about anything but getting away. I wished I could shed my old skin and that my life there had been a dream. But all of it was a nightmare: Jim; the consultancy firm; the desperate, futile struggle for Ma and Pa's love and approval—and I would have to return eventually. I understood this.

Grandma continued speaking, her eyes fixed upon the window. "I had hoped to put this into your mother's hands. But I knew she would not come. Not even now." There was so much grief in her voice that I took her hand.

"Ma thinks about you all the time, Grandma. She would have if she could."

"She stayed away not because she did not care enough. She stayed away because she loves too much," Grandma said. "I understand, but still it saddens me. You must take the treasure now, while you can."

I said only one word, "Helena." Helena, so jealous she could not see the sun shining upon the water. Out of the corner of my eye, I saw Lukas nod.

Grandma said, "That woman has eaten vinegar. She will always be spiteful. It is a pity that she glimpsed the gold all those years ago, but there had already been rumors. I am an arrow at the end of its flight. Once I am gone, she will rip this room apart looking for it. As the water recedes, the rocks will appear. There will be swords drawn and bows bent. Take it now and hide it in a train station locker or something."

Lukas huffed out a laugh.

I said, "You have been watching too many Hong Kong soap operas, Grandma. I am not a spy. Though she may be a toad lusting after a swan's flesh, she will never let it go, undeserving or not. She knows you plan to give it to me. She said she would do anything to stop you. If she does not find it in this room, she will know I have it."

Grandma set her triangular little chin, so like Ma's and Amy's. "So? Too bad for her. By then, the rice will already have been cooked."

I sighed, thinking of the cruel words I had spoken to Helena. "I suppose you are right."

Lukas said, "She will lose face. It will be an ugly scene. She might even demand to search your luggage or claim that you stole it from Grandma. Perhaps it is time for thunder from a clear sky. Grandma, maybe you should do things the Western way and tell my mother directly that you are giving your inheritance to Sylvie."

Both of us put on our huge eyes and stared at him as if we saw water burning.

Grandma said, "We are not Dutch, my heart stem. That would hurt her more than anything else I could do. I am not able to be a human being in such a way. We need to give her a back road for her escape even though she comes to loot a burning house. She also desires to attain it for you, Lukas. I hope you understand?"

Lukas shrugged. "What would I use it for?" But his mouth was strained and I remembered his dreams of owning his own studio.

I said, "She hungers for your love, Grandma."

"She has it, though she could have been nicer to me through the years. The things I have seen in this house, the way she treated you. You are two who could not live under the same sky." Grandma's shoulders drooped. She rubbed the heel of her palm against her bony chest. This was the first time we had ever spoken of it. "I could do so little for you then. This is also why you and your ma need to have the jewelry. It is the smallest boon I can give you, to keep you safe. I understand the problem of Helena. But now you must fight poison with poison, and I have an idea."

The next morning, I awoke exhausted again. Even with the prescription sleeping pills I had brought from New York, I could barely manage to make it through the nights. I was desperate for rest. I would sleep my entire life away if I could, but the more I longed for it, the more it eluded me, like everything else I desired. I had always been a bad sleeper and in the dark, still Dutch hours, the wreckage of my life caught up to me, worrying at the edges of my mind like a rabid dog—Jim and that girl, the whispers at work, those tender moments with Jim when we had both been so innocent, my phone call with Amy, her blind faith in me, and Grandma, moving further from me every day until she disappeared into the horizon. I took the sleeping pills at night for a bit of oblivion and then amphetamines in the wretched mornings to get me up and moving again.

I was cradling my head in my hands at the dining room table when Lukas entered the room. Grandma was napping upstairs and Willem and Helena had already left for the restaurant.

His gaze lingered on the shadows below my eyes. "Is it going all right?"

"Naturally." I tried to sound as steady and robust as the Dutch always did, but it only made my headache seem worse.

He scanned the cold kitchen. "You have not even made any tea for yourself."

"It is the jet lag," I lied, even though I had been in the Netherlands almost a week by then. It seemed like so much effort to make breakfast for myself, and I often skipped it at home anyway, running to meetings and presentations. "You know what? I used to long to take a vacation, but now that I have free time, I do not know what to do with myself."

"You were never very good at resting. Always acting, always doing. Sometimes you just need to be, Sylvie."

"Hamster in a wheel, that's me." Eighty to a hundred hours a week at work. The glow of the laptop keeping me company as Jim snored in our bedroom. Flights to city after city. Always another deadline, another crisis. And for what? When it mattered, no one had stood up for me despite all the money I had brought in for the company. I was beginning to realize that I had kept myself so busy to avoid examining my life, and now that I had the chance, I did not like it at all.

Lukas filled the electric kettle with water. The morning sunlight slanted through the window and lit the outline of his broad shoulders.

His silky dark hair, almost perfectly straight, had a slight curl to it where it hit the base of his neck. "It is a beautiful day outside and I would like to take some photos. Come with me. I can make us some sandwiches. I know just the place."

Pedaling away on the pink flowered bicycle Estelle had lent me, I breathed in the faint scent of hyacinths. The open landscape stretched before us, brightly colored fields of crocuses and daffodils waving in the breeze, and I felt something inside me unclench. A flock of wild geese slowly took flight around us, beating their wings, rising up into the air as we passed. I had forgotten how good it felt to have my body balanced on the bicycle's thin wheels, the freedom of the road speeding underneath me and the joy of the wind in my face.

Lukas took us along a tree-lined stretch by the Amsterdam-Rhine Canal where the deep water sparkled. We finally stopped at a little picnic spot with a bench overlooking the rippling currents. A tree hung low in the waves and there a few ducks floated, cradled in its branches.

As I locked my bike and set it against a tree, I said, "It is strange because I am naturally afraid of water but I love it too." Lukas unhooked his bicycle bags. Then he took off his shoes and peeled off his socks. He stepped barefoot around the picnic area like a big bulky flamingo. I giggled. "What are you doing?"

"Trying to find a dry spot. Why are you scared of water?" He stomped a few times on one location, grunted, and pulled out a thick pine-green blanket from his bags.

I went over to help him unfurl it over the ground. "Because I can drown in two meters of it, idiot." I slapped him on the arm, and then sat down cross-legged. I ran a finger over the soft fleece.

"Oh, I forgot." Lukas grimaced, looking sheepish. Everyone in the Netherlands could swim. He settled down on the corner of the blanket next to me. "Why do you love it, then?"

"It feels like freedom."

Now he stretched out and lay on his back. Strands of his hair spread over the blanket, shining with the iridescence of a mussel shell washed by the sea surf. He spoke with his eyes closed. "I was in the ocean for a few months during a trip to Alaska. The waves were enormous, so much greater than any of us. The sea was like a graveyard or a utopia, a cavern where ancient worlds were swallowed up and waited to be discovered again."

I leaned in. He smelled like freshly cut grass, basil, and earth. He was so familiar and yet at the same time utterly new. Such thick lashes, the small freckle underneath the sharp plane of his left cheekbone, the scar threaded through the hair behind his temple from when he had fallen from the jungle gym at school. His bare, hairy feet sticking out from his snug jeans. His full lips. His eyes opened and I jumped back.

I cleared my throat. "Your poetry is lost on me. I am but a simple girl." I leaped up and looked around for something to do. I stuck my hands in my pockets. I coughed again. Ah, yes, the food. "I will unpack the sandwiches."

He propped himself on one elbow, the top button of his shirt straining, revealing a sliver of smooth tanned skin. "Ha! Simple. You were devouring books before I even learned the alphabet. You remember everyone could not understand why you were looking at books without pictures? No one guessed you were actually reading already."

I forced myself to look away and started rummaging in the bicycle bag. I said, translating from Chinese to Dutch, "Dumb birds must start flying early."

I now plopped down as far away from him as I could. *Enough of that nonsense, Sylvie*. Out of sheer nervousness, I started humming as I poured tea for us from the thermos. I smiled when I found the cloth napkins, folded into perfect pinwheels. "Ah, you have used that ax more often. This is the work of an expert. I forgot you were the child of restaurant owners. I don't remember how to do this anymore."

"I spent many hours helping out there, while they were still hoping I would take over the restaurant."

I finally dared to look at him again. He was sitting up now, thank goodness. "Were they disappointed?"

"Very." His lips flattened. He imitated his mother. "'What nonsense, following your dreams. Survive. Make a living. Eat.' Except I think Pa understands. He is just afraid to speak up." Willem had been a mathematics teacher in China. His was the brilliant mind behind the success of the restaurant, balancing the input and output of goods and staff, knowing exactly when they had to hunker down and when they should diversify. When he had helped me with my homework, we would fly through the problems together, leapfrogging to the answer while Lukas was left to puzzle it out line by line. Still, the debt Willem owed Helena for releasing him from China's grip was one he would never be able to repay.

There was an awkward pause. I filled it with my senseless humming again, and Lukas said, "You have a nice voice."

"You should hear my little sister, Amy." I passed him a Brie sandwich on dark seed-mix bread and took one for myself. "If she hears a song on the radio, she can pick it out on her guitar or keyboard. And her voice, so rich and evocative, I would sometimes lean against the outside of the bathroom door while she was taking a shower, just to listen."

"She sounds pretty great." To my surprise, his eyebrows had furrowed into one thick line. Was that sarcasm in his voice?

I said defensively, "She is. There was never enough money or time to train her talent. I was not old enough to help her then."

He leaned over and laid his large palm over my knee. I could feel the warmth of it through my slacks. "What about you, Sylvie? Who was there for you?"

I shifted so his hand fell from me, then tore off a bit of my bread and pitched it into the water for the ducks. One dove for it, quacking wildly, while the rest fled. "I have always been fine, Lukas. Do not fuss."

"I think you should take a break, Sylvie. You cannot eat for tomorrow. Enjoy yourself while you are here and maybe find something relaxing to keep yourself occupied. Nothing productive or educational." He took a bite of his sandwich.

I tossed another piece of bread at the clueless ducks. They had gathered close again. This time, they all scattered. "But I am here for Grandma."

"You cannot be with her the entire day. Do you know who Estelle and I just had a beer with the other day? You should eat your sandwich."

Estelle. Of course, that was where he had been. I shook my head and wrapped my arms around my knees, suddenly weary. "I am not hungry."

"Filip. Do you remember him? He was in our class."

I cast my mind back and found a vague image of a small, dark-haired kid. "Yes, he always played the violin or something in the Christmas shows?"

Lukas shuffled to sit beside me and took my sandwich from my hands. "That is him. He is a professional cellist now with the Netherlands Philharmonic Orchestra. We became good friends after you left. He gives private lessons on his living-boat in Amsterdam. You could try it." He held the bread up to my lips. "Stop giving to others. Leave something for yourself. Take a bite."

I obeyed, then took the sandwich and blinked slowly at him as I chewed. He was suddenly very close. I swallowed. "Where on earth would I get a cello?"

His eyes were on my mouth. "I think most of his students rent one."

Self-conscious, I turned away, brushing my lips. Did I have crumbs on my face? "But I am not musical at all. Amy is the—"

Now he drew back as well and sighed. "I know it, you have said it. But that is precisely the point. Go and try something you have not done before. You never know where it will lead you."

CHAPTER 14

Amy

Friday, May 6

After the dispiriting talk with the police and the Tan family, I return to my room in the attic and call home to update my parents. Then I pace. Willem and Helena have left for work at their restaurant. I could lie to myself but the truth is that no one here knows Sylvie the way I do. Sylvie would never willingly disappear like this without a word, despite Helena's hints that she stole Grandma's jewelry and ran off, despite Lukas's conviction that she's just taking some time for herself. I remove my glasses and rub them against my shirt. I consider my image reflected in the lenses. Who are you going to be, Amy Lee? A useless, shy little sister? Or are you going to step up to the plate for Sylvie? Because, clearly, no one else is going to do it, not even the police.

I stand up straighter, go into the bathroom, and put in my contact lenses. It's a surprise to see my face without the protective glasses: all that exposed skin, stretched tight over my bones, vulnerable but stronger too. There's a fierceness to my mouth I've never noticed before. I look through my dormer window in time to see Lukas wheel a large black bicycle out of the smaller, garage-like house. That must be where he lives. He's my best chance at finding out what happened to Sylvie while she was here. He is not getting away from me today.

I hurtle down the stairs and fling open the front door, panting. "Hey, Lukas! Where are you going?"

He stops in surprise. "I am meeting Estelle in the center."

"Oh, d-do you mind if I come along?" I am pulling on my thin jacket and stick my feet into my shoes while I hold the front door open with my hip.

To my surprise, he waits patiently for me to come outside. "Okay. I should show you around anyway." Then he leans his bike against the house and leads me back to his cottage. "Thank you, by the way."

"For what?" I will never understand this man.

"For defending Sylvie." He peers at me from beneath his long lashes. For the first time, he truly smiles at me. It lights up his entire face and he becomes so handsome, I catch my breath. "I am sorry I was not very friendly. I am extremely worried about Sylvie and Estelle says I tend to act like an angry bear most of the time anyway. You know, Sylvie is always talking about you."

"Really?"

"'Amy is so smart, Amy is so kind. Amy can sing the birds from the trees. With her glasses, Amy has this funny habit of—'"

I don't recognize this version of myself. "Habit of doing what?"

He laughs softly to himself. "Nothing. So this is where I live."

"Do you like it here?"

"Well, I rent this place from my family and it is easy, because they take care of Couscous and watch the apartment while I am gone. I tend to be abroad more than I am in this country. But I am saving for my own workplace and house. That is my great hope."

Lukas unlocks his front door. He doesn't invite me in but I stick my head in anyway. It's not a living room, like I'd expected, but rather a large photo studio and storage space, filled with reflective umbrellas, tripods, and light stands.

"I'd love to see your work sometime," I say.

"Sure," he answers, without any enthusiasm. He pulls on a chain hooked against the wall and an adult-size pink bicycle descends from a pulley on the ceiling.

"That's surprising," I say. "I didn't expect it to be up there."

"Space is costly here so we have to store a lot of things vertically. Like my washer and dryer." He gestures at the two machines in the back corner, which are stacked one on top of the other. "Especially because we usually do not have any basements. The ground is too soft and wet. The entire country is below sea level."

"Nowhere to stash the bodies, huh?" I say, and want to face-palm myself. That came out all wrong. Lukas freezes and I follow with a weak "Ha ha."

He doesn't answer. A breeze gusts against my jacket as he steps outside with the bicycle. I squint my eyes against the brilliant, piercing sunlight. The clouds are swirling in unpredictable patterns within a vast Van Gogh sky.

Lukas has brought a few tools with him and starts to lower the bike seat for me. The bicycle is covered with hand-painted white flowers. "Sylvie is taller than you are."

I realize that I'm supposed to ride on that thing. "Much more athletic too. Is this her bike?"

"Borrowed from Estelle. But Sylvie will not mind. We can reset it for her easily." A bit of the constant ache in my neck eases to hear his calm certainty that Sylvie will be back.

"What do you think has happened to her?"

His eyes dart away from mine. "I think something upset her and she wants time to consider everything."

Why is he not looking at me? Was he the one who upset her? "Really? You think she's okay?"

"Yes, I do." His voice is so intense I wonder if he truly believes this or if he needs to be certain of Sylvie's safety so much he's convinced himself of it. Or maybe he's a brilliant actor and he's covering something up.

I try to sound casual. "What could have upset her that much?"

He shrugs and waves one hand at the main house.

"Right," I say. "Lots of options there." Maybe Helena had accused

Sylvie of stealing the jewelry and Sylvie had left. But why wouldn't she have come home? In the pit of my stomach, my longing for my sister intensifies. *Sylvie, where are you?*

Lukas has fixed the seat with quiet competence and now adjusts the handlebars. I notice that despite his apparent calm, his knuckles are white with tension.

"C-couldn't we just walk?"

"No, it will be much easier for you on the bicycle."

Right. A few minutes later, I am wobbling on the treacherous pink bicycle, barely managing to stay upright. Which idiot said you never forget how to ride? Lukas didn't even give me a helmet. But then I manage to find my balance and follow him into the brick street. I can tell he's holding back for me because soon an old lady with a walker attached to the back of her bike zooms past us as if we were standing still. My bike sways as I fight the wind that threatens to blow me backward.

"You are doing fine," Lukas calls over his shoulder. "We are going to make a right at the next corner, and after that, it is straight along the River Vecht. Very easy."

I grunt, too stressed from concentrating on the bumpy road. There are a surprising number of people on bicycles for a Friday. Doesn't anyone have to go to work here? A mom and her tiny child weave past me. He's pedaling away on his own little bicycle without training wheels and is the only one wearing a helmet. She shoots me a sympathetic smile. Then comes a businessman in a charcoal suit, sitting bolt upright, speaking into his headset, elegant leather briefcase strapped to the back.

I manage to make the turn onto the river road and take a moment to lift my head and look around. I can smell the water. The sparkling sky is admiring its own reflection on the surface of the rippling green waves where the rowboats and sailboats are docked, waiting to whisk their passengers away on an adventure. The tree-lined, small brick street merges with the sidewalk, only a different color and stone pattern distinguishing them, and I almost veer onto the walkway. I barely miss a young woman who leaps out of my way, uttering what must be a Dutch curse. I speed past old and new houses with pointed gables, none taller than three stories, which line both our side of the river and the opposite bank. It is completely foreign and almost unbearably charming at the same time.

As we pass a little white church, its high bell tower chimes the hour. With the urgent peal of its bells behind us, we pass a bridge and pull up to a café nestled on the bank of the river. To our right, large rustic barrows filled with pink begonias, and to the left, potted shrubs guard a number of square wooden tables shaded by dark green parasols that read HEINEKEN. I spot Estelle sitting in a checkered sage-and-white chair with her eyes closed, sunlight caressing her upturned face. She is wearing some kind of blue blazer and there's a clunky black bag on her lap. Despite the brisk breeze, a few other customers are seated at the outdoor tables.

My legs almost crumple as I get off the bicycle and leave it at the rack. Give me a nice subway any day. Estelle smiles as we approach and stands to give Lukas another lush smack on the lips. Then she kisses me three times, alternating on each cheek, as everyone else seems to do in this country. "I am so glad you came! Did you remember to lock your bike, Amy?"

Lukas tosses over my bike key and sits down beside her. "I did it for you."

Estelle pretends to tsk. "This is a very safe country. I have left my handbag with wallet inside in the basket of my bicycle by accident and come back after shopping to find that no one has taken it. Of course, that was a stupid thing to do. But if you leave a bike unlocked, watch out!"

I have settled into the chair across from them. "Why is that?"

Lukas shrugs. "Everyone has had so many bikes stolen themselves that if they see one unlocked, they feel it is fair game."

Estelle winks. "It turns into the wild west here. One minute and your bicycle will be gone."

I study them for a moment. The anger Estelle displayed at the airport when she asked Lukas if he had fought with Sylvie is gone. She hasn't said anything about Sylvie. He must have already talked to her and somehow convinced her that he's in the clear. Is that true or is Lukas just an incredible manipulator?

When the waitress comes, Estelle suggests I order a *koffie verkeerd*, which she explains means coffee the wrong way around, so it's more milk than coffee, and an *uitsmijter*, which has something to do with eggs and the Dutch cheese Gouda. She pronounces it like *Houda*.

After she and Lukas place their orders, Estelle says, "So are you surviving that house?"

I chuckle. What a relief to talk to someone normal again. "Barely. I mean, my cousin Helena means well, but . . ."

"I know. And Lukas can be prickly too, especially these days."

Lukas throws his hands up. "Just talk about me like I am not here."

"Will do," Estelle agrees, with a wink at me. "Well, it has been very hard for him, first with Grandma's death and then the disappearance of Sylvie." Her face turns serious. She wrinkles her forehead. "Though Grandma was not actually his grandmother by blood, right? That always confuses me."

"She was my grandmother and Sylvie's too, but not Lukas's. In Chinese, we often call a close older woman 'Grandma.' It's a sign of respect and love."

"Well, Lukas was crazy about Grandma too."

"Fine." Lukas stands. "I will go use the toilet so you can discuss me. When I come back, you will stop." He gives Estelle an affectionate tug on her hair before he leaves, so I know he is not truly angry. This is my chance to get some information out of her.

He passes the waitress, who is walking to our table with the drinks. She sets down a very small cup of coffee for Lukas. My *koffie verkeerd* is served with a little cookie. Estelle tells me it is a mini *stroopwafel*. Estelle's Coca-Cola Light comes with a wedge of lemon and a long plastic stirrer.

I ask, "Are Lukas and Sylvie close?"

She pulls the stirrer out of her drink. A flat circular base with spikes is set perpendicular to the stem. "From the time we were little. They were always together."

I take a sip of my *koffie verkeerd*. It is creamy and delicious. "Why did you think they might have argued, then?"

Her green eyes are startled. "I did not say that."

I set my jaw. "You asked him about it. At the airport." I am not backing down anymore.

Now she uses the base of the stirrer to mash the lemon into her cola, avoiding my gaze. "It is normal for two friends to fight sometimes, is it not?"

I place my hand gently over her long, elegant fingers. They are cold and slightly clammy. "Estelle, please help me." I stare at our hands so my tears won't overflow.

"Oh, Amy." She is beside me then, hugging me tightly, her blazer rough against my cheek. I am pathetic. Even people who are practically strangers pity me. But still, I close my eyes and squeeze her back. She gives me a quick kiss on my temple and then sits back in her chair. "I truly believe Sylvie is all right."

Is that really true—*oh please, Kuan Yin, goddess of mercy, let that be true*—or has Lukas convinced her of this? I fan my eyes with my hand and put the *stroopwafel* in my mouth. It turns out to be a waffle made from two thin crispy layers of dough filled with sticky caramel syrup. I chew slowly as I compose myself.

"We are a close friendship group," Estelle is saying. "And sometimes things can get complicated. There can be misunderstandings. But believe me, none of us would ever hurt Sylvie in any way, and especially not Lukas."

I hear some sort of *ching chong* sound behind her and catch sight of two young guys and a pretty blond girl walking past us. One of the guys gives me a sly smile. It was him, I'm sure of it. Estelle whips her head around and gives him the finger. Good to know that some gestures work here too. He stops, angry, and takes a half step toward us, but the girl with him grabs his arm and pulls him away.

"I am sorry. We have our problems here in the Netherlands too. There is stupidity everywhere and we are not used to having many foreigners here," Estelle says. "This is Mother's Day weekend and every idiot has returned to our village to see his mom."

My heart is pounding in my throat. I am used to this aggression back home, and had noticed some Dutch people staring at me curiously, but still hadn't expected it here. "You're so close to Amsterdam."

"The big cities are another story, but this is still a small village in many ways and it is very old and white. Some of these houses were built in the Middle Ages and it sometimes seems like the thinking is from then too. It was not easy for Sylvie and Lukas, being the only Asians in the area."

Poor Sylvie. She'd had to fight her entire life, just for being born as she was. "What do you mean?"

Estelle takes a long sip of her cola, leaving a faint lipstick ring on the glass. "I remember some boys stole Lukas's bike key and were throwing it back and forth as they insulted him."

A slow anger begins to burn in me. I am grinding my teeth. What morons. Had they done that to Sylvie too? "How?"

"That he could not see out of those slits for eyes, his parents lived in a garbage heap . . . that kind of thing. But then Sylvie jumped one of them and took him down, and that unleashed Lukas. By then, I had gotten there as well so it turned into one big kicking, scratching, and punching fight." Estelle's smile is fond at the memory. I watch her with unfolding awe and gratitude. She had fought for Sylvie, by Sylvie's side. What would it be like to be as fearless as the three of them? "It was great. We told the principal and they got into so much trouble."

I startle as Lukas speaks and slides into his seat. "But my mother also punished Sylvie because she said that Sylvie started it. She has always drawn Sylvie with black coal."

Perfect Sylvie, punished? And Ma, Pa, and I had had no idea what her life had been like. I want to march back to the house and smack Helena. I don't know this sister being revealed to me, but I love her more fiercely than ever before. I finally ask the question that has bothered me since I landed. "Why does Helena dislike her so much?"

Lukas rubs his hand over his forehead. When he faces me, he looks defeated. "I honestly do not know. Sylvie was such a good girl."

The waitress appears, arms laden with plates of food that smell heavenly. Despite my doubts, I feel brighter from Estelle's reassurance and find my appetite has returned. My *uitsmijter* is an open-faced sandwich composed of three slices of thick white bread, sunny-side-up eggs, and a thin layer of ham and tomatoes, all smothered in melted Gouda cheese. Lukas has two *krokets,* breaded, deep-fried cylindrical rolls with a creamy meat ragout filling, served with mustard and white buns. I am a bit dubious about Estelle's *filet americain* sandwich, which she tells me is a crunchy fresh-baked whole wheat baguette spread with raw minced beef and spices.

As I tuck into my food, I say, "When I was little, she saved me from being kidnapped once."

"No," breathes Estelle.

Lukas pauses with his *kroket* halfway to his mouth. "What happened?"

"I was four years old. Pa was home but he was busy fixing the lock on our front door, and I guess I must have decided I missed Ma and wanted to go find her by myself. When he went to grab some tools from another room, I left our apartment and toddled downstairs and out onto the sidewalk. Sylvie must have been only about eleven then, but she was the one who figured out I was missing. She flew off to find me before Pa even had his shoes on. When he finally caught up to us at the corner down the street from our place, Sylvie had put herself between me and a strange man. I was wearing this gold necklace with a carp pendant. He'd grabbed it when Sylvie pushed me away from him. He pulled it off my neck and ran. We never found out if he was only after the jewelry or if he'd wanted me too." I shivered. I had nightmares for years about the sharp angles of that man's face, how Sylvie pushed me behind her, how I'd clung to her, hiding my face in her familiar soft strands of hair. I'd wake crying and Sylvie would pull gently on my ears and nose, and recite the rhyme Ma had taught us, one of the few Chinese phrases I had managed to learn: "Pinch the ears, pinch the nose, wake up, wake up. Let Beautiful Jasmine be as brave as a grown woman."

"Was Sylvie hurt?" Lukas asks. He appears riveted by my story. I warm to him again. Maybe he truly does care for my sister.

I shake my head. "Your food will get cold."

"You never replaced the necklace," Estelle says, glancing at my unadorned neck.

"Ma and Pa were afraid to. They didn't want to make either one of us a target. The funny thing is, we wear gold or jade for protection, so maybe that necklace saved me from that man." But I know the truth. Sylvie rescued me. And now it's my turn to rescue her.

I set my flapping napkin underneath my saucer to stop it from blowing away. I turn to Lukas again. "Can you tell me what Sylvie's husband was doing here?"

Lukas is smearing his *kroket* with mustard. "No idea." Now he takes a big bite.

I pinch my lips together. Okay, he is really irritating after all. I take a deep breath to calm myself. "Did Sylvie seem upset by it?"

He scratches his head. "Kind of. I cannot say."

I roll my eyes at Estelle, and then leave to find the restroom. I cross the street to enter the café itself. I need a moment to adjust after the bright sunlight and see that the interior is cozy and warm, paneled with dark brown wood. As I pass, I stop to feel one of the prickly miniature embroidered rugs that are lying on the tables as placemats. I spot a waitress making a cappuccino behind the bar, so I ask her, "Where can I find the powder room?" When she blinks at me, I say, "The bathroom?"

"Ah, the toilet. It is at the back, to the left."

I open the door to the tiny bathroom and am confronted with a statue of Buddha. He sits on a shelf behind the toilet.

"I am so sorry you have to live here," I say to him.

When I return to the table, I tell Estelle and Lukas about what I have seen. "To a Chinese person, it's very disrespectful because we believe the Buddha actually inhabits the statue when he comes to visit."

"Well, my brother has the Virgin Mary in his toilet," Estelle says.

"To the Dutch, it is just like a pretty plate or a carving of a yin-yang symbol or something." Lukas sounds resigned.

I say in a small voice, "Everything's so different here. I-I don't know why I came or how I could possibly help Sylvie. She's always been the brave, competent one. I was planning to leave in a few days." I slump in my chair. "Stupid, right? A part of me thought that if I came here, she would show up and we could fly home together." Because Sylvie would never let me be lost, alone, and afraid in a foreign country. For the first time, I wonder what it must have been like for her to be uprooted and move to the United States, to act as babysitter and mother to a two-year-old toddler when she was a child herself.

The flesh on Lukas's face sags. His eyes are rimmed with red. "Stay longer, Amy. Sylvie would want you to."

The thought of returning home without Sylvie makes me want to cry. "Will that be all right with your parents?"

Estelle's eyes flash. "No, do not think like that. Screw what everyone else thinks of you, screw what they want from you. You go out there and you do what you need to do, whatever that might be. People think being a pilot is glamorous, but when I used to fly cargo, a lot of times there was not even a toilet in the plane. The male pilots peed into a bottle, so I did too. You just do what is necessary—pee in a bottle if you need to."

We all laugh at this. Something inside me lightens for a moment and I stop feeling so alone. Lukas and Estelle love Sylvie too. Maybe everything will turn out all right.

Estelle reaches across the table and gives my hand a warm squeeze. "Listen, Lukas and I need to visit my mother. He is helping her set up her new digital camera. But let me give you my number and if you ever need someone to talk to, you let me know."

I pass her my phone and watch as she stores her contact information. Then we leave the table and head toward the bicycle rack.

Lukas rubs his eyes and I glance up at him, wondering if he could be brushing away a tear. There is pure anguish on his face, though I can't decipher the reason for it. He drags his hands through his wild hair. "Can you make it home by yourself or shall I bike with you first?"

"Oh no, it's really simple. I'll be fine." I don't want him to accompany me because I'm planning to walk the whole way. "We should ask for the bill."

Estelle waves a hand. "We took care of it when you were inside. Just get back safe and do not worry about Sylvie. I am sure she is all right."

From: Jim Bates
To: Amy Lee
Sent: Friday, May 6
Subject: Bills

Hey Amy,
Have you heard anything from Sylvie? I had a locksmith get me into the apartment after we spoke and was pretty shocked by the state of it. She hasn't paid any bills at all since I left. I also can't believe the credit card bills she's racked up. Everything is in a state of limbo, especially now that she's missing. What the hell is going on?

I need to talk to Sylvie as soon as possible. There are things we need to straighten out. I deserve some explanations too.
Jim

From: Amy Lee
To: Jim Bates
Sent: Friday, May 6
Subject: RE: Bills

Jim, there's been no word from Sylvie and I was just told you were here in the Netherlands. Why didn't you tell me? Did you see Sylvie? How did she seem? When was the last time she used her credit card? That's very important because it can tell us a lot about what she's been doing and if she's okay.

Please, if there's any information at all you could share with us? It might help us find her.

From: Amy Lee
To: Jim Bates
Sent: Saturday, May 7
Subject: RE: Bills

Jim, did you get the email I sent you below? It's really urgent that you respond. I know you guys were having some problems but I'm sure you can work things out. If you won't talk to me, at least let the police know what you saw. Just please tell me if she's used her credit card recently.

From: Amy Lee
To: Jim Bates
Sent: Sunday, May 8
Subject: RE: Bills

Jim? You're not answering my calls and you're not responding to these emails. Just drop me a line, anything you know might help, we're desperate, okay? Please.

Jim, please.

CHAPTER 15

Sylvie

Saturday, April 9

Lukas's friend Filip said he could give me a sample lesson right away, so the next morning, Lukas took me to meet him in Amsterdam. This time, we rode on Lukas's black Vespa scooter. It felt good to have an excuse to wrap my arms around his waist, the smell of his leather jacket in my nostrils, the steady purr of the motor underneath me. The temperature had dropped since yesterday and we passed pedestrians bundled up in their bulky coats again. As the chilly wind whipped against my olive hooded jacket, I closed my eyes and felt the air promise me rain.

When we passed from tree-lined views of the waterways into the steady stream of bicycles, trams, and autos in Amsterdam, I felt like a heroine in a movie. The city exuded that same sense of wild freedom and possibility of New York, but in a gentler way. A father wove through the red light district on a cargo bike filled with two tiny children. A beautiful woman talking on her mobile strode past a construction site without receiving a single catcall. Lukas stopped as a tram swerved in front of us, then he maneuvered through the narrow brick streets until we turned onto the Brouwersgracht, one of the most beautiful routes in Amsterdam. I could feel the muscles of his body shift as he navigated the turns.

It was so beautiful and peaceful here, as if nothing could ever be wrong with the world. Graceful seventeenth-century residences edged the wide canal and living-boats bobbed in the water. Here and there, pots of crocuses and daffodils bloomed and dotted the street. I loved flowers, though I could never manage to keep them alive. One living-boat looked like a pirate ship, complete with an upturned red prow, while its neighbor resembled a rectangular train car, painted blue and white. Lukas parked his Vespa beside this one and we walked past a tiny garden on the water side of the street.

As we stepped onto the rickety wooden walkway that connected us to the living-boat, Lukas saw I was biting my lip and reached out a hand to steady me. I always felt vulnerable over water, and Lukas noticed this. I recalled the last cocktail party Jim and I had attended together, the one my engagement manager, Martin, had hosted—a drunken Martin standing too close to me, casually resting his hand on the bare skin between my collarbone and my neck under the pretense of having to yell in my ear to be heard through the babble of voices around us, and me looking for Jim, spotting him chatting with a bunch of men a few meters away, trying to signal my distress. Jim only waved and raised a glass to me in a silent toast. He must have completely missed the sexual connotations.

We walked onto the boat and Lukas rang the doorbell. After a few moments, the door opened. Oh my goodness. I took a half step back. The diminutive, pale boy I barely remembered had grown into this? Filip was about the same height as Lukas, except leaner, with broad shoulders and a narrow waist. His hair fell in dark, cropped waves across his forehead. Chiseled jaw with a deep dimple in the middle. Intense, intelligent eyes the color of the Dutch sky flickered over me, assessing me until his thin lips—sensual, a bit cruel—quirked in a half smile. I realized I had covered my mouth with my hand and lowered it. Lukas was watching me with his brow furrowed, one hand rubbing his neck. He had not missed my reaction either. He and Filip greeted each other, and then Filip shook my hand: a hard grip, determined and unrelenting, with calluses on his thumb and perhaps one of the fingers.

Then Filip stepped aside to let us in. I grasped the doorframe with one hand as the boat swayed gently. We were standing in a small kitchen with a large silver refrigerator. A sink and a fancy espresso machine sat underneath a bright window. The smells of olive oil and spices perfumed the air, and now I saw that a neat row of herbs and a garland of dried garlic lined the shelves, alongside patterned ceramic plates that looked like they might be Armenian. So he cooked too. Or was he married? I quickly checked both of his hands—here, the Catholics tended to wear their wedding rings on their left hands and the Protestants on their right—but I found no ring at all. Interesting. He and Lukas continued chatting to each other but I caught both men glancing at me when they thought I wasn't looking.

The door to my right was closed and I imagined it led to his bedroom. We squeezed through the narrow hallway on the left, practically bumping into one another in the cramped space, and stepped into a long living room that was flooded with light. I caught my breath. What a view. An expanse of water all around us, the waves rippling, while seagulls flew overhead, cawing, sparkling in the sunlight like jewels before landing on the arched stone bridge that spanned the canal. In the distance, storm clouds gathered.

Filip stood beside me, but instead of gazing out the window, he was examining me with his vivid, lucent eyes. "Sylvie. My, you have grown up."

A rush of heat swept upward from my neck. "I was just thinking the same about you. Although I must admit I do not remember you very well."

He bent his head toward me to say in a hushed voice, "You are very clear in my memories." I stared up at him as if mesmerized. What did he mean? Did he remember the awkward, homely girl I had been? "Let us measure your hand to see how large your cello needs to be."

He held my right hand up to his left one, palm to palm, finger to finger—his tapered ones far longer than my own. Was that another callus on the side of his thumb? Then Lukas grabbed my wrist and pulled my hand away from Filip.

"Ho, ho. Enough of this." Lukas's smile said he was kidding but there was an intense look in his eyes. He turned to face Filip and tapped him on the chest. "Cello lessons, nothing else. You keep away from my beautiful cousin with that deadly charm of yours."

Lukas thought I was beautiful. I chuckled at this, charmed by his protective instincts, though my skin still tingled where Filip had touched me. "You have nothing to worry about. I am married." Then, when Filip arched an inquiring eyebrow at me, I pulled at the collar of my shirt. "Separated. I am separated."

Now Lukas's eyebrows rose even higher. "Sylvie, he is as infamous as a mottled dog with a blue tail. The girls in our high school ran after him, even the female teachers were captivated by him, not to mention all those fans he picks up at his concerts. Always keep an instrument between you two, you hear me?"

Filip batted his eyes at Lukas. "Oh, I would love to keep my flute between us."

I laughed as Filip slung an arm around Lukas and shepherded him back to the front door. "We will behave. Come back in an hour to pick her up."

I heard the door close behind him, and then Filip called, "Just a moment, Sylvie. I wanted to see how long you were and the size of your hands before I chose a cello for you. I will get it now."

I could still see Lukas on the sidewalk, unlocking his Vespa and craning his neck to peer in through the window before driving off. I felt flutters in my stomach, whether from anticipation or nerves, I was not sure. I was now alone with the stunning cellist and I had never been any good at music or, indeed, any of the arts. Creativity required a leap of faith I was unwilling to make. I walked around the upright piano against the wall and settled into one of the two chairs. They sat facing each other, alongside two cello stands. One stand cradled an antique instrument, the wood burnished and scarred.

By my side was the windowsill, where an ashtray and a row of photos stood. Filip in a diving suit, a bright orange oxygen tank, his lashes spiked with water. Ah, a yellowed photo of the boy I remembered, probably about six years old, sunburned, wearing only a thin white undershirt, holding a child-size violin under his chin, playing barefoot on a rocky beach—and then another of an adult Filip with a little blond girl, around seven years old. She had his forehead and eyes, and they both stuck out their tongues at the camera.

"My daughter," he said from the doorway, holding a newer cello in his hands.

I refrained from asking if he was still married. "She is very cute. And this photo, this was you, right? I remembered you playing the violin."

"Yes, that was taken while we were on holiday on Tenerife." He strode over and placed the cello in my stand, then seated himself facing me.

I tentatively stroked the shiny wooden neck with my finger. "Why did you switch over to cello?"

"I heard one at a concert and after that, it was all I wanted. I begged my parents to let me take lessons." He maintained his distance now and his tone was friendly but professional. So the flirting had been for Lukas. It was always easier to play at love when there were safe limits. A voice whispered in my mind, *He saw the real you when you were younger, Sylvie. Why would he want you now?* My chest tightened and a heaviness descended over me.

He started tuning our cellos. The deep tones rang like a human voice, singing its darkest secrets, startling me. The floor shifted as a boat passed, rocked by the waves. I gazed upon him, another man I had known as a boy, his perfect profile impenetrable, but his hands—what tenderness and pain flowed from those hands—and just this, a gifted musician tuning his cello, began to unburden my heart. How Jim had loved me once and, so help me, how I loved him still. The sky outside grew dim and rain began to patter against the roof.

He paused and I quickly dashed a hand across my cheek, wondering how much my expression had revealed. He closed his eyes and, instead of continuing his task, played a slow piece, filled with all the longing and unrequited love I felt. I leaned my head back in my chair and let the melody swirl through me. *I am broken,* the cello said. *I am lost.*

When he stopped, his face revealed none of the emotion in his music. He gave me a tiny curt nod, and said, "Spread your legs."

I gulped. "What?"

He came over to me, pulled me forward so I was sitting on the edge of my chair, then spread my thighs wide with a bold hand on the inside of each knee. I was still gasping as he swung the cello in between my legs. "Be glad you are not wearing a dress. I forgot to mention it to Lukas and sometimes women come in these tight skirts, which can cause quite a problem. It is also good you do not have overly large boobs."

I was still staring at my chest when he placed the bow in my right hand and showed me how to hold it. "First, we will start with playing the loose strings. Only the bow, no left hand. Follow me. We will start with A."

He sat back down and played a long note on one string and I tried to do the same. We repeated this several times, playing A, A, A, A, D, D, the cello vibrating through my bones.

He sighed. "The cello picks up everything you are feeling in your body, and you are as tense as a cane. Close your eyes."

I did as he directed and felt the cold coming in through the floorboards. I suppressed a shiver, imagined the icy water beneath our feet. His voice was strong and resonant. "Let your shoulders and hands hang. That is it."

When I opened my eyes and tried to play, it sounded better but not enough to satisfy him. Filip went to the kitchen and returned with a ceramic bowl filled with water. He came over, picked up my right hand, and placed it inside the bowl. The water was warm, his fingers light against my wrist. This close to him, I caught a whiff of smoke and bergamot. "Does that feel good?"

I nodded.

"Now, take out your hand and flick the droplets off. As you do that, imagine all of your tension falling away with the water. Very good." Then he gently dried my hand with a small cloth, massaging every digit, and placed the bow in between my loosened fingers. "Hold it lightly, do not tense up. Now you are ready."

And when I began, for the first few moments I could hear the difference, but then I started to stiffen. I was learning that this was my natural state: stressed. His spine was rigid, bracing him against the sounds I made, though his expression remained neutral. Outside, lightning flashed as the rain turned into a downpour, splattering against the sundeck.

I winced and laid down the bow. I could not do this to him any longer. "This must be torture for you. I should stop."

He came and knelt before me on one knee so we were face-to-face, his eyes intent. He laid a hand on my arm. "Oh no. You have only just begun, Sylvie. That is why it is called an instrument. It is a tool for you to express whatever you want, good or bad."

"I must be filled with badness, then," I muttered, smiling a little. I leaned toward him. I had a sudden wild desire to lay my cheek against his. Here was a man who understood heartbreak. Here was a man who also knew what it meant to be devastated, and who somehow kept it all contained. I pulled myself back and searched for a reason to keep him talking. "Is your daughter musical too?"

He glanced over at their photo together. "Oh no. Zoë's passion is competitive alpine skiing, which happens to be a very expensive sport. My ex-wife is a musician as well and between the two of us, we can barely manage to afford it." He stood. I blinked back my disappointment. "Our time is almost up. Why do you not take the cello home so you can practice and not torment me so much next time?"

"You would lend me your cello?"

He shrugged and pulled out a hard cello case from a sliding cabinet beneath the window. "This is a cheaper one that I rent out to students sometimes. You cannot improve if you do not practice."

As he flipped open the lid of the case, I eyed the huge instrument. I was not substantially taller than it. "I do not have a car here."

He bent down to place the cello and bow inside. The case was mostly black, with streaks of dark blue running through it like a river. Two padded straps on the back allowed it to be carried like a backpack. "No problem. I take mine on my bicycle all the time."

I waved a hand at his long legs, the muscled arms. "But you are Dutch." People carted Christmas trees on their bicycles here, balanced on the steering bar.

"So are you." He stood and set the case upright. "You rest that on your baggage rack on the back of your bike and you will be all set." The doorbell rang. Filip handed the cello to me. "Your chauffeur is here."

I staggered a bit to get the cello through the tiny hallway and into the entryway. The whole thing was heavier than I thought. Filip had the door open and Lukas stood there drenched, dripping onto the tile floor. Droplets rolled off his hair and traced the line of his jaw. Behind him, a torrent of rain fell as thunder boomed.

I asked Filip, "When should I come back? I am only here a few weeks at most." Now that our lesson was over, I was like someone who had smoked opium for the first time. I did not *want* to see him again; it was a *need*. I felt lighter, looser, and something about him or our lesson had done that for me.

Filip glanced at Lukas, then bent and gave me three deliberate, lingering kisses on my cheeks. The charming playboy had returned. "As often as you like," he drawled. "Come every day."

Lukas took the case from me and scowled. "Do I need to hit this guy with my camera for you?"

"It would be easier to use the cello." I gave Filip a slow wink to show I was sophisticated and unaffected by him. "But it is not necessary. When he flirts, it is nothing personal."

I was unprepared for the flash of pain on Filip's face or the way Lukas flushed dark red to the roots of his hair. Had there been some other woman between them in the past? Someone they truly loved?

Lukas swung the case over one shoulder and turned on his heel to leave. "Yes, that has been my experience."

With the cello strapped to my back, the Vespa scooter caught so much wind that, at times, it seemed like we would take flight. The Dutch called this dog weather. Above us, the heavens opened while hard gusts of rain sent rivulets of cold water down my back. The shifting air currents caught the broad instrument at an angle and Lukas swerved to avoid a sudden bicyclist. Blinded by strands of my hair in the whipping wind, I was barely able to stay seated, clinging to Lukas with all my might. My shoulders ached from the weight. When we finally arrived at the house, I dismounted and tried to race inside to get out of the storm. But even though I was fairly tall, the cello still hit me at mid-calf, so I could only take tiny, mincing steps.

Once inside, Lukas stifled a guffaw at my half-drowned appearance. Water drizzled from us both onto Helena's marble tiles. He took the case off my shoulders, then removed my jacket and hung it over the radiator to dry. I propped one arm against the wall and bent to pull off my soaked shoes. When I straightened, locks of my wet hair were plastered to my face.

Lukas reached over and gently cradled my jaw and cheekbones in his large warm hands. He tucked each lock of hair behind my ears with his thumbs. My eyelids fluttered closed. He bent down and pressed a tender kiss to my forehead.

When I opened my eyes again, he had already turned away. "I will take your cello upstairs for you," he mumbled, leaving me staring at his retreating back.

Later that evening, after I had changed into dry clothing, I heard the door downstairs click closed. Lukas was back. All of a sudden, it seemed more attractive to practice in the living room rather than the lonely attic.

"Hey, Lukas, is that you?" I called.

"Come down and join me," he said.

I tried to walk downstairs with the cello case on my back, but it kept hitting the stair directly behind me, causing me to lurch forward. I made it down one flight and saw Lukas standing at the base of the other staircase, waiting for me, chuckling at my predicament. I was three-quarters of the way when the cello slammed into the stair behind me again and I started to tumble.

"Whoa!" He spanned my waist with his hands and swung me, cello and all, off the stairs. He carefully set me down on the floor.

Once I caught my breath, we both doubled over with laughter.

"Are you all right? How many times a week are you taking lessons again?" Lukas gasped.

"Every weekday," I said, giggling. "Unless this thing kills me first."

"I could bring you."

"Yeah, right." I snorted, thinking of our wild ride home. Our soaked jackets still hung from the radiator, though the floor tiles were dry. Lukas must have mopped after I went upstairs. "Filip said I could bicycle with that monster. He made it sound very simple."

"I hate that guy. You need to rent a car."

"I need to rent a car," I repeated. Luckily, my credit card still worked. Jim was probably paying our bills. I sobered as I thought of him. Had he been back to our apartment? Was he with her? I pictured her, waiting outside his office for him. They saw each other every day. I chewed on my inner cheek. There was an ache in the back of my throat and it was difficult to swallow. How could I hate him and still wish he were mine? The last time we spoke, he'd been so angry with me, as if I were the one who had done something wrong. I had never paid attention to his ugly side before, despite that horrible drunken night at Princeton. My eyes had been firmly closed to it, idiot that I was.

"Sylvie?" Lukas touched me on my forearm. "You seem far away."

"It is nothing." I placed my hand over his fingers and gave them an affectionate squeeze. "I am glad you suggested this. I think these lessons with Filip are truly going to help."

Five days later, the weather was warm and clear, perfect for a burglary. It had drizzled in the night as I lay in my bed, staring at the ceiling for hours, worrying that Isa would decide not to take Grandma for her daily walk. However, I knew the Dutch. No amount of rain, sleet, or snow stopped them.

We had planned it carefully. Early that morning, before Isa arrived,

Grandma pulled me toward her by the sleeve so she could whisper, "When you ride a tiger, you must not try to get off halfway."

It was still dark outside and the fear of a downpour made me extra prickly. I rolled my eyes. "I know, Grandma. Why do you two think I cannot be a good thief?" They needed Lukas to help Grandma navigate the stairs safely, so I had to play the burglar.

Lukas, standing by Grandma's bed with his arms crossed, switched into Dutch so Grandma could not understand him. "When it comes to being naughty, you are a floppy dick in rosewater. Let me do it."

I raised my voice. "No, I do not want Grandma to fall. I can stand strong in my shoes."

"Sssst! My parents will hear." He blew out a noisy breath. "Isa took her out alone before I came home."

"Grandma was stronger then," I hissed.

He said slowly, enunciating each word as if I were feebleminded, "You have to make it real."

Grandma said sweetly in her melodious Chinese, "When the sandpiper and the clam oppose each other, it is the fisherman who benefits."

As one, Lukas and I protested, "We are not fighting."

"Fart!" she said. Great, now even Grandma called me on my bullshit.

After Helena and Willem left for the restaurant, I pretended to go to my daily cello lesson, then parked the rental car on another street and returned via the back door, which I had left ajar. However, this door was normally locked and required a key—concealed in the kitchen drawer—to open it, so we decided to make it seem as if the burglar had entered and exited from the front door, which often did not close properly anyway without a hard push. Since we did not want to get Isa in trouble, Lukas made sure he was the one to leave the front door unlocked. The neighbors were always watching. Last Monday, Helena hadn't opened the drapes early in the morning and the woman across the street rang us. "It was so strange, I wanted to make sure you were all okay." So I stayed hidden inside the house, my heart leaping in my throat as if I were a real criminal, until I heard the slow, creaky sounds of Lukas, Grandma, and Isa leaving.

Then I climbed the stairs with gloves on, like a thief from a movie. I felt completely ridiculous, as out of place as a cat in a dog kennel. My prints were all over the room anyway, not that they would bother to fingerprint for such a petty crime. Staying out of sight of the windows, I rummaged through Grandma's things and pulled everything out of the closet. We had taken the jewelry a few days ago. Before I left her room, I quickly bowed to the altar to Kuan Yin and apologized for the mess.

But she who says A must also say B, so I went into the bedroom of Helena and Willem and examined it with the eyes of a hoodlum. This was my chance to wreak some revenge. I could hurt Helena for a change. What would a petty thief take? What did I want? I scanned the scattered evidence of their relationship, accumulated year after year like the bulky rings of a tree. If there was a map to their hearts, it would be here in their bedroom. I remembered how Willem and Helena would sometimes go for bike rides together on their free days: "just like the Dutch," Helena liked to say. She loved him, I was sure of it. And Willem? He certainly needed her and her family's money—perhaps need casts even stronger chains than love.

How could I possibly understand Willem and Helena when I had no grip on the relationship between my own ma and pa? They had nothing personal in their tiny bedroom back in New York. They never went to dinner together, never cuddled in front of the television. Those horrible fights they'd had when we were little, when Pa would get drunk and call Ma a whore and a liar. But still, there was tenderness when they looked at each other, though it was quickly hidden away again. Ma stayed up late mending Pa's work gloves. Pa put the choicest pieces of abalone in Ma's rice bowl. An ocean of love, guilt, and duty surged back and forth between them, stroking both their hearts even as it kept them apart.

There were no photos or books in Helena and Willem's bedroom either. Instead, a vase of fake flowers, Helena's jewelry case, a collection of expensive ties in the closet. A few of Lukas's childish drawings hung in cheap frames. A shelf filled with complex modular origami figures made from tiny bits of folded paper. I stepped over to examine the designs more closely: a green-and-white peacock with its magnificent tail unfurled, a dragon boat, an orange-and-white model of Couscous. What did it mean? A mug that read WORLD'S BEST MAMA. Had I not saved my pocket money and bought that for Helena, all those years ago? Why had she kept it? A woman's Rolex watch. Bought for herself? A gift from Willem? The more I saw, the less I understood.

I went to their dresser to steal her jewelry case and my eyes were captured by my own image in the mirror instead. For a moment, I was little again, creeping into their bed after a nightmare. Sometimes they let me stay there, snuggled up to their warmth. More often I was sent away. *You must not disturb Grandma in the night. You are trouble enough for her all day long.* I would then sneak up to Lukas's room and fall asleep curled on the floor beside his bed, holding his hand in mine. I leaned closer to the mirror and the reflection of the woman in her expensive clothing faded away. There was my weak eye, already pulling to the outside with the stress of the burglary, the strain in my lips, the fake tooth that was a bit lighter than all the others, the desperation etched on my face. *Who are you, Sylvie Lee?* I whispered to myself.

In the end, burdened by guilt and indecision, I took nothing. How could I remove something of theirs and never give it back? Lukas's voice: *That is what it means to steal something, Sylvie.* I threw some of their clothing around and made a mess. I knew I should stomp on a few of Willem's origami sculptures, but then I thought of his pleasure in the hobby, the way his eyes glowed with happiness when he finished a creation, and I could not bear to do it. I was a terrible, unbelievable thief, just as Lukas had predicted. Finally, I went downstairs and snuck out via the back door. Lukas would later lock it and hide the key again when he returned.

I went to my cello lesson with Filip for real this time and by the time I returned, the police were at the house, along with an agitated Helena and Willem. I set down the heavy case in the hallway and followed Helena's shrill voice into the living room, where Lukas and Willem were both leaning against the walls, doing their best to be invisible. Lukas and I did not dare to meet each other's eyes.

The uniformed police agent, a small, tubby man with a kind face and round spectacles, turned to me as I stepped in the room. "You must be the daughter." He waved a pudgy hand at Willem. "You can always tell family."

We all froze. None of us dared to breathe as we waited for Helena's fury. People had always assumed I was their child, and Helena would fume and sputter for days afterward.

She said acidly, "Just because the Dutch think all Asians look alike is no reason to believe we are all family. Sylvie is just visiting."

I was of course related to both her and Lukas but found it prudent to remain silent.

The police agent turned an eggplant color. He bumped into the cup of coffee beside him and almost knocked it over. "It causes me regret. I did not mean—" He stopped and straightened his glasses, then cleared his throat and returned to trying to make sense of the entire bizarre situation. "So nothing was stolen."

"A fortune has disappeared," said Helena, her voice rising to a screech.

"Aha," he said, scratching his balding head. "Do you have any photos of the missing jewelry? Insurance reports?"

Helena's mouth was a tight red line. "No. Grandma never showed it to us so we did not officially register it."

He peered at his handwritten notes. "That is the elderly lady upstairs? So she is the only one who knew about this missing treasure?"

"I saw it too once, many years ago." Helena gestured at me. "She used to let Sylvie play with it, right?"

All the attention in the room turned to me. I acted confused, tugging at a lock of my hair. "What has happened?"

Willem finally spoke up. "Someone broke into the house."

I gasped. "Oh no!" I brought my hand to my mouth, trying to be the murderer playing innocent. Across the room, Lukas widened his eyes at me, signaling me to tone it down. "I was very little then. I have no idea if it was real or costume jewelry. I do not think Grandma would have let me play with anything valuable."

Now Helena narrowed her eyes, as if turning things over in her mind. Uh-oh. Did she suspect me? My heart started to race, nearly exploding in my chest. Her head tilted like she was mentally cataloging the evidence.

Lukas quickly changed the subject. He seemed calm. "I should not have left the front door ajar."

Willem threw his hands in the air. "We have reminded you a hundred times, Lukas. How could you do that? You know it sticks. It has been like that for years."

Lukas cast his eyes downward, the picture of regret. He always seemed so guileless; I had no idea he could be such a good actor. "This is all my fault."

Helena replied, "Leave him alone. He had enough to do with taking care of Grandma, her portable oxygen tank, and her wheelchair." Why had she never defended me like that? I had been a child under her care too, once. When I was little, how many times did I daydream of Helena hugging me, telling me I had done something wonderful?

The police agent said, "But the back door was left open as well, correct? It has a blind covering, which means it cannot be locked or picked from the outside. So the thief entered from the front door and exited through the back."

Lukas had forgotten to lock it after I was gone. And such a crucial clue too. This would lead their suspicions directly to me. Could nothing go right today? The hair lifted on my nape and arms.

Helena tapped a finger against her temple. "It is strange because the key is always hidden. What a clever thief to have found the key so quickly."

She was not stupid. I could go to jail. The air was bursting in and out of my lungs. I jammed my hands into my armpits in a self-hug and asked, "How is Grandma?" What if all of this excitement hurt her?

"She is as fine as you would imagine, under the circumstances. She is with Isa. It was hard for the police to question her, with her limited Dutch and scattered memory." Helena deliberately lowered her head to stare at me. She gave me a false smile. "But something like this is such a violation. It is unforgivable." She knew. My legs were shaking so much, they would all see. I dragged my sweaty palms across my pant legs.

Then Helena asked with forced nonchalance, "How was your cello lesson today, Sylvie? Isa mentioned you were gone a long time."

I spoke despite the sour taste in my mouth. "Fine. I stayed a bit longer for a chat with Filip."

Lukas's expression tightened. He cracked his knuckles so loudly I jumped. "Oh? Do you do that often?"

He was upset with me about this? Today of all days? "Sometimes." I often stayed if Filip did not have another student directly afterward. I would drink Earl Grey tea or his excellent espresso while he smoked.

The round policeman shifted his weight from one leg to the other. "So aside from the jewelry, which no one except for Grandma has seen in recent years, was anything else taken?"

"Is that not enough?" demanded Helena.

Meanwhile, Lukas was frowning at me, his lip curled. Because I was hanging out with Filip or because I had been a poor thief?

"I will make a report of the supposed missing jewelry, but with cash and jewelry, there is a very limited amount you can claim without preregistration and proof of possession. You will have to resolve that with your insurance company," the man said.

We all knew what the insurance company would say.

After the policeman left, I asked, "Is Grandma very upset?"

Helena's eyes were cold and flinty. "Surprisingly, no."

The next day, I watched as Filip's long, capable fingers tuned his cello, which to my eyes was far uglier than mine. I had a modern instrument, with a warm glow to the maple. The varnish on his cello was uneven and burned in some places. It looked like it had been worn thin by centuries of use. Small bubbles had formed in those spots, and they'd filled with dirt over the years. I had come to cherish these moments as he concentrated on tuning and I could watch him unobserved: the intensity of his focus on each string, the grunt of satisfaction he made in the back of his throat when the tune was just right, the texture of his rough knuckles against the wood. I was completely unimportant then;

to him I did not exist, and this gave me the freedom to utter whatever flew into my head.

I asked, "What happens if I break your cello by accident? How much would it cost?"

He slapped the Y-shaped metal tuning fork against his knee, and then set it on the bridge of his cello. He listened to the hum of the note and then adjusted the pegs. "The one you are using? It is an inexpensive one. I think around three thousand euros."

My lips parted. I was glad I had not yet succeeded in dropping it down the stairs. "How much does that old thing of yours cost?"

"Fifty thousand euros." He smiled at my incredulous look. "It was made by Cuypers in 1767. Listen to the sound." He played a quick melodious phrase that sounded like sunlight shining upon gold. Behind him, the waves outside took on the color of his intent eyes and slivers of clouds crowned his finely shaped head. He lifted his bow off the strings and the spell was broken. "This cello cost me a rib out of my body but I love her."

Had he ever cared about anyone like that? What would it feel like to have all that intensity focused on me? He was the sort who loved seldom but deeply. He would be faithful, to the point of being consumed by his passion. I shook my head, cleared my unruly thoughts. "You have expensive taste."

He looked rueful. "Yes, between my competitive skier daughter and my beautiful instruments, I need to find a pot of gold somewhere."

Today, the water and sky had melded into a single blue expanse that cradled the two of us on his boat, rocked by the waves, submerged in the liquid voice of his cello. Into this intimacy, I said, "There was a burglary at the house yesterday and Grandma's jewelry was stolen. It was worth a great deal."

He cocked his head, and moved to tune the next string. "Oh? When did that happen?"

"During her daily walk."

"How coincidental." He placed his cello on his carved wooden stand and started on mine.

As he struck the tuning fork against his knee again, I asked, "What do you mean?"

Instead of using the fine tuners at the bottom of my cello, he fiddled with the giant pegs at the top of the neck. "Good God, Sylvie. What have you done to this thing?" He shuddered. "I do not know how it is possible you made it so out of tune in one day. I am glad I do not live where you practice."

I grinned. "I revel in imperfection." I was learning from Lukas to relax my standards. Then I asked airily, "But what did you mean, coincidental?"

He was still muttering to himself as he worked but paused to say, "That they knew exactly the right time. Was the jewelry just lying around?"

"No, I believe it was hidden." I traced the embroidered velvet of the chair where I sat with my index finger.

"So they found it quickly too. Sounds like an insider was involved. She is not well, right? Was there some sort of conflict over who would inherit it? Who was she going to leave it to?"

I fixed my eyes on the upholstery. "Me." In two seconds, he had made clear every weakness in our plan. I rubbed my hand over my eyes. In two more seconds, he would have figured out the whole thing. I cast about for a change of subject. I pointed to his stand. It was engraved, and I asked abruptly, "Is that a menorah?"

"Yes. My mother gave that to me. I am surprised you know what it is."

"I grew up in New York City. Many of my friends are Jewish."

Filip finished tuning my cello and began to play a melancholy piece on it, a low accompaniment to his words. I sensed that talking while playing made it easier for him to share, just as my own pained music somehow eased my mind. "That is quite different from here. Most of us have been killed or left for other countries. The Jewish community here is small and very aware of being survivors. Do you remember that kid Rafael from our class?"

"The name, yes, but I cannot recall a face."

"Well, he used to chase me during our lunch breaks, yelling, 'You stink, you dirty Jew.'" Filip said this in a sardonic way, as if reciting a story about someone else.

I recognized a kindred spirit in him. I too could talk as long as I did not need to admit that any of it had ever hurt me. "Fun. Some of the girls used to call me a 'poop Chinese.'"

"Oh yes, there was a phase when everyone was saying that on the elementary schoolyard. As we grew older, Lukas got into trouble for fighting too. They would call him a cunt Asian or a fat samurai, as if he were ever overweight."

My lips flattened. I did not remember those particular insults. I must have already been gone then and Lukas had endured it alone. So many years I had missed. "It is like people become blind and they just yell things that have no connection to who you are."

Filip segued seamlessly into a sharp, fiery melody. His left hand flew from string to string, trembling, as the bow relentlessly sawed against the instrument, cutting the blazing music out of the cello piece by piece. "My grandfather was part Indonesian. During the war, he sat in a camp run by the Japanese and, to the end of his life, would never buy a Japanese car. My grandmother was hidden here in Holland, moved from house to house. She wound up killing herself. My mother found the body." The bow lifted off the strings with a flourish, and then a soft, lilting refrain began. *Nothing to see here,* it said. *No grief. No rage. Just move on.*

I made my voice as casual as his expression. This, I realized, was what attracted me to him: his need to control all his demons, to wrap them up and confine them neatly in a locked compartment never to be opened. Still, the beasts we tried to tuck away writhed, twisted, and wailed to be free. "It is sad how trauma gets passed down from generation to generation. Helena, my own ma and pa: They taught us to keep our heads low, to hold our secrets as closed as an oyster. Keep ourselves apart from everyone else. At a certain point, you wind up dividing yourself internally into so many different people you do not even know who you are anymore."

Filip stopped playing and looked up at me. For once, his eyes were vulnerable and his voice filled with emotion. "That is it exactly. My mother told me everyone was anti-Semitic. Do not stick out your head in case it gets cut off. Never trust anyone outside of the family, while the family itself was, of course, completely untrustworthy. Do not reveal what you are truly feeling or thinking. Never show who you are. She wanted me to become a rabbi."

I asked softly, "And now?"

"She still wants me to become a rabbi."

We both chuckled. Then an awkward silence fell over us. He rubbed his jaw and I twisted a loose button on my shirt. When he finally spoke, his tone was brisk. "All right, let us do a call-and-response exercise now."

He played D, A, D, A, A and I answered with A, A, A, D, D. As we played, my instrument answering his, I felt as if our cellos were speaking to each other, like we were still communicating, only without words. I had progressed to playing notes and simple melodies. I frowned, concentrating on finding the note with my left hand as my right drew my bow across the string.

"The cello is difficult because unlike the guitar, it does not have any frets. You must search for the note on the string yourself. But before you can find the note, you must be able to hear it."

Filip stepped over to the piano and began to play. It was a simple scale and he sang along in a strong baritone. He indicated with a gesture of his head that I should join him. I got up, stood beside him, and began to sing, our voices merging. He played higher and higher, until the music slipped past his range, then he fell silent as I continued—each note pure and full.

When I finally stopped, he quirked his lips in a half smile and said, "You can sing." Was that admiration in his gaze? I thrilled to it. It felt like I had been submerged in a warm bath.

"A little. My younger sister used to stutter quite badly and sometimes, when she couldn't get the words out, we would sing together. It calmed her down. Amy is the one with the real talent in the family. Singing is something we share."

He nodded in approval. "Well, that is a huge step. Hearing where the notes should be is a great advantage."

I shrugged. "Or disadvantage, because, actually, I am hurting myself as much as you when I play so badly. I can hear it in my head and I wish I could put it into my hands. Well, if dogs could pray, it would rain bones."

He wrapped his hand around my wrist and my pulse quickened to a drumroll. Could he feel it? Without releasing me, he stood and led me back to my cello. "That is because your shoulders and arms are too tense. Let me do the left-hand fingering." He straddled my chair behind me and took hold of my cello with his left hand, and wrapped his right around mine on the bow. I was enveloped by his scent, the hard muscles of his chest and thighs, the firm gentle grip of his hands, the faint stubble on his cheek against my temple. His lithe body cradled mine. I closed my eyes and we played together.

Grandma had been warned to turn off her hearing aids whenever I practiced at the house. As I had known it would, my playing drove Helena insane. This gave me great pleasure. She asked me to practice at Lukas's apartment, which I only did when she was not at home. I was horrible at something for the first time in my overcontrolled life and I reveled in it. I poured my grief, pain, and ugliness, my misformed eye into my playing. I lost myself in the clumsiness of my fingers, the awkwardness of my body, the peeping, cracking sounds that came from my cello. This was indeed my instrument and it voiced all the rage and frustration that I could not.

I took off my wedding ring. I had always been too consumed with my ambitions, had never been boy crazy. Yet now there were two new men in my heart. I no longer recognized myself. I always warned Amy, when she fell in love with one guy after another, "You will not find happiness that way. You are just trying to distract yourself." I never understood why she yearned to find love and affection with strangers when, in my eyes, she already received so much from Ma and Pa. I was such a prude. With Jim, I had started dreaming of our future together almost right away. When I had read fairy tales to Amy, I was the one truly captivated by them. The gods help me, I believed that if I worked my hardest, if I was the best in every class, if I made myself beautiful, I would find someone who would love me like no one else ever had—and I had succeeded with Jim, my affectionate blond prince in tattered jeans. But he had only taught me that in these modern times, the distinction between hero and villain was often in the eye of the beholder. Instead, the spell had been broken in reverse: the kiss had revealed the truth of the frog underlying the prince.

No, this time, I loved not to remember, not to bring us together into some imagined future, but to forget. What was love but the most potent and addictive of all drugs, more powerful than pills or alcohol? I was still taking more than the recommended allowance of my sleeping pills each day; the habit had made them less effective. And drinking was no use because I found alcohol bitter. It made me feel flushed and itchy, my heart and mind racing like a hunted animal. I longed for peace, sleep, and forgetfulness—so I threw myself into thoughts of Filip and Lukas; they were a barrier holding my memories of Jim at bay.

I did not dream of a future together. I no longer trusted that rope bridge to hold. Therefore, I did not have to choose. They were from before I became everything I was now, good or bad. They were in both my before and after photos. It was like I had finally come home. It felt like they had a prior claim, a right to me that preceded everyone else, even my husband. Perhaps it was the intensity of knowing my time here was limited, the wonderful safe boundary of the inevitable goodbye. I kept my attraction a secret because I had learned that to do otherwise was to invite the gods to mock you. My relationship with Jim had been a mad rush, out of control and consuming everything in its path, like an avalanche. From the day we met, we had been inseparable. No more of that for me.

Lukas was forbidden fruit. He was my cousin and my friend, and what would it do to Estelle? When it all went wrong, as it invariably would, I would be left weeping among the ruins of our friendship. Filip was off-limits too, because I was mere sport to him, like the rabbit used as a lure in a race. Once he had exhausted himself, I would be of no more use, if he had not devoured me already. I was using them as a distraction and part of me knew it. But it did not matter. I held on to the images of their faces, their bodies, their hands, their voices.

None of us acted on our attraction, as if afraid to disturb this tenuous happiness, as fragile as a soap bubble floating upon a surface of water. Love was an asymptote I neared but could never reach, edging ever closer for eternity. This strange triangle of affection was my final chance at happiness and I chose to cling to it with my toes like a tightrope walker balancing above an abyss.

Dutch Local Newspaper

NOORD NEDERLANDS DAGBLAD

Tuesday, 17 May

This past Saturday, 14 May, the body of an unknown woman was found in the Amsterdam-Rhine Canal in Diemen. She was located inside her rental auto. Her identity has not been confirmed, though sources at the scene report the possibility that the body could belong to Sylvie Lee, a dual Dutch-American citizen, who was reported missing two weeks ago by her family.

It is believed that the victim might have been under the influence of alcohol and miscalculated the distance to water in her auto.

CHAPTER 16

Amy

Friday, May 6

I realize it is much farther to the house than I'd thought, especially when I keep ramming my shins into the pedals of the bike as I walk it. Bicycle after bicycle passes by me. It's not like in America, where mainly athletic, young people ride as adults. Here in the Netherlands, it seems as though everyone is on a bicycle, from tiny toddlers to the decrepit senior citizens you'd think could barely walk. The bike lanes have their own traffic lights. At an intersection, I spot a woman on a huge chestnut horse, peering at what appears to be a traffic light set high on the pole for equestrians. A man rides by with a crate of beer loaded onto the back of his bike and shopping bags hanging from both of his handlebars. Steering without hands, a teenage girl cruises with her arms at her sides, listening to music through her earbuds.

She seems so relaxed I decide to give my bruised shins a break and ride my borrowed bicycle the rest of the way. It goes pretty well until a pimply kid passes by, turns his head, and winks at me. He's completely turned around on his bike, jerking his eyebrows suggestively and pursing his thick lips into kisses. He seems to be doing just fine without looking where he's going, but I'm thoroughly distracted by this. He looks about thirteen and I wonder how old he thinks I am. I'm surprised by the attention, but I suppose I'm a rarity here. I stick out, in both good and bad ways. He obviously believes everyone can bike like the Dutch. I can hardly manage to steer and swerve as a car comes too close, honking at me.

Thankfully, this surprises lover boy enough that he turns around and soon disappears into the distance. I am passing a crowd of people, all standing around, drinking and laughing by a café, when, to my shock, another guy launches himself onto the baggage rack of my bike so he's sitting behind me. What is it with Dutch men and bicycles? He is enormous and the extra weight unbalances me. We swing like crazy. Luckily, the road is empty of cars at the moment.

"Hoi!" he says cheerily, and then a bunch of nonsense words I can't understand.

"I don't speak Dutch!" To my horror, we are heading straight for the edge of the canal, which is not secured by any type of guardrail. If this were the U.S., someone would drown there every five minutes, but in Europe they seem to believe that if you're dumb, you deserve to die so you don't pass your genes on to the next generation.

We both holler. I brace for the impact, tell myself that at least I can swim, when the stranger reaches past me to jerk the handlebars with one hand. He manages to crash us into the trunk of a large tree planted on the bank of the canal. We fly off the bike as we impact.

We are piled together—me, the man, the poor bicycle—and my rib aches where the handlebar grip struck me when we fell.

"W-what were you thinking?" I sputter.

He shakes his head, dazed, and gets to his feet, collecting his leather messenger bag as he does so. He offers me a hand, which I refuse. He then says in excellent English, "I did not realize you were not Dutch." *And can't ride a bicycle properly*. I hear the words he didn't say as clearly as if he'd spoken them out loud.

I brace myself on the fallen bicycle as I stand, still shaken. "Even if I were Dutch, why in the world would you throw yourself onto the back of someone's bike?"

He gives a short little cough and busies himself picking up my bike and fixing the stem of the handlebars. Despite my anger, I notice his fine shoulders, and how his wavy brown hair gleams in the sunlight and that he has a very nice profile. "Ah, it is sort of a custom here. I had a few beers with lunch and I changed back to my student days when I saw you."

"I still don't understand."

"Well, you see a pretty girl go by, you jump on the back. I just wanted to come along." He shoots me a hopeful look that manages to seem both self-mocking and charming.

I am speechless. This man thinks I'm attractive. The wind whips my hair in my eyes. I brush it away and take a good look at him. He is probably a bit older than me, closer to Sylvie's age. He's wearing a dark jacket over a button-down shirt and his jeans fit snugly over his long legs. But more, there is vulnerability and trepidation in his sensitive face, as if he's taking a great gamble by standing here, talking to me like this, but he's risking it anyway.

"I am very sorry about the bike and the crash and the possible swim and all that. At least your bicycle appears undamaged. Could I possibly take you out for coffee to make up for it?"

I want to go, very much. But I have been brought up in New York City. In fact, I have never spoken to a stranger to this extent before today. Serial killers abound. What would Ma or Sylvie say?

He reads my answer on my face. "Okay, I understand. Never go out with a man you do not know and all that." He rummages in his bag and pulls out a crumpled flyer. "Well, I happen to be giving a free lunch concert tomorrow at the Noorderkerk in Amsterdam. There will be many other people there to keep you safe if you should want to come. And there is a nice farmer's market outside on Saturdays."

The flyer is in Dutch but I can read the words *J.S. Bach, Zes suites.* "Are you a musician?"

He inclines his head. "I'm a cellist. My name is Filip."

Part 4

CHAPTER 17

Amy

Saturday, May 7

I float in a haze. Did the handsome cellist really invite me to see him today? I find his full name on the Bach Cello Suites flyer and, after Googling him on the laptop Sylvie gave me, now know everything about him. Is there anything I own that wasn't given to me by my sister? I can hear her now: *Slow down, Amy. You don't even know him yet. It's not possible to fall in love six times a year.* I'm not that bad. I just enjoy liking guys. It's my hobby. Each man is a potential doorway leading me out of my boring life and into theirs. Most of the time, I don't manage to speak to them much, let alone have them take a real interest in me. It's more about the fantasy. With the help of online translating programs, I learn that Filip (such an elegant and European name) is an established cellist with the Netherlands Philharmonic Orchestra—so definitely not a serial killer.

Sylvie. Is it wrong to spend my time going to a concert? How can I like a guy while she's still missing? What is wrong with me? But there's nothing I can do until Monday, when I can contact the police again. The stress of waiting has caused a constant ache in my shoulders and neck, and I can barely eat or rest. I sleep and wake with a weight upon my soul. I need a distraction from it all, even just for a morning. I could go listen to a concert given by a gorgeous musician—and the Bach Cello Suites are some of my favorite pieces. Even if Filip isn't actually interested in me—and I'm sure he's not—I can enjoy the music if nothing else. It might help clear my mind.

I study how to get to the Noorderkerk in Amsterdam by public transportation. A train, closely related to the subway, is something I trust and understand. It's surprisingly easy since the map program shows me exactly when and where the train arrives and Helena has given me an OV-chipcard, which I can use for any type of mass transit. I'm scared but excited too. I'm not telling Helena, Willem, or Lukas. If they're anything like Ma and Pa, there would be an interrogation and they would probably send Lukas along to make sure Filip isn't a murderer. Living at home, I've only managed a few dates under Pa's watchful eye, a bare minimum of a love life.

This is the new, independent Amy. I hear Sylvie's voice in my head—*Just go, you'll be fine*. I pull myself together. I put in my contact lenses and apply a tiny bit of makeup. There are new and unexpected dangers in this country, like flirtatious Dutch men on bicycles. I can no longer afford a fog of blurriness, not while Sylvie needs me at full capacity.

I go downstairs and call out to Helena and Willem, who sip coffee as they work on their paperwork at the dining room table. I tell them I'm heading out to explore Amsterdam. They don't seem surprised or alarmed. Don't they realize I'm not Dutch and could get lost forever?

The train station is quite close to their house so I don't have to take the bicycle, thank goodness. The weather has changed again and now feels like spring. I love the smell of fresh-cut grass. The wind is warm and playful today, tousling my hair with caressing fingers, though the sky is edged with a hint of darkness. Even the people I pass on the street seem to be smiling—that is, until they see me. I'm not sure if it's because I'm a stranger, or Chinese, or because of the way I avert my face to avoid eye contact, a necessary habit learned in New York, where hustlers and aggressive men lurk.

At the little red kiosk on the train platform, I manage to buy myself a cup of coffee and a warm *saucijzenbroodje*. I indicate by pointing. I make sure to speak English right away so they won't assume I'm Dutch and start speaking it to me. There's a rectangular sign next to the tracks that shows when the train will arrive and lists all the stops—truly a very civilized country. I sip my hot coffee, which is smaller and much stronger than I'm used to, and nibble on the flakey sausage pastry as a white train with bright yellow doors and blue accents pulls up.

I stand there waiting for the nearest door to slide open but it doesn't budge, even though people are getting in and out of other entrances. I race to another doorway and barely slip inside before the door closes. The conductor blows the whistle and we're off. I learn by watching at other stations. The doors only open if you push a button. Half of New York City would be trapped on the subways if we implemented that. There would be riots. The Dutch landscape is in full bloom, fields filled with tulips and hyacinths, rioting in red, yellow, and magenta over their carefully cultivated beds. There, lines of workers are decapitating the flowers. I assume it's to strengthen the bulbs. I crane my neck to watch as the train roars past. Trails of sacrificial blooms litter the earth, their delicate petals already wilting.

The train rides into a long covered space at Amsterdam Central Station, overarched with panes of glass and metal that glitter in the sun. People wait politely outside the train for us to get off before crowding in. I flow along with everyone until I find myself in the large central hall. It is part medieval cathedral, part modern age—I've never seen anything like it. There's no graffiti or litter anywhere. Tourists drag their wheeled suitcases into sandwich and pasta shops, while backpackers stride past teenagers chatting on cell phones.

My sense of being foreign eases a bit here, among all the diverse races and nationalities. I hear jazz piano music and realize it's coming from a shiny black grand piano that has painted on its side: *Bespeel Mij / Play Me*. A Moroccan man in a janitor's uniform is playing Thelonious

Monk's "'Round Midnight" with great feeling as his pail and bucket rest against the pillar nearby. A small group of people have gathered to listen.

I step outside and find myself in the midst of a mass of tram tracks. I did it. I went to Amsterdam all by myself. The maps app on my phone shows that it's only a fifteen-minute walk to the Noorderkerk. I look back at the station and see that it is indeed a long cathedral built on the water, lit golden by the morning light. For a moment, I close my eyes. *Please, whatever gods roam this land, please let my sister be all right.* Passengers are disembarking from flat ferries. I cross the street without looking both ways and am almost run over by a bicyclist who swerves to avoid me at the last moment. Then I pick my way along a road where literally thousands of bicycles rest against each other on both sides of the street. To my right is a tall modern building, entirely scaled with small squares of thick glass like some mythical snake.

In this beautiful city, I can feel that Sylvie will return to me, safe and sound. She will hug me and laugh that I was worried enough to come all the way here. We all go out for drinks together: Sylvie, Lukas, Estelle, and me with my new boyfriend, Filip. I giggle at the idea of this. I can't wait to see Filip again and hear him play. I cross an elegant modern arched bridge and pass an interracial couple, both men, necking by one of its pillars.

Then I stroll along the Brouwersgracht, a canal lined with tall and thin canal houses—each bearing soaring gables and long sleek windows. Pale green buds speckle the trees and houseboats are docked all along the waterside. How Sylvie must love it here. She always wanted to play boat when we were little, which meant sitting on our tiny bed and pretending we lived at sea together. I would leap onto the floor and thrash around to catch the fish and bring them back to Sylvie, who expertly fried them up. We had no idea she would grow up to be such a terrible cook.

On the corner, I spot a large, cross-shaped Protestant church. That must be the Noorderkerk. I have some trouble finding the entrance because the square in front is smothered with market stands, each with a little sloped cloth roof to protect it from the rain and sun. I can smell the fresh bread and roasted nuts, but I don't stop to browse. I hurry inside to find a good seat.

I spot Filip at the front, busy tuning his cello. His shoulders strain against the tuxedo he wears. He's sitting underneath the short staircase that leads to the pulpit, his hair lit by a large circular chandelier. Behind him, a massive pipe organ gleams silver and gold and stretches toward the arched ceiling. He stands to adjust his cuff links, and I stop so suddenly the woman behind me almost bumps into me and then stares at me curiously as she steps around me. I catch my breath. Those long legs, the narrow, tapered waist, the elegance of his hands, his chiseled, kind features. A line of well-dressed ladies admire him from the first row. The pews to the left and the right are filled already. I hurry to an empty seat in one of the rows of wooden folding chairs arranged down the middle of the church. He scans the audience as if he's looking for someone, and I feel myself glow as he sees me. Then he lifts a hand in greeting.

I move my chair slightly and it catches on one of the long gray stone slabs that line the church. There's a number engraved onto it, plus a hole to lift up the stone. I almost jump out of my seat as I realize we are sitting on tombstones. Ma: *Never walk over a person's grave. Very uncomfortable for their soul*. At the cemetery, we always take care to maneuver around the graves. This would be the greatest form of hell for us Chinese, to be buried in a busy church where hundreds of people tromp over our bodies. *What if Sylvie's*—I break off the thought. Just for one day, I will try not to worry.

A man in a suit speaks to the room in Dutch and presents Filip with a flourish. The audience claps loudly. Filip inclines his head, then sits and lifts his bow to his cello. The familiar strains of Bach's prelude of the first suite for solo cello in G major fill the hall, the soft, translucent tones of his baroque instrument resonating in this holy place. His phrasing is sensitive, yet intense and quietly perceptive. Despite Sylvie's disappearance, I feel at peace as the melody undulates, flows into the ragged edges of my soul. It's like I can sense Filip's passion and vulnerability in his playing—and, just like that, my stupid and frustrated heart is his.

After the concert, Filip is immediately ringed by his fans. I hesitate.

I long to approach him but even the thought of speaking to him turns my tongue into a log inside my mouth. I wait for a few minutes. The crowd around him shows no signs of thinning. He's a god and I am nothing. I shouldn't mistake politeness for anything more. My shoulders droop, and I turn to make my way to the door. But just as I step outside into the brilliant sunlight, I hear him call, "Amy! Wait!"

My joy sprouts wings and takes flight. I turn to see him hurrying toward me with his sleek silver cello case slung onto his back like a giant backpack.

"That's quite a talent you have there, being able to run with that thing on your back," I blurt out.

He stops a moment, surprised, and then starts to laugh. "Not quite the cello-related compliment I was hoping for, but thank you. Look, I really do want to make it up to you for almost drowning you in the river. There is a café right on the corner here that supposedly has the best apple pie in all of the Netherlands."

Could this truly be happening to me? I want to squeal with joy. "I-I'd like that."

As we make our way through the crowded market, I can't help craning my neck to stare at the huge round wheels of Dutch cheeses stacked on top of one another, and the mounds of crusty bread with names like *desembol* and *rustiek stokbrood*, and spectacular flowers in beige plastic crates being sold at ridiculously low prices. At one of the stands, a man is making large fresh versions of the *stroopwafel* I'd eaten, smearing caramel syrup between two pieces of wafer-thin waffle dough that he then toasts in a flat round iron. My stomach rumbles as the sweet fragrance wafts toward us.

Filip doesn't seem to mind our silence but when the crowd eases a bit, I say, "Your playing style reminds me of Starker."

His head whips around to face me. "You are full of surprises. Why do you say that?"

I scrunch my head down into my jacket. I always put my foot in my mouth. I mumble, "I felt bad I only complimented your running with your cello, though you did that very well too."

He shakes his head, his eyes clear and insistent. "I meant, why did you compare me to him? He happens to be someone I admire greatly."

I perk up. "So much darkness and passion beneath a cool and elegant surface."

"Ah yes. You are the musical one in your family, aren't you?" He's scanning the street, figuring out where to go.

I stumble over my feet and stare at him. "How did you know that?"

He stares into the distance. "Just a guess. Oh, here we are. This is Winkel."

We are standing at a packed outdoor café. Filip pronounced it "Vinkel" instead of "Winkel" like it says on the striped green-and-white awning. Diners sit at tiny wooden tables laden with meat pies, club sandwiches, thick slices of apple pie, and tall glasses of layered espresso and foamed milk.

We join the line of people waiting for a table. Across the street, a long-haired calico cat blinks at me from inside one of the windows, sitting among a nest of orchids. Behind the cat, an older woman watches us, probably because of Filip and his tuxedo. When she realizes I've seen her, she moves away from the window, but I can follow her movements through her living room. It's something I noticed earlier: the way the Dutch throw their curtains wide open, if they bother to have any drapes at all. Behind every pane of open glass, I imagine unseen faces examining me and everything I do.

I ask, "Why do so many houses keep their drapes open? I thought it was because I was staying in a village, but I noticed it here in Amsterdam too. In New York City, someone would break into your place right away if they could see inside."

He furrows his brow, thinking. "That is typical Dutch. There is plenty of crime here, but somehow the tradition still persists. It is like saying, 'We have nothing to hide here. We are very normal, decent people, look all you want.'"

It's our turn and the waiter leads us to a sunny little table in the corner. Filip takes his cello off his back and balances it against the pillar beside us. After I tell him what I'd like, he orders two slices of *appel-*

taart, a double ristretto for himself, and a fresh mint tea for me. I venture to ask, "Are the Dutch really that open?"

"We are and we are not. People here are extremely direct, which means if you ask them if they like your new shirt, they will say, 'I have never seen anything so ugly.' But when it comes to things like sharing problems, there is a real tendency to say, 'Everything is fine. I can handle it.' Even if that might not be the case."

His voice has a lovely, resonant quality that makes it sound like he's singing. He peeks at me once or twice as he talks, as if he's unsure of me. I thrill to this—he's somehow nervous around *me*. He's open and thoughtful, a sensitive soul hurt by the rigors of the world. He squints a bit in the direct sunlight and even this is charming, the way his lashes turn golden, his light liquid eyes.

He is looking at me strangely and the tips of his ears are bright red. Oh no, I have been staring at him like a fool. "I-ah, I . . ."

Fortunately, the waitress arrives then with the *appeltaart* and drinks, so I am saved from having to speak, though I am cringing inside. Why can I not be cool like other people? Sylvie would never do anything like this. I distract myself by pretending I am fascinated with my food. It does look delicious. My generous slice of *appeltaart* is made with thick, cakey, moist dough still crispy around the edges. The apples have been sliced thinly and layered with raisins. A dollop of freshly whipped cream accompanies the dish. My tea comes with a delicate little log of meringue filled with buttercream and dipped in chocolate at both ends that Filip tells me is called a *bokkenpootje*, a goat's foot.

After we've each tried the *appeltaart*, which tastes as good as it looks, Filip asks, "So why are you in the Netherlands?"

I cup my hands around my steaming mug filled with a large bundle of fresh mint leaves. Its fragrance soothes my embarrassment a bit. "I have some things I need to do while I'm here."

"You are not just a tourist?"

I stir in the little package of honey that came with my tea. I hardly know him. But I feel like I can trust him. I scratch my cheek and decide to take the plunge. "No, my sister, Sylvie, was here and then she disappeared." As I say these words, my fear wells up in me again. How can this not be a bad dream? What will I do now? I was deceiving myself earlier. This isn't a misunderstanding. Something has gone terribly wrong.

Emotions I can't quite read flash in his eyes: concern, discomfort, fear. Oddly, he doesn't seem surprised. I'm relieved he doesn't react with shock or horror, though, which would only scare me more. He pauses for a long moment, as if he's hesitant to speak or is trying to make some monumental decision, then says, "Oh, that is terrible. What happened?"

So I tell him the story of Sylvie's trip to the Netherlands. He listens intently.

Then he asks, "Have you spoken to the police?"

I sigh. My voice thickens and my shoulders sag. "Yes, but they didn't seem to have a real plan." What am I supposed to do if the police can't act?

Filip leans back in his chair and steeples his fingers. Nice hands. "I do not think they are going to do much."

Hearing him say it confirms my fears. "How do you know?" I don't quite manage to keep my voice from breaking.

"Well, my passion is diving."

I mutter, "That would explain your amazing body."

He is about to take a sip of his ristretto and sputters.

Mortified, I clasp my hands to my mouth as if I could force the words back inside. "I am so sorry for treating you like a sex object." I gasp again. "Uh, no, I mean, what—what I'm trying to say is I either stammer or stuff like that comes out of my mouth. It's one or the other."

"Right." He can't meet my eyes and is rubbing the back of his neck. His ears are now purple. "So I do many types of diving and, once in a while, I volunteer as a diver for a group that searches for missing people."

Of course he does volunteer work in his spare time. He's good and generous. Then the rest of what he said penetrates and my hand flies to my chest. "Do you work for the police?"

He finally looks at me again. The color in his face has subsided. "No, it is a nonprofit, independent organization. People go to them after the police have given up. So I have seen situations like this before. There are very strict rules here about what types of disappearances get investigated and the privacy laws prohibit much gathering of information. If they think she ran away or that it is suicide, they will just go and drink coffee with the family for a while so you do not feel bad. They are forced to give priority to criminal cases, but that is no help when someone you love is missing."

For once I am listening to his words instead of watching his lips. "So true."

He brings out his wallet and searches through it until he finds an old business card, then hands it to me. "The organization is called Epsilon. They have their own boats, dogs, everything."

I want to bounce up and down—finally, people who could help us. I could kiss this man. It was fate that brought us together. The gods are helping me bring Sylvie home again. "Thank you so much. This means everything to me." Forgetting my past blunders, I reach out and squeeze his shoulder. "Really."

He shifts a bit so my hand falls from him, and continues, "They just solved a case that had baffled the police for more than twenty years."

"How?"

He says simply, "They found the corpse."

What? My chest tightens and a clammy sweat breaks out over me. He must not have understood my story correctly. "But we're not looking for a body. We just need to find Sylvie."

He looks taken aback for a moment, then holds up his hands. "Of course, of course. They also recently found someone alive who was lost in the woods. Memory loss."

"Really?" Memory loss. Hope bubbles up in my chest like champagne. If only that were the reason Sylvie is missing. This could change everything. But why was he talking about a body? There couldn't be a body. That's ridiculous.

He scoots his chair a bit closer and leans in. "If you want more help finding your sister, they are the people you should call. The director is named Karin. If you decide to approach her, tell her I sent you. Here, let me give you my mobile number too." He takes the card and scribbles his cell on the back. "Since I dive for them, it would give me the chance to see you again as well." He gives me a devastating half smile that makes my heart flutter again. "We could go out in the boat together."

Thirteen Years Ago

THE DAILY PRINCETONIAN

Monday, November 18

In the early morning of Sunday, November 17, the Department of Public Safety (DPS) responded to a report of assault on the University campus. The alleged assault was reported at 2:16 a.m. and is claimed to have occurred sometime between 2:00 a.m. and 2:16 a.m. Director of media relations Nicole Thompson explained, "Regarding the assault reported in the November 17 log, DPS received a report from the Campus Security Authority that an act of violence occurred on campus perpetrated by a male student against a female and a male student. It is not known at present if any of the students was under the influence of drugs or alcohol at the time. We will not disclose the names of the parties involved or the details of the alleged incident."

An unnamed source reported that the alleged conflict arose over the victim's flirtation with the attacker's girlfriend and that the girlfriend suffered a minor injury as well in the confusion. The alleged male victim was treated by University Health Services for multiple lacerations, bruises, a fractured rib, and a loose tooth.

CHAPTER 18

Ma

Sunday, May 8

I was a mother alone on Mother's Day. Pa brought me a soy sauce chicken from Chinatown, which was his way of showing affection. I was glad Amy remembered to call me, but such strange reports she brought of her sister, saying Sylvie had gone to Venice with someone. Who? Jim? Another man? My Snow Jasmine, what has happened to you?

Women. Love. How can something so beautiful turn wicked? They say that once you see the ocean, no other water can compare. My love story started so many years ago. Pa and I began our marriage with the strength of a tiger's head but it slowly transformed into the weak tail of the snake. How could it be that I placed the green hat upon his head?

I had known him for so long. We were friends until something else grew in between us, something strong and binding. He made me gasp when I caught sight of him unexpectedly, standing with his friends—the blazing sun, the dust on the empty roads, the bustle of farmers going to market. I carried my basket and saw him looking, from underneath the shade. I had never seen a man so tall and broad, strong yet fine. I had never had a man look at me the way he did, with longing and desire, though I did not know then what that was.

One day, I was passing by him when I stepped on a stone and lost my balance. He reached out and grabbed me by the arm, stabilized me with a hand on my back, his focus on my lips. I met his eyes and felt like I had been kissed. Now I look back and wonder if these were the dreams of a young girl.

It was as if I had been empty and did not know it. Suddenly, here was the food I had always craved and I turned into a hungry ghost, devouring all but unable to be satisfied. Our first time, I never wanted to let him go—the discovery of small intimacies, like the birthmark behind his ear, the soft skin of his neck. Despite the pain and the sweat and the strangeness of it all, I wanted to keep him with me forever.

But then the burden of years weighed upon us. Love can change. It can grow and twist until the most beautiful sapling in the wild turns into a prison of stunted wood.

Telephone Call
Monday, April 18

Estelle: Hey, Sylvie, it is me. I am so happy you are back. Lukas told me it will be next weekend your birthday. I just looked and I can book us a few free tickets to Venice!

Sylvie: But I do not know. Grandma is so sick now. The palliative nurse is with her twenty-four hours a day. That is not a good sign.

Estelle: I must be honest. You looked terrible the last time I saw you. The skin under your eyes is like that of an elephant. We need to get you out more. Come up, it is your birthday and it will only be for a few days. My father died a couple years ago of cancer. It just ate at me inside day and night. I can take care of all the reservations. You would just have to pay a basic fee.

Sylvie: Are you sure? I have never been to Venice.

Estelle: Absolutely. Lukas flies with me all the time. We would technically be standby, but as a captain, I almost always get on the flight. Oh, and shall we invite your delicious thing too? Four is a better number than three.

Sylvie: I do not know who you mean?

Estelle: Right. Filip, of course!

CHAPTER 19

Sylvie

Thursday, April 21

Estelle and Lukas had decided to educate me on all I had missed by not growing up here and were holding a cursing contest. We sat inside the packed local pub, so unlike the elegant cocktail lounges I used to visit back in the city with my acquaintances and colleagues, where we sipped twenty-dollar dry martinis and mojitos while posing on sleek leather couches. Here, everything was wood-paneled. The bar was littered with paper Heineken coasters and there was not a single cocktail in sight. Only Belgian beer, Filou, *witbier*, Straffe Hendrik, and red and white wine, all for less than five euros a glass.

I perched on a wooden bar stool between Estelle and Lukas as they tried to outcurse each other. They began with the typical sicknesses: cancer dick, plague head, epilepsy bringer, get the syphilis, biliary cancer idiot. Then they moved on to anus curses like anus potato, anus pilot (Estelle had rolled her eyes at that one), and anus tourist. Now they were free-associating while I tried to stop laughing long enough to breathe.

"Coconut tree screwer." Estelle's cross-body Yves Saint Laurent Soho bag was slung over her shoulders, long jean-clad legs crossed, ending in cute black ankle boots.

"Slipper lover." Lukas leaned back against the counter as he took a sip of his beer. A pretty brunette with curly hair down to her butt deliberately squeezed in beside him to grab some coasters. Who needs extra coasters? They were everywhere. She gave him a sideways glance, clearly noticing the way his black T-shirt stretched across his chest and lingering on his strong neck and lips. He remained completely oblivious. Good boy.

"Intestine frog," Estelle said.

Lukas shot back, "Sewing box."

I held up my hands. "Wait, violation. How is that a curse?"

Lukas waggled his eyebrows at me. "Sewing does not just mean with a needle and thread."

Estelle made a graphic gesture with her fingers. "Sex. And a box also refers to a woman's—"

"Ah," I said.

It was Estelle's turn. Her white-blond hair had not changed since we were kids. If only I could have had her with me for all the intervening years. Her turquoise silk tank top shone like her eyes as she drawled, "Horse dick."

"Horse penis polisher."

With a triumphant smile, Estelle said, "Easter bunny pubic hair collector."

Now I almost fell off my stool from laughter. "You are just making these up."

In unison, they both protested, "No!"

A man with a ruddy face and straw-like stubble who had been hovering behind us said, "I called my boss that yesterday."

Estelle winked at the guy as Lukas deliberately turned his back on him. This was not the first man who had tried to join our game tonight, much to Lukas's annoyance.

"Oooh!" Estelle cried. "Dancing!" It was late and the crowd was drunk enough that a few people had started swaying and jumping in the middle of the room—and another small group tromped around doing the polonaise in a line with their hands on each other's shoulders, singing loudly out of tune. In most countries, this could not really be called dancing. "Come up." Before I could protest, she dragged me off to join them.

"No, no, I cannot. I really cannot," I protested, but it was too late. The polonaise line had tromped off to the other side of the room. We stood among the tiny dancing group as Estelle sashayed around me. I groaned and tried to claw my way back to the bar, but Lukas now stood before me, moving to the music. He looked good. Estelle turned so that her butt was pressed against his front and started to undulate, her hands gathering a cascade of pale hair above her slender neck. A bolt of jealousy struck me in the chest. They probably did this all the time, all the years I had been gone.

Above her head, his eyes met mine and he smiled, teeth white in the dimly lit bar. "Do not go. Dance with us."

Dutifully, I tried. My hips did not sway. I marched up and down in place like a robot. Although I had learned to find the beat, I did not understand what people meant when they said I had to "feel the music." What was there to feel?

Lukas's mouth slackened.

Estelle paused her sexy swinging. "Sylvie!" she screeched. "What. Is. That."

"Dancing," I retorted. I was a terrible dancer in a land of terrible dancers. Even here, I was unusual. But this was what they wanted. I marched harder.

The ruddy man from before came shimmying up beside me. "Looking good to me, little treasure."

"You are too drunk to see anything," Lukas snapped. He took my hand and pulled me to him, swinging us around so the man was hidden behind his broad back. Then, slowly, he lifted my palm to his lips and kissed it. My skin throbbed. I stared up at him with my lips parted. Then I remembered: Estelle.

I peeked around him, but she was dancing with two other women with her back to us. Thank goodness. She had not seen. Lukas's head swiveled to follow my gaze, his expression pained.

"I need to get some sleep, especially if we are flying to Venice tomorrow." Was that my voice? So breathless.

He leaned down and said, "Do not go yet. Or let me come home with you." I shivered at his breath against my ear. He had wrapped my hand in both of his and imprisoned it against his heart.

Heat rushed through my body. Now Estelle was turning toward us. I pulled my hand out of his grasp before she could notice. She was heading our way.

I made myself sound assured and breezy when she arrived. "No, of course not. I am not made of doll poopie. I am heading to bed and I can manage the little bicycle ride home. You two enjoy yourselves and I will see you tomorrow."

I kissed Estelle and then Lukas three times on their cheeks, breathing in Lukas's scent of sweat and ginseng, then made my way past the red-faced man, who blew me a kiss as I left.

I had only drunk one glass of white wine, yet still swayed a bit on my bicycle. I sobered quickly, though. Lukas and Estelle were probably dancing, entwined around each other, back at the bar. The weather had turned bitter and cold these past days and the night wind wrapped her empty arms around me. I passed living room windows. Something else I had not held on to: open curtains everywhere, bare of obfuscation and gray areas. There, a middle-aged couple watching a game show on television, a man ironing a pile of baby clothes while his wife worked on a laptop at the table behind him, an old woman sitting alone in her armchair, staring into the darkness. It was hard to watch Grandma worsen by the day, gasping for air, her skin turning gray, fading while still clutching at life. Was that how it ended for all of us? Everything was slipping away from me, walking out of my hands.

Rest continued to elude me most nights. I simply could not bear too much happiness, even when I was with Lukas and Estelle and Filip.

Even small amounts of light peeking through my curtains in the morning had started to irritate me. I was not used to companionship, and like a dog that had been abused as a puppy, I shied away from it. Joy was no longer something I could trust.

I locked my bike by Lukas's apartment and walked up the path to the main house. The moon hung low and full, caught within the tangled branches of the birch tree. The tree's white bark gleamed in the light. As I approached, I saw that it was pitted and scarred, peeling to reveal the wounded wood underneath. The sharp wind whipped my hair against my cheeks, merciless and blinding, and the lights inside the house had been put out like eyes.

I fumbled for my keys beneath the outside wall lamp and then stifled a scream as a low voice said, "Sylvie."

A bulky form emerged from the shadows, then a light mop of hair and I realized it was Jim. It took me a moment to switch into English. "What are you doing here?"

"Waiting for you." He reached out and trailed his hand along my cheekbone. He looked tired and disheveled, but his touch was familiar, dear to me. For a moment I leaned into his warm fingertips, until I remembered to draw back.

I still loved him and gods, it still hurt. "Why didn't you wait until I came back to New York?"

"I wasn't sure you would be coming back. A part of you always wanted to return here, didn't it?"

Despite everything, Jim did know me. What could I do with him now? I could not just send him away. I might wake up Helena and Willem if I brought him inside. Then all sorts of awkward questions would follow. Lukas was not home yet and who knew? Maybe he would not come home at all tonight. I pressed my lips together. "Come this way. My cousin lives here and we won't be disturbed."

I led him to Lukas's place, opened the door, and took him upstairs to the small living room and kitchenette.

"I like it," Jim said. "Efficiency infused with a careless insouciance."

As he wanted me to, I laughed. He seemed to me two different people: the man who had cheated on me, and my Jim, whom I still loved. Despite everything, it was good to see him again. If only we could erase the past year. I leaned back against the kitchen counter, weary all of a sudden. He took a seat on the sofa. "Where are you staying?"

"With family in the Hague."

Oh, right. Jim had an uncle who worked for the International Court of Justice there. "You shouldn't have come. I'm not ready to talk to you yet."

He looked up at me, his face filled with regret. He stood slowly, as if afraid to spook me, and came closer. Reaching out, he touched me on the elbow. Although my mind revolted, my body remembered only that this was my husband. I closed my eyes and took his hand in mine. He threaded our fingers together, as he always did. "You've been avoiding me for months. I am so sorry, Sylvie. Please give me another chance."

"It's not that simple." I stared at the tiled floor. "I wish none of it had happened."

He bent his head until we stood forehead to forehead. "I would give anything to undo what I did. I love you." He lifted my chin to kiss me.

His lips were soft and firm. I tasted salt and realized I was crying. As we drew apart, he wiped my tears with his thumbs. A wet shimmer clouded his eyes as well. "Sylvie. I was so, so wrong. It's your birthday this weekend. Let me take you away. Let's start afresh and we can have our lives back, both of us." His voice was so earnest, convincing.

Why not? To undo everything that had happened these past few months, like reverse animation in a movie. I saw all the pieces of my life fly backward and fit together to form the perfect picture it had seemed before. Back to the way it had been before I returned to the Netherlands—before Grandma, Lukas, Filip, and Estelle. I drew a shaky breath and pulled away. "I can't. I've changed. It's like there's been a shell around me and it's finally starting to crack."

He clenched his jaw and his eyes narrowed. "You've met someone."

I clutched the counter behind me, still silent.

He stepped closer, looming over me, feet planted wide. He stuck his face in front of mine. "I'm too late, aren't I? Who the hell is he?"

I lifted my chin, though my stomach clenched. "I'm going to Venice for my birthday. But not with you."

"With whom? Alone?" His voice grew deceptively soft. His eyes blazed with hurt and anger. "Tell me his name." He had looked this way that night at Princeton, when he had thought I was flirting with that guy at the party. The same animal fury, the dizzying flash of white behind my eyelids when he hit me, the reddened face and curled lip as he pushed the other guy through a window. We broke up for a few months after that, but he was so sorry, repentant, swearing over and over he would never do it again. He even went to therapy. Afterward he decided to study psychology.

Beads of sweat formed on my lip. My knees were locked and my hands trembling so hard I could barely grip the counter. This. This was why I was separated from this man. My fear washed over the tenderness he had rekindled, leaving only cold ashes behind. I set my palms on his shoulders and shoved him hard; he stumbled backward a step. "Fuck you, Jim. You have no rights to me anymore."

Half-crouched, he looked like a predator ready to pounce. His voice was hoarse with fury. "You're still my wife. If that bastard touches you, I'll—"

"What?" I said coldly. "Hit him the way you did me?" I had been stunned when he struck me the second time, during our initial screaming match about his affair, worrying about the neighbors hearing, not smart enough to be afraid of him, on the floor, sobbing, as he stormed out. By the time he returned, I had already changed the locks and thrown all his stuff out on the curb. That was the last time we had spoken to each other, though he had sent a steady stream of apologetic emails and flowers.

As if in slow motion, Jim's face crumpled. He straightened and reached his arms out to me, imploring. "I'm so sorry, Sylvie. I was afraid and I lost my temper. I don't deserve you. I've done everything wrong." He tore at his hair with his hands, his voice frantic. "I'm always pretending to be a nice guy, but in the end, I'm a selfish asshole. You're the best thing that's ever come into my life. Please don't throw it away."

"Like you did when you had an affair with a sixteen-year-old student?" I had been trying to forget, but there, I had said it. It was true.

There were not two Jims. How I wished there were. My voice was crisp, crackling with unshed tears. "I wonder if you truly regret the things you did, or if you're sorry our marriage is over, or if you're just scared shitless about what will happen if this gets out and the holy Bates name is tainted."

His arms dropped to his sides. His voice was a whisper. "Sylvie, don't do this. My mom and dad . . . it would ruin our reputation."

Still only thinking about himself. What a selfish bastard I had married. "And what about that poor girl?"

He snorted. "She wanted it. She's been after me all year, wearing low-cut shirts and miniskirts and hanging around my office. It was completely consensual. If you could see her, she looks like a full-grown woman."

The blood pounded in my ears. "You disgust me." My vision blurred. I bit down on the inside of my cheek so hard I could taste the blood. This man could see a splinter in someone else's eye but missed the wooden beam in his own. "You were the adult in this situation. She trusted you and you abused her trust."

He laughed, bitter. "She's a slut."

I slapped him in the face, hard. His head snapped around, blind fury in his eyes, and he grabbed me by the shoulders so hard I knew I would bruise.

I almost cried out from the pain and my toes were nearly lifted off the floor. I hissed, low and fierce, "We're never going to agree about this, so let's talk legal terms. Under the age of seventeen in the state of New York, a minor cannot give sexual consent in the eyes of the law. Whether or not she consented is completely irrelevant. You are guilty of statutory rape, a Class E felony which is punishable by up to four years in prison and a five-thousand-dollar fine. Yes, I looked this up. You have a hell of a lot more to worry about than your precious Bates name. Now hit me again if you dare."

He released me so abruptly I staggered and almost fell. I caught myself with one hand on the countertop. He held his hands up in the air. Innocent Jim. "She won't tell anyone. It's completely over now. No one else knows."

"Except me."

He pressed his palms together, beseeching me, blond hair glinting in the overhead light, dark blue eyes limpid and sorrowful—a beautiful praying angel. He spoke softly. "Sylvie, please don't do this. I made a terrible, stupid mistake. I've learned my lesson. We don't need to get a divorce. Everything will be like it was."

I swallowed hard. The words fell out like stones. "The thing is, Jim, you didn't just rob her of her innocence, you took mine as well. I loved you more than anyone. I let you into my heart and I trusted you." A dry sob escaped me.

"I was so wrong, sweetheart. I know you feel angry and betrayed. I was just lonely. She meant nothing to me. I'll spend the rest of my life making this up to you." His voice rang with sincerity.

He was such a manipulative jerk, even if I could hear a glimmer of truth in his words. That only made it hurt more. Our failure was my fault too. He took a step toward me. I held up a hand. Enough was enough. "Stop. Don't try those counselor tricks on me. They don't work anymore. Even if I could forgive you, I can never be sure that you won't do it again, to some other innocent student."

He scrutinized me until the resolution in my face seemed to convince him, and, like a mask, the pleading lover fell away—and the hurt too. How many times would I allow this man to put a blade through my heart? How had I never seen the chameleon before?

Now he was calm and businesslike, a negotiator in a contract arbitration. "Look, if you have to divorce me, leave this whole thing out of it and we'll get rid of the prenup, okay? All your bills, Amy's student loans, your parents. You'd never have to worry about money again. But don't destroy my life for no reason."

And just like that, he accepted the end of our marriage. I scoffed at this, irrationally hurt. "Great, you're trying to buy me. No reason? You still don't believe that what you did was wrong. And that's exactly why the truth has to come out, Jim. I'm sorry."

He took a step toward me, and then another, his muscles and veins straining against his skin. His breath was quick, the whites of his eyes prominent, his fists raised. I backed away, truly afraid for the first time.

His control had snapped. The last time he struck me, my head had whipped back from the force of the blow. He towered over me now, his face mottled with rage. I cowered. Footsteps. A blur of black. A loud crack, then Jim thudded against the floor.

Lukas stood over Jim's sprawled form, heaving, his huge hands clenching. "Get the hell away from her."

Jim stared at Lukas, then at me. He slowly raised a hand to the blood flowing from a cut on his cheek. He shook his head in disbelief. "So this is him." He gave me a long, pained look, filled with hurt, betrayal, and fury. Jim staggered to his feet and glared at me. "This conversation isn't over, Sylvie." He shoved past Lukas and stalked out of the house.

I sank down on the floor, suddenly weak. "How much did you hear?"

Lukas came over and knelt beside me, his voice gentle. "Very little. Something about bills and money. I came upstairs to find him threatening you. Are you all right?"

I held out my arms to him like a small child. "No." Then I was crying big heaving sobs as he held me. I felt safer in his arms. I had made such a mess of everything. My marriage was truly over. What would I do now? *Oh Jim, how did we come to this?* Lukas smoothed my hair and patted my back, murmuring indistinct sounds of comfort.

As I calmed, he handed me a box of tissues but kept one arm around me. He stayed on the floor next to me, leaning back against the kitchen counter. I blew my nose and took a deep breath. I rested my cheek against his shoulder.

"Husband?" he said.

I tried to speak, had to clear my throat. My voice was hoarse. "Soon to be ex-husband."

He nodded. "Do you want to talk about it?"

I shook my head and then chuckled, giddy after all the emotion of the evening. "Do you know when my happiest moment was?"

"Changing the subject?" There was a smile in his voice.

"I had had the worst day. It was soon after I had moved to the U.S. and I hardly spoke any English. I missed you and Estelle and Grandma. All of the kids there teased or ignored me and that day, one of the girls had pinched me so hard it left a purple bruise on my hand. The worst was, the teacher yelled at me for fighting, not her. I went home, trying so hard not to cry, and Amy jumped into my arms and everything was all right. She felt so warm and happy and alive. I knew she would always love me, no matter what. She saved me then. Like you just did."

He rested his cheek against my temple. "Are you not going to tell me what happened?"

I sighed and closed my eyes. "Not now. All I want to do these days is forget."

I lay in the dark, comforted by the knowledge that Lukas was in his apartment next door. I wanted to stay with him, but my heart was a desert landscape filled with mirages and quicksand, nothing in it trustworthy, and I loved him too much to lure him into a hallucination with me. As was my habit when I was stressed, I rubbed at the birthmark behind my ear. It was barely visible—a distinctive spiraled circle with a bit of a tail. Amy said it reminded her of a snail. Ma had always draped my hair over it when I was a child to hide it, and so I had developed a slight awkwardness about it. The sleeping pills were not working tonight. The life I had so carefully knitted together with Jim was falling apart. I was not truly surprised. In a way, I had been waiting for this unraveling my whole life. Deep down, I had known true love was not for me.

I had loved Jim with all of me that was innocent, the part that still believed in a fairy-tale ending for the immigrant Chinese girl. I was starved for affection and he, my chance at redemption, had been generous with it. I loved the way he was so unabashedly himself. It was not until much later that I realized what I thought was confidence was actually a form of selfishness, a refusal to believe that not everything in the world revolved around him.

I was an impoverished, awkward girl who got into Princeton on good grades, unlike another girl I knew whose father had enclosed a check for half a million dollars with her application fee. She could fish with a golden hook. We were so poor, they had even waived my fee—always the scholarship student, the brain of the class, the girl in the ill-fitting clothes. But those who wish to eat honey must suffer the sting of the bees. Methodically, I had fixed every flaw I could find in myself. In high school, I skipped lunch so I could save for a few good pieces of clothing. In college, I worked several jobs at a time so I could have my crooked tooth pulled and replaced with a fake one, too vain and impatient to wait for braces.

The other kids respected me because they had no choice. I made sure I was at the top in every class, but no one liked me. Unlike Amy, who had brought her little girlfriends home regularly. I allowed myself no vulnerabilities. I told myself I did not need friendships. When you were different, who knew if it was because of a lack of social graces or the language barrier or your skin color? I read etiquette books and studied designer brands as intently as my statistics textbooks. But I never mastered the art of the graceful shrug, the careless indifference of those who summered on private islands and tied clove hitches on sailboats. I was the recipient of critical stares, the kind that were the defining characteristic of those born into certain classes. I learned that there were people who knew of no other existence than their own, a path cushioned by wealth and breeding from birth onward.

Intellectually, some of the kids in college were far beyond me—as far as the stars were from the frog at the bottom of a well, as Ma would say. My freshman-year roommate, Valerie, had debated the importance of Immanuel Kant and John Stuart Mill with her Yale professor parents. I had never heard of either. That was partly why I chose the solid fields of mathematics and the sciences. I did not have to overcome a mountain of books or a vast cultural past that I had neither read nor heard of. With some talent and a lot of hard work, I felt I had a chance. Although Valerie and I never fought, we did not become friends either, and after freshman year, she chose to room with a group of other girls who smoked and wore heavy black eyeliner.

Guys only liked me for the outside. I understood that I ticked the *young*, *pretty*, and *bright* boxes, but so did many other girls. I did not want to be replaceable and, truth was, I was too much of a nerd inside to differentiate when a man had an abstract or personal interest in me.

In the dining hall, I once had a long, interesting conversation with a guy about our mutual class on the Cultural Revolution in China, and then was caught unprepared when he asked me out. I lied and said I already had a boyfriend. He never spoke to me again. Clearly, I had not been that fascinating after all.

But then I met warm, affectionate Jim. I had thought he was like me, a poor kid who made his way on his own. How thirsty I was for his attention and touch. Other boys had liked me but I never felt as if we spoke the same language. We were always, as Grandma would say, a chicken talking to a duck. But with Jim, everything was different.

Then he brought me home for Christmas and I was stunned by the mansion his parents called home. Much later, I recognized that our relationship had been defined by duplicity and silence from the start.

"You never told me," I had said, feeling awed and betrayed. My boyfriend was a member of the groups that disdained me.

"I've always felt guilty and stupid about it," he said, "being so privileged."

His parents, both products of centuries of breeding and expectations, were wannabe hippies yet still spoke only French in front of Jim whenever they discussed "vulgar" subjects like money. They were unfailingly polite and refined, too intelligent to be overtly racist, too well-bred to show any sort of derision for the poor relation that I was. But there was never to be any shouting, no inappropriate feelings. The worst crime was to be unrefined or to serve the wrong person first at a dinner party. They had bred into Jim's bones all the rules I had studied so theoretically in my etiquette books. I understood they were disappointed that Jim had not gone to Harvard like his father, but found Princeton acceptable. I wondered how an exuberant little boy had felt growing up in such a controlled environment.

We had sex for the first time in their indoor swimming pool while his parents were at a dinner party. We reclined in the shallow, warm water, surrounded by hothouse ferns and blooming plants like a jungle. The glass walls overlooked the windswept lake where the waves crashed against their boathouse. Jim's hands pulled down my bikini bottom, then his hands fisted in my hair, his lips tender against the hollow between my breasts. I gasped, my legs wrapped around his waist, his groan soft as he buried himself inside me.

Their wedding gift was the one time Jim's parents had relaxed their discipline of austerity with their only son. They had thrown us a lavish wedding and crowned it with the gift of the apartment in Brooklyn Heights.

Those days, we were both so busy. I came home exhausted and bleary-eyed. We hardly made love anymore. But we still loved each other, or so I thought. Despite the men who came on to me at the management consultancy firm, I had always looked forward to going home to Jim and our life together.

It was almost like playing with dolls, pretending to own a life I had dreamed of. I did not have a child-wish like the other women I knew, but soon, I thought, we would have kids and we would never have to send them away to be raised by someone else. I would be a fresh Sylvie, a beloved Sylvie. I brought Amy into our lives as much as I could. She never wanted to stay overnight when Jim was home for fear we were having sex or some such. I wanted to give her an oasis of peace, for her to lay down that burden of guilt she always carried. It was not fair that she had that stutter when she was little, or that she was so often in my shadow.

I was ruthless enough to climb to the top no matter what. In my work, I was sometimes responsible for the firing of hundreds of people. If it was better for my client, I did it without a pang. The older man who had come to plead with me once, "Please, I'm almost eligible for retirement"—I had asked security to escort him out.

When Amy was younger, she went through a phase of asking me questions: *If you could have a mountain of doughnuts or a mountain of gold, which would you choose?* The gold. *If you had to bathe in blood or poop, which would you choose?* Gross, Amy, I'm not answering that. *If you had the answers to a test, would you share them with your best friend?* No. Amy stared at me. *Not even your very best friend?* No. But I'd share them with you.

One weekend, after I was married, Jim was away for a conference and I invited her over. Amy was an excellent cook, her dumplings tender and soft, her soy sauce chicken fragrant, her red bean ice drinks creamy and sweet, but since Ma had never used our oven, Amy had never learned to bake. I decided we would make brownies from a mix.

"No, it can't be that hard to make them from scratch," Amy protested, ever the cooking princess. "What could go wrong?"

I gave her a hard stare. "I'm involved."

She sighed. "You're right. We'd better not risk it."

An hour later, we both had our elbows propped on my cook-island, a box of brownie mix and all-new baking tins and equipment spread around us that I had bought for this venture.

Amy expertly stirred in the water and eggs. "I shouldn't do this. I'm going to get fat."

I eyed her lustrous hair, the tanned glow of her skin, her bright eyes. "Ridiculous. You're beautiful. You have to step into yourself, grow into the woman you are meant to be."

She blew a lock of hair out of her face. Her forearm had a big smudge of flour on it. "I don't know. It's been pretty long and I still don't feel like a woman."

"Come on, let's finish this and I'll do your makeup and hair." I always felt clumsy and useless in the kitchen, probably because I never paid attention when I was there. At least I could do her face.

But of course, Amy resisted my attempts to play fairy godmother to her Cinderella. "Stop it, Sylvie. I'm not a doll. And I don't want any fashion advice either, my clothes are fine. But can I ask you something?"

I beamed. I loved giving advice.

She poured the brownie mix into a square tin. "Why did you choose Jim? I mean, there were always boys calling the house. It drove Pa crazy."

I stuck a finger in the mix for a taste. Amy slapped my hand away. With my pinkie still in my mouth, I thought back. "Oh, they just wanted help with their schoolwork. And none of them had any idea who I really was. The thing I noticed about Jim on our first date was that he was such a good listener. He wasn't looking around. He was only paying attention to me. He asked questions."

"Like what?" Amy pulled on the oven mitts and slid the brownie tray into the oven, which she had somehow remembered to preheat.

I watched her wash her hands. I started filling the dishwasher with the dirty dishes. I found the wooden stirring spoon she had used, still covered with batter, and licked it thoughtfully. "You know, 'What was that like for you? Why do you think that happened?' I felt like he really saw me for who I was, not just the surface of me but all of me."

Amy took the spoon and tossed it in the sink. "Stop that. You can get salmonella." She pushed up her glasses with her middle finger. "Well, he may be good at listening, but he's not that adept at remembering. He's had the same conversation with me three times. He asks me exactly the same questions each time and reacts with the same amount of surprise at just the right moment too. And he talks on and on, like one big monologue."

My face grew tight and I jerked back, surprised and angry. "What do you know? With those loser boys you fall in love with, sneaking around Ma and Pa as if they didn't already suspect."

She flinched, her mouth falling open. The moment I saw the hurt flash in her eyes, I was sorry. That was me, lip service to how great Amy was one moment and putting her down the next. No wonder she had such low self-esteem. When she was little, Amy had once run up to a girl who called me *Chinkerbell* on the street and kicked her hard in the shins.

But now, of course, I realized she was right about Jim. I had been blind. He had seemed warm and kind but he did it to be admired and loved, not out of any true generosity of the soul. He was not that observant either. More than once, we had fought because he was much more social than I was. Like a golden retriever, he loved everyone, or at least wanted them to admire him, whereas I did not have much use for most people. I networked when I had to but never wanted to waste my own time listening to others trying to impress me—and most thought I was cold and stiff anyway.

How could two people move so far away from each other without ever sensing it? How could they lose each other while seeing each other every day?

It started when I found the leopard-print thong mixed in our laundry. *It has to be a mistake,* I thought. Was it mine somehow? Or Amy's? Was Jim secretly a cross-dresser? But the part of me that had always relied on no one but myself took over. I hid the thong from him. I controlled the part of me that wanted to confront him immediately because I knew that if I did, I would never have proof.

I started making mistakes at work. I could keep only so much of myself under control—sloppy errors, forgotten emails, unprepared-for important presentations, incomplete financial records. When my engagement manager, Martin, asked if something was going on at home, I lied and said no. I could not admit the truth to anyone because I could barely face it myself.

I did not find anything on Jim's electronics, so I finally added spy programs to his laptop and his phone to log every keystroke. I watched him with the hundred eyes of Argos. I was the technical one in our relationship and had set up all our gadgets. I had given myself access so I could recover our information if Jim ever inadvertently locked himself out, which he had done before. Meanwhile, I smiled at him as if my heart were not breaking inside.

It did not take long. A colleague on the verge of a divorce had once said to me: *If a man takes his phone with him into the bathroom or to shower at night, watch out*. But when Jim had started doing those things, I had rationalized them away. I had been completely taken in.

The text messages came in as I was preparing to leave for a late morning meeting. First from her: *Got my phone back today. Thinking of licking u, this math class's so boring*. Then his response: *You make me lose my mind*. The cold rose from the floor to meet me, as if I were falling. First the betrayal, that my Jim could do this to me, and then the slow realization that the other "woman" was a child of sixteen. I had sunk to our unrelenting living room floor, my entire life disintegrating around me, all the pieces flying away like leaves from a tree.

In love and life, we never know when we are telling ourselves stories. We are the ultimate unreliable narrators. If we desire to forgive someone, we tell ourselves one version—he did not mean it, he is sorry and will never do it again. And when we are finally ready to walk away, something else—he has always been a lying bastard, I never should have trusted him and you could always see the lie in his eyes. That day, I called in sick to work and read their texts to each other, each one dropping like a brick against the wounded flesh of my heart. I waited for Jim to come home. He was late. He stopped short when he saw me sitting at the table with my computer open, my head leaning back against the wall of our kitchen. I turned the screen to show him the record of his text messages.

I did not need to say a word. His face froze and slowly flushed a deep red. Then all of my composure left me and I started to keen like an animal: Sylvie, who hated to cry. He came over and held me in his arms and I let him. He, the man I had allowed into the most intimate, hidden part of myself, still felt comforting.

I kept saying, "You cheated on me, you cheated on me," as if to convince myself.

"Oh my God, Sylvie, what have I done? I am so sorry. It's over, honey. I'll never see her again."

For a few minutes, we formed a truce in which we held each other. Until the memory of what I had seen that day crawled into my mind. *I'm counting the hours until we can be together again. Nothing else matters when I'm with you.*

I pulled away, still heaving as I spoke. "I can't believe you did this."

He pinched the bridge of his nose, closed his eyes, and sighed. "Please believe me. I don't love her. You were always gone and she was there, and I missed you so. She was just a stand-in for you, for the way things were with us."

But instead of mollifying me, this only enraged me further. I jabbed my finger in his face, my voice rising. "A sixteen-year-old girl could take my place? I looked her up. She's a student at your school, Jim. She's half your age. What the hell are you doing?"

He froze, and then gripped the sides of his head as if he could block out my words. He groaned. "What a goddamn mess. There's no excuse. I know. It's just you're always so competent, so brilliant at everything. You don't really need me."

I pounded my fist against my thigh. "And this child did. You can't handle a successful woman, so you had to find a girl who thinks you're really something. Fuck you."

His jaw hardened and a cold, hard glint flashed in his eyes. "Sylvie, don't do anything rash. I could lose my job."

He dared to warn me? "Shouldn't you have thought of that before you decided to have an affair with a minor?" I was almost yelling. The neighbors must be having a fit. I pressed my nails into my skin so hard I was afraid I would start bleeding. He should suffer as much as me. "Don't underestimate me, Jim. I'll see you pay for this."

"You vindictive bitch," he said, and slapped me across the face so hard my head slammed against the wall. I fell onto the floor, stunned by the blow, my vision unfocused. It was all too much. How had this happened? How could this be real? I curled in on myself, sobbing.

There was a slam and he was gone.

CHAPTER 20

Amy

Sunday, May 8

It's Mother's Day morning and Lukas's real grandma and grandpa are coming to visit. Lukas calls his grandmother *Oma* and his grandfather *Opa* in the Dutch way, so I do the same, in accordance with the Chinese tradition of following along in naming family. Oma is tiny and round with a fritz of hair she dyes jet-black. Opa is only a bit taller, but skinnier and white-haired. They remind me of a set of matching garden gnomes.

When they enter the house, I stand and wait to greet them as is proper, but then none of us know which traditions to use. Oma closes her eyes and purses her lips to kiss me three times at the same time I open my arms for a hug. I drop my arms to my sides and extend my hand while Opa places his palms together and bows to me. We all shift on our feet, and Oma says something to me in Chinese. Her accent is really weird. When I look at her blankly, Opa chirps in Dutch.

Finally, Oma gives me a weak little wave of her hand and says, "Hello."

I follow them into the living room. Willem pats me on the shoulder and winks. I wish he would stop touching me at every opportunity. I am dismayed to find that all of the chairs have been arranged in one large circle. I am forced to sit between Willem and Lukas on the couch. We all face each other, every expression, gesture, and word laid bare to everyone else in the group. If this is what Dutch parties are like, how in the world do they manage to flirt here?

Silence again. I clear my throat and say to Willem, "Are your parents coming too?"

Helena enters the room with the coffee and tea and says, "They died in China. Long ago."

Oh. We sit in silence as Helena passes around a plate of *boterspritsen*, swirled buttery shortbread cookies that melt in your mouth. I missed breakfast, since the family ate extra early today, so I take two, even though I notice Opa watching me. When the plate gets to Oma at the end, it is empty.

I cringe in my seat.

Oma waves her pudgy hands like she didn't want a cookie anyway, but Helena, careful not to look at me, goes to the kitchen and returns with a single *botersprits* on the plate, which she then gives to Oma. Opa waggles his eyebrows at me.

"I didn't know we were only supposed to take one each," I whisper to Lukas. I try to ignore Willem, who sits close to me, his legs pressed against my thigh and knee. He has swiveled his head to stare at me.

Lukas snickers. "Welcome in Holland. People count the number of cookies here."

Willem taps me on the back of my hand and says, "Did you do something with your hair, Amy? You seem different today."

I try not to move away too abruptly. "No. It's just that I'm wearing my contact lenses."

Willem throws his head back and laughs as if I've made a great joke. "Ah, that is it. You look very much like . . ."

"Sylvie," Helena finishes for him when his voice trails off. The lines around her lips and eyes tighten. She bares her teeth in a way that is more a gesture of aggression than a smile. "How are you enjoying Holland so far?"

"Very much. But why do your parents live in Belgium?" She had told me they drove in this morning. Is it safe to have Opa behind the wheel of a car?

"I grew up in this village, but when Willem and I married, we took over my parents' restaurant in Amsterdam. They had a business opportunity in Antwerp, so they moved away. They have a number of restaurants there now." So that's why Helena had to hijack our grandma to care for Lukas and Sylvie instead of asking her own parents to help.

Oma leans forward and says to me, "How you sister?"

My stomach churns and I feel my insides quiver. I wring my hands. "We don't know. No one has heard from her."

Lukas translates for me while Oma clucks sadly, shaking her head. He rubs his hand over his face and massages his eyes, as if he's as worried as I am.

I'd been hoping to bring this up later, after Oma and Opa left, but I can't wait any longer. We have to take action before it's too late. I turn to Helena. "Actually, I've been considering something. I heard about an organization that searches for missing people."

Helena's head jerks back and she gives me an incredulous look. "What is this?"

I continue anyway. They have to agree. We have no other choice. "They have a very impressive website, in both Dutch and English. I could show you."

She taps her lipstick-reddened lips with a finger. Her voice is high. "And who will pay for it?"

Is that all she cares about? They're rich and Sylvie was practically their daughter. What does money matter at a time like this? I'm fuming and cross my arms as I stare at the two uneaten cookies on my tea saucer. "I don't know yet. We'll figure it out, but the most important thing is that Sylvie might need our help."

"She is fine." Lukas's eyes are feverish and overbright. His gaze darts around the room. "She has to be fine."

"I thought you were on my side," I snap. I thrust my arms out wide. I hate them all. "Don't you want to find her?"

"No one wants to find Sylvie more than I do!" Lukas yells. He dares to jab a finger in my face. Oma and Opa can't understand a word and appear alarmed. "Where the hell do you think I go every night?"

I slap his hand away. I'm shouting as well now. "What? You're looking for her by yourself? That's fine, but why can't we bring in professionals too? Why are you all resisting me on this?"

"Calm down." Willem tries to put his arm around both me and Lukas.

I jump up off the couch, upsetting the saucer on my lap. My cookies fall onto the floor and break, leaving crumbs everywhere. "Oh, I'm sorry." I am almost in tears. I fall to my knees to clean up the mess.

"Stop, I will do it." Helena grabs me by the arm and pulls me upright. She settles me back on the couch and quickly removes the saucer and cookies. She speaks slowly and clearly, as if I am an imbecile. "This organization is not necessary. It is a waste of money. She will turn up. You mark my words."

I need to remain calm; alienating them won't help. "I know you want to believe that, but what if it's not true?" All of my despair sinks into the pit of my stomach. I've been trying Sylvie's email and phone nonstop and there's been no response. It's been too long. My hope is deflating like an old balloon. The possibilities for a happy ending are dwindling.

Lukas, stiff, uptight prick that he is, says, "We should not involve extra people. We will get in the way of the police. I have heard of these types of organizations and I do not trust them. They specialize in finding people who are—" He swallows his words suddenly and hugs his chest, rocking on the couch. There is such a look of despair and anguish in his eyes that I almost feel sorry for him.

Willem says in his smooth voice, "I do not think we should interfere either. The police know their job. We should let them do it."

Opa, who has probably only understood the word *police*, says, "We want no trouble."

And everyone takes this as the final word on the subject. I sit on the couch and try not to scream. This is just like dealing with Ma and Pa:

everyone afraid of any tiny change. Why are they all so scared? I can't get rid of the nagging feeling that there are things no one is telling me about Sylvie's visit. But she still hasn't come home and if I don't do anything, it's possible that she never will.

It's now Monday morning. The neighbors have heard rumors of Sylvie's disappearance, and yesterday evening, after Oma and Opa's strained visit, Helena found a casserole and a bouquet of tulips by the front door. Only a few of the people in our building in New York even know who Sylvie is. I am grateful for this kindness.

"That is the thing about a small village," Helena said. "We are all dependent on each other."

Willem and Helena had taken the weekend off for Mother's Day and plan to go to their restaurant today. "If the workers don't see the bosses regularly," Helena says, "they get up to no good." They start their car to leave, and I notice the next-door neighbor, a tall, stooped older gentleman, waving for them to stop at the end of the driveway. Willem rolls down his window, and the man says something and then clasps him on the shoulder before Helena and Willem drive off. The neighbor catches sight of me watching from the window and gives me a friendly nod before returning to his house.

There's no sign of Lukas. I go into the kitchen and light some incense at the altar for Grandma and the gods. As I bow to the photo of Grandma, I see Ma in the shape of her face, this woman I never knew. *Grandma, please keep Sylvie safe*. I called Ma yesterday to update her and to wish her a happy Mother's Day. She sounded so frail and sad, with both her daughters far away. After I change the water in the little vase of flowers in front of the altar, I phone the police again.

Danique sounds surprised to hear from me, but she is warm and polite. There have been no further developments. Yes, they are checking all possibilities and if they find anything, they will certainly contact us right away. Have a nice day, goodbye.

My hands are shaking when I disconnect the line. Then I take out the card Filip gave me and call Epsilon.

The connection is bad but I reach the Karin that Filip had mentioned and she sounds smart and competent. I explain the situation with Sylvie, and she says, "I will come to your house and we can talk further. Is tomorrow all right?"

A wave of relief floods through me. At last, someone willing to take action. "Can you tell me what your fees are?" I hold my breath, waiting for an answer. I have never wanted anything as much as I want this woman to come and help me. I would pay anything, somehow.

Her soft voice fades in and out as she says, "We are [*static*]—not need to worry."

I decide to leave it at that for now.

The next day, after Helena and Willem leave, I wait anxiously for Karin to arrive and text Filip again to thank him—in case he missed my earlier texts. He still hasn't responded. I'm sure his schedule is busy and he forgets to check his phone. I am pleased to see Lukas roar off on his Vespa as well. He's carrying his camera bag. I hope this means he will be away for much of the day. I shouldn't be sneaking around their house like this when I'm a guest. But Sylvie's more important. *Please let this woman not be a fraud.*

Karin pulls up a few minutes early in a black minivan with a pet barrier and two large dogs inside. She strides toward me and shakes my hand with a firm grip. She's probably in her midforties, with short tawny hair and stocky, muscular legs. She is dressed like a hiker in heavy-duty climbing pants and solid boots. "Can I bring the dogs inside?"

Her eyes are direct, her grip firm. She seems solid and dependable. Maybe this will work out after all. I relax a little. "We have a cat. Would that be a problem?"

"Oh no, they are very well-behaved." She clicks leashes onto the dogs, one brown and one black, and leads them inside. Despite their tails, which are waving furiously, the dogs are calm. I hear a hiss from the staircase and see a flash of orange as Couscous bolts upstairs.

The dogs sit quietly at Karin's feet. I make coffee while we chat a bit. She's warming me up before we get to the real deal. I learn that the smaller black dog is named Feyenoord and the brown one Ajax, after two rival Dutch soccer teams.

I take the coffee to the dining room table. After she sits, I pour us each a cup and then start to pace in front of her. I should sit to be polite, but there's too much adrenaline coursing through me. The dogs perk up at the motion and follow me with their heads, wagging their tails. This could be it. This could be our breakthrough. Or it could be yet another big disappointment. "So can you tell me a bit more about how you work?"

Karin leans back in her chair and gestures with her left hand. "We are mainly a volunteer organization. It depends on the case, but mostly we use our dogs, which have been specially trained. In addition we also employ sonar, underwater cameras, GPS, ground radar, metal detectors, and magnetometers. If we need to search in the water, we have our own specialized diving team. The dogs can greatly reduce the possible area and then our divers, for example, can do a more specialized search."

Yes! This is exactly what I'd been hoping for. I start bouncing from foot to foot. Ajax gives a little bark, wagging his tail, but quiets after Karin shushes him. "That's wonderful! You'll be able to follow Sylvie's trail and bring her back from wherever she's gone." I am beaming.

Karin's face turns severe. "We will do our best. Do you know why we are named Epsilon?"

I shake my head. Why does she look so serious all of a sudden?

Her brown eyes pierce straight through to my heart. She says gently, "Because while we approach the limit of what the human soul can bear, we always attempt to remain a small positive force. Sometimes, Amy, we are the takers of the last hope. Do you understand me? We cannot take on a case unless the family accepts this possibility."

I draw in a shuddering breath. She thinks Sylvie might be dead. It's not true. I know it's not but I need to play along so she'll help me. In a small voice, I say, "I understand."

Then she asks me a number of questions about Sylvie, and takes down the license plate of her rental car, which the family also gave to the police. "Can you tell me about her daily habits? Does she have a job here? Any hobbies?"

"Sylvie mainly came to see our grandmother before she passed away."

"So Sylvie did not leave the house much?"

I scratch my head, trying to remember. "I don't really know because I wasn't here. I was told that she was taking some kind of music lessons. Bass or cello or something, I think. But I don't know where."

Karin purses her lips. "That could be important. I would like to know where the lessons were and the route she took to get there. Also if you could find out if there were any spots she liked to visit in particular."

"All right, I'll ask." I worry my lip with my teeth. "What about your fees?"

Karin waves a square hand. "Oh, that is not a problem."

I know it is unwise, but I let it go. I want her help too much. I cannot bear anything else on my shoulders right now.

She wants to walk the property with her dogs. I follow along as the dogs sniff all of the bushes and trees. It is a cloudless day and the air smells like spring.

We pause underneath one of the trees in the front yard. The dappled light plays over our faces, first light, then dark.

Karin asks, "Is there anything else about Sylvie that might be useful? Places or people she likes? Things she is afraid of?"

I lean back against the rough bark of the trunk and fiddle with my hair, trying to think. "She can't swim. There was a prophecy that Sylvie would die by water and so she's supposed to avoid it. When a baby is born, Chinese parents sometimes ask a feng shui master, a kind of mystical specialist, to write their destiny. It's just superstition."

"We should search the water, to be sure."

I tip my head to the side, giving her a sidelong glance. She doesn't seem to be the mystical type. "Why? Do you buy into that stuff?"

She stares into the distance. "It does not matter if I believe. What matters is if Sylvie believes."

After this, Karin bids me goodbye and tells me they will begin combing the area immediately but that their most intensive search will start the following weekend. *Please let Sylvie be back before then.*

As she pulls out of the driveway, I realize she didn't ask for an item of Sylvie's clothing or anything else with a scent on it. I am about to run after the car and call her back when understanding strikes like a blow to my chest.

Karin is not looking for Sylvie. She is searching for her body.

CHAPTER 21

Sylvie

Friday, April 22

Lukas and I were packed and about to leave for the airport. But when I went to Grandma's room to say goodbye, it seemed like she was hardly breathing. She had shrunk so deeply into her bed that the shape of her body was barely visible beneath the sheets, as if she were already starting to leave us. I could feel death in the room, like a presence waiting behind the heavy curtains to claim her fully. Isa hovered over Grandma, a strained look on her usually cheerful face, fussing with the oxygen tank.

"Maybe we shouldn't—" My eyelids felt hot and gummy. How could I leave Grandma like this? My time with her was precious. Every bite I fed her, every song I sang to her, I feared would be the last.

She opened her mouth but no words came out. She started to cough, a delicate skull fighting for air. I helped her sit upright. She held on to my arm and pulled my ear toward her lips. "Go."

With a barely discernible gesture, she pointed toward Tasha, who sat on the bedside table with her serene smile, and then to the Kuan Yin in the corner altar. "I am in the hands of the goddess."

Lukas bent over the two of us, his forehead furrowed. "We could still cancel. It would be no problem."

"It is your birthday weekend," Grandma said. After all these years, she had remembered. "I did not call you back here to watch me die. I would never wish that burden on the ones I love most. I only wanted to see you live. Go. For me."

I took her frail body in my arms and murmured into her wispy hair, "I love you. We will be back in a few days."

She nodded and made an impatient gesture with her hand for us to leave. When Lukas bent down to say goodbye, she caught his shirt. "Take care of her."

He hugged her and said, "I will."

Her next words were a whisper of air. "Open your hearts, be happy."

At our meeting point at Schiphol Airport, I spotted Estelle from a distance. She wore an exotic linen dress that accentuated her defined collarbones underneath a fringe-trimmed opera stole in rich beige, the same color as her golden skin. She grabbed me first, kissing me fully on the lips, practically sticking her tongue down my throat. That was Estelle. "I always wanted to do that, you gorgeous thing."

Laughing, I pushed her away. "Where did you get that dress? It's lovely."

"I have a tailor in Bombay who designs them for me. I go to him whenever I fly there. I will get one for you next time." Then she turned to Lukas. "And now you." She kissed him thoroughly as well until a masculine hand landed on Lukas's hair and pulled him away from her.

"I have had enough of that," Filip said, eyes bright, fingers still tangled in Lukas's black locks, looking fine in his straight-legged dark jeans, tailored black jacket, and a navy slim-fit button-down shirt decorated with a tiny diamond pattern. Seeing the two of them together almost stopped my breath. He gave Lukas an affectionate swat on the back of his head.

"You saved me," Lukas said, pretending to wipe sweat from his brow.

"Yeah, right. You look as proud as an ape with seven dicks," Filip said. "And what the hell are you wearing? Could you not find something a bit nicer?"

"What?" Baffled, Lukas looked down at his battered leather jacket and faded jeans above the solid low hiking boots he always wore. I hid a smile.

"It might be a good idea to pack a little more in there," Filip said, gesturing at the small canvas backpack Lukas had slung over his shoulder that somehow held all his clothing and toiletries. "And a bit less of that." Filip pointed to the giant black camera bag filled with lenses and equipment Lukas took everywhere.

"I brought clean underwear," muttered Lukas.

"Come on, you delicious thing," Estelle said, linking her arm through Lukas's. "We had better go through security." She paused to let a flock of Asian tourists pass. At the end came an elderly woman in a wheelchair, pushed by a young, attractive woman, probably her granddaughter.

"Wait." I stood there, frozen amid the bustle of the crowd. "I cannot stop thinking about Grandma. Maybe I should stay."

They all stopped. Filip reached out and rubbed a piece of my hair between his fingers. "It is your decision, belle Sylvie, but I think your grandma would want you to enjoy your birthday."

I cast my eyes over my little group of friends—surprised they looked concerned for me—and covered his hand with mine. "You have it right. And I have never been to Venice before."

I dozed on the airplane against Filip's shoulder. He woke me as we were about to land at Marco Polo Airport. Were Estelle and Lukas snuggling in the seats behind us too? I craned my neck to look out the window. I saw large islands set in a turquoise sea, and a wide water highway set off by long wooden pilings, where boats and water taxis sped in two directions. I was in an alternate reality.

We grabbed our luggage after we disembarked. Outside the terminal, even the air smelled different, like seaweed and cut grass. Here, I would forget about Jim. Here, I would become a new Sylvie, happy and free with her friends. We walked to the dock, where we debated the ferry or a more expensive water taxi. In the end, since there were four of us, we decided to splurge on the taxi.

Our driver, a cute Italian guy wearing a tight T-shirt and sunglasses, cast longing glances at Estelle the entire trip to our hotel. She laughed and waved at the boats that passed while her hair tossed in the wind. On the same water highway I had seen from the air, we sped past the Alilaguna water bus. It was jammed with tourists pressed against windows, clicking pictures. Lukas came and stood beside me, his shoulder solid against mine. We watched Italian teenagers cruise by in speedboats, and wealthy older couples enjoying their rides in luxurious yachts.

By the time we passed the island of Murano and then curved around the coast of Castello, the sun hung above the horizon like a molten gold medallion. I had expected Venice to be overrated. Everyone knew it was inundated with tourists, the authentic Venice eradicated by money-making shops, the city slowly sinking beneath the weight of its own clichés. I too had read *Death in Venice*. And yet I was captivated by the skyline of thirteenth-century buildings lit by globes of light, the silhouette of the winged Lion of Venice atop its tall granite column against a pink-streaked sunset. A yellow-and-orange craft sped past painted with the words *Ambulanza, Venezia Emergenza:* an ambulance boat. Yes, Venice was a myth. But its magic was real too.

Lukas was taking photos, his competent hands caressing his camera. We cruised past long alleyways of water lit by small cafés where people chatted amid the glow of candlelight. Tiny bridges crossed tranquil canals while tourists thronged and packed into stands with glittering souvenirs. The water taxi drew up to our hotel, right on the Grand Canal next to Piazza San Marco.

Estelle and the guys headed out for a late dinner but I decided to go to bed. The trip had drained me. Once inside, I never wanted to leave my hotel room again, an oasis of velvet sage and gold trim. Thick curtains kept the night at bay while hand-blown glass lamps bloomed on the walls, elegantly arched confections of spring green leaves. The hotel clerk had left a bottle of chilled Pellegrino on ice, covered with a fine embroidered napkin. I lay back against the plush pillows on the bed and wished I could live from hotel to hotel, never stopping, never allowing the rest of my life to catch up with me.

The next morning, I found Lukas in the hotel restaurant leaning over the terrace railing, snapping photos of the covered gondolas docked nearby. Gondoliers in their typical black-and-white-striped T-shirts stepped from boat to boat, checking and cleaning before their workday began. The cool morning air played with his shaggy hair as rays of sunlight caught the gold and red strands among the dark.

"You are up early," I said.

He jumped, and turned to face me. "Congratulations." He bent and kissed me three times. His freshly shaven cheek smelled of citrus, cedar, and a hint of vanilla. "Thirty-three years. And just yesterday, you were only nine, it seems."

I looked into his eyes. I could not recall the last time I had felt this content. "I am glad we decided to come here."

"Come on, I am hungry. Estelle and Filip are not what you would call morning people."

We filled our plates from the buffet—fresh croissants and pastries, scrambled eggs and fruit salad—and settled on a sun-drenched table next to the water. The waiter brought us tea and coffee with warm milk, along with fresh *jus d'orange*.

I cracked open a little jar of strawberry preserves and smeared some across my croissant. "This must be the most beautiful place I have ever been."

Lukas looked out over the begonias that flowered along our railing to the dark cyan waters underneath a cloudless cerulean sky. Then he smiled at me, his eyes warm and dark. "I have never seen anything lovelier."

"Not flirting so early in the morning, I hope." Filip's tone was dry. He now stood beside our table with Estelle. They both wore dark sunglasses. "Congratulations, little treasure."

They each kissed me three times, and then Filip went to find food while Estelle sat and slowly sipped her black coffee. "Oh, I really needed this. Now, what are we going to do to celebrate Sylvie's birthday?"

"I do not really want to do anything special," I said.

She pushed her glasses up onto her head to stare at me. "Nonsense."

Filip set his plate down, pulled out a chair, and said, "Shall we go exploring during the day and maybe a nice dinner tonight?"

"I have always wanted to see the Palazzo Ducale," Lukas said.

"Both Sylvie and Lukas are in Venice for the first time, right?" said Estelle. "You know what that means: gondola ride! Our gift to you."

Lukas and I both groaned.

"I cannot swim," I said.

"Really?" said Filip. He leaned in close, lowered his lashes, and murmured, "I will have to teach you sometime."

"No one falls out of a gondola," said Estelle, throwing her hands up in exasperation. "Not even the really clumsy tourists. And if you did, I would save you. I have six swimming diplomas."

"I refuse to let an Italian guy sing to me," I said, crossing my arms in front of my chest.

"Me too," said Lukas, nodding emphatically. "Especially if he is hairy."

Filip lifted one eyebrow, his tone turning wicked. "Which is exactly why you must both undergo this most stereotyped of tourist experiences. Think of it as a rite of passage."

We spent the morning at the lavish Palazzo Ducale. After we climbed the twenty-four-carat gilt staircase Scala d'Oro, I stopped before a stone face of a grimacing man with penetrating eyes and an open mouth.

"Afraid?" asked Filip, leaning in close. I could feel the warmth of his tight muscles through his thin shirt, pressing against my back.

"What is it?"

"*Bocca di leone,* the mouth of the lion. This was a postbox for secret accusations, where people would slip notes about their neighbors. The

Council of Ten would then lead an investigation by the dreaded security service."

I shivered. "Ominous."

"Every secret has its price. Come on, let us go to the Bridge of Sighs."

He took my hand and led me to the bridge where it is said the prisoners sighed at their last views of Venice before they were led to their darkened cells. Inside the dungeons, the bits of graffiti etched into the stone walls were the only evidence of the lives that had been exhausted there.

For lunch we only had time to grab slices of thin, crispy pizza from a woman with leathery skin and a flowered scarf covering her hair before we were off to the Basilica di San Marco, with its lavish spires, Byzantine domes, and patterned marble. On all of my business trips, I had never taken the time to enjoy the places I had visited. There had always been a client or a colleague to impress, another presentation to prepare. Now I could just be. We hopped on the *vaporetto* water bus for a tour of the Grand Canal, gliding past ornate buildings while the canal itself was crowded with cargo barges, kayaks, delivery boats, and water taxis. I was delighted to see a Total gas station set by a dock, serving boats instead of cars.

In the late afternoon, Estelle announced it was time for our gondola ride. She had already secured our *vaporetto* and museum passes, and now she bargained efficiently with a gondolier before calling us over. Naturally, she told him it was my birthday, so I had the seat of honor with Lukas, the other Venetian virgin, as Estelle called us. Estelle and Filip settled into red velvet cushions across from us. Instead of the flirtatious Italian singer I had been dreading, a small white-haired gentleman climbed aboard. He wore a plastic union card pinned to his neat button-down shirt. The gondolier shoved off, and the elderly man turned on the speaker at his feet and began to sing in a beautiful baritone, his voice amplified by the surrounding buildings and the narrow canals.

Even Filip closed his eyes to listen, a small smile signaling his professional approval of the musical proceedings. He was almost unbearably good-looking: dark lashes against fair skin, the cynical quirk to his full lips. My phone pinged with a text from Amy, wishing me a great birthday and asking when we could chat. I quickly wrote back with an excuse, not wanting her to know I had left Grandma, then put away my mobile and resumed studying Filip. If Amy ever met him, she would fall hard. He was exactly her type: musical, funny, smart.

Lukas wrapped his arm around me and I snuggled into his side. No one made me feel safer than Lukas.

"Do you remember the valentine I gave you? Before you left?" he murmured.

I wrinkled my forehead. "You never gave me anything like that."

"Yes, I did but I did not sign it. I left it in your desk on Valentine's Day."

I thought back. There had been something. I had been surprised to find it, especially since, in those days, Valentine's Day was not really celebrated here—a crumpled piece of red construction paper in the shape of a heart. What had it said? I started to laugh. "That was you? I think the note compared me to a toe or something?"

He nodded, satisfied. "'Without you, I am like a sock without a foot.' Now you know how I felt about you."

I chuckled, and then surrendered to the music floating between the buildings, the lapping of the water against the hull of the boat, the rhythmic stroke of the gondolier's oars. This close to the houses, I could see the way they tilted, the crumbling brick sagging into the waves, the moss that grew and multiplied along the waterline, bits of graffiti scribbled here and there. The vulnerability of this place only made me love it more.

Lukas pulled me closer and rested his cheek against my hair. Though Estelle chattered away and Filip seemed to be asleep, I realized they were both watching us: Estelle out of the corner of her eye and Filip from under half-closed lids. My face, neck, and ears began to feel hot. I stretched and pulled myself out of Lukas's arms. At his surprised glance, I shrugged a little and sat up straighter, putting some distance between us.

When the singer took a break, Filip spoke to him in fluent Italian.

Lukas turned to me and mouthed, *Show-off*.

Estelle knocked her loafer against Filip's shoe. "Okay, we are impressed enough. You may stop now."

Filip looked at us for a moment. "I had a good Italian friend once." Then he said something to the singer that made the man throw back his head with laughter.

Estelle gave me a look and pointed at our gondolier. I turned to find him taking a selfie with his mobile. Filip caught the gondolier's eye and blew him a deliberate kiss. The man blushed and almost dropped his phone.

I chuckled and Estelle leaned forward. "You should smile more, Sylvie. It suits you."

I stared out at the water and wondered what it was that Estelle saw in my face most of the time.

That evening, we went out for dinner at a restaurant that specialized in Venetian delights. We sat underneath red umbrellas on an outdoor terrace on top of the canal, surrounded by water. The meal was my treat, of course, a custom that had tripped me up when I first moved to the States. For the Dutch, it was customary for the birthday person to take out everyone else, while in America, this was reversed.

Estelle, as organized and practical as ever, told the restaurant about my seafood allergy, then took the seat beside me, and we all toasted with a bottle of prosecco.

I leaned my elbows on the table, entwined my fingers, and rested my chin on my hands. I cocked my head at Estelle, so lovely, independent, and uninhibited. Everything I wanted to be. "You have come so far. A female pilot. Was it hard for you?"

She twirled a finger around the rim of her glass. "You have no idea."

Filip scoffed and rolled his eyes. "Ah yes, it is so difficult to be the only woman in the cockpit with all those men in uniform. Come up, you know you love the attention."

She grinned and took a big sip of her drink. "It is nice sometimes.

Like when we fly to Africa and go out at night, they all watch out for me. But then my copilot will knock on my door and ask for sex, and if I say no, he tells everyone I am a shitty pilot. Men have come right out and said to me that this is no job for a woman."

"Well, it is not a great career if you want a family." A passing gust of wind ruffled Lukas's hair as he spoke.

Our food came then and everyone was silent as we admired our meals, inhaled the rich aromas, and shook out our napkins.

Estelle had ordered scallops with wild fennel. She took a bite and chewed thoughtfully before she answered. "True. If you are a woman who wants house, tree, and pet, then being a pilot is not for you, unless you can find some nice man to be your house husband." She wrinkled her nose at Lukas, who grinned. Had they talked about this? *Stop it, Sylvie*. It was none of my business.

I took a bite of my tagliatelle with artichokes and pecorino and sighed; the sharpness of the cheese highlighted the silkiness of the pasta. "This is so good, as delicious as an angel peeing on your tongue."

The others murmured their agreement.

"But I can imagine it is not easy for you sometimes," I pressed.

Estelle's usually expressive face grew still and she dropped her breezy facade for a moment. "Everyone always thinks I am a flight attendant. The airlines are saying how they would love to hire more female pilots but the truth is, there are no laws regulating it and they would rather have a man. When I took the exam for my commercial license, the examiner opened the door and he said to me, 'Oh, you are a woman. Do you know what color the sky is?' Ha ha. I showed him how good I was. But I cannot imagine it was all smooth sailing for you either, Sylvie." In her face, I could see that she remembered how homely I had been, how awkward and isolated.

I emptied my glass and held it out for Filip to refill. How much should I tell her? Years of habitual silence seemed to block my lips, but the lapping of the waves, the warm haven created by the candlelight, the full moon hanging like a ripe fruit over us, and their sympathetic faces made me reconsider.

"You want a bite?" Filip asked, pushing his plate of squid ink linguini at me.

I held up my hand in refusal. "Allergic, remember? I do not want to go to the hospital on my birthday." I turned to Estelle, who was tilted back in her chair, cradling her glass in her hands. I had held so much inside with Jim and look at where that got me. A new Sylvie would be born in Venice. "It is still difficult, actually. My engagement manager on my last project said to me, 'I admire you people so much. I mean, Chinese immigrants.'"

Filip shook his head ruefully. "Not a compliment."

"The next thing is, 'You people are ruining our economy' or 'You people smell.'" Lukas pushed his salted codfish around his plate.

I remembered the teacher in my New York elementary school who sometimes called me *Miss Ching Chong*. "I think that wherever you are, to live in the world as a white person is a completely different experience than a person of color. Discrimination is invisible to them because it does not affect them. They are truly shocked."

"Or if you are a woman or gay," Filip added, tapping his finger against the tabletop.

The waiter appeared then to take our dessert orders. Filip asked, "Shall I just do it?" and we all nodded. He glanced at the menu and fired off a stream of rapid Italian.

After the waiter left, Filip leaned back and crossed his legs. "You know, there was this yellow-face character on TV for many years. It was after you left."

"I heard of it." I had read Dutch news all the time I was gone. "Was there not also a film?"

Lukas cupped his hands around the candle on the table. The light played across his straight nose, his high cheekbones. "Yes, a white woman dressed as an Asian who spoke terrible English and said embarrassing things to international celebrities. There is a kind of naiveté here. Or you could call it ignorance. Maybe the Asians simply do not protest enough."

Dessert came then, plates filled with crumbly *zaeti* cookies, *ciambelle* ring doughnuts, a pie of *amaretti* biscuits and almonds, and fried sweet Venetian dumplings.

I took a bite of one of the *ciambelle* and said, "In the U.S., people may be racist, but at least they are usually aware that it is wrong."

Estelle said, popping one of the dumplings into her mouth, "Sometimes I think that because we Dutch believe we are so emancipated, we become blind to the faults in ourselves."

Filip tilted his head to the side and looked at me with his clear blue eyes. "So how goes it with this engagement manager of yours?"

I took a deep breath and reminded myself, *New Sylvie*. "Actually, he got me fired."

Lukas froze with his *zaeti* cookie halfway to his plate. Estelle reached out and took my hand in hers. "What? Oh, little darling. What happened?"

I could not meet their eyes. "He had wanted to get rid of me for a while—after I made it clear I was not interested in fun and games with him in bed. So when I was foolish enough to give him an excuse, he did." I hunched my shoulders. I was a failure at everything. What must they think of me now?

Lukas tilted up my chin in his hands. His face was blurry. I blinked to clear my eyes as he said, "It was not your fault."

I gave a choked laugh and brought a shaky hand to my cheek. "He was not the only one who wanted me gone. I do not really have friends back home." My throat felt thick, as if I were having an allergic attack.

Estelle gave me an incredulous look. "How can you say that? Why not?"

"People use me for my connections, and the ones who do not, stay away." I hugged my shoulders, my chin resting on my neck. I suddenly felt chilled.

Lukas asked, eyes fixed on me, "Why is that?"

It hurt to admit everything, but it felt good too. No more hiding. "It is my fault. I keep them at a distance. I am cold and unfeeling. I always have to play first violin."

Filip smiled and pretended to shudder at the idea of me playing any instrument, then picked up my hand from across the little table and pressed a warm kiss onto it. "Ridiculous. You are not that bossy. Remember, high trees are attacked by strong winds."

Estelle wrapped her arm around me. "I have the solution: Do not go back, Sylvie. Stay here with us."

I hugged her and looked across the table at the two men: Filip, with his elegant eyebrows arched in challenge, and Lukas, with his heart in his eyes. *Stay.*

Later, when we tried to cross Piazza San Marco to return to our hotel, I was amazed to find it under at least ten inches of flooding, the lights that hung from every archway now reflected in the glistening water. The enormous square had become a sea, with no dry spots anywhere. Some tourists wore plastic sheeting on their feet and legs while others waded barefoot. A few reclined in the partially submerged metal and bamboo chairs that had been set out earlier for dining, their shoes dangling from the armrests.

"What happened?" I asked, breathless at the transformation.

Estelle said, "*Acqua alta*. Occurs during certain phases of the moon when tides are strong."

"You knew this was possible?" said Lukas, swatting her on the arm. "And you did not warn us?"

Estelle opened her black leather shopping tote and pulled out a pair of rubber boots encased in a thin plastic bag.

"Incredible," said Filip with a bark of laughter.

"You kept boots in your Prada bag?" I said, wide-eyed. I shook my head in disbelief.

"Bought these rain-shoes for an apple and an egg at the HEMA, only ten euros," she said happily, pulling off her Rockstud ballerinas and slipping them into the plastic bag she had used for the boots.

Lukas sighed. "In the land of the blind, she with one eye is queen."

She pulled on the khaki rain boots. I looked down at my champagne satin mules, my blue linen wide-leg pants. They would be ruined by the water.

"I would have mentioned it to you," Estelle said, "but I knew you could not fit anything in your little knot clutch anyway. I love it, by the way. That woven silk is so cute."

Estelle began to wade across the plaza. I took a breath and was about to plunge in behind her when Lukas stopped me with a touch on the shoulder.

"Please allow me to carry you," he said, his head haloed by the street lamp behind him. He stood there, broad and handsome, holding out his hand in invitation, a small smile playing at the corners of his mouth.

But before I could step into his embrace, Filip swooped me up from behind. I clung to his neck, laughing, as he twirled in circles until the world spun and I was dizzy and gasping. Then he strode across the dark water of the square, his strong arms holding me tight, while Lukas was left behind.

By the next morning, the floodwater had drained away as if it had never been there. This was our last full day in Venice. We tried to purchase tickets for a concert that evening, but the only showing available was performed by musicians in period costumes.

Filip pretended to stick his finger down his throat. "I refuse to see this Punch and Judy show."

"'Masquerade dinner and dancing beforehand,'" Estelle read from the brochure. "'Masks required.'"

"Can you say 'tourist trap'?" Filip said.

"I think it sounds fun," I said, peering over her shoulder. "And are not we shopping for gifts and souvenirs anyway today?"

To appease Filip, we first visited the renowned opera house Teatro La Fenice. We decided to follow the audio tour, but at some point Estelle and Lukas disappeared and I found myself growing bored. Instead, I followed Filip around. His face was aglow, his grumbling manner entirely dissipated.

"It is amazing to be here," he said. "Monteverdi was hired as choirmaster. *La Traviata* and *Rigoletto* premiered here. Rossini, Bellini."

By this point, we had climbed the stairs and could hear music coming from the stage below. The door was ajar and we peeked through to find one of the central opera boxes, half-filled with tourists watching a rehearsal in progress. We squeezed into two empty seats. At first, I was too astounded by the beauty of the theater to notice the opera. The room glowed with elaborate golden moldings and paintings beneath a huge chandelier.

The woman on the minimalistic set was dressed in a simple all-black shirt-and-pants combination with stiletto heels, which I could tell were Louboutins from their signature red soles. The two male singers wore bathrobes and slippers. I could not tell if they were in costume because this was a modern opera or if these were their normal clothes. When they sang, the music reverberated inside my soul.

As we left to rejoin Lukas and Estelle, I said, "I think I follow now."

"What?"

"Music. My sister, Amy, lives for it. I never truly understood before." I traced a finger along the wall as we passed.

We started down the elaborate staircase and Filip took my elbow. "Watch your step. And what have you learned?"

"That it can express something beyond words, beyond logic and rational thought."

"The first time I heard the cello, I felt recognized. Like the music was greeting something inside of me, something no one else could see." He slung his arm around my shoulder in a loose hug.

It was unusual for Filip to be this open about something that mattered to him. I reached up to give his hand an affectionate squeeze, then gazed down the stairs to find Lukas staring up at us. Estelle was busy checking her phone at his side. His face was tight. He sent me such a long, pained look that I tried to edge away from Filip, who only tightened his grip.

"Where have you guys been?" asked Lukas, his tone casual despite the strain around his lips.

"We were lost," answered Filip with a satisfied smile. "But now we have been found again."

We headed over to the Ponte di Rialto to do some shopping at the little stands and boutiques on both sides of the Grand Canal. My legs ached by the time we arrived. I had not realized that all of the charming arched bridges in Venice were composed of steps, like staircases. Tourists everywhere huffed and puffed to haul their heavy luggage to their hotels.

Estelle and I wandered arm in arm through the elaborate crowded market, licking our dripping *gelati*. I noticed a shop window near us was filled with masks and carnival costumes. Inside, artisans were hard at work.

"A real mask maker," I said. "We could all find something."

"It is hard to catch hares with unwilling dogs," Filip said.

Estelle grabbed him by the arm and yanked him into the store. Lukas followed meekly. We watched an artist paint details on a full-faced harlequin before Estelle and I started trying on eye masks. She bought one made of velour and embroidered with swirls of green and silver flowers. Mine was covered in gold leaf and macramé lace; a plume of black feathers embellished the forehead. For Amy, I purchased a delicate laser-cut black metal filigree decorated with crystals. Meanwhile Filip and Lukas were laughing their heads off, trying on different looks. Finally, Filip chose a half face in silver leaf and Lukas a full face red-and-black Japanese-style Kabuki mask.

In a boutique selling authentic Murano glass, I purchased a bright green watch for Ma—its large round face edged in tiny beads—and, for Grandma, found a white-gold keychain with a dangling Sommerso key. Streams of amber blue flowed through the glass. I was at a loss to find a present for Pa but then Lukas showed me a Solingen pocketknife with an engraving of the Venetian winged lion. I could not wait to give my family their gifts.

That evening at the masquerade dinner, a white-faced mime drifted from table to table, resorting to speaking when he failed to sell his roses through gesture alone. The flowers were everywhere, on the tables, braided into the canopy, their heady sweet scent filling the air. The music from the live band drifted over the cobblestones as masked couples, drunk on wine and anonymity, fondled each other in dark corners. At the table next to ours, a man in a white diamond skull mask dipped his fingers in red wine and let his female companion wearing a bronze Egyptian cat face lick them off, one by one. A woman in a glittering ball gown and elaborate sun-goddess headdress twirled around the dance floor with a man in a plague-doctor mask, his long beaklike nose buried in the feathers of her hair.

When Estelle asked me to dance, I shook my head. She seemed to remember the last time, giggled, and tried to pull Lukas to his feet instead. He too refused, leaving Filip, who gave me a lingering glance as he and Estelle left the table, his eyes gleaming behind the silver mask, his sensual mouth quirked in a half smile.

Without a word, Lukas's hand found mine underneath the table. He stood and led me to the shadowy area behind the musician's stand, and pulled me close. As I swayed in his arms, the night seemed to be a hallucination: the masked dancers, the eerie labyrinth of streets that led away from the small square, the soft glow of lamps creating our own universe. I could not see his face through his mask and knew mine was hidden as well. Glimpses of flesh served as my guide: a flash of his eyes, the underside of his jaw, the column of his neck. As I turned beneath his arm, the feathers on my mask brushed against his sleeve. Then he was leading me into a darkened alleyway—and my back was against the brick wall, his hands cupped around my head, his fingers caressing the hollows of my neck. I was breathing quickly. He towered over me. His mask hid him from my sight.

"Sylvie," he breathed. His voice was filled with heat and sweetness. "This is making me insane."

He pushed his mask to the top of his head and then he was kissing me, his lips warm, demanding. I entwined my fingers in the silky mass of his hair as I had wanted to for so long. My mouth opened to his, and he half lifted me off the ground, pressing me against his supple body. The kiss felt like an edge we had tumbled off and we were falling, falling. His hands, callused and long-fingered, caressed my skin, pushed the straps of my top off my shoulders. His eyes were dark with desire, urgency, and claimed my own. I still wore my mask and felt like I was swimming in honey; there was nothing but feeling. I was drowning in it, with my last chance, my only one.

"Buy a rose for beautiful lady?"

I jumped, and we sprang apart, both gasping for air as if we'd run a marathon. It was the incompetent mime.

"Tomorrow is Festival San Marco. Tradition is man gives woman he loves a rose," the mime continued.

"No!" Lukas barked, then we both burst out laughing as the mime held up his hands and left on exaggerated tiptoe.

"Is he not supposed to stay silent?" Lukas growled.

"'Talking mime.' That tells you enough." I smoothed my hair with my fingers. They were still trembling. "We had better get back."

He reached out and helped me straighten my mask and clothing, and murmured into my hair, "Tell me before we go—Filip?"

I pressed a final, gentle kiss to the back of his hand. "Only a game."

We tried to compose ourselves on the way, but when we reached the others, their glittering eyes and set mouths told us they were not fooled at all.

I did not hear a note of that concert. I sat trembling, reliving every moment of our kiss while the ensemble in period costume played Vivaldi. Everyone had removed their masks and I knew my face was flushed, my eyes wild. Lukas sat beside me. I felt the heat emanating from him. I was aware of every flex of his arms, the tilt of his head, the way his fingers drummed on the armrest that separated us.

As we were leaving, most of the audience put on their masks again. I assumed they were going on to other festivities. I was shrugging on my wrap in the doorway when I stopped, frozen by the sight of a blond man in a full-face *bauta* mask with a jutting chin and no mouth. The way he moved, the set of his shoulders, the line of his neck: it was Jim. I was sure of it. Our eyes met.

What was he doing here? Was he spying on me? I began to squeeze through the crowd in his direction but he had turned away. Then a laughing group blocked my view, a woman in a tight black cocktail dress cackling.

"Pardon me," I said, pushing my way past a man in a red-and-white harlequin mask. "Please let me through, it is very important."

But Jim was already gone.

I gasped as someone grabbed my wrist from behind and spun me around. It was Lukas.

"What is wrong?" he asked.

I let the crowd press me up against his hard chest. I rubbed my cheek against his shirt and said, "I thought I saw someone I knew."

His arm crept around my waist. "Your ex-husband?"

I stiffened as I pulled away. My life was such a mess, and now I was jumping at shadows. Was what I felt for Lukas even real? "Actually, we are still married. Come on, it could not have been him."

On our way back to the hotel, Estelle and I walked ahead as the men lingered behind. Their voices drifted to us on the night breeze. They were arguing about the concert.

"Do you want to talk about it?" Estelle asked in a low voice. I stared at the ground and shook my head. She placed a gentle hand on my shoulder. "It is okay, Sylvie. I am not upset."

I hooked my arm through hers and linked our fingers together. "You are too good to me. I do not deserve a friend like you."

She stopped and held our hands up like a trophy. "Men are delightful, but we will never let one come between our friendship."

I opened my mouth to respond but stopped when I heard raised voices behind us.

"You are so arrogant," Lukas said. "Everything has to be so artistic with you."

"The man was dressed in red brocade and a white wig. No self-respecting musician would wear that. Plus his phrasing was atrocious, pure melodrama. But you do not need to be pure, do you?" Filip's voice was biting.

They were approaching us now and I saw Lukas curl his lip. "What do you mean by that?"

"How much commercial photography work have you done in the

past year? And how much of your own?" Filip said. His eyes were small and mean in the lamplight, filled with bitterness.

Lukas flexed his shoulder and said in a deceptively soft voice, "Some of us need to make a living."

"While entertaining our lovely cousins. You should stay the hell away from her."

They had both stopped and now faced each other, bodies tense, their hands clenched.

Lukas's nostrils flared. His voice was low and intense. "You have no right to tell me what to do. You can better take your own advice. I know what is going on here."

Filip gave a harsh laugh. "Oh, really? You understand the situation so well, do you? Such a clever boy."

They sprang toward each other as Estelle and I rushed toward them. They were grappling, swinging, kicking. Filip pushed Lukas up against the pole of a streetlamp. Lukas scrambled to his feet and shoved him back. Filip fell on the sidewalk and hit his temple. By now, Estelle and I stood between them.

"Stop," Estelle cried, tears in her eyes. She helped Filip to his feet. "You will both have regret for this tomorrow."

I already did. What had I done to our group of friends? The two men straightened and, without a word, Filip turned on his heel and walked back toward the center while Lukas stalked off in the direction of our hotel.

Estelle and I did not speak after that and I made my way to my hotel room, alone.

Despite my fears and worries, I hoped Lukas would come to me that night. Was he sorry for what we had done? Had it been an impulse of the moment? Should I go to him? Perhaps he was not alone. Maybe I would not be welcome.

When I had felt his hand underneath the table—indeed, when I let Estelle and Filip leave—I understood there was no choice to be made. It had always been Lukas, from the beginning. Filip was sexy and delightful company, but it was nothing more than a flirtation, a way to pass the time, to keep our demons at bay. But now the doubts crept in about Lukas as well. Was I merely feeling weak and unbalanced and Lukas was here? I had never felt so connected to anyone, not even Jim. Maybe Helena was right about me: maybe I was only a taker, using people. Perhaps I should not have given in to my rash desire. Now I had wounded the people I loved.

I lay awake for hours, still hoping for a knock on my door. But this lonely night in Venice, it never came.

When I finally slept, I dreamed that death was near, like a great wind carrying my beloved Grandma away from me. Then Grandma turned into Amy and Ma and Estelle and Filip and Lukas, their faces shifting from one to the other. They were in an abyss, crying out my name. I was afraid of the storm and then I was the storm itself, destroying all that touched my periphery—Jim, sitting in his office, menacing, violent, jealous, a mean drunk; the faces of my former colleagues; professors who had believed in me. A stack of unpaid bills toppling, the look on Amy's face when she too realized I had failed.

When I cracked open my door the next morning, I found a perfect red rosebud, half-open, caught right at the moment of blooming. He had not forgotten me after all. I brought it inside the room and cradled it in my hands. The scent was sweet, intoxicating.

I was already packed to check out, so I pressed the rosebud carefully between the pages of a notebook and slid it into my handbag with a little prayer. *I cannot afford to nourish you, but may you survive regardless.*

I was the only one of our group on the restaurant terrace. I leaned out over the water, thinking of the anger and disappointment of the previous night, wondering if I had ruined all of our friendships for good. I heard a click and there were Lukas and Estelle. They stood a few meters away from me—Lukas and his photography again. I had been swallowed by the lens of his camera the entire trip.

"You look so sad." He seemed tired and his T-shirt was wrinkled, but my heart still leaped at the sight of him.

"More people drown in the glass than in the sea," said Estelle, rubbing her temples. She wore her sunglasses on top of her head and the lines around her eyes seemed deeper this morning.

"Did you drink last night?" I asked.

"We had a few before going to bed," said Lukas.

I pinched my lips together. I tried not to feel left out and failed. So he had been with Estelle instead of me. Had they talked about me? Had Filip been there too? Was that why I had been left alone? So much for the new Sylvie.

Lukas saw what was written on my face and came to stand beside me. His voice was gentle. "You should have joined us."

I gave a little airy laugh. "You guys are a bad influence. Those who associate with dogs get fleas."

I was not fooling anyone. Breakfast was quiet and Filip did not come at all. He met us after we had checked out. His face was closed, an angry scrape on his cheekbone below his dark sunglasses. When I touched him on the elbow, he shrugged my hand away.

Piazza San Marco was packed with people waving the Venetian flag in celebration of Liberation Day and Festa di San Marco. Men and women worked the crowd selling single roses to couples and lovers. Estelle and I chattered about meaningless things. The guys did not exchange a single word.

I sat in the water taxi, speeding toward Marco Polo Airport, and breathed in the salty air as the sun shone relentlessly upon the turbulent waves. Venice was hauntingly beautiful. I would never forget the images of the limpid canals and sparkling sunshine during the day, the labyrinthine alleys at night, redolent of passion and secrecy, flickers of bright gold against absolute black. Small details returned to me: the ice that came in a separate little bowl when you ordered a soft drink, signs forbidding gondolas from certain waterways, the way Lukas's lips had felt against mine. I watched as the magic of Venice faded behind us, and wondered when I would come back and if I would return with him.

CHAPTER 22

Amy

Saturday, May 14

The rest of the week crawls by, the spring sunlight slowly turning into wind and rain, until it is finally Saturday and Epsilon can do a full search. It has been two weeks since anyone has seen or heard from Sylvie and I am a quivering wreck, worn thin by despair. Every morning, I wake certain that Sylvie's safe and I imagined the whole thing. Ma and Pa sound more helpless each time I speak to them. I want to go home to New York but I won't leave without Sylvie. I have a faint spark of hope that she's run off. But deep inside, I know something has happened to her. I am beginning to realize we might never find out the truth. It's like the Sylvie I knew has slowly spiraled away from us, out of sight and hearing and memory—the center of our little domestic world unraveling with the vacuum of her absence.

I hardly see Lukas, Helena, and Willem, but when I do, the strain of Sylvie's fate reveals itself in the slow, careful way we maintain our distance from each other. No one wants to dig too deep, reveal too much. The police have no news. I found out from Helena that Sylvie had been taking cello lessons in the Brouwersgracht in Amsterdam, the area where I'd seen the houseboats. She gave me the likeliest route Sylvie would have driven with her rental car.

Filip finally returned my many texts with a suggestion that we get together but now I am too distressed to be distracted by a crush. Karin told me they've already gone over the main areas with their dogs and will start their intensive search this weekend.

I had phoned Karin yesterday to share the information about the music lessons, and asked if I could accompany her team today.

She hesitated. "We do not usually allow family members."

Two weeks ago, I would have apologized and hung up the phone. But everything was different now. "Why is that?"

"Because if we succeed in our search, it can be . . . upsetting."

The pit of my stomach dropped away. I tried to speak but had difficulty swallowing. I'd forced myself to face this possibility yet could barely utter the words. "You mean if you find a body."

"Yes." Her voice was quiet and compassionate.

"I know that Sylvie might be dead." Was that my voice? It shook so badly, I wondered if she could understand me—just saying it made me want to burst into tears—but we still didn't know anything yet. I would keep my hope alive until the very end. I tried to still my trembling by wrapping my free arm around myself. "I understand the situation. It's just that I might think of something during the search that could help. I'd like to be there. None of us can predict how we'll react in a bad situation, but I promise I'll do my best not to become hysterical. Please. I need to do everything I can to help you find my sister."

After a moment, she said, "All right. One of our divers is coming along too, which is unusual at this stage. They do not usually join until the dogs have found something. Since he is willing to help, I can give another member of my crew the day off."

I had a suspicion. "Anyone I know?" Would he come?

"His name is Filip. I believe he is a friend of yours." My fear for Sylvie had burned away my desire, but I was still glad he cared enough to come. I'd at least have someone I trust there with me.

Now I know why Dutch painters were obsessed with the sky. Stretched above the flat landscape, the morning boils and eddies, the roiling clouds battling a single sharp patch of obstinate sunlight. Filip's eyes are bright against the gray water as he stretches out his arm to help me onto their floating rigid boat. His hand is warm and strong. I'm glad to have him with us. Karin holds on to the leashes of the dogs Ajax and Feyenoord, who are eagerly perched on the hull. I feel the craft sway as it adjusts to my weight and then we push off from the pier. I feel I am leaving all I have known behind.

Both Filip and Karin wear high-visibility one-piece waterproof coveralls, though I catch a glimpse of a black diving suit beneath Filip's. He settles down behind the wheel, where a sonar screen is bleeping, as I take a seat in the middle of the boat. I pull on the life vest Karin hands to me. They've picked me up close to the café I visited with Lukas and Estelle what seems an eternity ago, and we're heading toward Amsterdam alongside the roads Sylvie would have taken to her music lessons. Ajax and Feyenoord wag their tails, antsy and impatient, at the front of the boat.

I huddle in my seat, chewing my nails to the quick. "How can the dogs smell anything in this? The police seemed to think that there'd be no scent trail with a car. Is that why you use two dogs?"

Karin is busy checking some piece of equipment against her map, so Filip answers me. "Ajax is the lead dog. The little one is in training. We are not actually trying to track her scent. We are checking to see if she has gone into the water."

For a moment, I'm confused. If she were in the water, wouldn't we see the boat? Then I understand and feel like there's a thick woolen blanket smothering me. "You mean if she's drowned." This is a dream, a nightmare. This can't be true. *My beautiful sister, where are you?* This strange country, this landscape of water in the air, water in the sky, and water beneath our feet. We sail past once-vibrant flower fields now fading, their sagging blooms pulled back toward the earth.

He nods and there's genuine grief in his eyes. He seems older today, the lines on his face etching his distress at accompanying me on such a dark day. He reaches out to give me a quick pat on the arm. "It does not mean she has done so. Just to rule it out. Human remains emit specific gases for a long time that rise to the surface. The dogs are trained to zero in on that scent. If they find something, they will jump in, but there can often be false alarms, which is why we have all this other equipment on board."

Karin finishes fiddling with her gear and joins our conversation. "Then we search with sonar and if there is enough reason to believe it would be worthwhile, the diving team is called in, though we are lucky to have our own diver here today."

I scratch at a small cut on my hand until a droplet of blood oozes onto my skin. My heart beats so quickly I can hardly breathe. How can we be having this discussion about Sylvie? "I thought—I thought bodies floated to the surface."

Karin answers, "It depends on the time of year. Yes, if it has been warm, the chances of a body being washed ashore are greater, or that a fisherman would find it. But if it is a cold spring, like it has been this year, a body could never be found. It can be underwater, eaten by fishes, stuck in a hole or a cave."

I bury my head in my hands. This is all too much. I refuse to believe this could be true. *Please, please, please, let this not have happened to my Sylvie*. I feel a comforting arm around my shoulders and realize Filip's now sitting beside me.

I cling to him, trying not to cry, until I hear him whisper in my ear, "I know this is difficult. But Karin has that look on her face. You need to pull it together or she will remove you from the boat."

This wakes me up. I take deep breaths and wipe my face. I sit up and indeed, Karin is assessing me with her sharp eyes. "I'm all right. It just got to me for a moment." I try to think of something to say to distract her. I gesture to the expanse around us as a relentless drizzle begins to fall from the sky, soaking us. "The area is huge. How can you ever search it all?"

Filip pulls up his hood and says, "We try to proceed very logically. If it was suicide—"

"Sylvie would never kill herself," I interrupt. I know my sister. She would never give up. So talented, so dazzling. Never.

"Okay, but to explore all the possibilities for a moment. Most people choose a spot where they liked to go. A place they went fishing, for example, or close to their family home, or a spot they met their lover. One man drowned himself near a fish stand where he always went with his son."

I say in a small voice, "I was hoping you were trying to catch her scent from the trees or something, that she would be lost in the forest." I was so naive.

Karin crosses over to kneel before me. Her weathered face is kind. She takes both my hands in hers. "We went through the area on land yesterday and came up empty. That is why we are searching the water today. If we do not find anything, we will look there again. Most of the time, Amy, if we succeed, then people can move on. Sometimes that is all we can offer."

Hours later, the weakened sunlight fading, the rain finally stops. There's so much water in the air I can taste the humidity in the wind that whips through my clothing, hunting for gaps. We have stopped twice for restroom breaks, where Filip, to my surprise, pulled out a package of cigarettes to smoke. They offered to share their thermoses of tea and coffee with me, plus a lunch of salami sandwiches on light brown bread. I could not eat a bite. The mysterious expanse of water surrounds us, swelling and ebbing, and a cold dampness crawls underneath my clothing and burrows itself next to my heart.

This is the third time we've passed over the same territory. Karin explained that the breeze could be blowing the wrong way or the precise area obstructed by a passing vessel. The dog in training, Feyenoord, has grown agitated and jumped into the water twice now. My heart almost stopped each time until Karin indicated a false alarm.

She says, "Even if we find something, most of the time, it will be a mistake. So do not get alarmed if the dogs act. If there has been a lot of human contact inside a vehicle, the dogs could be reacting to that. We do hope to find our victims alive. The dogs are trained to search for life as well as corpses, so if there is a sunken automobile that has had many passengers, they might jump. And there are a large number of cars hidden in Dutch waters. People drive them in by accident or to cover up crimes like insurance fraud or carjacking."

"Or to hide a body." Filip stares into the distance, his posture rigid and tense.

I'm wondering if I've wasted everyone's time and we are on the wrong track altogether when we turn onto the Amsterdam-Rhine Canal. The water feels surprisingly deep despite the fact we are not far from shore. The bank is lined with tall trees, swaying in the wind. I spot a grassy area behind a small group of ducks bobbing on the waves.

I press my lips together and cover my mouth with my hand. I will not burst into tears. Karin will make me leave. Still, my voice is broken as I say, "Sylvie loves places like that. She's always had a thing for picnics."

Karin says to Filip, "Can you take us closer to that spot?"

His face grim, he steers us toward the shore. Nothing happens. We draw closer and closer and then, for the first time, Ajax starts to wag his tail and bark. Feyenoord follows his lead. I am holding my breath. Both dogs jump into the water at the same time. They swim ahead of us, surprisingly quick, and then start turning in circles, barking maddeningly the entire time.

My chest seizes. Despite everything, I pray this is a mistake. I wish I could turn back the clock to a few minutes ago. I realize I prefer ignorance. If Sylvie is truly gone, I don't want to know because the grief will tear my heart into pieces. I wish I wore my glasses so I could take them off for a respite from all this clear air, the sharpness of the waves in the water, the icy fear of what we might find. But I cannot. I must be as brave as Sylvie. I will not look away.

Karin is checking the machine she told me was the 360-degree sonar. "I can see from the Humminbird that there is something down there—probably a car." She narrows her eyes at the bank. "If someone had driven off the road at high speed, aiming between the trees there, they would land right about here."

At my stricken face, she says, "There is no indication that this has anything to do with your sister." She whistles and the dogs clamber back onto the boat, spraying water everywhere.

Filip's face is hard and unrelenting. "Except that this was described as a place she often passed on her route. I want to go in."

Karin shakes her head. "Alone? We should wait until at least one other diver gets here."

I am chewing so hard on my lips, I taste blood. My hands are clammy and I can't seem to stop blinking. My heart is about to explode out of my body. I can't sit here waiting for more people to come, not knowing. "Please. Please let him go. Just for a quick look."

Karin hesitates, and says, "All right, but be careful. If there are any difficulties at all, come back up."

Filip is already stripping off his waterproof coveralls. He pulls on the rest of his diving gear, his goggles. His eyes meet mine for a moment before he splashes into the water.

He doesn't come up and he doesn't come up. I can hear Karin calling people and speaking in Dutch. I pray to the gods. *Please, let this not be Sylvie. It's not possible.* Maybe this has nothing at all to do with my sister. It's some drug lord or, like Karin said, insurance fraud. I deeply regret ever having called Epsilon. I should have left it alone, like Lukas wanted. For the first time, I understand his denial. I would not be sitting on this boat then, wondering if my sister . . . I cannot even finish the thought.

Suddenly, Filip breaks the surface beside me. I jump. He hangs on to the side of the boat and pulls up his goggles. His dripping face is bleak. He gasps, "I can't see much down there but one of the windows is open and I could feel something through it. There's a body."

Oh gods. No. I gasp. "W-was it—"

"I cannot tell anything yet. Give me the screwdriver and crowbar." Karin rummages in the tool kit, hands them to Filip, and he disappears again.

I am still gaping, trying to process what he said: a body. But it can't be Sylvie. We're close to Amsterdam, which must be filled with criminals. Anything is possible. I am gulping down breaths to stop from screaming. "Why-why did he take the tools?"

"He is going to remove the license plate."

Now I understand why she wanted that information about Sylvie's rental car. *Please let it be the wrong car, let it be someone else in the car.* How could there be a body here, underneath this cold, merciless surface? I've never even seen a dead person before. *Let Sylvie have run away with the gold, let her now be starting a new life somewhere.*

I jump at every movement in the water—but Filip doesn't reappear. It seems to take much longer this time. Is he all right? What is he doing down there? Karin drops a buoy in the water to mark the spot.

After what feels like an age, Filip's dark head reappears, with a warped yellow license plate in his hand, some of the paint flaked off. Karin takes it from him and helps him climb into the boat. I am absolutely still as she checks her notes. I can't breathe.

Finally, she looks up at me. "It matches."

It is almost dark now. The sun is setting and the water is like the inner recesses of a dark mouth, a tomb, its depths as implacable as eternity. I am numb from standing on the bank for so long, watching the divers, firemen, and police at work. Danique and Pim have arrived. They've not said much to me. They're too busy with the recovery project. The emergency responders have set up an enormous crane and are trying to pull the car from the canal. Filip has been in the water or on the boat most of the time. The divers went down earlier with an underwater camera but there was too little light and the water was too murky.

Lukas comes roaring up on his scooter with Helena and Willem's car right behind him. He runs to me, too much white in his eyes, wild and desperate.

I am relieved to see a family member, but he cries, "What have you done?"

Stunned, I am speechless.

He's almost foaming at the mouth, his nostrils flared. "Why did you have to stir everything up? Why could you not just leave it alone?"

I turn away. I understand the anger and accusation in his voice. It is because I have stripped away the comfort of ignorance for us all.

Helena comes and wordlessly links her arm through mine. I hug it to me; her warmth is all I have now. I haven't called Ma and Pa. I won't until we know what's below the surface. I have no energy for anything but the emergence of that vehicle. I have no thoughts anymore. I can't think. I won't.

Finally, slowly, the small blue car is pulled upward. A flood of water cascades from it. Then the crane rotates and sets it upon the ground. Rescue workers rush to the doors as water streams onto the grass under the harsh and unyielding artificial lights they have set up all around the area. I let go of Helena and push my way to the front, where Lukas already stands, his chest heaving. Water still streams from the windows and indeed, I catch a glimpse of something that could be human limbs in the front seat. A shroud of hair swirls like a curtain around the face, blocking it from view. I can't breathe. I am gasping like a fish on land—no air enters my lungs no matter how hard I try. I catch a glimpse of Lukas out of the corner of my eye, his face a skull of fear. This, I thought, this is what horror is.

They open the doors. Water gushes out. They are pulling out the person. My brain rejects this; how can a human be underwater for so long? The slender arm, it's a woman. Logically, I know she's dead but I want them to try to resuscitate her anyway. Tangled black hair. The woman—I can't call it a body—is Asian, but she isn't Sylvie. Sylvie's taller; her hair is shorter, features sharper and more beautiful, not bloated and obscene like these. Oh gods, is a part of her face missing? It can't be Sylvie. It isn't her. But it is.

Part 5

CHAPTER 23

Ma

Saturday, May 14

I could not understand Amy at first. She was heaving with grief. I sucked in a breath of cold air and then I was the one who was howling. In one frantic thrust I pushed all the plates from our table, the rice and fish crashing onto the floor, shards of ceramic jagged and raw. This should not have been thunder from a clear sky, I should have expected it, and yet I was completely unprepared.

For a long time, I had no words, only pain. Pa gripped my hand, the two of us for once united in our grief. As his face dissolved into tears, I saw something else in his eyes, though—wariness, a part of himself he still held back from me. How long had it been there? Too long. He retreated into the bedroom and his quiet sobs added to my burden. This suffering has made us cough up blood and yet we cannot share our pain.

Why could the gods not have taken me instead? I deserved it. Heaven's net is wide and none can escape its mesh. This was my fault. This could not be true. I had seen Sylvie so recently. It was the greatest torture for a parent to outlive a child. If only I were dead instead—stupid, reckless woman. Our family was like grass that had been pulled up by the roots: eradicated, my mother and daughter dead.

I burned incense by the altar. *Mother, Kuan Yin, please embrace the spirit of my daughter as I could not. My Snow Jasmine, forgive me for placing you in a mountain of blades and a sea of fire. You were but a kite with its string cut, blown away without recall.*

I was going back there. By Monday evening, we would be in Holland to bury my daughter in that same dark landscape where my mother had died. And I would see him again.

CHAPTER 24

Amy

Saturday, May 14

I retch and stagger to the side of the crowd. I throw up everything inside of me. A gentle hand smooths my hair back. Helena. She gathers me into her arms. Between my hoarse sobs, I hear her murmur over and over, "I am so sorry," but instead of saying my name, she says, "Sylvie."

I recover enough to wipe my face with a tissue, and see that Willem has one arm around Lukas, who clutches his stomach like a man who's been kicked repeatedly and can bear no more. Tears stream down his cheeks. Willem is whimpering and biting his other fisted hand, as if to restrain himself from lashing out, as if to ease some of his pain. When Lukas straightens, his skin is splotchy, bunched around his red, swollen eyes, his face ravaged by grief.

On the periphery of my vision, I spot a dark figure climbing out of a boat that has just docked. I call out, "Filip!"

I release Helena and stumble, heavy-footed, toward him. I can barely walk. He wears a silver thermal blanket over his diving suit and, in the shadows of the trees, looks haggard and worn.

My teeth chatter uncontrollably. I hug myself. "Th-thank you for leading me to Epsilon."

He gathers me into his embrace. "I am so sorry."

He is cold and soaking wet, but I am comforted by his closeness. "I-I am glad we know what happened. And that she is out of the water."

Behind me, I hear a low snarl, like that of an enraged animal. I whip around. It's Lukas. There's a murderous gleam in his eyes. "What the hell are you doing here? And with her?"

Confused, I detach from Filip and swivel my head back and forth between the two of them. Filip has both hands raised and slowly backs away. "You know each other?"

Lukas stalks forward, throat rigid, every muscle in his body tense and ready to fight. He keeps his eyes fixed on Filip and spits out, "He was the cello teacher of Sylvie! And one of my oldest friends too, or so I thought. But he talks out of two different mouths like the vicious snake he is."

The handsome cello teacher Helena thought Sylvie had liked. Lukas's friend. My Filip. I open my mouth a few times before I can form words. My entire history with Filip rips apart, exploding into the air, and when the remnants land, a divergent and barren landscape takes shape. Our story is not a romance then, but a tragedy. "W-what? B-but you never told me."

"I can explain—"

Lukas shoves Filip so hard he falls a few steps back. A vein in Lukas's temple protrudes. His face is twisted with fury. He looms over Filip with fists clenched. "Both sisters? You went after Amy too?"

Filip flinches. He spreads his hands wide in a gesture of appeal, begging Lukas with his eyes. "No, you do not understand."

Suddenly, Lukas launches himself at Filip. He's flailing away at him, hitting him in the stomach, the ribs, his face, trying to knee him, and then Willem and the police are there, pulling them apart. Filip is bleeding from the nose and mouth from the brutal blows. He's not made a move to defend himself and stares at Lukas with a look that says he's sorrier than he could ever convey. Lukas tears himself away from the men holding him and falls suddenly, twisting his ankle. He stands quickly, gasping for air, then half stumbles, half runs to his scooter and rides away. I see him wipe the tears from his face with his sleeve. Without another word to me, Filip hobbles away as well.

I can't believe they are both gone. I can't believe anything that has just happened. My teeth are chattering and I am trembling. But slowly, the shakiness catches fire inside me and I start to smolder. I am shuddering so hard, I am nearly convulsing. I am filled with rage. I hate this country and every person in it. This place took my beloved sister from me and I will know why.

Couscous prowls around my bed. I pick her up and cry on her until her fur is wet and spiky. Then she lies beside me and purrs in her funny, staticky way until I fall into an exhausted sleep.

In the morning, the ocean of grief that has engulfed me begins to recede. Not the weight of it—I fear I am only feeling the first ripples of what will become a tsunami—but the dense opaqueness that blinded me to all else. I hold back the tide of emotion through sheer willpower. I need to function. I've begun to think again, and I must, for Sylvie. If this happened to me, she would move heaven and earth to uncover the truth. I realize I have always taken refuge in the lie that Sylvie would take care of everything, that I could do nothing on my own. Perhaps I am more like Sylvie than I ever realized.

It is a long holiday weekend here called Pinksteren. It has something to do with White Sunday and White Monday, and everything is closed. Lukas has disappeared. I've hardly seen Willem or Helena either, except to discuss when Ma and Pa would arrive for the funeral. How Ma and Pa had cried last night when I phoned with the terrible news. Willem and Helena went to Antwerp to visit Oma and Opa for Pinksteren. They invited me along but I begged off. Helena has been extremely kind ever since we found Sylvie, and asked if I was sure I'd be all right before they drove off.

I take a deep breath and ring Karin. I cannot keep running any longer. When she answers, I hear what sounds like a family gathering in the background.

"I want to thank you for what you did." To my shame, I begin to sob uncontrollably.

She waits until I can breathe again, and says, "I am sorry it was not better news."

I wipe my eyes and nose on my sleeve. "I've been afraid to ask, but how much do we owe you?" I brace myself. How will we pay for what must be an astronomical bill—the dogs, the boat, the fancy equipment, the divers, the time spent searching—and now with Sylvie gone? My bills, her bills, I can't even think.

"No, there has been a misunderstanding. You owe us nothing."

I must have heard her incorrectly. "What?"

"We are a volunteer organization. We cannot ask money for what we do. We pay for it with donations, volunteers, and quite a bit of our own money. It is a good thing that when I am not searching for bodies, I am a doctor. And my wife is a veterinarian, so she trains the dogs."

"Oh, Karin." That is all I can say. I give a half sob, so relieved that at least one burden can be laid aside.

"No price may be set on life or death, Amy."

At that moment I understand why Sylvie loved the Netherlands so much. Then I call the police.

I ask for Danique. As soon as she answers, I say, "When will the autopsy report be available?" I feel a desperate desire to know every detail. What could have happened?

Her voice is distant and tinny on the phone. "Actually, it is not likely that we will conduct one."

"What? My sister has been found dead inside her car and you won't investigate further?" My voice rises and I practically shriek into the phone. I can't believe the police didn't find her body and now they still do nothing. My heartbeat pounds so loudly in my ears I have to strain to hear through the rush of fury that washes over me.

"Family members always believe the case involves murder, but the vast majority of the time, the most likely cause is suicide. We do not at this moment have any reason to suspect criminal activity."

Oh, so we're the stupid, misguided family members. Majority of the time! No reason to suspect! Trying to stay calm, I tell her about Filip, how suspiciously he's acted, how there's a missing fortune in jewelry.

She says, "Well, men do strange things sometimes when they meet an attractive woman. Sadly, there is no proof the jewelry ever existed. And if he was involved in a murder, why would he lead you to the body?"

"I don't know. That's your job," I grind out through clenched teeth. "Maybe he tampered with the evidence underwater. He was the first one to reach the car and he was alone. He misled me for our entire relationship and pretended he didn't know either one of us. Don't you think that's a bit suspicious?" I am growling into the phone. I bite back the words: *You imbecile. You uncaring bitch.*

"It would be if there was a possible motive. Lying in a personal relationship is not very honest but it is also not a crime. Perhaps he thought you would not like him if you knew he was acquainted with your sister. Now if there is not anything else . . ."

She's going to hang up on me. Getting angry won't get me an autopsy. I somehow need to convince this idiot of a police agent. I have to be smart, like Sylvie. "Look, Sylvie was a young, healthy, successful woman. Our family needs to know if she was drugged or under the influence of alcohol. Her husband was here. They were having trouble. Maybe they had a fight . . . were there any bruises on her body? I am not accusing anyone of anything but there are still so many questions. Even if she died of a heart attack or stroke and lost control of the car, for example, I need to know that for my own health reasons." I hold my breath, waiting for her answer. *Please, please, please.* I can't be left never knowing what happened to Sylvie.

The silence over the phone is long and heavy. Then she says, not unkindly, "I am very sorry. The case is closed. Amy, let me give you some advice. It is over. Stop asking questions, stop pushing. Find your peace. Just go home and live again. Not everything in life has answers."

I hang up and want to scream. That's easy for her to say. Lose the person you love most in the world and see how accepting and peaceful you are then. I am no longer the Amy who would have crawled back to Ma and Pa and pulled the covers over her head. No more.

I try to think everything through. Is it possible Sylvie killed herself—but then why? The problems with Jim and her job had started before she left for the Netherlands. Something must have tipped her over the edge. If she didn't do it, did someone drug her and place her in the car? Did it have something to do with Grandma's jewelry? No matter what the Dutch police say about the gold, my Chinese instincts tell me it existed—and what about Jim? He had come to the Netherlands and Lukas said that Jim had asked Sylvie not to destroy his life. Jim had threatened Sylvie. But that was probably because Jim didn't want Sylvie to leave him; he must have felt desperate at the thought. Jim has enough money of his own and I can't think of another reason he would want Sylvie gone. Helena? Out of rage, if Sylvie had indeed taken Grandma's gold? Willem? He's so strange and creepy. Could he have done something to Sylvie as a child and she'd threatened to come forward?

Then there were the two men, Lukas and Filip. Perhaps Lukas wanted the gold for himself? He's said how much he wants to own his own place, and there could have been some kind of tussle or an accident. But his grief has been so desperate, so vicious. I can't believe anyone is that good of an actor. Between the two of them, Filip is the obvious suspect. I still can't believe he'd known Sylvie and manipulated a meeting with me. He must have jumped on my bicycle knowing full well who I was. The flesh on my forearms breaks out in goose bumps. I'd thought he was cute, open, and vulnerable. I'd thought he liked me. Fortunately, I am so exhausted from my grief and rage that I have little emotional space left for embarrassment. Did he have a relationship with Sylvie? Did he need the money? Or was there some sort of love triangle and things got out of hand?

I've been calling and leaving messages for Filip. I think over everything I've learned since coming to the Netherlands. What had Helena said about a trip to Venice? Who did Sylvie go with? I could ask Helena and Willem about it, but Sylvie might have lied to them. I am realizing that my sister hid so much more of herself than I ever knew. *Sylvie*, I pray, *I am ready to sacrifice my imagined ideal of you if only I can find out who you really were. Please help me.*

Then the answer comes to me. Estelle.

Telephone Call

Sunday, May 15

Estelle: I am so very sorry. My parents saw it on the television. I see you rang me a few hours ago but I was flying. We just landed in Kuala Lumpur. I am in shock. I could barely concentrate on the flight.

Amy: Thanks.

Estelle: Sylvie was the loveliest, most loyal person. Many people only saw her from the outside. I cannot believe it. [Voice breaks] And I was with her so recently.

Amy: Yes, that's what I wanted to ask you about. Did you know about that trip she took to Venice?

Estelle: Of course. I was there. I arranged the tickets.

Amy: Really? Who else went with you?

Estelle: Lukas and Filip. We had a wonderful time. Well, except for a terrible fight the guys had.

Amy: What did they fight about?

Estelle: Nothing. It was stupid. Something about a show we had just seen—came out of nowhere.

Amy: Actually, Filip introduced himself to me without telling me he knew any of you. We saw each other a few times.

Estelle: What?

Amy: To be honest, it's kind of creepy. Do you know why he would have done that?

Estelle: Amy, I do not have any idea. But Filip is a good man. You should ask him.

Amy: I'm trying, but no one's talking to me. Lukas has disappeared; Filip's not picking up.

Estelle: Yes, Lukas is not answering my calls either. Filip can have a terrible temper too. Lukas, well, he and Sylvie have always had a special relationship.

Amy: I don't mean to pry, but does Lukas disappear on you often?

Estelle: Sure. There are often long periods when I do not know where he is, because we both travel so much. But usually he returns my calls. I imagine this must be horrible for him. I am worried.

Amy: Estelle, were Filip and Sylvie romantically involved?

Estelle: . . . Honestly, I do not know the answer to that, but if they were, it was only a surface love. I think you better ask him yourself. I have no idea where Lukas is right now but I can tell you that most weekends, Filip performs with the Netherlands Philharmonic Orchestra. I am so sorry, Amy. Truly I am. But I am sure that neither of them had anything to do with Sylvie's tragic passing.

CHAPTER 25

Sylvie

Monday, April 25

The house felt strangely empty when Lukas and I opened the front door—and where was Isa's coat, which she normally hung on the rack? Perhaps she was at the store. Lukas and I tiptoed upstairs, in case Grandma was sleeping. I clutched her present, the white-gold keychain and Murano key, in my hand. Her door had been left ajar. I pushed it all the way open and a sudden wave of cold swept over me. Her bed was made and empty. Her medicines and oxygen tank were gone. No, it could not be. If there had been an incident, Helena and Willem would have called us.

Lukas stopped midstride. Then he was calling over the staircase, "Ma, Pa! Where is Grandma?"

Willem emerged from their bedroom, unshaven, still wearing his pajamas.

Something was wrong. I could not get enough air. I pressed my knuckles against my sore, aching heart. My voice was small and tight. "Did you move Grandma to a hospice?"

He shook his head and his crimson, swollen eyes said enough.

Lukas whispered, "No."

I gripped the left side of my head as if to cover my ear, as if that would stop Willem from confirming what I already knew. My breath rasped in my chest. I started to lurch into Grandma's bedroom but my knees gave way and I bumped into the doorframe, the glass key digging into my palm. I staggered forward until I fell facedown, arms splayed, onto Grandma's bed, where I had spoken to her only a few days ago. The key fell from my stupefied fingers, hit the wooden floor, and shattered. I pressed my face into the coverlet that had once warmed Grandma, and that was still here while my grandma was dead, and sobbed.

The bed shifted, there was a weight beside me, and then Lukas was stroking my back. He said, "Oh, Sylvie," in a voice clogged with tears. Poor Lukas. Grandma had cared for him his entire life.

He sniffed, and I pushed myself upright so I could wrap my arms around him. We held each other while we convulsed with grief.

Then Willem's arms were around us both and I stiffened. He smelled of sweat, his flesh too warm through his thin pajamas. The embrace was intimate and I shifted away.

Lukas asked, his face tear-stained, "How? Why did you not call us?"

Willem straightened and raked his fingers through his disheveled hair. "She instigated the euthanasia procedure the moment you were gone. She did not want you to be notified. Do not feel bad. She planned it that way. It was what she wanted."

At this, I hid my face in my palms. Grandma did not want me with her. Even she had rejected me in the end. She had died with only Willem and Helena around her. I had taken her Lukas away too. Because of me, she had died essentially alone.

Lukas croaked, "But we did not get to say goodbye."

Willem raised his arms as if he wanted to comfort us once again, thought better of it, and let them drop to his sides. "She wanted to go with as little fuss as possible. She arranged it months ago with the euthanasia commission once she knew she was terminal."

I managed to ask, "How did it happen?"

"Very peacefully. She started the procedure as soon as you left. Two doctors came yesterday—her own and the one from the commission. They spoke to her separately to make sure she was doing it out of her own free will, and that she was in her right mind." Willem was rubbing the back of his ear, a nervous tic he had.

Yesterday: while Lukas and I were dancing and kissing, and I was off having fun with my friends. I can barely squeeze out the words. "And did it go quickly?"

"Two shots. One to put her to sleep and the other to stop her heart. She did not suffer at all. She is at peace."

A hard, brittle voice came from the doorway. "Did you enjoy your time in Venice?" It was Helena, her eyes aflame, skin pale and blotchy, jaw clenched as if to hold back her anger and grief.

Lukas said, his voice breaking, "Mother, we did not know. We never would have gone."

She came over to the bed and put her arms around him. "I am not blaming you." Her eyes were on me. It was clear who she blamed.

I longed to have Grandma or something of hers in my arms again. I looked around the bare room. "Where is Tasha?"

"Who is that?" asked Helena.

I said in a quiet voice, "You know. The doll Grandma made for me. She was on the bedside table when I left."

She shrugged. "We must have thrown it away by accident."

I recoiled as if she had struck me. I pressed my fist to my mouth to keep from crying out. Tasha, Grandma gone. It was just like the day I had left the Netherlands, losing everyone I had loved. I realized suddenly, of course Helena had taken Tasha then too. What a cruel thing to do to a child. Now she knew I had Grandma's treasure and had stolen Tasha from me. Lukas looked between us and reached out for me but I stood suddenly. If he touched me, I would break down again and I refused to do that in front of this woman, who had always hated me.

I stumbled out of the room and let the grief take me once I was alone in my attic room.

Venice had been a beautiful dream but now I was confronted by reality again. Grandma was gone. Her things had been either thrown away or hidden somewhere and Helena would never allow me access. Tasha, the doll Grandma had made for me with her own hands, had been tossed in the trash. I had not been here for Grandma for all these intervening years and was not here to hold her when she died.

I lay on my bed all day and night. I sent Filip a text message canceling the rest of my lessons. Lukas tried to see me, but I would not let him in. I loved him, but it could not go any further. I had been burned enough. I savored our time in Venice: the longing, the awareness of him, his skin, his smell, his touch . . . but after this came passion and then, inevitably it seemed, betrayal. I knew this desire, to edge closer to the cliff, to tempt fate. I had leaped off before and barely survived it. I was not sure I had. My grief consumed me and I could not bear any more risk to my wounded heart.

Estelle left me messages, but I did not respond. Friendship had failed me. In a way, I was angry at all three of them for tempting me to go to Venice, though I knew it was my own fault. Besides, I had already done enough damage to our group.

When I could speak again, I called Ma and told her that her mother was dead. She keened, each cry hitting a tender spot inside of me. I did not dare tell her that I had not been there at the end. I failed in my original purpose in coming to the Netherlands. When Amy's voice came on the phone, I said, "Take care of Ma for me," and she promised, "I will."

Two days later, it was King's Day, the birthday of King Willem-Alexander. Even though I stayed inside the house, I had to endure the knowledge that hordes of Dutch in fluorescent orange clothing were celebrating and drinking throughout the land. They painted Dutch flags on their faces; dressed in orange boas and huge sunglasses that read KING; wore hats that could hold a liter of beer, which they then piped to their mouths with a siphon. It was an excuse for the ever-controlled Dutch to cut loose. Some people saved up the entire year for their partying on this day. It was the worst day for grieving.

When I was little, it was called Queen's Day, since Queen Beatrix still reigned. Grandma loved this holiday. It was the one day in the year when everyone could sell their old junk on the street, without a permit of any kind. She would wake me and Lukas early, so that we left the house by seven in the morning.

"Quickly, or all of the good things will be gone," she said. She wheeled her large shopping cart along with us. The square in the center would have been transformed, covered with children and parents huddled against the early morning wind, each guarding a tarp mounded high with old toys, books, teacups, bicycles. People would be sipping coffee bleary-eyed, dressed in unbearably bright orange shirts and hats. Grandma loved a good bargain and would stop at every stand. She always gave Lukas and me some money to spend as well—fifty cents for a puzzle, a guilder for a toy car. Sometimes people sold freshly baked cookies or cupcakes. Lukas always spent everything at once, on marbles, plastic dinosaurs, Lego sets, but I liked to save my money, knowing I might find something more expensive. It was at the Queen's Day street markets that I bought lavender-scented candles and delicate tea cups for Grandma, Helena, and Willem. Despite my fear of Helena, I still loved her and tried my hardest to please her. Grandma bought us cups of hot chocolate or warm, freshly made caramel waffles to munch on as we shopped. She would fill her shopping cart with miniature china ballerinas, bronze clocks, crystal glasses, and then we would walk home together, with Lukas pushing the cart and Grandma and I following, swinging our hands.

Before she died, I had spoken to Grandma about Dutch burial laws and her wishes. This was not very Chinese. We did not like to speak openly about death, but I wanted to make sure everything was done in accordance with what she, and not Helena, wanted.

"What? They can dig you up after ten years? And then throw your bones away?" This had not occurred to Grandma. In China, the burial site was of utmost importance. Families fought for the best spots on the mountain for their loved ones because it was the only place with good feng shui. This way, they believed, the departed could continue to bless the living. The forces of wind, water, and earth were in harmony there. Grandma shook her head. "Barbarians."

"Customs are very different here. The burial rights need to be renewed in Holland and within cemeteries because it is so crowded. There is not enough room. They often will not permit a renewal after ten years."

Grandma leaned back against her pillows, her cheeks and eyes sunken and still. "You decide, Sylvie."

A pang went through me at the thought of Grandma's death. How could it already be so near? I had to pull myself together. The most important thing was that she was happy. "I cannot do that, Grandma. This is too important. I want to know your wish. There is the possibility of a natural grave. That means that you would be placed somewhere in nature, without a tombstone. Many Dutch love this option."

She huffed and waved her frail hand around. "Nameless and forgotten, in the soggy mud of this country? I do not think so."

I hid a smile. "We could try to transport you to another land."

She sat up and I placed a pillow behind her back so she would not tire herself out. "Where? To the Beautiful Country, where I have never been? Back to the Central Kingdom? No, I have been away too long. I would like to fly free, like the phoenix. I wish to see your grandpa again. Dragon and phoenix, yin and yang, man and woman. A death should be floating clouds and flowing water: natural, beautiful, free." Her voice drifted away. The tirade had exhausted her.

I took her hand in both of mine. How happy I was that she was still with us. I had to savor each moment with her, no matter how bittersweet. I cleared my throat to rid the thickness. "Would you consider cremation, then?" This was what I would want for myself. Good riddance to this body.

She thought for a moment and nodded slightly. "Yes. I am a modern woman. Our rituals must fit the lands we live in. Our old feng shui master would have a terrible time here in Europe."

On the day of Grandma's funeral, we drove through a wooded area to a long one-story rectangular building set like a concrete block within a flat meadow. April was sweet but wore a white hat. Despite some initial warm days, this one had turned out to be the coldest in years, closer to the depths of winter than any rebirth of spring. The sky stretched over the horizon, gray and clear, like the iris of an unblinking eye. When Lukas and I stepped from the back of Helena's car, our breaths turned to mist. We were as cold as newly shaven sheep.

"At least Grandma would be happy it is dry," Lukas said, his breath disappearing into the air like a ghost.

Grandma had always carried an umbrella bigger than she was on rainy days. She hated the chilly wet weather. Other parents had often remarked that they expected her to take off on the wind like an airplane during storms. Lukas and I had both fit beneath her massive umbrella. He had always been a long boy and had helped her hold it as I clutched her arm on her other side.

We entered the reception hall, where the guests were supposed to wait. To my surprise, Oma and Opa were there. I had completely forgotten about them. Oma started when she saw me. I did not think she had expected to see me either. It had been so many years. They used to visit us from Belgium every birthday and major holiday. Where Helena had grown harder, Oma and Opa had grown smaller and softer. Their skin and eyes had faded to white, though Oma's hair was still dyed black. I had not known them well. They had never been around enough to enforce discipline. I did remember that they always brought large sacks of chocolate with them for Lukas and me.

I was longer than both of them now. I bent to kiss Oma three times on her cheeks.

Tears sprouted in her eyes. "I know how much you loved her."

"Thank you, Oma." I had never noticed their Belgian accents when I was little, but they had only just moved to Antwerp then. This was how I could mark the years: Oma and Opa had lived there long enough to develop accents.

Opa patted me on the arm. I took a moment to look around the chilly and depressing reception area. There was only a long modern sofa with flat leather cushions. Its hard seats were dark brown and the multicolored beige and orange backrests had been added in an attempt to bring some cheer to the room. Everything was nondenominational. There was no sign of a cross or a Buddha anywhere. We had been asked if we wanted to have a priest and politely declined. This room was as pragmatic as the Dutch, with nothing to suggest anything as nebulous as heaven or an afterlife. I closed my eyes and offered a prayer to our gods. *Please take Grandma into the company of our ancestors.*

The funeral director, a stubby man in a dark suit, greeted us and led us to the room reserved for immediate family. It resembled a typical Dutch living room, with a few square indigo fabric couches arranged around two mismatched coffee tables. We sat and were served tea and coffee. It felt like we were visiting distant relatives, not saying farewell to the woman I had loved the most, the only real mother I had ever had.

Then the director told us that if we wished, we could take leave of the departed privately in the mourning room. Oma, Opa, Helena, and Willem stood but I remained. Lukas stayed behind with me, shifting closer on the sofa. I would not share my grief with Helena and did not think she wished me to witness hers either. After an awkward pause, they left.

When they returned, their eyes were swollen and most of Helena's makeup had worn off. I had not bothered to put on any cosmetics. Then Lukas and I entered the mourning room together. It was tiny, barely enough room for a few people to stand around the closed red mahogany coffin set on a high table in the center. Two lonely chairs leaned against the wall, which had been painted a calming beige.

I could not comprehend it: Grandma was inside that coffin. How could she breathe? It made no sense. How tiny she must be inside there. I felt a sudden urge to open the lid, to release her, to set her free. "She does not like that clunky Dutch-size thing."

Then a large hand took mine and Lukas wrapped me in his arms. "She is already gone. She is free." I closed my eyes and rested my cheek against his shoulder as he stroked my hair. He said softly, "No more pain. No gasping for air."

Then we were racked with sobs again, our arms around each other, the two children Grandma had tended.

"We were not here," I whispered. "I let her down. It was all my fault."

"No." He held my chin in his hand and bent to brush away my tears. "She wanted it this way. Do you remember the last thing she said to us?"

"'Open your hearts. Be happy.'" And with those words, my burden lightened just a bit. In my mind, I said, *Grandma, I know you can hear me. I love you.*

I heard her answer in my heart: *I love you too, Snow Jasmine.*

When it was time for the ceremony, Lukas, Willem, Opa, Oma, Helena, and I acted as the pallbearers. We took the six handles on the coffin. It was heavier than I had expected. The wood probably weighed more than Grandma herself. Opa and Oma stood at the front, Helena and I were in the middle, and Lukas and Willem took up the rear.

The handle burned into my hand. The pressure was unbearable. I was carrying the body of Grandma. A tear rolled over my cheek. She was truly inside. I would never see her again, feel her hands holding mine. I would never get to take her on a luxurious holiday, treat her to a restaurant, or take her home to China. It was too late.

As we entered the main room, I was surprised to find people in attendance. I had not expected anyone. Estelle and Filip sat in the front row. It was clear Estelle had been crying, and Filip gave me a small sympathetic smile. Perhaps I had not completely ruined our circle of friends. Our neighbors were all here, the good faithful Dutch. Even though Grandma had never learned how to speak to them, they still came. The music was some generic classical assortment that the crematorium had chosen. Grandma never told me if she had a preference.

As we approached the front, I was pleased to find the table for the coffin laid out in the Chinese way, with a large framed picture of Grandma at the front. I examined it more closely and realized it was one of the photos Lukas had taken the day I had done her hair and makeup.

Lukas whispered to me as we took our places, "She picked it out herself."

The room was austere—rows of chairs in a neat line facing the coffin and the podium, which would remain unused. For the Chinese, a funeral is a time for grief, tears, breast-beating, folding of sacred papers to be burned that will then turn into gold and silver for the deceased. The room should be thick with incense smoke. Where were the chanting monks, the mourners overwhelmed with pain? *Oh, Grandma,* I thought, *we have come into a strange foreign land.*

Her flowers had not been made into Chinese funeral wreaths. Helena and Willem had never followed the old customs here. What would the neighbors say about us burning ritual papers in the backyard? I thought with gratitude of Ma and Pa, who had always followed our traditions in their little back garden, where the anonymity of New York City protected us—no one had ever said a word if they noticed us at all—and of the kind monks in our temple in Chinatown, where we went to find out our fortunes for the year, each prophecy shaken from a bamboo jar. How I wished I could have taken Grandma. How much room could there be for regrets in one person? Mine were infinite.

Estelle dabbed her face with a tissue and Filip linked his arm through hers. I had known this day was coming. How, then, was it still so bitter? It hurt to leave Grandma behind in her coffin as we left the room.

In the other room, everyone was served tea or coffee and a slab of cake. It was very civilized. The neighbors, embarrassed by any strong emotion, including grief, gave us all the eternal three kisses on our cheeks, said, "Condolences," and left. None of them had truly known Grandma. She was just the funny little Chinese woman who lived on their street.

There was a tap on my arm. It was Filip. I let him draw me outside the room under Lukas's watchful gaze.

When we were alone, he said, "Is it going all right?" He did not wait for me to answer before pulling me into his arms and holding me tight. "Do not blame yourself."

I sniffed. "I am so sorry, Filip." I had treated him so badly.

His voice was muffled in my hair. "It was always only a jest between the two of us, darling. I knew that."

I let him leave it at that. But if that was true, why had he been so angry in Venice?

As I returned to the room, I thought of the Dutch children's song:

In a green, green, green, green tuber tuber country
There are two hares, very dapper
And the one blew the flute-flute-flute
And the other hit the drum
Then suddenly a hunter-hunter-man came
And he shot one
And that made—you must know—
The other sad and worried

Now with Grandma gone, one of my two lifelines had disappeared, the security of her arms, her smile, her love for me.

Lukas was all I had left here.

Telephone Call
Thursday, April 28

Sylvie: She did not wish to die a dog's death, Ma. And, in the end, she shed the red dust of the mortal world with the grace of floating clouds and flowing water.

Ma: I am glad you were with her, Snow Jasmine. I only wish— [sobs]

Sylvie: Oh, Ma.

Amy: Sylvie, it's me. Talking is too much for Ma right now.

Sylvie: Hey, I've missed you.

Amy: Are you doing okay?

Sylvie: Oh, sweetie. Actually, it's been pretty hard. [Voice breaks] I loved Grandma so much.

Amy: I know, Sylvie. But she's still with you. I'm sure of it. When are you coming home?

Sylvie: I'm not sure. My work here's not quite finished. I'll fly back as soon as I can.

Amy: Of course, Sylvie. I can't wait to see you.

Sylvie: Take care of Ma for me, okay?

Amy: I will. See you soon.

Sylvie: Love you. I'll be back before you know it.

CHAPTER 26

Amy

Sunday, May 15

The Netherlands Philharmonic Orchestra has a website in English. I check their program and see they're performing tonight in Amsterdam at the Dutch National Opera and Ballet. *Got you now, Filip*. They're set to play Dvořák's *Rusalka,* a favorite of mine, an opera about a water nymph who leaves her own kind and thereby gives up the power of speech. But the show is completely sold out, and I wouldn't be able to speak to him there anyway. I'll have to confront him afterward or during one of the two intermissions. I think back to our ride on the Epsilon boat. He's a smoker. Everything indoors in the Netherlands is nonsmoking, so he'll likely be outside during the break. I know the first act takes about an hour. If I hurry, I might be able to catch him today.

I take the train to Amsterdam Central Station, and transfer to a subway to Waterlooplein. It's now past eight o'clock in the evening and still light outside. I have to squint against the setting sun.

I walk past the sweeping, blocklike mass of the main building to reach the curved facade of the opera house facing the Amstel River. I lean against one of the dock posts and watch as the skies darken, the white marble front evolving from a golden sunlit glow into columns of brilliant sapphire, lit by blue artificial lights. Several boats are docked along the waterfront. Beyond them, the river has turned brooding and black. The large windows reveal curved interior foyers and multilevel terraces barren of people.

Someone's propped open a few doors and I can hear the faint strains of "Song to the Moon" from Act I. I haven't missed the first intermission then. The singer's melancholy voice floats across the water, yearning for love:

Moon, high and deep in the sky
You travel around the wide world,
and see into people's homes.
Moon, tell me where is my dear.

It reminds me of Sylvie. The Autumn Festival, which falls on the fifteenth day of the eighth lunar month, was always her favorite holiday. She would stand at our window and gaze out at the full moon. I once heard her whisper, "Uncle Moon, come down and have a piece of cake." She had told me, "When I moved to America from the Netherlands, the moon was the only thing that came with me." It was one of the few times she spoke about the life she had before I existed. Out here, in the lonely night, the tears run down my cheeks, where no one can see.

I hear a gong and the crowd of well-dressed people inside begin to approach the doors. It's time. There are several exit points. I pace back and forth, afraid to miss him, and wonder what I'm doing, confronting a man I think might be involved in my sister's death. But who could I have brought as backup? The police think I'm being ridiculous and Lukas has disappeared. The sounds of Dutch and laughter drift like a cloud all around me. I stare carefully into each person's face, hoping to find Filip in the half darkness. There, a bunch of people in black tie walk out of a side door that looks like it could be the exit for the musicians. I circle them, but he is not a part of the group.

Then I catch sight of a lone cigarette's glow and recognize Filip at once: his athletic build, the tilt of his head. He stands by himself at the water's edge on the periphery of the crowd. A raw breeze whips through me and I shiver. People chatter loudly to one another and drink champagne. Would anyone see or hear if he pushed me in the water?

As I step up to him, he jerks and drops his cigarette. "You startled me."

"You owe me an explanation."

He waves his hand in a dismissive gesture. "This is not a good time. I have to go back inside soon."

My neck goes stiff and my pulse pounds in my ears. I shove him in the chest, hard, despite the fact that he's almost a foot taller than me. He stumbles backward. My voice comes out in a furious hiss. "My. Sister. Is. Dead. You lied to me. You must have lied to her. How dare you try to get rid of me now?"

His eyes flare and his face turns into something hard and furious. He raises his arm as if to strike me and I am suddenly afraid. It's so dark. I'm sure no one can see us. The waves lap at the dock and the water seems sinister and vast. I step back.

The anger drains from his face and he presses a fist against his chest. He squeezes his eyes shut. "I am sorry. For everything."

I am still trembling and wrap my arms around myself. "W-why did you jump on my bicycle?"

He stares into the distance, unable to meet my eyes. He scuffs his foot against the ground. "I was back in the village, seeing my folks. I had a concert on Mother's Day, so I would not be able to go home. I went to give my mother her gift early. I was on my way when I spotted you with Lukas and Estelle outside the café and I understood immediately who you were. So I followed you. Once you started going back to Lukas's house, it was simple to figure out where I could intercept you, especially since you bike slower than a snail." A small smile creases his lips at this.

A sudden gust of wind sweeps my hair forward. I gather it back out of my face impatiently. "But why?"

He swipes a hand over his face. "I cared about Sylvie. I was hoping you would hire Epsilon. I have no right, but you do because you are a family member. I had suggested them to Lukas, but he would not listen to me. He was still angry over something that happened in Venice. I was afraid if I told you the truth, you would ask Lukas about me and he would stop you. He pretty much went out of his mind when she disappeared. I have never seen him like that, like a beast had taken him over. I think he was in denial that she might be dead." He throws his hands up.

I cross my arms and try to make out his expression. "Why didn't you tell me who you were after we got to know each other a bit? I would have done anything to help Sylvie, including keeping a secret from Lukas."

He sighs. "It began with an impulse and then I was caught in the lie. I was trying to find the right moment to tell you, but then—" He breaks off and tugs at his ear.

There is a moment of awkward silence. I finish for him. "I developed that ridiculous crush on you. I stared at you and called you a sex object and sent you a million texts. You were embarrassed." My cheeks must glow in the darkness. But it doesn't matter. I need to figure out what happened to Sylvie. "Why did you and Lukas fight? I mean, what was the real reason?"

He wraps both arms around his head, an unusually gawky, graceless move for him. "The truth? I was jealous."

I furrow my brow and bite my lip, trying to assimilate everything he's saying. "Because you were afraid Lukas would take Sylvie away from you? Even though he's with Estelle?"

Filip doesn't answer and covers his face with his hands. He starts to heave. At first, I'm afraid he's crying, but then I realize he's laughing, long and bitter.

I stare at him. Lukas's crazed grief. How Filip let Lukas hit him over and over again, not lifting a finger to defend himself. "You were never romantically involved with Sylvie."

He shakes his head, his eyes still clouded, but not with humor, with pain. His gaze is fixed on me and I understand.

"You thought that if she was found, he would be able to move on." He had done it all for Lukas. Filip hadn't been jealous of Lukas. He'd been jealous of Sylvie. I ask gently, "How long have you been in love with him?"

His face in the shadows is unspeakably sad. "Forever."

I reach out my arms and he goes into them. We hold each other for a long moment. I breathe in his smell of cigarette smoke and Earl Grey tea. I mutter into his shirt, "I just want to make it clear that you were never my type."

He breaks into a surprised chuckle. As we separate, we both have tears in our eyes. The air between us feels lighter now, as if a great weight has fallen away.

There is a thickness in my throat as I ask, "Did you ever tell him? I mean, you're Dutch, for goodness' sake. You live in Amsterdam."

He rolls his shoulders and blows out a series of short exhales, as if to regain control. "Everyone except Lukas knows. I made it very clear to him once. We were the last ones in the locker room in high school and we'd just gotten out of the showers. He looked so beautiful, with the water crusted on his eyelashes, I just—" Filip breaks off and sighs. He works his jaw. "I made it perfectly obvious how I felt about him and he was horrified."

I lay my hand on the silky fabric of his tuxedo. "I'm so sorry. He was young."

He places a hand over mine and gives it a warm squeeze. "I know. We weave our own webs. Then they trap us. After that, I tried hard to convince him, myself, and my family that I was not gay, that the incident had been a joke. I married a wonderful woman. But it never works when you deny who you truly are. You know what she said to me when we got divorced? She said, 'Lukas is your French Revolution. Once you loved him, everything in your life fell into a before and after. Nothing would ever be the same.'"

Filip looks me directly in the eyes. I shiver under the weight of his stare. He leans in close and whispers to me, "Lukas was my French Revolution and Sylvie was his."

Text Message

Amy: I just spoke to Filip and a lot of things are clearer now. Okay, I'm sorry, I have a stupid question. Is Lukas your boyfriend?

Estelle: Oh, honey. Absolutely not.

Amy: But you always kiss him on the lips. You hold each other.

Estelle: I am physical with many people. Mothers kiss their children that way here. It does not mean anything. I am not the one for Lukas.

Amy: Sylvie.

Estelle: Yes.

It's late when I get home, and Helena and Willem have already gone to bed. I have bitten all of my nails to the quick. My mind has been churning the entire trip over everything I've learned from Filip and Estelle. Could Lukas possibly have something to do with Sylvie's death? Jealousy? I think about his wild eyes, his enormous hands. Was that why he didn't want anyone to find the body? If there were any marks on her, we'd never know since the police refused to do an autopsy. Or was it something with him and Jim? But Jim has no real motive. I remember all the talk about the gold. Helena suspected Sylvie of faking the burglary. What if Lukas had deliberately cast the suspicion on her so when she disappeared, Helena would assume she had taken it? Could he possibly be such a good actor? But I can't believe Lukas would have hurt my sister. If what Estelle and Filip said is true, then Lukas has been lying to me and everyone else about his relationship with Sylvie—but confronting him directly will only alert him to my suspicions.

I tiptoe into the unlit house and know what I have to do. I'll search Lukas's apartment while he's gone. I wedge the door open with my foot so the outdoor light illuminates the key rack that hangs in the entryway. One key is labeled LUKAS. Probably so his parents can look after Couscous and his apartment when he's traveling. Easy.

I take a deep breath. My fingers are numb with fear but I have to do it now while I have the chance. I take the key and gently pull the front door closed behind me. Half of the moon hovers suspended in the hollow sky, the other half obliterated by darkness. The sharp white stones paving the front lawn glint in the moonlight like bones. I take a step toward the converted garage but freeze as I catch sight of Lukas's scooter parked in the driveway. The lights flick on inside. He's back.

I stomp my foot on the hard earth, but a part of me is relieved as well. I rake my fingers through my hair and turn around, defeated for now. I whisper into the night air, "If only you could tell me what happened to you, Sylvie."

CHAPTER 27

Sylvie

Friday, April 29

My grief and disappointment overwhelmed my system. I was listless with despair. The sharp edge had been dulled. I felt as if I were carrying a great weight on my back that dragged me toward the earth. Now that Grandma was gone, I had no excuse to stay any longer—unless Lukas asked me to, and I was not going to hang around waiting for him. He had not given me any indication that he felt the same way now that he had in Venice. I thought of that night over and over, but it was, in the end, nothing but a kiss. Who would want me now? I was a broken woman saddled with the prospect of a messy divorce.

When evening fell, I packed my things, took my cello, and went to Lukas's apartment to tell him I was leaving the next morning. He could return the cello with its case to Filip for me. I rang the doorbell. No one answered. His bicycle and scooter were parked in the driveway. He was probably working and could not hear me.

I used my key to let myself inside and set my cello beside his front door.

"Lukas?" I called out.

I heard a faint noise from the back of the studio, where he had his darkroom. I walked toward the double-hinged doorway and knocked on the door. This time, he said something indecipherable from inside. I cracked open both doors and waited behind the dark curtain.

"Who is there?" he asked.

"Me. The lights are off. You do not need to worry."

His voice grew warm and intimate. "Come in. Let me show you what I am doing here."

In the glow of the overhead red light, I could just make out his tall figure. He stood beside one of the large washbasins. The scent of chemicals tickled my nostrils. He was hanging a photo to dry on a line. The darkroom was covered with pictures. I squinted to see but as I recognized them, let out a shaky breath. Perhaps I had not been as delusional as I had thought.

I stepped up behind him and wrapped my arms around his waist. "These are all of me. That one is my weak eye."

His voice was husky. "I love your eye."

It was a tight shot of my right eye, probably taken during our time in Venice: the almond shape, the long fine lashes, the iris lit up by the sun and ever so slightly tilting outward toward a landscape no one else could see.

Why had I waited so long? I leaned my cheek against his back, so broad and strong. I felt him strip off the thick rubber gloves and rinse his hands. He turned around and I was in his arms again, where I had always wanted to be without ever knowing it.

I leaned my forehead against his chest and took a deep breath. I had to say it. "My flight is tomorrow. I just finished packing."

He stiffened and gripped me by the shoulders so hard it hurt. "What? No. Sylvie, what about us?"

I shook my head, my hair brushing against his hands. "Lukas, you do not know everything about me."

He growled, low and urgent, "I know enough. When you came back and I saw you again at the airport, I felt like I had been struck. Every piece of my life fell into place in that moment."

My voice was so small, it almost squeaked. "Why did you not come to me that last night in Venice?"

He sighed and pulled me close to him again. His large hand stroked my hair. "I was afraid you were not ready. You were newly separated from your husband. You were seeing him everywhere. And then we returned and Grandma—it did not seem the right time. I suppose I still was not sure you wanted me instead of Filip."

My legs were weak and I felt the tears behind my eyelids. "You have to understand. I ruin everything."

"Not true." He rested his cheek against the top of my head.

I put my heart on my tongue, wise or not. I laid my trembling hand against the side of his neck. I had to give him the chance to say no to the real me. "I always try so hard and yet, it all goes wrong. No one really likes me. Not after they know me, anyway. One colleague took me out to lunch just so she could let slip that everyone thought I was sleeping my way to the top. When you are a woman, people always assume success comes from your bedroom and not your boardroom skills." Despite myself, my voice cracked. "Before then, I had thought I was getting along well with people at work. I believed I had friends." How I wanted that to be true. "After that, I learned to keep my distance."

Lukas drew back to look at me. His eyes were tender.

"Then my marriage went down the drain."

He caressed the side of my face with his callused palm. "Did you really think any of this would matter to me?"

Despite myself, I sniffed and sagged against him as I struggled to find the right words. "My own parents did not want me, Lukas. I never fit in anywhere. The only people who ever truly cared about me were Grandma and Amy. Now Grandma is gone and Amy is grown. She no longer needs me. Amy got the love and I got the success, but I do not have anything anymore."

He bent down, his lips a breath away from my own, and said in a hoarse whisper, "You have me."

CHAPTER 28

Amy

Monday, May 16

Ma and Pa are scheduled to arrive this afternoon. I pretend to have a migraine from all the stress to avoid picking them up from the airport. It's not far from the truth. In the bathroom mirror, I see that my eyes are sunken into their sockets, the skin around them red and abraded from my constant rubbing. My lips look as if a layer of white wax has melted over them, now flaking off. Lukas will accompany Helena and Willem. This is my chance to look through his apartment without anyone around.

As soon as the car leaves the driveway, I race over to his apartment with the spare key in my hand. I decide to start my search upstairs. I am surprised by how neat it is for such a shaggy, unshaven person. I head for the desk, which supports a massive monitor attached to a laptop. I hesitate before opening the first drawer. I can't believe I'm doing this. I've broken into my cousin's apartment and suspect him of having something to do with Sylvie's death, maybe even of murdering her. I am ridiculous.

Frantic with energy, I search his desk anyway—cables, an old cell phone, flash drives. Papers that look like invoices he's sent to people, with his name in big black letters in the letterhead. Everything's in Dutch. One drawer's filled with receipts filed in different folders. If I were a real detective, I would figure out something clever from this. He still has a thick paper agenda. I flip through it but can't read a word. Then I open the laptop and try a couple of passwords: Sylvie's name and birthday. But they don't work.

Why did I ever think I could accomplish anything by coming here? Ma and Pa will arrive soon and then we'll leave for New York and we'll never know how Sylvie wound up at the bottom of the Amsterdam-Rhine Canal. I choke back a sob and press my hand against my chest. How can this be real? *Pull it together, Amy. They'll be back soon.* I tackle the agenda again, this time going through it page by page, checking the days when Sylvie was here.

There, wedged deep into the inner crack of the book, is an irregular slip of yellow notebook paper. It looks like it's been torn from a larger piece. I pull it out gently with my fingernails and gasp.

It's Sylvie's angular, clear handwriting. It's just her signature, as if this is the end of a note she wrote, but instead of *Lee* she's signed her name as *Sylvie Tan*. Lukas's last name.

So it's true. It had been Lukas and Sylvie all along. She must have really been in love with him to pretend his last name was hers. She hadn't even taken Jim's surname after they wed. Perhaps this was a tiny bit of proof. No wonder he'd looked so distraught. I tuck the slip of paper into my jacket pocket and go through the other papers more carefully. I don't find anything, so I return to the computer.

I'm startled by a soft scuffle and then a meow from downstairs. Could it be? I type in *Couscous*. The laptop unlocks. I immediately go into his email, but again, everything seems to be written in Dutch. I don't know what I'm expecting. That he wrote a confession in English and sent it to someone? In the *Sent* folder, I see what must be dozens of emails to Sylvie. None of them have a reply. I pick a few and send them to myself. I can try a translation program on them later. I'm afraid he'll be back at any moment so I quickly go through the rest of his laptop.

The Dutch documents are equally mysterious and, with a sigh, I click the computer closed.

I scan the room. A cello is propped up against the corner, next to its black-and-blue case. A sharp pain shoots into my heart—had that been Sylvie's? I spot an enormous messenger-style bag next to the broken coffee table. The edge of what looks like a portfolio peeks from underneath its gaping flap.

I yank the bag toward me. I open it and pull out the portfolio. Tears spring to my eyes as I press my knuckles to my lips. Inside is photo after photo of Sylvie. Sylvie in what must be Venice, with a gondola in the background, smiling, radiant with happiness. Sylvie's wandering eye—her throat and lips. Strands of her hair, black in the wind against an Italian cathedral. Sylvie lying on the sofa bed behind me, stroking Couscous, stretched out across her stomach. If I hadn't suspected it before, these photos would have revealed Lukas's love or obsession to me. But I am taken in by the open warmth and vulnerability in Sylvie's eyes as she gazes at the photographer.

Between the glossy photos, I find an old Polaroid. The edges of it are worn as if it's been handled often in the intervening years. It's yellowed and fading but the image is still clear: an awkward, homely Chinese girl, about eight years old, sitting on the floor and tucking herself into the corner like she wishes she could disappear. Her shoulders are hunched as if to ward off a blow that she knows is coming. One eye is hidden by a dark blue eye patch, the other glares from beneath her uneven bangs. She's scowling, staring at the camera as if daring it to unveil her secrets. She is so different from the impeccably dressed, poised sister I've known most of my life that it takes me a moment to realize it is Sylvie. She's in handmade clothes, probably sewn by Grandma: a funny little shirt with a Chinese Mandarin collar. That shirt could not have done a better job of marking her as different in this country.

Her mouth is strange and thick. I realize it's because of the crooked front tooth that protrudes from her front lip. I'd completely forgotten. Sylvie had it fixed as soon as she went away to college. Was this what Sylvie had been—a child driven into the corner? I see resentment and a fierce intelligence on her expressive face, but there's fear too. What had

Willem and Helena done to her? I clutch the photo to my chest. This is why I have to find out what happened to her. This girl is counting on me.

More photos: Sylvie against the open Dutch sky, the flat fields laid out behind her. Sylvie on a bicycle in Amsterdam. Sylvie drinking tea at a café. Sylvie playing the cello in Helena's living room. Sylvie laughing beside a bunch of trees, water behind her, a half-eaten sandwich in her hand. I recognize the spot. That's where we found her body.

I look through all the photos and then rummage through the rest of the bag. Nothing.

I hear a car pull into the driveway outside. Oh no. I still haven't found anything, except for evidence that Sylvie and Lukas had an intimate relationship. What was I expecting anyway? I quickly replace the photos and slide the portfolio back into the bag.

Couscous has padded upstairs by now and is playing with a part of the cello case. She wiggles her butt and then pounces on the frayed shoulder strap that is lying on the floor. I pause. Why isn't the cello inside its case?

I hear voices from the lawn. They're getting out of the car. Lukas will be back at any moment and I'm still inside his apartment. I hesitate, then run over and swiftly flip open the case.

There's a worn velvet bag stuffed inside. I know what it is from the way it feels: Grandma's missing jewelry. I am frozen in shock before I make myself move. Oh gods. It can't be. It was Lukas after all. He took the treasure from her, then killed her. I can't be caught in here when he comes back alone. The only exit is through the front door. The family must have gone into the main house by now. They'll realize I'm not there and he might come looking for me.

I hear the key in the lock downstairs. I'm breathing so shallowly, I think I'm going to hyperventilate. As quickly and quietly as I can, I race down the stairs, still lugging the jewelry bag. The door is half-open now and I shove against it hard.

It bounces against Lukas, who lets out a yell, and then I'm through to the outside. He reaches to grab my arm. He has me, his grip bruising, he's pulling me inside. I'm twisting and kicking and then I'm loose and I run for all I'm worth.

He yells, "What the—? What is that? Amy! Stop!"

I hear his footsteps heavy and swift behind me, his longer legs gaining on me quickly. The stones are slippery and I slide, almost trip, then I recover my balance and keep going.

In front of me, the living room lights are switched on in the main house and I can just make out the familiar figure standing behind the gauze curtain: Ma.

I pound on the door. I ring the doorbell again and again. Now Lukas is upon me. His giant hands are grabbing the back of my jacket. He is pulling me backward.

I hang on to the doorknob. "Open up! Please!"

The door falls away and Helena is staring at me, her mouth open. Lukas and I both freeze. I tear away from him and burst into the house, heaving and panting. I am drenched in clammy sweat. Everyone's gaze is fixed upon us. I hear Lukas's ragged breathing, and then focus on Ma's and Pa's familiar faces. It's strange to see them in this foreign place. They're sitting on the couch; Willem has stopped short before them with a tray of coffee and tea in his hands.

Ma is deflated like an empty trash bag, wrinkled, old, and sagging in a way I've never seen before. It's as if the life has drained out of her with the passing of her mother and daughter. "Amy, what going on?" she says.

I catch my breath. I can't believe what I have discovered. Am I somehow wrong? How can I devastate them further? Should I stay quiet as I always have? I am clutching the bag to my stomach. It's hidden inside the folds of my unzipped jacket. I could take the treasure home with us and let it all be over. Except I can't go back to the person I used to be. Lukas murdered Sylvie. The shock and horror of it echoes through my mind. In a trembling voice, I say, "We need to call the police."

Lukas looms behind me. I can feel the heat of him, his rage and frustration. What will he do now?

Willem's face is a polite mask. He sets down the tray with a clatter, but his voice is deliberate and calm. "Why would we need to do that?"

I am breathing so shallowly, I can barely say the words. "Because your son killed Sylvie."

Helena gasps; her face blotches. Ma jerks as if I've dealt her a physical blow and Pa's eyes bulge like those of the fish he kills. Lukas lurches toward me. As I wince away from him, he grabs the back of a chair and uses it to brace himself. He hangs his head so his hair curtains his face.

The stunned silence is broken by a long peal of laughter. Willem says, "A very dramatic joke, Amy."

I open my jacket and reveal the velvet bag. The mocking smile disappears from Willem's face. From the stricken look in Ma's eyes, I know she recognizes it. I drop to my knees in front of the low opium table and pour out the contents. At first, a small plastic bag emerges and I'm afraid that I was mistaken. But then pouches of silk envelopes tied together with ribbons appear. I open one to reveal a gold necklace formed of apple-green jade droplets, each teardrop setting wrought in the shape of a lotus flower and studded with diamonds. Both Helena and Ma stare with longing on their faces, whether for the jewelry or Grandma's love, I cannot say.

I stare at all of them. "I found this hidden in Lukas's room."

"What the hell were you doing in my apartment?" he bellows. He has his arms wrapped around himself, his teeth bared like a feral animal's.

"That does not prove anything." Helena dares to come over and start stuffing the jewelry back into the bag, as if she plans to return it to Lukas. She doesn't meet our eyes. She speaks so rapidly I can barely understand her. "He has a right. Grandma raised him. Grandma must have given it to him. If Sylvie had the jewelry, she stole it."

"Stop!" I am screaming as I grab her by the wrist. She freezes and her entire body goes rigid. "How dare you? Sylvie's dead!" I cry out, keening. I dump out all of the contents again. No more hiding. "Why? What did she die for if he didn't kill her? He has a photo of her at the exact spot where her body was found. They had a secret relationship. Sylvie was in love with him." I hear Ma's sharp intake of breath. I pull out the scrap of paper from my pocket. "Look at this. She wrote 'Sylvie Tan,' like a schoolgirl in love. Grandma meant the jewelry for Sylvie. He seduced Sylvie, took the gold from her, and then got rid of her and made it look like she ran away with it."

Everyone except for Lukas crowds around to read the little scrap with Sylvie's precise handwriting on it. Even when besotted, she had been clear and exact.

No one speaks. They are like wax figures in a horror show, transfixed and aghast. Lukas works his jaw but he too is unable to speak.

I turn to him. "You played the lover and then you murdered her." My voice is shaking with rage now. I want to tear him apart.

He says in a hoarse voice, "You are right. I did kill her." He rubs his eyes with his clenched fists. His face is haggard. "I regret her death more than I could ever say." He convulses with ragged, tearing sobs. He moans, "Sylvie . . ."

Helena brings the back of her hand to her trembling lips. Then she steps to her son and wraps her arms around him like she would a small child.

I am shuddering so hard I can barely stand, but I am resolute. "No more silence. These secrets have taken Sylvie from us."

Willem has staggered backward, ashen, his eyes feverish and overbright. His hand is clasped over his mouth as if to stop himself from confessing. He stares, not at me, but at my mother.

To my great surprise, it is Ma who speaks. She shakes her head in denial, her shoulders curled, her spine bent as if to protect herself. Her voice is choked with emotion but strong. "You are right that a secret killed my daughter. But the secret is not what you think."

CHAPTER 29

Ma

Monday, May 16

I need to speak Chinese now so I can express myself truly. Helena, would you please translate for Amy? I must chop nails and sever iron to get to the heart of the matter.

This was my fault. I have wronged all of you in this room. But heaven's net is wide and none can escape its mesh. I too am punished.

Pa, I put the green hat of cuckoldry upon your head, although you did not deserve it. When I married you, I was already pregnant with another man's child. I did not know for certain at the time but there was no excuse. I can only offer an explanation.

I grew up knowing I would not be allowed to choose whom I should marry. Our families were friends and we were promised to each other from when we were little. I was betrothed to Pa but I was in love with Willem. I know how it is to desire that which you do not have.

I did not dare to speak until it was too late. By then, you had come back, Helena, with your sophisticated foreign ways, the open beckoning road behind your every move. You could offer Willem freedom, wealth, and your whole heart. I loved you too, Pa, and that was why I was so conflicted with my affections divided.

But then, Helena and Willem married. They were to leave together and Willem and I had cast longing glances at each other for years. If one often walks by the riverside, one's shoes will eventually get wet. Willem and I took our last chance to be together. Our heart blood rose in a tidal wave. We destroyed our cauldrons and sank our boats. We were leaving for separate countries, different lives, and would never see each other again, so we thought.

Pa and I married almost immediately afterward and then we too left China. The two of you moved to Holland, and we headed for the Beautiful Country. I did not expect to get the big stomach.

Soon after that, Snow Jasmine was born. Pa, I know that after her birth, you slowly grew to suspect. I thought at first she could belong to either of you and so I watched her like a hawk. That was barren ground for a mother's love. I scrutinized her every moment, wondering if she would betray my sin by a gesture, a mark, a word. But soon, I understood who her father was.

And yes, Helena, when the chance came to send her to you as a baby, I did it for many reasons. We could barely afford to keep her. She cried in the hot New York summers. I was afraid for her safety and mine. I knew that you, Helena, could offer her and my mother a better home than I could. But I also did it so her biological father could know his daughter.

The truth is, when I flew to Holland with Snow Jasmine, I did not know if I came to leave my baby or to take the treasure and my girl back home with me. I was jealous of you, Helena, with your large house, fine husband, and my own mother to care for your child, and now, I would give you my daughter too? The jewelry had belonged to me from the moment I married Pa. That was why Grandma could not give it to anyone else. As was tradition, it was her wedding present to me, but I felt too guilty to accept it because of what I had done. Pa never knew about it. It was for me to keep for myself, something a mother could pass on to her daughter, something a woman could use to save herself in times of dire need. I asked Grandma to take care of it for me.

When I came to leave Snow Jasmine here, I ate bitterness. It was common for our children to be raised by their grandmothers. Many of our friends in the Beautiful Country had sent their babies to live with their relatives in the Central Kingdom so their kids could learn the old ways and language. But Grandma could see how it made me cough up blood to think of leaving my child behind. She said to me, "My daughter, you have brought with you the extreme danger of a mountain of blades and a sea of fire. We must dispel the clouds and see the sun again. Sell the jewelry. Keep your child and leave this place, and this man."

I had the gold in my luggage, ready to tell you, Helena, that I had changed my mind. I felt new courage and hope. It must have shown in my demeanor, and Willem, who was always watching me, guessed the truth. I was staying here in your house in a state of mutual hostility, both of us with swords drawn and bows bent, and you never let him or me out of your sight. But one day you were both working at the restaurant and Willem told you there was an emergency and that he had to consult with your accountant. He circled home and spoke to me instead. He had seen Snow Jasmine's birthmark. He knew she was his. He begged me to leave his daughter with him, if only for a year or two.

I could not deny him. The burden of shame and obligation was too great. I staked all on one throw. My Ma knew then that I would not accept the treasure until she was dead and that Snow Jasmine would have to be the one to put it into my hands. But a fire at the city gates is also a disaster to the fish in the pond, and that decision claimed many innocent victims, the worst of all my Snow Jasmine, who had always been as lovely and pure as a crane in a flock of chickens.

Make no mistake, I am the true villain of this story.

CHAPTER 30

Sylvie

Friday, April 29

Then, finally, he was kissing me again. I was afloat with love and joy. His hands tugged gently on my hair to tilt my head back, and I felt his rough stubble at the sensitive skin of my throat. A flood of heat washed over me. Dizzy with desire, I braced one hand against the wall for balance. My fingers struck the ridge of something, and then I was blinded by white.

"Oh, I am so sorry, I hit the light switch by accident!" I gasped and raised a hand to my flushed cheek. "Have I ruined your work?"

He gave me a long, slow smile, blinking in the sudden brightness. He bent down and whispered, "Do not worry. I had already finished." Then he swept my hair back with his thumb and planted a deliberate kiss behind my ear. I shivered, closing my eyes. "We should move this upstairs—" He broke off.

"What is wrong?" I peeked at him through my lashes.

He was staring at my ear, his eyes wide. "How long have you had that mark?"

Was I deformed? Did he not want me anymore? I self-consciously rubbed the birthmark. "Since I was born. Why?"

His mouth was slack. He lifted both hands from my body and held them suspended in the air. "Because my father has the same one."

"What?" I furrowed my brows. I could not understand it. What was the problem, we were relatives, right? Oh wait, Helena was my cousin, not Willem. Willem had married into her family. How could I be related to Willem? Ridiculous. "It must be a coincidence."

Lukas held his body slanted away from mine. He shuffled backward on his feet. "It explains everything, do you not see? Why everyone always thinks you and Pa look alike, how brilliant you both are. Why he always loved you so much."

I rubbed a hand across my face. I felt stupid. Normally I was the clever one, figuring out the killer in movies long before everyone else. It was like my brain had been packed in cotton and I could not get the gears to turn.

At my silence, he placed his fist against his mouth as if he could not bear to say the words. "That is why my mother always hated you." His voice broke. "Because you are his child."

Willem's daughter? The air was knocked from my lungs. Was I Helena's daughter, then? Why would she hate me? But I had been born in the United States. I had a birth certificate. Born to Ma. Wait. No. Ma and Willem. It could not be. Lukas was not my distant cousin. He was my half brother.

A mangled cry filled the room, like some pitiful animal was being slaughtered. It was coming from my throat. Everything was blurry. "No!" I pounded my fists against his chest as he held my wrists in his hands.

I fought against him until I collapsed, sobbing, against his chest. He held me to him for a long time until I could breathe again.

Now he took my hand in his and brought it to his lips for a soft kiss against my knuckles. "This does not change anything."

I pulled it away and tucked it behind my back. I wiped my face, and moved aside so I could look at him. "How can it not?"

A flush stained his cheeks and he could not meet my eyes. "No one knows. We do not have to tell anyone." His voice seemed to come from across a great distance. "My mother may suspect but she will never say anything, and my pa and your ma have kept it a secret all these years." He spoke rapidly, trying to convince himself.

I reached out to touch his silky hair. "Lukas. You are the one good thing in my life. My only hope. I will not drag you down with me."

He cradled my face between his palms. "What do you mean?"

"You finally learned to speak up. I will not bury you in secrets again."

"Sylvie." His lips parted and he bent down. I turned so his kiss landed on my cheek.

"Look, this is such a mess." I forced my voice to sound rational, though it still trembled. I gave him a wan smile. I had to protect him from me. "Neither of us can think clearly right now. Shall we go to sleep and talk in the morning?"

"Do you know it for sure?" He peered at me intently, still so concerned for me, never thinking of himself. He took me by the shoulders. "Are you all right?"

I took a deep breath and shook my hair, straightened my spine. "Yes. Do not worry, I am fine. I am tired and overwhelmed, that is all. I only need some time alone to think and rest. Can you please give that to me?"

He nodded. "Of course, I will give you anything you want, Sylvie."

"We will talk later, I promise," I lied. I took a step back as his hands reluctantly released their grip.

I strode toward the door but could not resist one last peek at him. He was so handsome and vulnerable standing there beneath the stark lighting, staring after me with his heart in his eyes.

He swallowed, as if he could barely form the words, and asked, painfully, "Please just tell me one thing. Do you love me?"

At that, I broke and rushed back into his arms. I held him tight. "Forever."

My lifeline had been cut. From the moment I understood, I knew what I had to do—the long, slow grind of the past few months, Jim, my work, Grandma, and now Lukas. It was enough. Something instinctive and biological took over. He had been my last hope and a part of me had decided long ago that if I lost this final gamble, the game was over.

I scribbled a note for Amy, Ma, and Pa. I was being selfish yet again. I hesitated a moment before signing it, then decided to use my real name. I slid the note and the gifts I had bought for them in Venice into the velvet bag that held Grandma's jewelry.

I waited until it was late and Lukas had turned out his lights—and told myself, *Better a clear break than an eternal desire for someone you could never have, someone you never should have desired in the first place*. I could not bear to live wanting and needing him, to watch as he moved on, married someone else. Not all of us were like Amy, made for warmth, love, happiness.

When everything was quiet, I crept across the lawn. The night was bitter and still, the waning moon waiting for the darkness to overwhelm it completely. I opened his door, held the jewelry bag against my cheek for a moment, and then removed my cello and hid the treasure inside the empty case. I wished I could tiptoe upstairs and kiss him one last time.

They had always said I was destined to die by water.

I placed everything that belonged to me inside the small rental car and drove away as quietly as I could. I looked in the rearview mirror as Lukas's apartment disappeared in the distance. Death did not recognize sweet children. We all had to go, whether we had been good or not. The lies that had sustained me: if I did everything right, I could earn love; if I was perfect enough, I would cheat death. My painful truth: love would always leave me; I did not deserve to be loved. Even a donkey did not stumble over the same stone twice.

All of my designer things, buying into the myth that if you owned the right items, you would belong. That respect and friendship and the right skin color could be purchased. If you were born a dime, you would never become a quarter. When I met Jim, it was like I had finally attained the promised land. I had made it to the foreign shore I had spent so long attempting to reach and been allowed inside, only to find it barren.

This life of mine, given away as a baby. That was the beginning. And now, I was at the end.

I parked in the spot where Lukas and I had picnicked on the banks of the Amsterdam-Rhine Canal. There were a few scattered farmhouses in the distance and all of their windows were dark. I finally understood everything: Helena, Willem, Ma, Pa. How foolish, my hope for Ma and Pa to truly love me. Willem, my father, who took from me the man I desired most.

I was tired of wanting and choosing. Who we truly were and our rational selves were two different entities. The logical part of me knew I did not have to do this—but answers to questions of the heart were inaudible and incomprehensible. We could only feel them, like currents swaying us from beneath the surface, supporting us at their whim, until they decided to grab hold and pull us under.

I took the rosebud from between the pages of the book in my handbag. I pressed it to my lips and inhaled its faded scent. With Lukas, I had felt like I was finally home. The other men who had cared about me only loved the image I projected for them, like a floating helium balloon bound to my wrist by the most tenuous of strings. Lukas had been different. But I would not be like Ma, hiding an essential truth for my entire life.

Amy, I will not be around to watch out for you. You must learn to care for yourself.

I sat in the dark waiting as the sleeping pills took effect. As it grew murkier and the world around me faded into oblivion, I stepped on the gas. The headlights came on automatically and I switched them off. The icy water would make things quick. I started to fade and woke myself up. I did not want to be found here on the grass. I wanted to disappear, to return to the great oblivion of the sea, to our true home, the land of the unliving from which we had all originated.

The car lurched, picked up speed, launched itself from the earth, and was free.

CHAPTER 31

Amy

Monday, May 16

We are silent after listening to Ma's story. My head spins. I feel nauseous. I cup my nose and mouth in my hands and breathe deeply to stop from passing out. When I recover enough to look around, Pa's face is wooden and streaked with red, whether from embarrassment or anger, I do not know. Helena is blinking back tears and Willem stares at the floor. I slowly realize that I am the only one who is utterly astounded. The rest of them already knew.

"How did you find out?" I ask Lukas, who is still bent over, gripping the back of the chair.

He wipes his face with his sleeve, unable to answer, and taps his ear.

There is a pause, and then Willem touches his own ear. "She has the same birthmark. That is how I always knew she was mine."

Helena's voice is low and choked with emotion. "I hated her for it. I wanted to despise you too, but I love you too much. There was not enough room for hate. I am only a fool." She turns her face away.

Ma's hand flies to her mouth at Helena's revelation. She presses her lips together to hold back her tears. "If you know, if you hate Sylvie, why you not send her home?"

Helena speaks with her back to us. "I was afraid of losing Willem and Lukas. They loved her so much. And despite myself, I loved her too. Like I said, I am an idiot."

Willem walks over and tentatively rests the palm of one hand on her upper arm, as if he's afraid of driving her further away from him. "I am sorrier than I can ever say. I love you, Helena. I have always been yours."

Ma stares at him with anguish and heartbreak in her eyes. I realize she has been in love with this man all these years. She squeezes her eyes shut and I can see her dreams dissolve behind her lids. This, I now understand, is the reason Willem stared at me so, because I resemble Ma.

Pa clasps his hands together in front of his face so hard his knuckles turn white. His voice wobbles, unused to carrying the emotional weight of his words. "I knew what was between the two of you. I did not understand you had already acted on your feelings for each other, not until much later. But still, I spoke to Willem before we ever left China."

Ma's head snaps toward him. "What?"

Pa hits his forehead with his fisted hand and closes his eyes. "I wanted to give you your freedom. I wanted you to be happy."

Her breathing is shallow. She's hardly able to speak, and stares at him as if seeing him for the first time. "You never tell me."

Now Pa looks away and doesn't answer.

Willem glances at Helena's back, then hardens his face. "I refused. He did not wish to hurt you. That is why he said nothing. I chose Helena, all those years ago."

Slowly, Helena turns around. She still doesn't meet his gaze but lets him hold her by her shoulders. Ma closes her eyes and collapses against the couch, as if she can no longer hold herself upright. Then with her eyes still closed, she reaches for Pa's hand and grasps it in both of her own. He does not hold hers back but he does not pull away either.

I catch Willem's furtive, pained look at Ma and know that he may have chosen Helena, perhaps for her money, but he has always been in love with my mother. In this, I am wise enough to know when to keep silent.

Willem says, his voice thick, "I only regret I never held Sylvie after she knew she was my daughter."

Pa glares at him. "She was my daughter."

Their eyes meet, their frames are rigid. I am afraid they will come to blows.

"Ours," I say. "Sylvie belonged to all of us." I step over to Lukas and touch him on the arm. "I am so embarrassed by the accusations I made."

He takes a shuddering breath. His eyes are dark, intense, filled with an ocean of grief. "I should not have kept the truth from you. I should have been kinder to you, especially since I know how much you meant to Sylvie. The truth is that I have always been jealous of you."

I am taken aback. No one has ever envied me. "What? Why?"

He says simply, "You took my place." I hear in those words how much he loved her, how much he missed her when she left, and how much he will long for her the rest of his life.

"There was enough room for all of us." My breath hitches. I rub my temples with my fingers. "That's what her signature meant. She wasn't pretending to be married to you. She was trying to tell us her true name: Sylvie Tan."

I stretch out my arms. He steps into them and we hold each other for a long time.

As he pulls away, he says, "I never intended to keep the jewelry. She hid it in my apartment that last night. I was going to give it to your ma before you all left. I did not want any problems." He glances at his mother. "I only ripped off her signature because I was afraid of what would happen if our secret was revealed. Look, the note was still in the bag. I saw it fall out when you emptied the jewelry onto the table."

I pick up the plastic bag with the wrapped items. "Is it in here?"

He clenches his jaw and I see anguish overtake his face. "No, I think those are the presents she bought for you in Venice."

We search the floor and I find the folded piece of yellow notebook paper beneath the coffee table. When I flatten it out, the signed scrap is a perfect match.

Dearest Ma, Pa, and Amy,

You are the true treasure of my heart.

Love always,

Sylvie Tan

CHAPTER 32

Ma

Monday, May 16

I said to Helena, "You never deserved what I did to you. I wronged you."

Helena's face worked and then she said, "I committed evil as well. I did not treat Snow Jasmine as I should have. I could only see you and Willem in her face. Every time I looked at her, the same wound reopened."

She left the room and returned with a homemade rag doll in her hands. Helena's wan smile no longer contained a knife. "This was Sylvie's. She named it Tasha. Grandma and Sylvie would have wanted you to have it."

"Thank you, Helena." I turned to her husband, who watched me with his heart laid open in his eyes, as he always had. "Goodbye, Willem."

For so many years, I had loved someone who did not exist. I wronged Pa in more ways than one. A part of my heart had never been accessible to him, obsessed with the useless fantasy of a young girl. I had ignored the man with whom I had enjoyed the sweet and undergone suffering for all these years.

I stood beside Pa and took his arm in mine. Despite everything I had done to him, he gave me a small smile.

EPILOGUE

Amy

Sunday, December 25

This is our first Christmas since Sylvie passed eight months ago. We celebrate at our apartment. It is strange that a Christian holiday acts as a bookmark for a bunch of Buddhists. For us, it's an adopted holiday, like a pair of shoes that once belonged to someone else. It grows more comfortable with wear until it becomes ours as well. We used to think it was Sylvie who pushed the tradition on our family, but now that she's gone, we realize we are still drawn to it. This year, there is no burned pot roast or Western cutlery. No Jim either; he's quit his job and disappeared. No one knows why. We saw him for the last time at Sylvie's memorial service. Ma went up to him afterward and said, "Ah-Jim, you good husband for Sylvie. Thank you, you take care of her." He pressed his cheek to Ma's and then hurried away. Her former company also sent a large bouquet of flowers.

Ma and I have cooked a full Chinese meal and Zach, the cute guy from the music store, has brought traditional desserts he made himself—crispy gingerbread men, frosted Christmas tree cookies, a dark chocolate pie and a flakey pumpkin one. He's a grad student at NYU in music and we are slowly getting to know each other. I've reenrolled at CUNY for my teaching credential and I love it. I'm studying with a determination and focus I've never had before.

After dinner, Zach plays his guitar while I sing Christmas carols. Wonder of wonders, Ma and Pa sit together on our couch holding hands. I have overheard their long whispered conversations these past months. He gazes down at her hair with a gentle expression. She too shimmers with a contentment that overlies our ever-present grief. Some wounds will heal while others will never fully close. I did not have the chance to practice grief—no pets that died, and I never knew my grandparents. There should be smaller wounds to the heart before the killing blow is struck, and yet I have survived.

We are all thinking of Sylvie. She smiles down upon us from her photo next to Grandma's in the altar. Lukas sent us this picture of her. Her doll, Tasha, is tucked beside it. I touch the copy of *Time* on our coffee table that contains news of his photo exhibition. I know there are several images of Sylvie in it, but I cannot bear to see them. The last I heard, he has been working and traveling nonstop.

It turns out the Dutch police were right all along. It was suicide. Oh, Sylvie, if only you had allowed yourself to share your burdens with me, or maybe if I had gone to the Netherlands when you invited me. My love would have kept you safe. There could have been, there *should* have been another way. I envision, so clearly it hurts my eyes like dazzling sunshine, another future with a joyful, thriving Sylvie. The vacuum caused by her absence will haunt us forever. How my knowledge of Sylvie, of Ma, of myself has changed. We had all been hidden behind the curtain of language and culture: from each other, from ourselves. I have learned that though the curtains in the Netherlands are always open, there is much that can be concealed in broad daylight.

As Sylvie told me once, we are all ultimately unreliable storytellers of our own lives, whether we wish it so or not, whether we share a common language or not. The only reliable narrators are to be found in books. Much of Sylvie was hidden from me, but the loyal, generous sister I loved was also true—all facets of the same diamond: my sister, the woman without a country. Who could she have been if she hadn't been born into such a burdened existence? Now the gifts she brought back from Venice are precious to us: a watch, a mask, and a knife.

Earlier today, Ma gave me a gift as well. We have never indulged in this custom at Christmas. Even before I opened it, I could tell from the worn red silk envelope that it was part of Grandma's inheritance. Inside I found a gold necklace with a carp pendant set with vivid jade, wrought so masterfully that the fish seemed to come alive. Ma told me that while nothing can replace that which is lost, emptiness creates room for new growth. I clutch the warm jade against my skin and recall the myth Ma told us when we were little: the tenacious carp swims against the currents until she manages to leap over the dragon gate and turn into a dragon herself.

I wonder what would have happened if Sylvie had chosen to live. The truth is, it is impossible to hide from yourself. Another truth: it is possible to find yourself anywhere. I pull back the curtains as the Dutch do, and let our happiness and sorrow stream out into the dark night.

From: Lukas Tan
To: Sylvie Lee
Sent: Saturday, April 30
Subject: Call me

Sylvie, I cannot speak straight that which is bent but please give me but a chance. Why will you not answer your mobile? I must have rung you a hundred times. My mother is furious that you left without saying goodbye. You must be on your flight back to New York by now.

I can imagine how you must feel about the situation. I know what lies in my heart and hope yours is also unchanged. We must leave yesterday behind us. I will do anything to make things right. Can we talk? Please, Sylvie.

I know you do not want to hear these words but I love you. I will always love you.

Lukas

ACKNOWLEDGMENTS

First, I would like to thank my late brother, Kwan S. Kwok, who was the inspiration behind this novel. He was not only brilliant but also kind and generous. From the Chinatown clothing factory where we worked as children to the Ivy League, Kwan led the way for me until he died in a tragic plane crash. I miss him every day and will always be grateful to him.

I'm also grateful to my readers around the world for their kindness and support. Thank you so much for reading. To those who have reached out to me, it means the world to me when you share your personal stories with me and let me know what you think of my work. I'm also extremely thankful to all of the organizations, libraries, booksellers, high schools, colleges, and universities in both the U.S. and abroad that have stood behind me and my work. You've made the dreams of an immigrant girl from Hong Kong come true.

My agent, Suzanne Gluck of William Morris Endeavor Entertainment, has been with me from the very beginning of my career and has guided my steps with wisdom, courage, and fierce intelligence. I have the pleasure and privilege of having Jessica Williams of William Morrow as my editor. Jessica's tremendous emotional and intellectual insight brought out the best in this novel. Special thanks to the rest of my team at WME, especially Tracy Fisher and her foreign rights team, and to all of my foreign publishers.

I'm indebted to the wonderful people at William Morrow and HarperCollins: our great publisher, Liate Stehlik; Lauren Truskowski, Ryan

Cury, Kelly Rudolph, and the rest of the amazing publicity and marketing departments; marvelous copy editor Laura Cherkas; the production department; the art department; the entire hardcover, paperback, and digital sales forces, who serve on the front lines; and everyone else who did an incredible job bringing this book out into the world.

My immense gratitude to the people who were willing to share their experiences and expertise with me: Esther van Neerbos of Signi zoekhonden, Mieke Zinn, Inge Grandia, Ino Benschop, Frederike Maus, Alexander de Blaeij, Natascha Raaphorst, Shih Hui Liong, Agnes Lee, C. V. Petersen, Kelli Marcus, Emily Nolan, and Dina Nayeri. I asked you so many crazy questions and you had answers to all of them. You told me about searching for a body in the water, flying an airplane, Sylvie's doll Tasha, palliative care, the hierarchy within a management consulting firm, running with a cello on your back, homophobia, designer shoes, anti-Semitism in Europe, legal euthanasia, darkroom photography, being an Asian abroad, and much, much more. You were my inspiration and my knowledge base—thank you from the bottom of my heart. Any errors are my own.

My awesome early readers gave me the courage to continue: Katrina Middelburg-Creswell, Sari Wilson, Alex Kahn, and Julia Phillips. What would I do without you? I also need to thank all of the great folks at the Ragdale Foundation for providing the residency where this novel was born, and especially Hannah Judy Gretz and her eponymous fellowship. A huge thank-you to fellow writers and publishing veterans for your invaluable support and advice: Helen Schulman, Julie Otsuka, Scott Turow, Celeste Ng, Cheryl Tan, Sarah McCoy, Amy Hill Hearth, Caroline Leavitt, and, most especially, the brilliant and generous Marilyn Ducksworth, whose guiding light has always illuminated my career.

I am so thankful to my dear friends, who have somehow stuck with me through all of the moaning and groaning: Julie Voshell, Stuart Shapiro, Suzanne Demitrio Campbell, Rob Wu, Stephanie and Jonathan Kastin, Paula Schasberger, Judith Schasberger, the Beck family, Chimene and Peter Lam, Carin Gerzon-Koning, Jules Gerzon, Laurent Lédé, Meta van der Wal, Jan-Paul Middelburg, Natasja Moenen, and Doris Seibert. Your laughter and encouragement keep me going.

All of my love to the Kwok and Kluwer families, especially Betty and Gerard, and to my brothers Joe (Chow), York, and Choi. And finally, my deepest love and gratitude to Erwin, Stefan, and Milan, who put up with not only my months of traveling, but also the months when I'm at home writing and therefore burning all of our food.

P.S. Kisses to the cats for being furry and orange: Anibaba, Timoto, Sushi, and Couscous.

About the author

About the book

Insights,
Interviews
& More . . .

About the author

Meet Jean Kwok

Chris Macke

JEAN KWOK is the *New York Times* and internationally bestselling author of *Girl in Translation* and *Mambo in Chinatown*. Her work has been published in twenty countries and is taught in universities, colleges, and high schools across the world. She has been selected for numerous honors, including the American Library Association Alex Award, the Chinese American Librarians Association Best Book Award, and the Sunday Times EFG Short Story Award international shortlist. She received her bachelor's degree from Harvard

University and earned an MFA from Columbia University. She is fluent in Chinese, Dutch, and English, and currently lives in the Netherlands.

jeankwok.com
: /JeanKwokAuthor
: @JeanKwok
: jeankwokauthor

Behind the Book

When we moved from Hong Kong to Brooklyn, New York, my older brother Kwan and I lost our parents—not to death but to immigration—and so we meant more to each other than ever. Ma and Pa had transformed, now more lost and confused than we were, and as the youngest of seven siblings, quicker to learn English than our elders, Kwan and I were charged with guiding our parents through a complex new culture and language we could barely navigate ourselves.

There are few photos of us from that time because we could not afford a camera, but one stands out in my memory. I was five years old, toothless and exuberant, sitting at fifteen-year-old Kwan's feet with a bowl of rice and chopsticks in my hands. I would not learn to use a knife and fork until I was a teenager. Kwan's expression was thoughtful, one hand resting protectively on my shoulder. He had already started working at the clothing factory in Chinatown after school.

Kwan was, however, brilliant. He painstakingly crafted a way out of that cycle of grime and exhaustion, and in so doing, led the way for my escape as well. One night, I woke upon the mattress on the floor where I slept. Kwan had returned from his restaurant job and laid a small, wrapped brown package next to me. It was a present. To this day, I am amazed that he did not give me a toy or a piece of candy, but something that would change my life. It was a blank diary and he said, "Whatever you write in this, will belong to you."

From that moment on, I began to write: about my confusion in this country, my loneliness as an awkward, homely Chinese girl amidst my Nike-wearing classmates—and, after Kwan was accepted into MIT and left for college, about how much I missed him.

I lived for the moments when his orbit brought him home, always bringing me gifts—thick red MIT sweatshirts, books about Einstein and quantum theory, a computer to take the place of the manual typewriter I used, contact lenses to replace the thick glasses I desperately needed but never wore out of vanity.

Then, in November 2009, Kwan disappeared. I had moved to the Netherlands to be with the man who would become my husband and received a panicked phone call from my family. Kwan had not come home for Thanksgiving. He was the most responsible person we knew. An invisible hand clutched my heart. Something must be wrong.

I quickly took over the search, contacting his work and friends, and ▸

discovered he had gone to Texas to purchase a small plane. Flying was his passion and he had clocked more than 1,600 hours of flight experience. I hacked into his email and finally found the right airport. Kwan had taken off. . . . Then the plane vanished.

I broke down, sobbing to strangers, the police, politicians, cell and credit card companies, the FAA, anyone who might help us find him. We narrowed the search area to a hundred-square-mile expanse of mountains. My family raced there, driving around aimlessly, calling his name into the woods. A week after Kwan disappeared, the air force and search-and-rescue teams found his body. His plane had nicked a tree and he had died upon impact.

Searching for Sylvie Lee was born from my love for my tragic, brilliant brother. Even though I know he is gone, my heart will never stop searching for him.

Photo courtesy of the author

Questions for Discussion

1. How do the members of the Lee family deal with being measured against stereotypes, language barriers, and other people's perceptions? Have you ever felt like an outsider?

2. Discuss the relationship between Amy and Sylvie. How do the siblings both understand and mystify one another?

3. How is this immigrant family like others you've seen or read about? What about their experiences do you think are universal or unique?

4. How does Kwok represent the different languages in each chapter? Did any idioms or word orders surprise you or make you think differently? Why do you think Kwok chose to depict language this way?

5. This novel says a great deal about the influence our families can have on us. How did Amy's and Sylvie's different upbringings shape them and their choices? Did anything about your own upbringing strongly influence you?

6. Did your perception of Ma change when you read her chapters? How did she appear through other's eyes in comparison to how she sees herself? Do you think others see you the way you really are?

7. Do you think any of the characters in the novel are reliable narrators? Can any narrator be truly reliable, or are we all colored by our perceptions and misunderstandings?

8. What is the price of the American dream? Who pays for it? How does it compare to the European lifestyle?

9. Amy and Sylvie perceive the Netherlands differently. How do their impressions of the landscape and the people—especially Filip and Lukas—demonstrate their own characters?

10. Has reading this novel deepened your understanding of the implications of casual racism, even toward well-integrated people? Did any instances in the novel surprise you? Have you ever encountered situations like this in your life? ▸

Questions for Discussion ***(continued)***

11. Different men love Sylvie in this novel. How did their forms of love differ, and why?

12. Why do you think Helena resented Sylvie? How deserved do you think the resentment was?

13. There are so many secrets that the characters keep to themselves. What do you wish they had shared with each other, and how might this have changed the plot? Are secrets always bad, or are they sometimes necessary? Have you ever kept secrets from people you loved?

14. Do you think the novel's title, *Searching for Sylvie Lee*, has multiple meanings? ~

Recipes for *Searching for Sylvie Lee*

Scallion Pancakes with a Coconut Yogurt, Coriander, and Lime Dip

PREP TIME: 15 MINUTES • COOKING TIME: 25 MINUTES • TOTAL TIME: 35 MINUTES • SERVES: 4-6

INGREDIENTS:

¼ cup fresh cilantro leaves, chopped
grated zest of half a lime
1 cup unsweetened coconut yogurt
1 cup all-purpose flour
½ cup rice flour
1 tsp kosher salt
1 large egg, beaten
1 cup sparkling water
½ cup filtered water
3 scallions, finely chopped into rings
3-4 Tbsp coconut oil

*Optional: 1 Tbsp finely chopped chili pepper, if you'd like to add some heat

DIRECTIONS:

1. Start by making the dipping sauce. Chop the cilantro, and then zest the lime into a small bowl with the yogurt. Mix this together until well combined. ▸

Recipes for *Searching for Sylvie Lee* *(continued)*

2. For the pancakes, in a large bowl, measure in the dry ingredients and mix together. Add the beaten egg, sparkling water, and filtered water, and give this a good stir with a whisk, trying to eliminate any lumps. Add the chopped scallions, and chili if you are using that. The batter should be easy to pour into the pan. If it's too thick, it can end up stodgy and take longer to cook, so feel free to add a bit of water to make it into an appropriate pancake batter consistency!

3. Over a medium-high flame, heat a generous teaspoon of the coconut oil in a small frying pan. I used a cast-iron skillet. When the oil is hot, pour a ladleful of the batter into the pan and swirl it around so it touches the edges of the pan. Cook this for about two minutes. Check the underside of the pancake, and when it looks brown and crispy, it's ready to flip over. Cook for an additional two minutes. Repeat this process until you have used all of the batter. If you like, keep these warm on a tray in the oven set at a low temperature (120°F).

When all of the pancakes are made, serve them with the coconut yogurt dipping sauce and a sprinkle of scallions to garnish.

Recipe by Jennifer Kular, at The Well Travelled Kitchen.

thewelltravelledkitchen.com ▸

Recipes for *Searching for Sylvie Lee* *(continued)*

Dutch Apple Pie

Prep Time: 45 minutes • Cooking Time: 75 minutes • Total Time: 2 hours • Serves: 8–12

INGREDIENTS:

1½ cups all-purpose flour
½ cup oat flour
1 cup packed light brown sugar
2 tsp cinnamon, separated
1 cup unsalted butter, chilled, and cut into 8 equal pieces
5 lbs (about 12) Granny Smith apples, peeled, cored, and cut into thin slices
2 Tbsp freshly squeezed lemon juice
¼ cup gluten-free oats, to mix in later for the crumble top
2 cups heavy cream, whipped (for serving)

DIRECTIONS:

1. In a large bowl, mix together the flours, brown sugar, and 1 teaspoon of the cinnamon. Next, add the bits of butter and cut them into the mixture by using a pastry cutter or an electric mixer and blend until it comes together in pea-size crumble. Press ⅔ of this mixture onto the bottom and up 2in of the sides of a 9-inch springform pan.

2. Preheat the oven to 350°F. Peel and core, then slice the apples into a large bowl. (Should any liquid accumulate, pour it off.) When all of the apples have been sliced, drizzle with the lemon juice and the other teaspoon of cinnamon and toss all to coat evenly. Place them into the prepared springform, being sure to fit them comfortably into the base. Given the quantity, they may mound higher than the edge of the pan—this is fine, as they will shrink when you bake the pie. Now is the time to add the extra ¼ cup of oats to the mixture for the crumble topping, and sprinkle this remaining crumble on top.

3. Line a cookie sheet with parchment paper, place the pan on top, and bake for 75 minutes, or until the crumble top starts to turn golden brown. At this point, remove the pie from the oven, run the blade of a knife around the edge, and place the cake pan on a wire rack to cool completely before releasing from the springform. Serve at room temperature, in the traditional Dutch way, with a bit of the whipped cream on the side! ▸

Recipes for *Searching for Sylvie Lee*
(continued)

Recipe by Jennifer Kular, at The Well Travelled Kitchen.

thewelltravelledkitchen.com

For the full book club guide and more delicious recipes, go to jeankwok.com.